Second Wind

A novel
by Darlene Deluca

Other titles
by Darlene Deluca

The Storm Within
Book One, Women of Whitfield

Something Good

Meetings of Chance

Unexpected Legacy

Second Wind
All rights reserved. Copyright © 2015
by Darlene Deluca

ISBN: 1505681170
ISBN-13: 978-1505681178

Second
Wind

Chapter One

Dana Gerard's pulse quickened as she scanned the horizon. The sky glowed the murky greenish-gray color of a bruise, and a menacing wall of clouds rolled in the distance. She knew a possibility of rain had been forecast, and she'd been hoping for a good, steady shower – the kind that sank in deeply, nourishing farmers' crops, one that would wash away the dirty browns of winter and give life to the budding tulips and iris that had just begun to dot her neighborhood. But that scenario seemed unlikely now. These clouds carried an ominous threat.

Pulling her gaze away, she murmured to Mrs. Carlyle. "Try to get some sleep now. We'll check back a little later." Dana tucked the blanket around the frail woman who'd once been a much-loved third-grade schoolteacher, and gave the limp hand a gentle squeeze, then made a beeline for the door, emergency procedures playing in her mind.

At the nurses' station, she tapped the keyboard of her computer for a local weather report. She wasn't one to panic over bad weather, but she did like to be ahead of the curve. "Hey, Jeanie, have you heard any weather updates?"

Jeanie Thresher, one of the other nurses on duty, turned from her chart. "There's a thunderstorm watch. Brooke's mom said it was windy when she came in."

Earlier in the day, Greg Talisman, their chief surgeon, had removed six-year-old Brooke's tonsils, and her

1

parents, with three other children at home, had been tag-teaming ever since.

When the computer monitor sprang to life, Dana pinched her lip as she studied the screen. The flashing radar indicated a heavy line of storms heading straight for Whitfield. The thunderstorm watch had been upgraded to a warning, and a tornado watch had been added. She was no meteorologist, but it looked like tornado weather to her. A life-long Kansas resident, she knew the signs.

"Okay, listen, I don't want to alarm any patients, but I'm concerned about this." She walked toward the window as she spoke, then gasped. The sky had darkened considerably in the last few minutes. "Get Valerie in here, and let's—" Lightning flashed outside, quickly followed by a sharp clap of thunder. Dana jumped, her heart thundering as well.

She whipped the pager from her waist. "I'm calling Greg. I think we'd better start preparing to move patients. Those clouds are nasty." Dana mentally ticked through the patients on the floor. Thankfully, the clinic was closed on Sundays, and the fifteen-bed hospital was only about half full.

Adrenaline surged through Dana as she began implementation of the Whitfield Community Hospital emergency procedures. As head nurse, she was in charge until Greg or their administrator arrived.

"Let's move all ambulatory downstairs," she instructed. "Everyone else comes to the center hallway for now. Remember, charts stay with the patients. Start with maternity." Dana figured a new mother would want her baby in her own arms if things got tense.

When her cell phone buzzed, she checked the number. and took the call. "Hi, Greg. I wanted you to know that I'm moving patients into shelter zones. This storm looks bad."

"Is Brad there?"

"No." Even though Brad Berkley, their administrator, was next on her list of people to contact, she expected him to arrive on his own. Surely he, and everyone else in town, was watching the sky. "What are you seeing from your place?" Dana asked.

"Storm is definitely heading this way. It's probably a good idea to get a jump on moving people, just in case. You've got a few folks who won't be able to manage stairs."

"Exactly." She wanted to get as many people downstairs as she could while they still had use of the elevators. "I'm going to call Brad then—"

"I'll call him. You take care of the patients."

As soon as she ended the call, Dana motioned for Valerie. "Let's move Mrs. Carlyle down. We may not have much time."

Ten minutes later, her cell phone buzzed. "Hey, Greg. Did you get—" In that instant, the emergency sirens outside blasted to life, the loud horns screaming a warning of danger. Damn. That meant the elevators were off limits now. They'd have to have two shelter areas.

Greg's voice sounded over the noise, mirroring Dana's sense of urgency. "I'm on my way."

For a split second, Dana stood rooted to the floor, another alarm sounding in her head. Where was Chase? She said a hasty prayer that her son had gone to Paxton forty-five minutes away as planned, and was still there – safe and clueless to the potential danger unfolding in Whitfield.

She slipped her cell phone into her pocket, then charged into action. As she headed down the hall, Dana nearly collided with a wide-eyed Brooke holding her mother's hand and clutching her fluffy stuffed bunny. Dana stopped and gave them a reassuring smile, patting Brooke's arm. "Head to the stairs and down to the basement. Don't run. Everything is all right."

"What happens if the power goes out?" Brooke's mother asked.

"The back-up generator will kick in. Don't worry."

Mrs. Dryden let go of Brooke's hand and began fishing in her handbag, immediately drawing a whimper from her daughter. "Shh, Brooke, I'm just going to call daddy."

Dana put up a hand. "Mrs. Dryden, please don't take the time to do that now. We need to get you both to shelter." She gave Brooke a quick hug, then applied a tiny bit of pressure to her back to scoot them along toward Jeanie who was hovering near the main staircase with the new parents and their baby boy.

Seconds later, Mark Sellers, their security officer, called Dana's name. At the same time, Valerie dashed around the corner. Feeling like a traffic cop, Dana waved her toward the patient hallway. "Hey, Mark. I need you on the scanner. Find out how close this is and how big of a threat we're looking at."

The horns outside waned, but then blared again. Inside, it was organized chaos as Dana and the other nurses shepherded their patients to safety. Just as Dana and Valerie steered another patient and his heart monitor into the hallway, Greg appeared.

"Hey," Dana said. "We've got a group downstairs and the others in here."

"How many still in their rooms?" he asked, his voice low.

"Just one."

"Where's Brad?"

Dana shook her head. "Haven't seen him. It's possible he slipped in while I was with a patient. Did you talk to him?"

"Yeah. But by then, the sirens had gone off, and his wife was freaking out, I guess."

"Hmm. We don't have time for a freak-out," Dana said.

"We'll manage whether he makes it in or not. You were smart to start early. Something's brewing for sure."

As they wheeled the bed and equipment to the designated interior shelter, Dana gave Greg a rundown on the patients in the basement. "Mr. Hoffman has been a little agitated today. Why don't you take this area, and I'll head downstairs with Jeanie."

4

"Sounds good."

She and Valerie spun around and raced back down the hallway. One more patient to evacuate. As they hurried past the central nurses' station, more lightning crackled outside, lighting up the windows with an eerie green glow. Dana could almost feel the electricity around them as they rushed into the seventeen-year-old's room.

"Hey, Derek. It's probably no big deal, but since the sirens are going off, we've got to move you out of here," Dana said. Turning to Valerie, she added, "wheelchair to the stairs. It'll be faster. Grab his chart, too."

"Dana!"

Her head snapped around as Mark barked at her.

"Hurry up. This is bad. How many more?"

"This is it."

"Come on, come on." Mark pressed a walkie-talkie into Dana's hand. "Hang tight. I'll be in touch."

She clutched the mobile device, feeling the weight of it in her chest as well as her hand. Downstairs, Dana moved among the patients, making sure everyone was settled. Jeanie had given out bottles of water, and the lab technician was speaking softly to Mrs. Carlyle. Though not the most comfortable space in the facility, the room offered basic necessities.

Satisfied that everyone was doing well, Dana slipped out the door, and sprinted back upstairs. She wasn't about to "hang tight." She wanted to know what was going on.

Her mouth dropped open as she neared the security station and police monitor. Harsh, loud voices boomed from the speaker. Men shouting, yelling over each other. Holy shit.

"What's going on?" she asked, though it was obvious that something was very wrong. So much noise. The wind and the sirens roared in the background.

"Oh, God," shouted one voice.

"Look out!"

"It's on the ground. Go. *Go!*"

Dana stared at Mark, heart pounding. There was something chilling about hearing fear in a man's voice. "This sounds bad," she whispered.

Mark jumped to his feet. He placed firm hands on her shoulders, and turned her around. "You gotta get out of here, Dana. Get downstairs. Stay there until I give the all clear."

The windows rattled as if to enforce Mark's words, and Dana sprinted to the back stairwell, her no-nonsense orthopedics cushioning her pounding steps. She stopped short in front of the door. She was a professional, and would do everything she could to keep her patients safe, but she was a mother first. If Chase was home he could be in danger. That kid could sleep through anything – including tornado sirens.

Snatching up her phone, Dana punched in Chase's number, willing him to pick up quickly. On the third ring, she slumped against the door, about to give up. Then his voice came on the line. "Hey, Mom."

"Chase! Where are you?"

"Paxton. At Luke's," he said, puzzlement in his voice. "What's the matter?"

Her tone had obviously sent him a message, but apparently he knew nothing of the weather situation. Her words rushed out as relief surged through her. "Oh, good. Stay there. We've got tornado sirens going off in Whitfield. I'm at work. I just wanted to make sure you're safe."

"I'm fine. It's–"

"Okay. That's all. Can't talk. I'll call you later. Love you."

She slipped the phone back into her pocket and raced down the stairs. No point trying to call her dad. By now, the manor staff would be doing the same thing she and her staff were doing – securing patients. He was in good hands.

All eyes turned to her when she stepped into the concrete storage area. Dana smiled, and glanced around. "Everyone doing all right?" she asked. "Hopefully we won't be down here long." She leaned closer to Jeanie and whispered. "There's definitely a tornado. I heard the police on the scanner. It's touched down."

Without a change in the expression on her face, Jeanie nodded.

Dana tamped down the fear in her chest, and pushed her own concerns aside. She had to be mentally present here. Her gaze landed on Derek. A teenage boy would put on a good front and try not to show emotion, that she knew well. Inside, though, he probably wished one of his parents were there. Too bad they'd had to turn away the bouquet of balloons his grandmother had sent. Due to allergies, the hospital could no longer allow latex balloons in the building. Of course a teenager wouldn't care so much about the balloons, but oh, could they have some fun with the helium. Not so many years ago, the gas was a standard of comic relief around there. She nearly laughed as she imagined a tornado and Munchkins from The Wizard of Oz combined with a little helium.

"Hey, buddy, how are you doing?" Dana asked "Hope we didn't jostle you around too much. The leg okay?"

Derek shrugged. "I'm good."

A shrill wail interrupted them, and Dana could see the frustration in the young mother's face as she tried to calm the newborn. The baby's howls filled the crowded room.

"I don't know what's wrong," Shannon cried.

Jeanie's glance met Dana's. "I'll get this," Jeanie whispered. She stepped away and repositioned the baby against his mother, her soft voice trying to calm them both.

When Dana scanned the group a few moments later, she caught Mrs. Dryden's eye. The woman glared at her. "There's no cell service down here," she snapped.

Dana's stomach dropped. Of course there wasn't. That meant none of them could contact their families. She'd forgotten about that when she asked the woman not to make a call earlier. With a twinge of guilt, Dana turned toward Brooke. The girl's chin quivered, her mother's tension obviously triggering some anxiety. Dana stroked Brooke's tangled hair. "You've been such a brave girl," she told her. She patted the stuffed animal that Brooke had nestled into her neck. "And bunny, too. Super Brooke and her best buddy, Bunny."

Brooke's head bobbed. She leaned into her mother, but gave Dana a shy smile.

Dana glanced at Mrs. Dryden. "I'm really sorry," she said. "But your safety is my top priority."

"What about the safety of my other kids?" she said, her voice pitching to a high whine.

"Aren't they with their dad?"

Mrs. Dryden covered her face with her hands. "Yes, but he'll have his hands full, and they'll be crying for me."

Dana crouched beside them. "I know it's not ideal to be separated, but you'll be together soon. The storm will be over before we know it."

As she spoke the words, Dana was reminded just how fast a storm could wreak havoc. Then again, she'd heard these sirens go off many times before. She'd gone through this same routine, hunkered down in this basement with dozens of patients over the years, and it never amounted to much of anything. That was life in tornado alley.

Seconds later, they all jumped when a loud crash came from outside. And another.

Mrs. Dryden screamed, sending her daughter into a fit of crying.

"It's okay, Brooke," Dana said softly, trying to soothe the girl. Her mother certainly wasn't helping the situation.

"Sounds like something hit the building," the baby's dad said.

Yes, something was pounding the hospital. Dana couldn't tell if it was a hard rain or something else. Tree branches? There was a line of beautiful red maples along the south side of the building, and redbuds dotted the green areas. To her, it sounded more like trash night, when gusty winds played kick-the-can with all the neighbors' trash barrels at the curb, bumping and rattling them until they fell into the street.

Funny thing was, Dana couldn't remember ever being able to hear anything from outside in the times she'd waited in the basement before. Now, even over the cries of Shannon's baby and Brooke, noises rumbled around them.

The voices she'd heard on the scanner ran through Dana's mind again, and she drew in a deep breath, steeling herself for the possibilities. It didn't sound like nothing this time.

Chapter Two

Though the hospital's lower level housed the lab and brightly lit supply rooms that Dana visited often, it seemed more like a cellar as the group hunkered down waiting for the storm to pass. The baby's inconsolable cries made the minutes stretch like hours. Trying to keep a smile on her face while gritting her teeth was becoming more difficult by the second. Thirty minutes into the ordeal, Dana's walkie-talkie crackled to life. "Ms. Gerard?"

Jumping from her chair, she responded. "I'm here. Go ahead."

"All clear," Mark said. "You can come up now."

When cheers and applause broke out around her, Dana grinned. "Copy that."

A few moments later, the elevator doors opened with a welcome swoosh and Val met them with wheelchairs.

"Everybody okay up there?" Dana asked.

Val grimaced. "We're fine, but I can't say that was any fun. Doesn't sound good out there."

As they emerged from the basement to the second floor, the only sound Dana could hear from outside was the shrill whine of sirens. She gave a cursory scan of the area. As far as she could tell, the hospital interior appeared unscathed, and they quickly shuffled patients back to their rooms. Then Dana took a moment to stop by the police monitor. "Whew, what are you hear–" She stopped short. Mark's eyes were wide, his face ashen. "Oh, no. What–"

"I gotta go see what's happening," he said, his voice wavering.

Dana nodded, straining to understand what was being said over the static and sirens in the background. The adrenaline that had flowed through her system a few minutes earlier was replaced by a cold chill as she struggled to make sense of the words coming from the speaker – words like EF-Five, crushed, and blown apart. A shudder ran through her. After all these years, after all the dodged bullets, had a big one finally hit Whitfield?

She yelped when her phone buzzed in her pocket. Pulling it out, she saw several missed calls – each of her children had called, and so had her father. It'd take too much time to try and figure out how to send a group text message to all of them. Instead, she took a moment to text Chase. He could contact everyone else.

"I'm ok. Let the others know. Call Poppa. Luv u." That would have to do for now. The staff needed to regroup, and Dana wanted to take a look outside.

"I'll be right back," she told Jeanie.

Outside, the cool air felt damp on Dana's skin, even though she was protected from the pelting rain under the hospital's covered circle drive. She squinted, trying to see in the dim light. It was dusk now, and the cloud cover made it darker than it should've been. When she stepped outside, she already knew there'd been a tornado, and some damage. Still, she needed to see it to process it. But she could hardly make out the shapes and sounds around her – until people began running toward her, crying, and yelling.

"Oh, dear God," Dana whispered. When the horns stopped, and Mark called to say they could come up from the basement, they thought it was over. She shook her head as the reality sunk in – it was only the beginning.

Brace for impact, she thought. Whirling, she ran as fast as her shaking legs would move. She yelled, sprinting up the stairs, no longer caring if her words alarmed their patients. Panting, she grabbed Greg's arm. "Oh, my God, we've got to call for help. Get ready for the ambulances. People are hurt."

Valerie turned from the television, and stared at her, a stricken expression on her face. Dana pulled Val into a tight hug, her hand circling her colleague's back. "Come on, Val. These people need us." She pulled back and gave Val's arm a squeeze. "Switch on your auto-pilot, sweetheart. Get everyone in here. *Now*." Dana headed for the first empty room, hollering back over her shoulder. "Call everyone – even the part-time nurses and all the facilities staff. Greg, we need beds." The hospital staff was first-class, and Dana knew the entire crew would most likely report in. But everyone might not realize the extent of the situation immediately. They'd need all hands on deck.

They met the first victims as they rushed through the sliding glass doors. A young man carried a limp woman in his arms.

Dana's eyes locked with Greg's for a moment, then everything else was forgotten as they turned their attention to the people streaming in – people moaning and bleeding. And all wearing the dazed, blank look of shock. Greg helped lower one victim from the arms that held her onto a bed, while Dana slid her arm round a woman holding a shirt to her head, blood spreading like tie-die through the fabric. She leaned in close, trying to hear over so many people talking and crying at once. From what she could make out, the woman and her husband hadn't made it to their basement, and instead ducked inside a closet. A metal box had fallen, its sharp edge connecting with the woman's forehead.

Dana glanced around, trying to quickly assess and prioritize patients. The hospital had an emergency room, but it wasn't a trauma site. Serious injuries would have to be sent to Paxton or other locations. Even traveling at high speeds, it would take their ambulances thirty minutes to arrive. Whitfield's two ambulances could soon be overwhelmed.

She guided the injured woman to a chair, then Dana gathered her staff, giving assignments in terse commands, aware that she probably sounded like a drill sergeant. Oh, well. She could apologize later. "Val, you stick with Greg. Jeanie, you help Tiffany process patients. Did you get Pamela and Hillary?"

"On their way," Val called, already in motion. "Sarah, too. Couldn't reach Abby."

Okay, three more . . . Dana swallowed hard as her eyes flickered toward Greg where he examined the woman on the gurney. A moment later, they dashed down the hall toward the operating room, with Val close behind. Dana said a prayer that their blood supply would hold out.

Hillary hurried inside then, followed by a breathless Daniel, one of the other doctors. Thank God.

Daniel rushed toward Dana. "What have we got?"

Dana jerked her head toward the double doors behind her. "Greg's got a patient in the O.R. I'm triaging patients as they come in. You'd better look at the man lying down first. He has chest pains."

Daniel nodded. "You heard much from outside?"

"No. Can't even think about it."

"Everything south of Sixth Street is gone."

Dana froze as her stomach dropped to the floor. "What? What do you mean – gone?"

Daniel spread his hands in a quick, horizontal motion. "I mean destroyed. Flattened."

Dana's heart pounded as she tried to comprehend the words. She lived south of Sixth Street. *A lot of people lived south of Sixth Street.*

Daniel reached across the counter and yanked up a box of surgical gloves. Snapping his hands into them, he pushed past Dana. "It's a nightmare out there."

Closing her eyes, Dana took a second to collect herself. Focus, focus, she chanted inside.

Thirty minutes later, all of the clinic examination rooms were full, there were two people in each hospital room, and they were running out of beds. People with minor injuries were resting on couches in the waiting areas. And anxious eyes followed her every move.

Then Brad strode through the doors, shirt sleeves rolled up, hair that looked like it'd been pulled in every direction, and a harried grimace on his face.

Dana couldn't decide whether she was relieved or annoyed. They could use the help, but she wanted to shake him, to give him a 'what the hell?' and remind him that they all had family. What about her son? And her dad? But there was no time. Besides, he was her boss. Those questions would never cross her lips.

He headed straight for her.

"You all right?" she asked.

"Fine," he said, his voice clipped. "Fill me in."

Ooookay, Dana thought. Guess they were keeping it strictly business. Turning, she headed back toward the exam rooms, giving Brad the scoop as they walked. "All of the patients who were here during the tornado are fine, and back in their rooms. We've got all the staff we could get a hold of here or on their way." He nodded, and gave a few mm-hmms. She stopped outside the room where another doctor who'd arrived was stitching up John Eckerd. With a broken nose and multiple cuts, the man's ear had nearly been ripped off. People would be wearing scars from this for the rest of their lives.

"Where do you want me?" Brad asked, raking a hand through his hair.

The question took Dana off guard. He was looking for marching orders from her? Her mind went blank for a moment, then she unleashed all the questions that had been worrying her. "Why don't you check on the supply of blood and tetanus shots? We need to cancel all routine appointments and scheduled procedures. Follow up with any staff who hasn't come in yet. And try to find out how many ambulances are out there, and where they're going. I've seen a couple go by, but I'm still hearing a lot of sirens and helicopters. Are people being airlifted out? Are there any fatalities? Mark is talking with Police and Fire. Try to get a status check. How many more can we expect tonight?"

Brad's blank face told Dana the man was trained in management but had never actually worked a serious emergency situation. He looked at her as if he didn't understand what she was talking about. Just as she was about to repeat herself, he seemed to remember what his job was, and came to life.

"Right. Let me see what I can find out. Looks like you've got things under control down here."

Did it? He must be seeing a different scene than she was, but she didn't have time to argue the point.

As soon as they finished with Eckerd, Dana hurried out to get the next patient. She glanced at her watch. Shift change was in less than an hour. That wasn't going to happen, for sure. They'd all be there through the night. Still, she'd have to figure out a way to give her nurses a few hours' rest on some kind of rotation. Looked like the break room and its lone sofa were going to stand in as bedroom tonight.

In the next second, Dana did a double-take, sucking in her breath when her neighbor entered the hospital holding his young son. With a mounting sense of dread, she watched them move to the counter where Tiffany was processing patients more quickly than the medical staff could see them.

Dana moved forward, and saw that Micah's hand was wrapped in a towel. "Ron," Dana said. "What happened?"

Ron's Adam's apple bobbed, and she thought the young dad might actually break down and cry. He pressed his lips together against the top of his son's head.

"Haven't you heard?"

"I heard it's bad south of Sixth. What about our block?" She unwound the towel as she spoke. "Oh, ouch. What happened here?"

"Fell on a nail as we were trying to get out."

"Yeah. Let's get that cleaned up. I know Jessica stays on top of check-ups and shots, so there's no worry about tetanus."

"Stitches?"

It was a deep puncture wound, and the boy's hand was already bruised and swollen. "Probably. We'll see what the doctor says." Her eyes met Ron's, and he squeezed her shoulder. "Your house is bad, Dana. Just like ours. The whole block. Like a pile of sticks. Was anyone at your place?"

She sucked in her breath, willing herself not to lose control of the hot tears that sprung to her eyes. "No. Chase is in Paxton. Are Jessica and Cole okay?"

"Yeah. Just a little shook up."

Nodding, Dana whispered, "Thank you for telling me." She forced a shaky smile for Micah. "We'll get you all fixed up in a few minutes, big guy."

Oh, God. A pile of sticks? She had to tell Chase, to let him know he couldn't come home. Dana glanced at the waiting area. Still crowded. She kept thinking she'd wait until they'd taken care of the patients to check in with Chase, but there were just too many. This could go on for hours.

She pressed an ice pack to Micah's hand, then stepped aside, reaching into her pocket for her phone. Hoping no one would notice, Dana slipped down the hallway and bolted upstairs, where Sarah was single-handedly covering the floor. Dana gave her a quick thumbs-up, then ducked into the break room. The first thing that registered was that someone had had the presence of mind to make fresh coffee. They were going to need it. With unsteady hands, she poured a cup, took a gulp, and tapped in Chase's number.

He picked up even before it rang on her end.

"Mom?"

It took only that one word for Dana to lose her hold. Trembling, she sank into a chair. "Hey, sweetie."

"You still at the hospital?"

"Yes, honey. I'm going to be here all night." She swallowed hard. "Listen. You can't come home." *Home*. The word hit her like a punch in the gut, and she slid an arm across the cool surface of the table, as she closed her eyes. According to their neighbor, there was no home to come back to.

"It sounds bad, Mom. Whitfield's all over the news."

"Yeah. It *is* bad. And I've got to get back to work." She couldn't keep her voice from quivering. "A lot of people are hurt. Stay with the guys there. If you can't do that, just find a motel and put it on the credit card. Everything is a mess here." No sense telling him the whole truth when she didn't really know the extent of it herself. She let out a shuddered breath. "I'm so glad you weren't here. Did you call the others?"

"Yeah. Left messages."

"All right. Stay in touch with Poppa. I love you. I'll check in tomorrow morning."

"Okay. Bye."

Dana ended the call and swiped her fingers under her eyes. Leaning against the counter, she took two more sips of coffee, then she squared her shoulders. Ready or not, she had to get back out there.

**

With a deep breath, Dana opened the door to the waiting area. Usually calm and quiet, it looked anything but "under control." Across the room Jeanie motioned to people as though she were conducting an orchestra, and Daniel was on his knees with the defibrillator, pumping a man's chest. She bolted forward, ready to assist, but before she'd taken two steps, Brad appeared from the other direction. His hand on her arm stopped her mid stride.

Her eyes shifted past Brad where a news crew hovered in the background. What the–? She shook her head. Was he crazy? They couldn't be in here. Couldn't take photos of hospital patients. That wasn't allowed. "We can't let–"

Brad tightened his grip on her arm, and leaned in. "News people from Paxton. They want a quote. Want to know about the injuries and how many people we're treating. How many people were here during the storm? Was anyone hurt?"

Really? Dana thought. They sent a news crew? How about sending some doctors. They could use some extra physicians on hand. She took a step to the side. She couldn't stand around talking to reporters or Brad with so many people waiting for medical care. "We can't deal with them right now. Tell them we're busy. Tell them we followed emergency procedures, and everyone came through the storm just fine." And tell them to stay out of the way, she muttered under her breath.

When she glanced back at Brad she couldn't believe her eyes. The man had actually stopped in front of the glass partition, and, using it as a mirror, he smoothed his hair. Under these circumstances, he was taking time to primp for an on-camera interview? Her respect for her boss plummeted to an all-time low as she hurried to more important matters, and crouched beside Dan.

After stabilizing the man who'd gone code blue, they admitted him to the hospital. Though they were over capacity, twenty minutes later, they admitted a young girl who'd been hit by flying debris and appeared to be suffering a concussion. And Brad was still talking with the news crew in the hospital lobby.

What in the world was he doing? While he was wasting time answering their questions, she was still waiting for answers to hers. Had he followed up on any of the things she'd asked him to?

If they needed blood, someone was going to have to make that happen. Soon. If they ran low, and the blood bank sent frozen plasma, they'd have to wait for it to thaw. In an emergency, that could mean precious seconds. Dana yanked off her surgical gloves and headed for the lab, wishing she'd thought to check it while they were down there earlier. She'd add that to the procedures for next time.

She surveyed the bags in the refrigerated case. Looked like a normal supply to her. But this wasn't a normal situation. Her instinct said they should have a bigger back-up supply, especially of type-O blood. Pulling out her cell phone once again, Dana made the request, and hurried back downstairs. She stopped abruptly at the sight of Brad speaking to Jeanie, his hands flailing.

"What's going on?"

"Oh, Dana. Hey, you should probably be the one answering these questions," Jeanie said, obviously relieved. "I know we're swamped down here, but we've got to handle the bedtime meds on the floor."

"Absolutely," Dana said. "You see to that."

As Jeanie headed upstairs, Dana turned to Brad. "I've ordered more blood. What did you find out?"

"I haven't had time to check with the field services, Dana," Brad said, his voice taking on an edge. "I've been talking to the news reporters."

She blew a hair off of her forehead. "Yeah, what's that all about?"

"They seem real concerned about the emergency procedures, what we did, and how hard that was on the patients. I don't know, I think it's some kind of hot button because of the horror stories after Katrina and Sandy."

"Oh, for God's sake," Dana sputtered. "We're not flooding. We don't have a damaged facility, and no one has died."

When she started to turn, Brad held her arm. "But we *did* follow procedures, right? Everything by the book?"

Irritation flared inside Dana, and her hands tightened around the water bottle she held. Was he questioning her competency? There wasn't a doubt in her mind they could play Trivial Pursuit with the emergency handbook, and she'd be eating pie while Brad Berkley was still thinking.

"Of course," she said. "We can go over it later if you want, but right now, we've got patients to take care of."

**

At three a.m., Dana left the clinic where people were apparently crashing for the night, exhausted bodies burrowed into assorted chairs and sofas, one man's snores practically reverberating around the room. Dana shook her head. The whole scene was like something out of a movie.

She tiptoed into the break room. They were on three-hour rotations, and it was time to wake Valerie. Jeanie would take the next shift, which meant it'd be almost daylight by the time it was Dana's turn to rest. On one hand, sinking onto the couch with a pillow sounded like heaven. Her feet were beginning to protest the hours she'd logged on them, but she wondered if it would be better to just stay up. A couple of hours' sleep could put her in worse shape if she woke tired and groggy. Another shot of caffeine might be a better choice.

She squinted toward the sofa, considering whether she should give Val some more time. Then she remembered Brad's conversation with the news people. Were they doing everything by the book, following every procedure to the letter? She certainly didn't want any glitches in the aftermath, not after all they'd been through.

With a heavy sigh, she crossed the room. But knowing Valerie, Dana kept her distance, ready to jump back as she patted Val's shoulder. She knew from experience that waking Val was a lot like waking a slumbering bear, and she tended to be just as grouchy. On the team for eight years, Valerie was her best nurse. She was thorough and efficient, and not prone to dramatics. Thank God she'd been on duty. It was rare for them both to work the same Sunday night. Dana marveled at the providence of that. She only worked one Sunday a month – and it just happened to be the Sunday of the biggest tornado in Whitfield history.

Typically, Dana spent Sunday evenings quietly winding down the weekend at home with a glass of wine and a good book or at the manor with her dad. She shuddered at the thought of being alone in the basement of her house during the storm. Would she have survived? Would she have made it to her basement in time? That thought had her skin prickling. She'd been known to stand on her front porch and scan the sky during storms. Being at work was probably a good thing. Being here today would be better, too. Soon, though, she needed to get to her house – or what was left of it. She'd have to face what the disaster meant for her personally, but right now, this is where she needed to be.

She tapped Val's shoulder. "Hey, Val? Time to get up," she said in a loud whisper.

After some gentle coaxing, Val swung her legs to the floor and pushed back her hair. "What?" Sleepy eyes blinked up at Dana. "Oh. Already?"

"Afraid so, darlin'"

"You taking over?"

Dana shook her head. "Not yet. Think you're ready to get back out there?"

Valerie rubbed her temples, but looked up at Dana with a wan smile. "You giving me a choice, boss?"

Dana gripped the back of a chair, determined not to sit down. "Sorry, my friend. Gotta crack my whip, and keep this place running."

Val stood, rolling her neck. "Always the slave driver."

"That's why I get paid the big bucks," Dana said, giving Val a playful nudge. "Get a snack and some coffee, then relieve Jeanie on the floor."

"Sure." Val started to move past Dana, but rested a hand on her arm. "What about you? Doing all right?" she asked softly.

Dana took a deep, shuddered breath. "I'm okay, as long as I keep moving." That was the key, she told herself. Just keep moving.

At the first glimmer of pink light from outside, the hum of activity started up again. People shifted and woke. Those who'd been treated but decided to stay put for the night began gathering their things. Dana figured they'd have a new wave of patients soon. All of the people with minor injuries, who'd decided to tough it out through the night would begin filing in. Hopefully anyone who needed emergency services had already been taken to other hospitals.

While Dana and Hillary checked patients out, and made sure they had prescriptions, gauze and other supplies, a Red Cross volunteer stood at the door, ready to direct people to the shelter at the high school, if necessary. And sirens from emergency vehicles still screamed in the background. Dana's ears rung with the noise, and she wondered if she'd ever get that sound out of her head.

She turned, startled when someone tapped her arm. Jeanie jerked her head toward the stairs. "Your turn."

"Hey, Jeanie," Dana said. "Did you get some rest?"

"Yeah. I'm good. You want me down here?"

Dana glanced around as the people came to life. She wished she knew if another wave was about to hit. Somehow she'd gotten a second wind and felt less tired now than she had four or five hours ago.

"I'll stay here for now," she told Jeanie. "We'll need extra people upstairs to get through breakfast and morning rounds. Why don't you and Val do that. Hillary can stay down here."

"Sure. Has anyone heard from Abby?"

Dana's shoulders sagged. "Yeah. They lost their house. She'll be in as soon as she can, but she sounded pretty wiped out when I talked to her. I guess—"

Dana broke off at the sound of yelling as the sliding glass doors of the emergency entrance whooshed open. "Get Greg," Dana told Jeanie, then dashed to the lobby.

Oh, dear, God, Dana whispered. Who was that? White hair met white pillow, giving Dana an approximate age on the new arrival, but everything else that was visible was red with blood or blue from cold or bruising.

"She needs attention," an EMT shouted at Dana. "Can you take her?"

"Of course. Do you know—"

Cynthia Schroeder and her husband rushed through the doors, and Dana knew exactly who was lying on the gurney – Cynthia's mother. Adele Hawthorn, a wisp of a woman spry enough to still live alone in her own home though she was into her late eighties. She was a merry woman with two green thumbs who still tended to prize iris in her front yard and attended monthly garden club meetings without fail.

Cynthia's eyes were wide with horror. She clutched at Dana. "Oh, my God. Oh, God, Dana. We couldn't get hold of her last night. Cc-co-couldn't find her. We tried."

22

Dana rubbed the woman's back, and handed her a tissue. "All right, Cynthia. Calm down. We're going to help her. Tell me what happened."

"Un-under the bed," Cynthia hiccoughed. "Oh, God, she was under there all night long. Practically buried alive. Outside in the rain. We didn't know," Cynthia wailed.

"Oh, Cynthia." Dana's heart ached, and she pulled the woman into a hug. "I'm so sorry. Of course you couldn't know. Come on, let's get her checked in."

Dana handed Cynthia over to Tiffany to start on paperwork, then hurried after Greg and the EMTs.

Greg held up a hand as the technicians backed away. "Don't leave yet. We may have to send her to Paxton."

"We considered that, doctor, but we were afraid she was too frail, and the family wanted to get her here as fast as possible."

Greg nodded. "Just wait."

They worked quickly and efficiently, descending on the poor woman with IVs, oxygen, blankets, X-rays. Dana held her breath as Greg gingerly examined every inch of Adele's battered body, whispering soft expletives every few seconds.

"Jesus Christ," he exploded, finally. "I think every bone in her body must be broken."

Dana willed her hands not to tremble the way her insides were, prayed that it wasn't too late to help her. She worked alongside Greg for two hours before she let Jeanic take over.

In the lobby, she spoke softly to Cynthia. "We're keeping her sedated for now. The doctor is doing everything he can. Probably a little while longer before you can see her. Please let one of us know if you need anything, all right?"

On jelly-filled legs, Dana slipped inside the staff restroom. Splashing cold water on her face, she leaned against the counter, and let the tears come. They hadn't had such an overwhelming injury in months. She couldn't help wondering how many had been taken to other towns

– how many hadn't survived. How many others would be found in the rubble now that it was daylight?

By mid-morning Greg told Dana he'd done as much for Adele Hawthorn as he thought her body could handle. He swiped an arm across his brow. "Let's see how she does over the next few hours," Greg said. "Tell the family, she's resting comfortably. They can come up if they want to."

"Sure," Dana whispered.

"And you get some rest, yourself," Greg added. "It's time."

This time, Dana agreed. She ushered Cynthia into the room to sit with her mother, then, instead of heading for the couch, she pulled a padded chair into the small equipment room at the end of the hall. The break room would be too noisy now. Curled up in a ball, Dana closed her eyes as soon as her head hit the back cushion, the steady hum of the machinery from the room next door offering a familiar white noise in the background.

Dana started when a warm hand closed over her ice cold one.

"Dana," Greg said, his face just inches from hers.

Blinking, she registered the high afternoon sun finally making an appearance and shining through the windows. Apparently, she'd been asleep awhile. When she focused, and looked into Greg's eyes, the sadness she saw there was mirrored in his voice. "She's gone, Dana."

Dana came instantly alert, and her hand flew to her mouth. "Oh, no."

Greg shook his head. "We did the best we could. It was just too much for her."

Slowly, Dana rose. "Does the family know?"

Greg nodded. "Yes. They're with her."

A heavy weariness settled over Dana as tears spilled onto her cheeks. Gone. They'd done the best they could, but it wasn't enough. On lead feet, Dana moved past Greg, and trudged down the hall to Adele's room to give her condolences.

Fifteen minutes later, she quietly snapped the door closed behind her, and took a moment to regroup. Her stomach rumbled again, reminding her that she had to make time for a quick snack before returning to the floor. In the cafeteria, she spoke to Regina who appeared to be doubling as cook and cashier, then carried a piece of fried chicken to a small table, and pulled out her phone.

"Hey, sweetheart," she said when Chase picked up. "You still in Paxton?"

"Yeah. You still at the hospital?"

Dana let out a long, shuddered breath. "I am. We're swamped with patients. I haven't had time to watch the news in a while. Fill me in. What are you hearing?"

"That two hundred houses are gone, and four people are dead. Some others are missing."

Dana closed her eyes, fighting the sudden churning of her stomach. "It's so sad," she murmured. "We're doing everything we can, but . . ." She drew herself up, finishing the sentence in her head. *But there was more to be done.* "Listen, I took a nap, so I'm heading back out in a few minutes. I'm sure the streets are busy with people trying to get in and out, but if you can, why don't you come on back and stay with Poppa, okay? They're saying the manor is fine, but I don't want him to worry. You can just sleep on the couch in his sitting room tonight. Tomorrow I have to get out and take a look at the damage."

"I can come with you."

Dana managed to smile into the phone. "Sounds good, sweetie. I'll touch base with you later." Her head fell forward, and Dana rubbed her temples. She should probably decline her son's offer. No reason to put him through that. Except she wasn't sure she wanted to face it alone, either. That pile of sticks.

Chapter Three

A glint of light flashed in Dana's eyes as the sun hit something metal. What was that? The twisted shape resembled nothing that had been part of her home. Squinting, she shaded her eyes with her hand, and brushed against the yellow tape.

Oh, wait. Guttering, of course.

With a lump in her throat that she feared might choke her, Dana pulled her denim jacket a little tighter. She stood in the chilly spring breeze with neighbors surveying the kaleidoscope of bizarre shapes and piles that two days ago were their homes. It was almost her turn to go in with a group of volunteers and sift through the rubble to see what, if anything, could be salvaged.

She inched forward with the others. It was something she had to do, but part of her wanted to turn and run. She'd seen pictures of such devastation before, of course. And she'd seen aerial views of Whitfield's condition on the news. Somehow, though, a television screen didn't quite capture the scale of the ruins. The view was much different when you looked at it through watery eyes, when you were standing in the midst of utter chaos that made no sense, and when you could feel the anguish of friends and neighbors in the air.

At each new cry or wail carried on the breeze, the hairs on Dana's arms and neck stiffened. The initial injuries had been tended to, sure, but there was still such shock and pain. Such loss. Being at the hospital when the tornado roared through had spared her the terror of hearing her house ripped apart around her. But since she'd been working to save lives and limbs, she hadn't been able to save any belongings before the twister and the following deluge of rain got to them.

"Mom!"

Dana's head whipped around at the sound of the familiar voice. With her heart in her throat, she lunged forward to wrap her son in a bear hug, rocking as tears sprung to her eyes. Her hands clung to his shirt, and when he pulled back, she didn't let go. It was a full minute before she loosened her grip. Then, ignoring the scratchy five-o'clock shadow, she placed both hands on his face, she drew him down to plant a kiss on his cheek. "Oh, my gosh. I'm so glad to see you."

"Man, this is a mess," Chase said.

Dana turned and propelled him into line beside her. "To put it mildly," she agreed. "Did you have any trouble getting in?"

"Nah. Just had to show my ID a couple of blocks back."

"How far out did you see damage?"

"A lot. But it seems like everything's on this side of the highway. Took me an hour to get to the manor last night. Everything was backed up. Police and news people are all over the place."

Yes. Big news. The little town of Whitfield had hit national television. The only good thing about that was it would prompt others around the county to send aid. They were sure going to need it.

According to the last news report she'd heard, all residents had been accounted for. Taking hold of Chase's hand, Dana squeezed her eyes closed. Accounted for, but not saved. Now, fire crews and volunteers were going house-to-house, or rather, address-to-address, to help sift through the debris.

"Mrs. Gerard?"

At the front of the line, she recognized Stephen Reinhardt, a young police officer who was only a couple of years older than Evan, her eldest.

"Yes. Hello, Stephen." Dana said. She understood the title of 'Missus.' was simply a courtesy extended to a woman of her age. She hadn't been Missus anyone for thirteen years. Not since she'd discovered that her husband had been leading a secret life, gambling them into debt and entertaining himself with a medley of other women.

"You ready?" Stephen asked.

Ready as she'd ever be. Dana blew out her breath. "Sure."

He cocked his head toward a man standing slightly behind with an armload of flattened boxes. "This is Paul Duncan. He'll be leading your team."

She forced a smile for the stranger. "Good to meet you, Paul." She turned to Chase. "And this is my son, Chase. Thanks so much for your help."

"Happy to be here, ma'am. Least we can do."

With the pleasantries exchanged, Officer Stephen stepped back and let them proceed into the area. Five or six others fell in behind. Thank God people were willing to give up their personal time to lend a hand.

Dana swallowed past the lump and willed herself not to cry as she took in the scene. It was just stuff, after all. And not much of value. Still, she hoped to find some jewelry and photo albums, at least. Looking at the mess now, though, her hopes plummeted. Chances were, what wasn't already ruined was strewn across town.

Where to start? News reports said city crews had already taken pictures to document the losses. And her insurance company had been one of those named in the scroll across the bottom of the screen. Agents would be on site soon they said. She wasn't holding her breath, though. She dreaded speaking with the insurance people. That looming battle scared her the most.

Past experience gave her little optimism, but that ordeal was for another day. Right now, the challenge was gathering what was left of her possessions. She wiped a skillet on her pant leg, examined it, then tossed it into a box. Maybe it would clean up.

Even as she tried to focus, Dana couldn't help but think of the daunting tasks before her – all the things demanding her attention. Next up, she needed to find a temporary place to live. The Red Cross had set up a shelter, and FEMA was sending in some trailers. She could get in line for one of those, but it certainly wasn't her first choice. It'd be fine for her, but she couldn't imagine living in such cramped quarters with Chase.

The timing couldn't have been worse. Chase had just left the junior college and come back to live with her. She glanced at her son's pale face. Twenty years old, unsure of himself and directionless, the storm had shaken him. Luckily he'd had a few clothes and his new laptop with him in Paxton when the storm hit.

And there was Maddie's graduation and party, only a few weeks away now. At least she'd agreed to join with a couple of friends for a simple come-and-go in the park, and nothing at the house. Maybe they could still make that work – if the weather would cooperate. By then maybe people would be ready for the kind of relief a party could provide – something to take their minds off the losses at least for a little while.

Dana's head snapped up when she heard someone holler her name. In spite of the fact that she stood knee-deep in rubble, the smile was automatic. She waved at Mary Logan, and beckoned her over. With a nod at Stephen, still standing guard, Mary ducked under the tape and scurried into the wreckage. In only a second, warm arms wrapped around Dana. Mary rocked her, patting her back. "Oh, honey. I'm so sorry. I'm so sorry this happened to you."

Dana swiped at a tear. "Thanks, Mare." She spread her hands. "Would you look at this mess? I don't know where to start. Nothing even looks familiar. I can't believe I'm standing in my house."

"I know. But we'll get through it." She reached out and pulled Chase into a hug as well. "Hi, Chase. I'm glad you're here with your mom. The important thing is that you're both okay."

Chase nodded, grunted something unintelligible, and turned back to the box he was assembling. Mary sidled up close to Dana again.

"I know you could use some good news, hon. And here it is." She pressed something hard into Dana's hand.

Dana looked down at the key, then back to Mary. "What's this?"

"Key to Claire's place. She's in Wichita with Elise and her family, of course, and she wants you to stay at her house."

Dana stared at Mary. "Oh, my gosh. That's wonderful, but–" Her thoughts switched gears. "How's Elise?" Their friend's daughter had been in a car accident that had landed her in the hospital with serious injuries. So far, Dana's information was pretty sketchy. She needed more. She needed to talk to her friend, but hadn't been able to reach her.

Mary shook her head. "Still comatose. But the prognosis is good. The doctors expect her to recover. They say her brain is functioning, just needs a little time to re-boot."

"Thank God for that." Dana bit her lip. She could only imagine the fear her friend was facing. And here she was coming to Dana's rescue to put a roof over her head. At least for a while. Claire's house was on the market, sitting empty. With so many homes destroyed, though, it might not be for long.

Dana slipped the key into her pocket, and gave Mary a shaky smile. "That's really nice. She knows I have Chase, too, right?"

Mary patted her arm. "Of course. She said use the upstairs bedrooms. Not sure what all she took with her, or what's left. So if you need any kitchen or bath supplies, let me know. And tonight, it's dinner at my house for sure."

"Thanks. I'll be ready for that."

"But for now, let's get cooking on this. What's the procedure?"

Dana shrugged. "If anything looks like it's still useful . . . Hell, if you can even recognize what it is, dump it in a box or a plastic bag."

"You got it."

"And be careful. We've had as many injuries from the aftermath as we did from the tornado itself. These piles might not be steady."

"What? You don't want a lawsuit on your hands, too?" Mary joked, but shot an uneasy look at the tower of rubble beside her.

They both turned when shouts and hoorays broke out.

"Oh, that sounds like something good," Dana said. Jumping over a broken window, she hurried to the edge of the yard and looked down the street. David Teller held a fluffy gray cat in his arms while two children danced in front of him. Clapping along with the others, Dana hollered back at Mary. "The Tellers found their cat."

"That's wonderful! Come on. You're going to find some things, too."

Dana's chest tightened. Maybe. Thank goodness they didn't have a pet that'd been home alone.

Back to the task at hand, Dana pushed a loose strand of hair from her face and turned her attention to what had once been kitchen cupboards. A mosaic of broken dishes littered the area. She nudged the box toward Mary and spoke in a low voice. "Would you supervise this area? I'm going to attempt to locate my bedroom and see if there's any way I can recover my jewelry. And maybe a couple of pairs of shoes."

"Will do. Good luck, sweetie. Remember, lost and found is getting set up, and you can check over there, too."

"Yeah, just not sure when I'm going to get a chance." And even if she did, how could she prove what was hers? How could anyone? So many people from neighboring towns had come to help. Would there be scavengers as well? Stepping carefully, Dana picked her way back to the bedroom, hoping that the work crews and residents would be honest and turn in any valuables they found, but knowing things would be lost.

Hands on her hips, she surveyed the mess. Her bed was there, but stripped. She looked around a moment. No telling where the mattress had landed. News reports claimed the debris field was as wide as the miles of wheat fields surrounding the town. It gave her the creeps to think of personal items floating out there somewhere – and the way her toilet sat naked and exposed in the open air for all to see. She couldn't help glancing around, but was almost afraid to – afraid of seeing bras or panties hung up on trees or fence posts. That'd be the only way– Oh, whatever. Shaking her head, Dana made her way to where her jewelry box should've been. The larger of her two dressers had been upended, several drawers missing. The smaller dresser was just plain missing. Her stomach churned at the truth – the contents of her home were nearly a total loss.

"Mom."

She looked up at Chase. At six-feet, her youngest towered a foot taller than her. Dana's heart ached at the defeat on his face.

"This is shit," he said, his voice harsh. "We're wasting our time."

She swallowed hard. Of her three children, Chase was always the quickest to give up, the one she had to coax through life's troubles the most. It had always been that way. She'd never know why – whether she'd been too lenient or too preoccupied when he was little, whether she could've done anything differently. As the youngest, he'd been affected the most by his dad's departure. Chase had basically been raised by a single mom.

Reaching out, she squeezed his arm. "You know, baby, if there's nothing you especially want to look for, you can go see if anyone else needs help." She gestured over the rubble. "I want to spend some time in here."

"Where would I go, Mom? The place is crawling with people."

He ran a hand through his thick hair that was too long and hanging in his face. Before she could answer, he kicked at a piece of wood at his feet.

"What are we gonna do? There's nothing left."

She blew back the errant hair again, fighting to be patient. "Chase, I don't have all the answers right now." The tents in the background caught her attention. One probably had refreshments. "Hey, I could use something to drink, other than water. Want to see if you can get me

32

something warm? Coffee or hot chocolate?" She flexed her hands. "My fingers are getting kind of cold." She didn't *need* something to drink, but it would give him something to do. Everyone else was working. Hard as it was to do, he needed to pitch in.

Didn't take long for Dana to agree with her son's assessment, though. She hadn't located a single piece of jewelry or the box she'd kept it in. A chill swept through her. All of the pieces from her mother and grandmother, her sister's blue sapphire, all of her keepsakes, were in that box. And all of them were gone.

She looked up as Chase approached, and didn't bother to fake a smile. "Thanks, sweetie," she whispered. It was all she could do to take the cup he handed her and not fling it across the yard. She shook her head. The yard. It was ravaged as well. Her giant sunflowers, the ones that would eventually stand six to seven feet tall and always managed to cheer her, were crushed under . . . something. Chunks of the roof, she guessed. The only things left standing were the two large maples, their branchless trunks eerie silhouettes against the morning sunlight.

"I'm gonna help pass out water," Chase mumbled as he turned away.

"Yeah. That's good," she said, taking a sip of the bitter black coffee.

Dana set the cup on the back of the dresser, then stooped to recover an ornate brass frame. As she turned it over, her stomach fell, and she plopped down hard on the ground. Or whatever was underneath. Water had almost destroyed it, but she could make out faint images of her mom and dad. Her lips trembled, and the next thing she knew, Mary was beside her.

"You okay?"

The tears burned hot, and Dana wiped a sleeve across her face. "Is it too much to ask to have a couple of pictures of my folks left?" she asked, her voice breaking.

Mary propped a chin on Dana's shoulder. "It's not fair, sweetie. That's for sure."

Dana let out a groan. Did her dad know about the house? She hadn't specifically told Chase not to tell him.

33

She'd sent him text messages, and he knew they were safe. But a wave of guilt stole over her. "I've got to get over to the manor and see Daddy," she murmured more to herself than to Mary. "I know he's worried, but I just haven't had a chance yet."

She clutched the photo in her hands. Even though his mind was generally sharp, her father's body had failed him a few years ago. A stroke had left him mostly paralyzed on one side, and unable to care for himself. Now he had a space in the assisted living side of the retirement center. Dana had tried to be his caregiver when the kids were still around to help, but he was too heavy for her to lift by herself, and she'd moved him to the center two years ago. Guilt had been a steady companion ever since.

"Hey." Dana touched Mary's sleeve, as thoughts of her dad reminded her of the hospital's patients. "Did you hear about Adele?"

Sadness turned Mary's lips. "I heard she was crushed."

Dana nodded, her shoulders sagging. "Yeah. It was awful. A lot of people were hurt. They just kept coming," Dana said, her voice breaking. "I knew a lot of them, but some I didn't. So many people—"

Someone cleared his throat, and Dana and Mary both looked up. A man stood above them, dressed in khaki slacks and a navy jacket, his face twisted into an apologetic grimace.

"Sorry to intrude, ladies. I'm looking for Dana Gerard."

With as much grace as she could manage, Dana pushed herself up, brushing her hands across her jeans. "I'm Dana."

The man extended a hand and a sympathetic smile. "Good to meet you. I'm Kent Donovan from Heartland Farm and Home."

Ah. The insurance man. Would wonders never cease? He'd actually come calling.

But as she took in the man's appearance, a flash of annoyance surged inside her. Everyone else was in work clothes and boots. From his tidy cropped hair to his white smile, this guy had the looks of a smooth-talking front man. So they figured they'd send in some suave corporate guy for the job, to soothe everyone with platitudes. Still suffering from lack of sleep, and drained from the drama of the past two days, Dana was in no mood to listen to empty promises. It got her ire up. And it was pretty high already. With supreme effort, she extended her hand and lightly grasped his.

"Hey, I know you're busy right now, and feeling some stress—"

"Yeah, just a little."

"Well, I wanted to touch base, let you know I'm on the premises. Maybe we could set up a time to meet. This evening or tomorrow? No pressure. We want to make sure we're doing everything we can for you as quickly as possible."

Dana considered his request. She'd been working nearly forty-eight hours, and she felt it in every muscle in her body. Tonight, she needed to sleep. And she wouldn't be making any concessions for insurance people, no matter how sincere or friendly they were.

"Of course," she told the man, unable to keep the coolness from her voice. "I'm off tomorrow."

He glanced down at the clipboard in his hands. "You bet. How 'bout ten o'clock? We can meet over here in the trailer." He gestured behind him.

Dana looked past him. She could see now the Heartland logo along the side of a dark blue trailer. She frowned at the makeshift office. That's how they did this? "Oh—"

"Or, I'd be happy to meet you somewhere more comfortable," Kent spoke up quickly. "A friend's house or coffee shop."

His eager-to-please expression and consoling voice confused her. Was this guy for real? "Yes, let's do that." She'd probably need an entire pot of coffee. "Let's meet at The Coffee House on Main. Do you know where that is?"

"Sure do. I'll see you in the morning. Say, Dana, do you happen to have a video record of your home's interior or a list of valuables in a safe deposit box?"

She almost laughed out loud. He had to be joking. Who did that? And even if she'd thought of it, when would that have ever made it to her to-do list? She shook her head. "A list?" she echoed, pursing her lips. "Sorry. I don't."

Mary squeezed Dana's arm and smiled at Donovan. "Mr. Donovan, thanks so much for stopping by. Maybe you can go over those pesky details tomorrow after Dana's had a chance to rest. We're all a little tired and overwhelmed here."

Donovan flashed a smile. "No problem. We'll talk about it tomorrow. I sure am sorry about your loss, Mrs. Gerard. Hope you find some of your things in here."

Dana gritted her teeth. "Call me Dana, please."

With a quick nod, he turned, and Dana watched him zig-zag through the clutter. "Yeah," she muttered to Mary. "Bet he hopes I find a lot of stuff so he won't have to cough up the money for it."

"And I bet *he's* really looking forward to tomorrow." She reached over and lifted something from Dana's hair. "You've got insulation in your golden locks. Pink. Not your color at all."

With a scowl Dana kicked at the ground, her mind still on the conversation with the insurance agent. "Thanks for jumping in. Guess I was being a witch, huh?"

Mary chuckled. "Not that you didn't have cause . . . but let's say your broomstick may have been showing. Just a little bit."

Chapter Four

Rude or not, eating and running was all she could do. Mary's pulled pork roast and hearty potatoes left Dana full and satisfied – and about to do a face plant on the table. She glanced at Chase, who'd barely said two words through dinner. "You ready to go?"

With a shrug, he pushed back his chair. "Guess so."

Dana smiled at Grant and Mary. "Thanks for feeding the homeless tonight," she said, attempting a laugh as she picked up her plate and reached for Chase's.

Mary bolted out of her seat, and whisked the dishes out of Dana's hands. "Uh-uh. Stop right there. You're dead on your feet. You're not helping to clean up. You two need to get on over to Claire's and get some rest. I've got a few things for you to take with you." She turned to Grant. "Honey, could you get those groceries for Chase?"

While Chase followed Grant into the kitchen, Dana looked around for her purse, and fell against Mary when she wrapped her arms around her. How easy it would be to simply collapse right there. Her arms felt so heavy, Dana wondered if she could even manage the short drive to Claire's place without falling asleep at the wheel.

"You get some sleep, sweetie. Tomorrow will be better. Let me know how the meeting with the hot insurance guy goes, okay?"

Dana laughed as she stepped back. "You thought he was hot?"

Mary gaped at her. "Are you blind? Did you not see that smile?" She shook her head. "Of course you didn't."

"Guess I had other things on my mind. He sure was clean, though. Looked like he'd had a good night's sleep."

"And that is exactly what you need. Take a look tomorrow and see if he doesn't grow on you some."

Dana shrugged. She'd have to reserve judgment on that one. "Too bad it's coffee and insurance. Not a combination I'm fond of."

Mary squeezed her arm. "I know. Want me to go with you? I could stare him down, make sure he doesn't give you any crap, while you look sweet and wrap this guy around your finger, and let him know who's boss."

"Oh, please," Dana sputtered. "Have you ever known me to look sweet or wrap a man around my finger?"

"Are you kidding? You always look sweet, but I do realize it's a front. On second thought, be the Queen of Righteous Indignation that you are. And let him know that you have friends with mouths and we aren't afraid to use them."

Shaking her head, Dana couldn't help but crack a smile. She'd earned that Queen title after more than one showdown with teachers and administrators in the schools. Mary had coined the phrase after she'd witnessed Dana coming to the aid of some students during field day when a teacher had punished an entire class for the misdeeds of a few. Unfortunately, it hadn't done her much good dealing with past insurance issues.

"Seriously," Mary said, nudging her. "Do you want some back-up? I don't want this guy giving you the runaround."

"Thanks, Mare. I can handle it."

She just didn't want to.

"Okay, but call if you change your mind." Mary picked up a plastic bag and handed it to Dana. "Of course there's absolutely nothing in my closet that you could wear, but I raided the leftovers in Annie's, and found a few things that might get you by for now."

"That's awfully optimistic of you," Dana said. She appreciated the gesture but wondered if she could possibly fit into anything that belonged to Mary's daughter.

"Oh, hush, I've seen house cats bigger than you. Now, I rounded up some things for Chase, too. Let's see how the clothes in the washing machine hold up. Maybe this weekend we can get over to Paxton and get some new stuff."

"Listen, Mare, you don't need to do my laundry. I'll come over tomorrow and deal with that."

Mary nudged her toward the door. "Talk to the hand, babe."

Dana let it go. She knew her friend, and had no doubt that when she stopped by, there would be a pile of clean, folded, possibly mended, clothes for her to pick up. She wondered how many people Mary had taken under her wing in the wake of the tornado. Odds were, more than one meal had been delivered before she and Chase had arrived. Plus, she'd made the whirlwind trip to Wichita with Claire. Truth be told, Mary probably had as much reason to be exhausted as Dana did.

The drive over to Claire's house was quiet, and Dana's thoughts returned to Mary's comment. Shopping in Paxton? Buying all new clothes? She had a little money in savings, but that sure wasn't how she'd planned to spend it. She'd just gone halves with Chase on the new computer, and she was determined to keep enough cash for herself to take a trip with the girls this summer. They'd talked about it for so long, and she was so ready.

Her shoulders slumped as she pulled the car into the driveway. She'd have to wait and see about the insurance situation. Ignoring the pounding in her temples, Dana reached over and slid a hand down Chase's arm, and offered an encouraging smile. "Ready? Let's go in and call it a day."

"Yeah."

Dana hardly recognized the house as she switched on lights. What used to look like something out of Hearth & Home Magazine, with candles, pillows and a cozy personality, seemed bare and generic. It'd been packed up and pared down to only essentials and minimal furniture for selling. A wave of sadness rolled over her. Claire wouldn't be coming back to live here. Already the house seemed cold and empty without her.

Dana made her way to the kitchen. She knew the layout. She'd been inside that house so many times, had stayed in the guest room upstairs on nights when they'd stayed up too late or tossed back one too many. When would they ever share a carefree evening watching a movie or just talking again? It had been too long, and the way things were going, it could be much longer. She checked her watch. Before she fell into bed, she needed to call Claire.

She unloaded the perishables from Mary but left the other bag for tomorrow, then they headed upstairs to the bedrooms. Dana gripped the railing, pulling herself up one stair at a time. She knew exactly which room had belonged to Claire's son, and she walked past it. Whether it was cleared of Ben's possessions or not, she wouldn't feel right sleeping there. Her chest tightened as she thought about their situations. Her friend still had her son's lifetime treasures, but she'd lost her son. Dana had lost her children's treasures, but she had her children. They were safe, thank God. A shudder ran through her. Chase was only a few years younger than Ben had been when he was killed in crossfire in Iraq. Ben and Evan had been friends growing up, and it was that friendship that had cemented the bond between Claire and Dana. Oh, if only they could sacrifice every possession any of them had to bring back that boy. His death had left a deep hole in their lives, and had brought Claire such pain and anguish. Dana knew how her friend's arms ached to circle around her son again. Dana had experienced a mere fraction of that feeling this morning.

With a heavy heart, she continued down the hall to the other rooms. She took the one with twin beds, and pointed Chase to the other. "We'll share this one bathroom so we don't dirty up two, okay?"

"How long are we staying here?"

Dana briefly caught her son's hand as he passed. "I don't know. Try to be patient, Chase, while I get some of this figured out. I'm just glad to have a nice place for now. It's probably ours for at least a couple of weeks."

"We can clean two bathrooms, Mom."

Dana leaned against the door casing, conceding defeat. "Sure. You take that one."

She watched him for a moment, and when he turned back to her with questioning eyes, she gave him a weak smile. "It'll be all right, Chase. Try not to worry."

To her surprise, he nodded, then moved toward her. She wrapped her arms tightly around him, hugging him to her. Nothing else mattered. Her children were her life, not that twisted pile of boards and shingles on Wheaton Street.

"You, too, Mom."

She patted his cheek. "Night, sweetie. Thanks for helping out today."

Dana snapped the door shut then sank onto the closest bed, and for a long moment, maybe minutes, stared into space. She knew she was fortunate, should feel nothing but gratitude, but her resolve to focus on the positive waned. Fact of the matter was, she felt as though she were drowning, overwhelmed by the forces of nature. Maybe she should take some vacation time. God knew she had more days accumulated than she could ever use. But that was part of the problem – there was never time to take it all. Never a time when she wasn't needed at home or at the hospital. Taking off in the wake of the disaster would be selfish and would leave the hospital in a bind. As tears burned her eyes, she yanked up a pillow and hugged it against her, rocking. She refused to wallow in self-pity. It wasn't a luxury she could afford, but *dammit*, she could use a break here.

Her phone's cheery notes suddenly broke the silence. How out of place it sounded, Dana thought, as she dug it out of her purse. She recognized her daughter's number.

"Hey, sweetheart."

"Mooooom," came the long groan. "Oh, my God. I watched the news tonight, and the pictures from Whitfield are awful. Everybody's talking about the tornado. They're

41

saying people are dead and trapped under their houses. Did you *see* any of that?"

"No, but I saw a lot of injuries. I've been at the hospital since Sunday. Chase called you, right?"

"Yeah, I got a call from Chase that said, basically, nothing. Who died? Anybody I know?"

"Well, you remember Jack Hunter and Adele Hawthorne, right? A couple of teenagers were in a car and were killed. I don't know who the girl was, but the boy was one of the Marshall's grandsons."

"Oh, my God, I think I saw that car. They keep showing this smashed up blue car over and over."

Dana shook her head. Of course they did – because people would be drawn to such horrific yet fascinating images. "Yes. It's awful."

"What about our house?" Maddie's voice rose to a high pitch. "It looks like everything is gone."

With the phone at her shoulder, Dana rubbed her temples. She should've known she wouldn't get by with vague reports, that television crews would play the images on an endless loop. "Yeah, Maddie, the pictures aren't lying. A lot of stuff is ruined."

"Have you been to the house yet?"

"Spent all day there. It's a mess."

"Did you get the things out of my room?"

"Mad, listen, there's not much left. We got a few things, but–"

"Like what? All my summer clothes are there, Mom. And shoes. What about my dolls and all my books?"

"Yes, I found a couple of dolls, but, honey, they're in bad shape. And all the books are destroyed. Everything that didn't get blown away got drenched. It's moldy or rusty or coming apart. I'll check lost and found when I get a chance. I'm sure some of the dolls will turn up."

"This is great. I left all my good stuff at home so nothing would get stolen at college, and now it's gone, anyway."

Yeah, Dana remembered that conversation. Great plan. "There's nothing we can do about it, sweetie. We're lucky none of us were hurt. We'll replace as much as possible, but right now, we have to get it all cleaned up. And I still have to work, and I have to check on Poppa–"

"Is he okay?"

"Yes. Chase stayed at the manor with him last night."

"What are you going to do, Mom? Should I come home?"

"Of course not. You stay put, and try not to stress, okay? You just need to focus on school and finals. We'll get things figured out. And, hey, don't watch the news. You know they always show the worst parts, the most sensational. You'll see for yourself in a couple of weeks. Don't worry."

"I'll try. Hey, Tiff's here, Mom. I gotta go."

"Okay. I love you."

"Love you, too."

"Night."

"So much for getting right to sleep," Dana muttered, tucking the phone into her pocket. Pushing up from the bed, she kicked off her shoes, and dug inside her purse. Bottle of Tylenol in hand, she padded to the bathroom for a glass of water, then took a deep breath and punched in Claire's number on her cell phone. When the call went straight to voicemail, Dana was almost glad. She left a brief message and turned out the light. *Finally*. But when her head hit the pillow, it was as if she'd flipped a switch on, and dozens of thoughts crowded in, all vying for her attention.

She started a mental list. She absolutely had to get over to see her dad, and take care of some errands. That would have to be after her meeting with Mr. Insurance Guy, which would be after she made a trip to the bank to dig the insurance papers out of her safe deposit box – assuming they were there. And then, who knew how many hoops the insurance agency would make her jump through?

With a groan, Dana rolled over and pulled the sheet up to her neck. Was there any chance something wouldn't fall through the cracks?

**

At seven a.m. Dana woke to unfamiliar surroundings. Generally a morning person, she was used to waking with the sunrise, enjoyed the quiet stillness before the bustle of the day began. But *this* morning, she was having trouble getting her muscles to remember it. What they remembered, apparently, was seven hours of digging through rubble and pushing boxes around.

With a wince, and more than a little effort, she pushed off from the bed and peeked into the hallway. No light or sound from the room next door. Not that she expected any. She'd give Chase another hour or so.

Gingerly, Dana made her way downstairs and into Claire's kitchen. An involuntary groan escaped as she scanned the countertop. No coffee maker. She peered inside all the cupboards, and still came up empty-handed. Her meeting was at ten. No way could she wait three hours for her first cup. This early, maybe she could dash to the grocery store without being seen by anyone.

Groceries. She spun around and dug through one of the bags from Mary, grinning triumphantly when her eyes lighted on the small box of instant coffee bags inside. "Bless you, Saint Mary," she whispered.

While the mug heated in the microwave, Dana gazed out the window at the pink light of the morning sky. Somehow it always managed to ground her and help her face the day. She took a deep breath. This day she needed all the help she could get.

With coffee in hand, she retraced her steps, hopeful that Mary had come through once again and there would be something in that bag of clothes she could wear. She certainly didn't need to impress anyone, but she didn't care to look like a wayward vagabond, either.

After a steamy shower, Dana searched through the pile of clothes and slipped on a black skirt with an elastic waistband. A little snug, but she could probably make it work with a blouse that fell past her stomach. She was no taller than Mary's daughter had been in college, but she had a few pounds on her. Not to mention three pregnancies.

A bright pink top with tiny buttons up the front did the trick. Her hair she dealt with in the usual manner – a heavy-duty clip to keep the thick curls from falling into her face. Satisfied that she didn't look like the traditional homeless person, Dana glanced around for her shoes. *Oh, no.* The only shoes she had were her no-nonsense work shoes. She let out a heavy sigh. She was going to look ridiculous after all.

Shaking her head, she slipped them on, and took a gulp of coffee. Then she tapped softly on the door of Chase's room. When she got no sign of life, she cracked the door open and peeked inside. "Hey, Chase? Honey, it's time to get up."

He shifted, but didn't turn toward her. If she let him, Dana had the feeling Chase would sleep until noon. He had to kick that habit. And soon. "What's your plan for today?" she asked, knowing her voice was artificially sing-song. She refused to start the day with an argument. "I'm heading over to the bank, then I have an appointment with the insurance adjustor." She hesitated a beat before pressing on. "Do you have any interviews?"

He muttered something that Dana was pretty sure was a negative, and she rocked on her toes a moment, wishing she knew how much to push. Did the kid need more encouragement or tough love? She always had trouble with tough. "Okay, well, why don't you go ahead and get up. Have something to eat, then get started on some web searches. Maybe make some calls. When I get back we can take a look at your résumé." Wasn't that the point of the new laptop, after all?

Finally, he spoke. "What about internet?"

Oh. She had no idea how to access Claire's internet, or if she still had it. All these details . . .

"Not sure. I'll ask Claire next time I talk to her. For now, you might have to go to the li–" She caught herself. *No library.* It was one of the few public buildings that had been in the tornado's path. She heaved a sigh. He couldn't go to the coffee shop. That's where she'd be. "You might have to go to a friend's house or Bailey's. Pretty sure they have free WiFi now." Maybe that was best. He'd be forced to get dressed and out the door.

She crossed the room and ran a gentle hand over his shoulder to temper her words. "Come on. We both have a lot to do. Go to Bailey's for a while, then I bet they could put you to work at the shelter or the lost and found. I'll check in with you later."

**

She stopped at the bank first. Thank goodness it'd been spared. What a nightmare that would've been. Dana approached the bank, and even the business at hand couldn't keep her from smiling at Charlie Fast, a longtime Whitfield resident in his funny gold-checkered cap standing vigil outside as usual.

"Hey, Charlie," she said to the aging man who'd been slowly losing his faculties over the years. She wondered where he'd been during the storm. He could've been hit by flying debris in the tornado and never even seen it coming. She reached for his hand. "Sure is nice to see you out here."

He lifted his cap and gave her a slight bow. "Morning, ma'am. How are you today? Lot of strangers in town today. You be careful."

Yes, the town was crawling with cleanup crews and volunteers. Probably as unsettling for the elderly man as the tornado had been.

"No worries, Charlie." She took a deep breath. If only that were true.

"Best if I stay out of the way," Charlie mumbled.

Dana glanced around, wondering if someone had used those exact words with Charlie.

"Probably so," Dana said. Before she could proceed into the bank, Charlie took three red balls out of his pocket and began juggling, hopping back and forth on his feet.

Laughing, Dana clapped. "Look at you! I can't believe you can still do that. Charlie, you're amazing." When he caught all three balls and a wide grin spread across his weathered face, she pressed a five-dollar bill into his hand. The man didn't panhandle and didn't drink. He was just

46

lonely and had nothing else to do. "You have a good day, okay?"

Still smiling, she opened the heavy glass door and glanced inside, unsure whom to approach. She hadn't used the safe deposit box in years. In fact, it was a minor miracle she even had the key buried in her purse. That alone told her it might be time for a total clean-out. No telling what else was in the bottom of that bag.

Michelle, one of the tellers, waved to her.

"Hey," Dana whispered, sidling up to the counter. "Who do I see about getting into my safe deposit box?"

Michelle pointed. "All the way back." Then, leaning forward, she covered Dana's hand with her own. "How are you doing? I heard about your place. I'm so sorry."

Dana swallowed hard. "Thanks. I'm doing fine. Staying at Claire's for now." She held up her key. "Gotta see about the insurance. Cross your fingers for me."

"You got it. You're at Claire's? All right, I'm bringing dinner tomorrow night. Seven o'clock."

Dana sputtered out a laugh, and took a moment to enjoy the warmth that settled over her, reminding her that she loved the spirit of this town. People always willing to help their own. Blinking fast to keep tears at bay, she nodded. "We'll be there."

After signing in, Dana entered the small room filled to the ceiling with metal boxes. Alone, she rummaged through the contents of her safe deposit box. Her divorce decree flashed at her like a neon sign. Why on earth hadn't she burned that a long time ago? The accompanying documents had been thoroughly worthless. Her alimony and child support had been sporadic at best. How did you get money out of someone who spent it faster and in higher amounts than he could ever hope to make?

For a few years after he'd found another idiot to marry him, Dana had gone back to court and received almost steady checks – signed by the new wife. But it didn't last long. She had no idea whether the lazy bum was married now or not. And she didn't care. She hadn't heard from him in more than five years – no doubt he'd stay under whatever rock he was hiding until the kids were out of college.

She pushed that aside and came across her ancient passport that had never been anywhere. With a sad shake of her head, Dana thumbed through the empty pages. What a joke. One year they were going to Niagara Falls for their anniversary. The year Evan had started Spanish class, they were taking the kids to Mexico for vacation. Big talk. All talk and no action. They'd never gone farther than Six Flags over Texas. Once.

Instead of tossing it back into the box, Dana slipped the passport into her purse. She didn't know what kind of girls trip Claire had in mind, but she was going, come hell or high water – or tornado. And she'd have her passport renewed and ready, just in case.

Finally, her fingers landed on a bulky packet with the Heartland logo on front. With a sigh of relief, she pulled it out, and gave the papers a quick scan. She glanced at her watch. No time to read through them there, but maybe she could scoot on over to The Coffee House and get a few minutes to herself. She shoved the drawer back into place and locked it.

"Thanks so much," Dana called as she slipped past the receptionist. Inside her car, she tossed the documents into the passenger seat and said a quick prayer that those flimsy pieces of paper had what it took to put her life, or at least her house, back together.

Chapter Five

The bright yellow awnings of The Coffee House glowed in the morning sunshine, and lifted Dana's spirits as she stepped inside. Just like her sunflowers, the color yellow had a cheering effect on her. But a quick glance around had her faltering. Damn. Kent Donovan was already seated at one of the mismatched square tables about halfway back, and already had a mug and a stack of papers in front of him.

When he looked up, Dana remembered to mind her manners, and flicked a brief wave before moving to the back of the line. She rarely indulged in anything fancier than straight coffee, but today, she decided, called for something more. She ordered a caramel latte with whipped cream then made her way toward Donovan. As she approached, he stood and pulled out a chair for her.

"Thank you," she murmured. Just as Dana sank onto the chair, her name was called.

"I'll get that," Kent said. "You get settled."

Boy, they sure had sent the right person to make the clients feel cared for. She had to give them credit for that. Still, it made her uncomfortable – as if she were stepping into a trap. Dana nodded to a couple of people at other tables, noting that the shop was noisier than usual, and there were more people she didn't recognize. The regular crowd was probably on tornado cleanup duty. Maybe the strangers in town would make up for the lost business, she thought, smoothing the papers out on the table. Reaching for her Wal-Mart two-for-ten reading glasses, she suddenly wished she'd taken the time to get to the bank yesterday so she'd be more prepared.

Kent set a large ceramic mug in front of Dana then took the seat opposite her.

"Thanks," Dana said again, lifting the cup of liquid candy. She peered at the man over the mug. And froze. Without taking a sip, she set it down, her heart pounding. Unmistakable sympathy radiated from Kent Donovan's eyes. *Sympathy was bad.*

Dana's stomach churned, and for a moment she thought she might be sick. She closed her eyes, and inhaled a deep breath.

"Dana? You all right?"

Fighting back tears, she faced him, her fingers clenched tight around the mug. "Is it that bad?"

At least he had the grace to not pretend. He ran a hand over his jaw and regarded her with steady golden-brown eyes. "It's not best-case scenario," he said.

"Please," Dana said, her voice only a whisper. "Just tell me. In plain English. What's the problem?"

Kent drummed his fingers on the table then sat back. "Well, in simple terms, your insurance probably isn't enough to cover the cost of reconstructing and furnishing your home."

Dana shook her head as tears burned. "Of course it isn't." She leaned forward, a quick simmer flaring inside her. "And why is that? Why isn't it?" Her voice wavered as it grew louder. "This is paid through escrow. Why wouldn't the mortgage company make sure the insurance was adequate?"

"Well, that's the thing. In terms of the mortgage company, the insurance probably *is* adequate. As long as it's enough to pay off the loan, that's their primary concern."

"Uh-huh. Enough to protect them, but not me. So, you'll turn the check over to them." She lifted the oversized mug and took a drink of the coffee, even though the hot liquid would probably raise her blood temperature to a rapid boil.

"To you and the mortgage company, jointly. What you have left depends on how much principal you've paid. Here's the deal. You've got a cash-value policy. What that means is I'm going to need a list of all the items in your house and the approximate age. The insurance is paid based on the depreciated value of each item. If your roof was twenty years old, you'll get the value of a twenty-year-old roof. Not a brand-new one. Same with things like carpeting and appliances. I gotta tell you, you might end up with a hundred thousand in insurance, but new construction on a house this size is running about a hundred and forty-five thousand. And that doesn't include furnishings."

Dana lifted the cup again to hide her quaking lips. But she couldn't hold the cup and wipe tears away at the same time. The mug landed hard, sloshing brown liquid onto the table, and the papers. As tears escaped, she swiped at her eyes then brushed a hand across the thick multi-page insurance policy. "That's it?" she asked, lifting the papers. "All of these pages to say I might have a hundred thousand dollars' worth of insurance, but we're not really sure?"

Donovan heaved an audible sigh. "I know it seems like a lot of mumbo-jumbo, but it's a pretty standard policy. I talked to your agent this morning. He looked at the files, and said they contacted you about upgrading several times over the years, and that you declined."

His words stoked the embers burning inside her, and her cheeks flushed. The years had gone so quickly, and she'd been focused on raising and supporting her kids. And the truth was, with all the trouble they'd gone through when Maddie was a child and the insurance company fought them on payments, Dana never wanted to so much as speak to another insurance company again. Yeah, she'd probably ducked that one. But shouldn't her mortgage company have waved a red flag?

Even as she told herself Kent Donovan was simply the messenger, Dana's fingers itched to slap the man. She sent a scowl his direction. How dare he act as if she'd been negligent? How do you know what you don't know, for God's sake?

He hitched an elbow on the table and leaned toward her, apparently not realizing he risked personal assault if he came any closer.

"Look, Dana, I'm not saying you don't have some options. There are a lot of federal programs, loans and grants available. Don't worry. We'll help you file a claim and go through the process. John would like to talk to you, and asked if I could get your cell phone number for him."

Oh, sure. She figured John Fallon, her current insurance agent, would rather walk on nails than talk to her. He'd been the one in the hot seat after letting her dad's insurance lapse. Dana had little patience with insurance people. Just thinking about the phone calls, the paperwork, how they'd gone around and around with person after person during Maddie's childhood leukemia, could reduce Dana to tears. Instead of focusing on saving her daughter's life, she'd been forced to fight one battle after another over covered charges, allowable treatments and . . . the benefits cap. Ultimately, they'd written thousands of dollars' worth of checks to the hospital and specialists. In her experience, insurance companies didn't want to pay out. Why would homeowner insurance be any different?

Through clenched teeth, Dana ground out her cell number, fighting to remain civil. She knew without a doubt, she wouldn't qualify for a grant. Gainfully employed, she made too much money for that – but not enough to have any extra. As always, there was no padding. No, she'd be looking at another loan. And another thirty-year mortgage. What choice did she have? Sell the lot? Move into an apartment? No home for the kids to come back to? It was so wrong.

And, *dammit*, it wasn't fair. She'd worked so hard. She–

When her throat tightened again with unshed tears, Dana snatched up her policy and purse. "I'm sorry," she whispered. "I can't– I just can't do this right now."

She pushed the chair back with such force, that it nearly tipped over and threw her off balance. Lurching, she caught herself and rushed toward the door, ignoring the stares, and the "Dana, wait," from Kent Donovan. She had to get out of there.

**

Sensing that all eyes in The Coffee House were drawn to him, and aware that he was an outsider, Kent quietly sat back down, though his eyes tracked Dana Gerard's retreating form. He made a mental note of her car, a white Toyota Highlander with a University of Kansas Jayhawk license plate in front. That was good to know. Maybe he could use a different tactic with her, and break the ice with some Rock Chalk talk, the language anyone affiliated with the university would understand.

She hadn't done herself – or him – any favors running out like that. He was no stranger to small-town drama. No doubt people in the shop knew her, and would share the story – and it'd catch like wildfire, blazing a path until it had exhausted its fuel.

He rubbed a hand over his jaw. Most of the time, he enjoyed his job. Sometimes, he got to be a hero and watch families put their lives together again. Times like this were the worst. Here was someone in a tight spot, someone who needed help. And there wasn't a damn thing he could do about it. The rules and procedures were as clear as her low-grade policy.

No matter how many times he told himself not to – or someone else told him – Kent had a tendency to pull for the underdogs, to want to throw them a bone. He thought of the drawer full of thank-you notes and letters, the heart-warming stories of new homes and fresh starts, he'd received over the years. Usually, that did the trick, and put him back on course. Thinking of them now, though, didn't erase the image of Dana or the hurt and defeat he'd seen in her face. And something else . . . anger, maybe. Anger directed at him, but also at a system she didn't understand. And didn't trust. It wasn't unusual. Most people didn't know or care about the workings of the insurance industry until they had a problem. By then it was too late.

He'd have to talk to her again, no question. The only information he'd managed to get was her cell phone number. Didn't even know if she was staying in the shelter. He swore under his breath. Of all the clients they had in Whitfield, he had a feeling she'd be the most difficult to settle up with. If he were betting, he'd put money on Dana Gerard being the last to finish the process. And the biggest thorn in his side.

**

Dana slapped her hand on the steering wheel. "Un-be-*liev*-able," she hissed. As if having her house blown apart wasn't enough of a nightmare. It was exactly what she expected. Knew the insurance would be a huge issue. But that didn't make it any easier to accept.

She drove in circles until her chest stopped heaving, and her pulse calmed. The manor was only a few blocks away from The Coffee House, but she couldn't go in until she had her emotions under control. She re-clipped her hair, and dabbed a tissue under her eyes.

Finally, she sucked in her breath, and climbed out of the car. Tugging on the snug skirt, she slammed the door shut. It was so tempting to drive to Paxton with her credit card and buy a whole new wardrobe right that minute. But, as usual, reason prevailed. Spending money she didn't have would only make things worse.

Instead, she pasted on a smile, and stepped into the foyer of the manor. Waving at the receptionist, Dana glanced around the cozy living area. Sure enough, her dad was seated in his wheelchair near the window with Bobbie, one of the staff members, leaning over his shoulder.

Bobbie gave a cackle and, looking up, beckoned to Dana. "Mercy, this man is in a mood today," Bobbie said, still chuckling as Dana made her way over. "You should see the nonsense answers he's putting down on that crossword puzzle. That ain't never gonna work out, but it sure is funny."

"Funny guy, huh?" Dana said.

When her eyes met her dad's, a crooked smile lit up one side of his face, and he held his hand out to her. To Dana, that smile was therapy. And just what she needed. She moved in closer and grasped his hand, then planted a kiss on his cheek. "Hey, Daddy. How are you doing?"

He nodded, and squeezed her hand.

"Do you want to stay out here and visit, or go back to your room?"

He jerked a thumb. "Back."

"We'll see you later, Bobbie," Dana said, gripping the handles on the chair.

"Alrighty. Y'all take care, now."

Dana pushed the wheelchair to her father's small apartment, and maneuvered inside, then helped him into his large, overstuffed armchair near the television.

"You look good," she told him. "Looks like they've been feeding you well."

When her dad's eyes narrowed and focused on her face, Dana groaned inside. What a stupid thing to say. He couldn't very well return the compliment without lying. He looked good, but she looked like hell.

She quickly changed the subject. "I'm really sorry it's taken me so long to get over here, Dad. You know about the tornado, right? I'm sure everyone's been talking about it. Boy, what a mess. We were crazy busy at the hospital. A lot of people were injured. I think the first funeral is tomorrow. For Jack Hunter."

His eyes widened, and she could see him struggle for words. She gave an encouraging smile and pushed a table on wheels toward him. "Use the pen and paper if it's easier, Daddy." Dana knew he wanted to talk, wanted to hold a conversation, but he had trouble forming the words. His mind formed them much faster than his mouth could say them. He could still write, though, and often wrote his thoughts instead. In fact, he spent a good deal of time writing long letters to friends and family.

Dana had purchased him a laptop, which he used, but the pen and paper seemed easier for him than one-handed typing. While he scribbled on the paper, Dana surveyed the room. It was neat and clean. And smelled good. That was important to her. She didn't want his place to smell old, or like the hospital. His apartment consisted of two rooms – a combination sitting area with small kitchen, and a bedroom with a hospital bed and adjoining bathroom. It wasn't big, but it was spacious enough for him to move around easily in a wheelchair.

Often when she came to visit, he wasn't even in his room. Like today, he'd be reading in the common sitting area or enjoying the gardens in the courtyard, or hanging out with the staff. The staff at the manor had a soft spot for her father. Except for some occasional confusion, his mind hadn't deteriorated – he was still polite and appreciative. He didn't bark at them, and could laugh at their jokes. People like her dad made their jobs more pleasant.

Her gaze landed on a large basket on the kitchen counter. She kicked off her clunky shoes, and padded toward it. "What's this, Daddy?"

"For you."

"What?" She stopped, and turned in surprise. "Did you say this is for me?"

His head bobbed.

Curious, Dana lifted the card taped onto the cellophane wrapping. As she opened the envelope, she peered through the plastic wrap covering the basket. It bulged with bath essentials – scented soap, shampoo, lotion, comb, brush and more. Looked as though someone had gone down the aisles at Sheridan's Drug and Gift and picked up one of everything. They'd done a nice job, too.

Dana smiled as she read the card. The manor staff had pitched in. With the card at her chest, Dana turned to her father. "You're very lucky, you know. The people around here love you."

"You. Love you," her dad managed.

Did they? She hoped so. Sometimes she thought they were afraid of her because she was a nurse, afraid she'd find fault with their care. She wasn't shy in her expectations for her father's care. In that regard, her standards were high. But she always tried to be positive and temper any criticism with praise and reasonable suggestions.

Her father pushed the notepad toward her. She took his hand again, and read the note. *Do you need money?* Tears blurred her vision before she could finish. Her dad would give her all that he had, she knew that. Trouble was, he didn't have all that much. After Dana's mother and sister had died six years ago, her father had let the farm go. He was a good farmer, but he'd lost his focus and energy. The accident and then a couple of rough patches when the weather hadn't cooperated had done him in. When the stroke left him disabled, the farm had already been mortgaged.

So far, they'd managed to hold onto the land, but someone else was farming it. Their share of the farming proceeds was strictly earmarked for his care. Dana refused to touch any of it. It cost a lot of money to stay at the manor, and he'd been there less than two years. What if he were there for another ten? Or more? She couldn't bear the thought of lowering costs by lowering his quality of life or care.

Dana shook her head. "No, Daddy. I don't need any money." But as soon as the words left her mouth, her lips trembled. It was a lie, and she knew he'd see right through it. When didn't she need money? Two words from Kent Donovan echoed in her head. Not enough. *Not enough.* Before she could stop them, tears rolled down her cheeks, and her shoulders shook.

She turned, but her father's good arm shot out and stopped her, pulling her toward him. Her eyes met his, and like a little girl, Dana crumpled onto the oversized chair and cried against her father's shoulder, releasing the frustration and exhaustion of the past three days. So much loss.

She stayed there, pressed to his side, a good long time, though she knew she was soaking his shirt, and probably making him uncomfortable. But she couldn't move. Even though her father didn't have the bulk and muscle he once did, it felt good to be held for a change. She had so little physical contact with – anyone.

While her father made soothing sounds, and stroked her hair, Dana curled into his warmth.

"Shhh, Dana Dee," he murmured softly. "Shhhh. It's okay, Sugarplum."

Dana hiccoughed against him, the familiar nickname calming her sobs. When she became aware that she'd lost feeling in her cramped hand, she slowly sat up. Lifting her feet to the edge of the chair, Dana wrapped her arms around her knees. She offered a weak smile, unsure how much to tell him, unwilling to burden him with her problem. The last thing he needed was something to worry about. Some advice would sure be nice, though. Would he have any ideas or suggestions? She simply didn't trust these insurance people to be straight with her, or to act in her best interest.

Times like this reminded her how alone in the world she really was. She missed her mother and sister. Sure, she had great friends, but no one whose priority was looking out for her. She let out a long sigh. Maybe Evan could help. He was a smart kid, knew about business and finance. But the thought of dumping this on one of her children made her shudder. That would happen only as a last resort. Guess she'd better put in a call to Susie, a friend and real estate agent. Maybe she'd have ideas. She'd at least have information on the market, and might know about construction costs, too. Perhaps she could verify Donovan's numbers.

Dana started when her father nudged the paper toward her again. Forcing her eyes to focus, she continued reading. *You're a strong girl. You'll be okay. Call these people.* He'd written a couple of names. She lifted her brows. "Call these people about the house?"

Nodding, he took the paper from her, and began writing again. When he handed it back, a chill swept through her as she read his last words. *Yes. Don't worry about the house. What about Chase?*

Her eyes met his. "Daddy, what is this supposed to mean? What about Chase?"

Her father shook his head. "Not happy."

58

Dana's stomach clenched. Wow. Talk about hitting someone when she was down. Sniffling, she got up and snatched a tissue from the side table. What on earth had Chase said to Poppa? Ignoring the fear fluttering inside, she tried to keep her voice light. "He's trying to figure things out."

"Needs a job."

"Yes, of course he does. And he'll find one." She looked at her watch. This conversation could go south real fast. "We're going over his résumé and talking about some ideas later this evening."

Her father was writing again.

Get him back home. Away from those friends. Take his car keys if you have to. Don't let it get out of control. And don't give him any money.

Dana's heart pounded. "Oh, my God, Dad. What did he say to you?" Hands on her hips, she stared at her father. "Do you think he's in some kind of trouble?"

Her dad scribbled again then took her hand.

Not yet. Step in before it gets to trouble. Make sure he gets a job. And I want to see him.

"We're working on it. I don't think we have a crisis here. We have a kid who needs to figure out what to do with his life. He'll get there." Her voice had gone shrill, but she couldn't help it. "And I'm sure, now that he's back in Whitfield, he'll want to stop by and see you whenever he can. You two have always been close."

As she spoke the words she realized they hadn't actually been close for several years. Those days had been Chase's childhood. The tragedy they'd experienced had taken such a toll. Chase's high school days were a blur. Barely functioning, her father had withdrawn. He'd stopped attending sports events, stopped giving cash for good grades. Chase had been a victim of the timing.

Dana took a deep breath. She wanted them to reconnect. It'd be good for Chase to spend time with a male authority figure, and good for her dad to have the company, and maybe something to focus on. How was she supposed to control who her son hung out with or take his car keys? He was twenty years old, for crying out loud. She studied her dad a moment, taking in the hard line of his mouth, the worry in his eyes. He certainly had more time on his hands than she did. Maybe Chase could be *his* project.

**

Dana left the manor with indecision clogging her brain. Once again she considered calling her eldest son for advice. Was he far enough removed from the family and boyhood squabbles with his younger brother to be objective? Could he help? She didn't know how often the two of them spoke. Even though each of her children were two years apart, it always seemed that Evan and Maddie were much older than Chase, and closer to each other.

She let memories flood in as she waited for a green light. There were only a handful of traffic signals in all of Whitfield, but she always seemed to hit this one red. She'd been so looking forward to having all of the kids home for Maddie's graduation. Had wanted to focus on her family, and work with Chase. Wanted her family to be top priority. But a tornado had blasted in, forcing her to switch gears, fragmenting her attention. Not exactly the Hallmark moments she'd imagined.

When her phone chimed, Dana checked the number, and didn't recognize it. With a grimace, she dropped the phone back into her purse. If this call was from her insurance agent, no way did she want to take it. There were only a few people she wanted to talk to right then, and he didn't make the list. She wondered, though, thrumming her fingers against the steering wheel, if she'd hear from Kent Donovan again. Or had he done his job, and she'd now be turned over to her regular agent?

If she hadn't run out of The Coffee House so fast, she might know more. Obviously, she needed information about the steps involved – some sort of plan or timeline. He said they'd help with the process. But how much?

A smidge of guilt wafted over her. Leaving him sitting at the table had been rude. She glanced toward her purse again. The call could've been from him, she supposed. He and John both had her cell number now. She didn't love that, but she couldn't give out Claire's number or the number to the hospital. Unfortunately, that meant her cell phone was now her primary means of contact.

On autopilot, Dana pulled into Mary's driveway. She climbed out of the Highlander, and made her way from the beautifully landscaped circle drive to the curved red brick steps of Mary's porch. The door opened before Dana had a chance to ring the bell.

"Hey, how'd it go? Come on in," Mary greeted her. "Uh-oh. Looks like you could use something to drink."

"Yeah. What've you got?" Dana asked, following Mary toward the kitchen.

Mary stopped, eyebrows raised. "I've got everything. You want a big-girl drink?"

A glass of wine sounded pretty good, but Dana's thoughts turned to Claire, and she couldn't bring herself to go there. "Nah, too early for that." She glanced at her watch. Was it really only noon? Seemed like she'd been riding an emotional roller coaster for hours. "Got any iced tea?"

"Sure thing. Have a seat, sweetie."

Dana sank into a cushioned chair at Mary's kitchen table. As she looked around, she couldn't help but mentally add up the cost of furnishings in Mary's amazing home. Cha-ching, cha-ching. Dollar signs flashed everywhere. Mary and Grant had one of the nicest homes in Whitfield, and Dana figured the furnishings alone were more than the cost to rebuild her entire home. She wouldn't have enough money to rebuild the shell of her house, let alone furnish it with garage sale cast-offs. Everything in her house was at least fifteen years old.

She swallowed hard. She'd never been too concerned with material possessions, and had known better than to try and keep up with the Joneses, but at this stage in her life, shouldn't she have a few nice items? A decent mattress and comfortable chairs, at the very least?

Mary sat a glass of iced tea in front her, and pulled a chair close. "Tell me what happened."

Dana took a long drink of the cold beverage then blew out her breath. "I'm screwed."

The sympathy in Mary's eyes vanished, a fiery light replacing it. "That's bull," she exploded. "No way. This town is going to make sure you and everyone else lands on their feet. Now what do you need?"

That question again.

Dana shook her head. "What do I always need? Money, of course. Some things never change, I guess."

Mary squeezed her arm. "What did the insurance guy say?"

Dana shot her a wry look. "That I don't have enough insurance to rebuild or furnish my house."

"Why the hell not?" Mary demanded.

"Funny, that's exactly what I asked."

"*And?*"

With elbows on the table, Dana rested her head in her hands. "Bare bones policy, I guess. Depreciation. No replacement costs."

"What are they going to do about it?"

"They?" Dana echoed. "Who's they? No one's going to do a damn thing about it, Mare. What can anyone do?"

"Well, that's just bullshit."

As soon as she said it, her lips twitched, and Dana grinned, knowing exactly what they both remembered.

Mary laughed. "Where is Claire's bullshit button when you need it?"

"Oh, I think I'm going to need my very own," Dana said.

"Absolutely." With a heavy sigh, Mary pushed her chair back. "Listen, this is going to work out. I promise. Have you eaten anything? I've got some fruit and cheese."

Dana knew she should get up and leave, go check in with Chase. She wanted to go over his résumé, talk about interviewing and job hunting. She could go by the house again or pitch in with cleanup efforts. But, *ugh*, she needed more time – needed to process the events of the morning.

She scooted out of her chair, and joined Mary at the granite-topped kitchen island. Sometimes her brain worked better when her hands were busy. "Thanks, Mare. Sounds good." Picking up a knife, she sent her friend a grateful smile. "Tell me about Claire. I haven't been able to get hold of her. How is she? Tell me the truth."

A shuttered look passed over Mary's face. "Well, she was all right when I left Wichita, but I'm worried about her. I'll check in with her again this evening. Let's hope this will snap her out of it and keep her sober. She needs to be there for Elise. And believe me, I told her exactly that."

Dana nodded. Claire was one of her dearest friends. Unfortunately, she'd leaned too heavily on alcohol to get her through the trauma and tragedy in her own life. Looking back, Dana cringed with guilt. She couldn't count the number of times she'd taken a bottle of wine over to Claire's house, shared a glass – or more – with her. Hadn't seen it coming. "I miss her."

Mary stopped chopping, and turned her gaze out the kitchen window. "I know. We all do."

Dana touched Mary's arm. "Hey, didn't mean to be a downer."

Mary shook her head and shot Dana a wry smile. "You're not. I just want her to get well."

"We should send something for her new place," Dana said, trying to sound more cheerful.

"Absolutely. Bring the cheese, would you?" She picked up the tray of fruit and headed to the table. "Now, what about Chase? He's okay with staying at Claire's?"

"Oh, sure. He doesn't have any more options than I do." Dana chewed her lip. She hated to unload all of her problems on Mary, but maybe she'd have some tips on how to motivate Chase. Her kids all seemed to be doing well. If she asked, Dana knew Grant would give Chase a job at the cement operation in a heartbeat. But something held her back. She wanted Chase to make something happen on his own.

Between bites, she filled Mary in on the conversation with Poppa, concerns about Chase trumping her pride.

"What about an apprenticeship or some kind of technical program?" Mary asked.

Dana nodded. "I said the same thing. I know college isn't for everyone. Problem is, he doesn't have any idea what he wants to do. Nothing seems to grab him. I'd hoped that after a year at the junior college, he'd find some kind of interest. But nothing's stuck. And now *he's* stuck, and I just don't know how to help him."

She paused to pop a grape into her mouth, but she couldn't seem to stop talking.

"I told him he could come home, thought it would help him get his feet on solid ground. I thought the safety of the familiar would make him feel more in control." She shook her head as her lips trembled. "Now look. There's no home. There's nothing for him here. Nothing is familiar. His room, his things . . ." her voice broke. "Everything is gone."

Leaning back in her chair, Mary eyed her. "Do you want me to talk to Grant?" she asked softly.

Before answering, Dana took a long drink of iced tea. "I'll be honest. I thought about that, and you're sweet to offer, but I want Chase to figure this out. We can't hand it to him."

"But we could suggest. Give him a nudge."

"Sure, but Mare, I want him to have a career, not just a job. Or a job that will lead into something more, like management or higher levels of responsibility. He's not stupid, just unfocused."

"That's right." Mary shook the fork in her hand. "Give him some more time. You never know, Maddie's graduation might inspire him. He might not want to be the only one without a college degree."

True, Dana thought. On the other hand, could it cause him to withdraw? Would his sister's graduation and all the fanfare that went with it make him more unsure or feel inadequate? The last thing she wanted to do was make her son feel bad about himself.

Dana considered her next move as she began carrying plates to the counter. What was really going on with Chase? Would it be wise to question him about his conversation with her dad, or would that cause him to clam up? She'd planned to spend the entire week working with Chase, helping him get his résumé and cover letters in shape, get a list of prospective companies to call on, maybe coach him a little. And to mother him a bit, make him feel special. So much for that plan. The time and energy for that had blown away with the twister. She couldn't expect to make any progress now, at least not this week. They'd have to be flexible. Not her strongest suit, she admitted. The only way she'd survived working and getting three kids where they needed to be all those years was by being organized – writing things down, and making lists. She lived by a calendar and schedule.

"Thanks for feeding me. Again," Dana told Mary. "I hate to think what your grocery bill is going to be this week."

"Hey, we haven't even got to the good stuff yet. I have chocolate."

With a wide grin and flourish of her hands, Mary produced two cupcakes with a thick layer of chocolate butter cream frosting and dark chocolate shavings on top.

Dana recognized them immediately as a specialty of Hannah's local bakery and cafe. "Oh, my God, Mary. Those things could send a person straight into a sugar coma."

"No, pal, you're looking at a sugar high. Just what the doctor ordered. Come on, you need this fortification."

She didn't have to ask twice. Dana took the fork and cupcake offered. Within minutes, she licked the fork clean – and reached under the back of her shirt to inch open the zipper on the borrowed skirt.

Then Mary poured Dana a fresh iced tea in a plastic cup. "I bet you haven't had time to brew any, so take this with you. I'll get the clothes. They cleaned up pretty well."

After they loaded the bag of freshly laundered clothes into Dana's car, Mary pulled her into a quick hug. "Listen, try to take it easy, my friend. You have a lot on your plate right now. Give the thing with Chase a little time. It'll all work out."

Dana had to smile. Mary provided a sugar high, therapy and a pep talk all in about an hour and a half. And at a very reasonable price. "Thanks, Mare."

Yes, she supposed it would all work out. But that was the kind of statement that made Dana crazy. *When* would it all work? And *how*? Open-ended comments like that didn't come with a schedule. Or a plan.

Chapter Six

Dana pulled into Claire's driveway, noting that Chase's car was at the curb, and immediately spotting the bright red cooler sitting on the porch. It hadn't been there when she left that morning. Looked like word had circulated, and she was on a meal program. Couldn't complain about that. Grinning, she opened the back car door, and retrieved the bag of clean clothes from Mary and the basket from the manor staff.

Buoyed by those things, Dana hurried up the walk, and mentally crossed her fingers, hoping to hear that Chase's day had been productive.

That thought lasted about a second. Disappointment settled in her chest as she walked into the living room and found Chase asleep on the sofa. She dropped the bag of clothes then headed to the kitchen with the basket, not bothering to keep its cellophane wrap from crinkling.

Irritation warred with her momma-bear instincts. What was wrong with him? Why did he need – or want – so much sleep? Was it a physical problem or an escape? Either way, it might be time for a checkup. It'd probably been a couple of years since he'd had one. She could set that up at the clinic.

She placed the basket on the table, then leaned against the counter, debating her next move. When her phone pealed from inside her purse, she snatched it up and automatically turned off the ringer. Didn't matter. Chase didn't even stir. Checking the number, Dana hurried back outside.

"Claire," she breathed. "Oh, my gosh. How are you? How's Elise?"

"We're okay. Sorry I didn't call back last night. It's been exhausting. But I have good news."

Hope surged through Dana. "She's awake?"

"Yes. Woke late last night. She doesn't remember much, but at least she remembers who she is and who we are. She still has the bumps and bruises to deal with, but her mind seems good as new."

Though the words were reason to cheer, Claire's voice quivered, and Dana heard the tears she was trying to hold in. If they were together, they'd probably be bawling and hugging. She wished they were. "Oh, Claire. That is the best news ever. I'm so happy. I can't even imagine how hard it's been."

"I could've lost her, too."

Claire's voice was hoarse, heavy with the strain of such raw emotion. Dana's heart broke for her friend, thankful that hadn't happened. Claire could not have survived losing another child. "Don't even think about that. Can she go home soon?"

"Probably another day or two, just to be sure, the doctor said."

"And what about you?" Dana asked softly. "How are you?" There was a long moment of silence before Claire spoke again.

"We both have some healing to do. You need to know that I have an AA sponsor here now. I can't get sick again. And I'm going to need all of you to help me through this."

Dana couldn't help but think that would be a lot easier if Claire came back to Whitfield. But she understood why that wouldn't happen – not with her grandkids in Wichita, and her ex and his new wife in Whitfield. "We're all here for you, girlfriend."

"I'm giving up the booze for good," Claire said, attempting a laugh.

"We don't need it," Dana told her. "Besides, think of all the money you'll save. You can spend it on clothes or, say . . . chocolate and ice cream, instead. Wish we could get started on that today."

"Me, too."

"Will you stay with Elise?"

"Yes. I'll help out while she needs me, and then . . ." Claire let out a long sigh. "Hopefully only a few more weeks and I can move into my place."

"I can't wait to see it. Let us know when you're ready for company."

"Definitely. Now, what about you? Settled in?"

"What would I do without you? God, I'd probably be in one of those nasty little trailers."

"That would not do at all," Claire said. "There's absolutely no reason for that house to sit empty. Not as long as you can use it."

"But, Claire, I have to pay you. After all, you could be—"

"Oh, for heaven's sake. If you're going to start talking nonsense, I'm hanging up."

It was the response Dana expected, and she couldn't even begin to express her gratitude. Still, she couldn't take advantage of her friend indefinitely. "Fine. We'll come back to that later. You'd better not hang up. I want to know what I can do for *you*."

While they talked, Dana peeked inside the cooler that had magically appeared on the porch. On top of a bed of ice was a tray of meats and cheeses and a large bunch of green grapes. Easy food. Exactly what they needed.

"Now, listen," Claire said. "I know Maddie's graduation is coming up. You do whatever you need to at the house. Take over the whole place. I want to be there, Dana, but I don't think I'll make it. I'm not sure Elise will even be able to drive by then."

"We all understand. You have too many other things to think about. We're doing a party with Rebecca and Callie in the park. No big deal." She bit her lip. "But,

Claire? Come down as soon as you can. Everyone misses you."

"I will. I can't think about it right now, but I want to make sure someone's working to get the library up and running again."

"Yeah, I'm afraid that's going to take a while. There's nothing left. It's–"

"I know, but we can't just let it go."

Dana didn't want to argue, but to her mind, the library could wait. There were much more pressing needs. People had to come before books. "You're the person to make it happen," she told her friend.

"I wish I could be there to help you," Claire said.

"You are helping. Don't worry about Whitfield for now. But come when you can."

"I will. Can I stay with you?"

Dana laughed. "You name the day, and I'll clear the dust bunnies."

"I'll be touch."

"Okay. My love to Elise. And, Claire?"

"Mm-hmm?"

"Take care of you."

After they said goodbye, Dana tapped the phone against her hand for a moment. They were all doing what they had to do and were where they had to be, but she couldn't shake the sadness that settled in her chest. Like the contents of her house, her friends and children were scattered across the miles. The holes in her life kept expanding, leaving voids that were hard to fill.

Dana picked up the tray from the cooler and wandered back inside. She stopped short at the sight of Chase standing at the kitchen sink guzzling a glass of milk.

"Hey, sweetie."

He ran a sleeve across his mouth. "Hey."

She slid the tray inside the fridge then turned to face him. "So how's your day going? Make any progress?"

"Nah. I ended up working at the school for a while."

"You did? Well, that's great, honey. I'm sure they appreciated it. Did you get anything to eat?"

"Yeah, someone brought in a bunch of sandwiches. I think they're using the school cafeteria, too." He ran a hand through his shaggy hair. "Man, a lot of people are camped out there. The gym is full of cots."

With a heavy sigh, Dana leaned against the counter. "It's so sad, but hopefully people will find other accommodations soon. I'm sure glad we aren't there." That thought collided with a fresh wave of guilt. They were lucky to have Claire's place all to themselves. She glanced at her watch. Three o'clock gave them several hours of daylight still. They could get back out there. She could check in at the hospital, or go to the school and make sure no one needed medical attention. They could hand out water, or dig through rubble. The list of needs was long, but she hesitated. The tornado would consume their lives if she let it. Besides, with the Red Cross and FEMA and all the volunteers from out of town, they might just be in the way.

"Did you see anyone you knew?"

"Lots of people." Solemn eyes met hers as Chase nodded. "It's bad. Lots of old people and little kids. I think they're trying to have day care."

That was the second tragedy of the tornado. The older neighborhoods were the hardest hit, so the people who could least afford it were the ones most affected.

The cloud of uncertainty on Chase's face cemented Dana's decision. Maybe he'd witnessed enough devastation and despair for one day. She rested a hand on his shoulder. "Let's take a little break from the tornado, sweetie. "Why don't you grab your computer and let's have a look at your résumé."

Dana jumped when Chase's fist connected with the counter.

"I don't *have* a résumé, Mom. I don't have anything to *put* on a résumé."

Gripping the edge of the table, Dana counted to ten. She knew the outburst wasn't really directed at her. It was a symptom of the stress and doubt he was feeling. Instead of reacting to it, she attempted a smile and level voice.

"That's not true. You're a high school graduate. You have a year and a half of college under your belt. You had good test scores. That's all relevant."

Dana pushed up her sleeves, and pulled out a chair. She didn't understand his lack of self-confidence, but she was determined to get his feet on solid ground. "It's all in the way you present it. Come on. We can crank this out now. It won't take long."

With a reluctance that was palpable, Chase set his computer on the table and opened the two-year-old document he'd created in high school.

Dana did a quick scan. It wasn't bad. "Okay, here's the deal," she said. "You have about one page to sell yourself. You're not just going door to door looking to fill out applications. You're looking for an entry-level professional job that has some career potential."

"Mom, no one's going to hire me without a degree."

"That's not true," Dana countered. "You have to make them see your positive attributes."

Dana started typing while Chase appeared to stare into space.

When she looked up again, her heart ached, and she touched her son's arm. "You know what else," she said softly. "You're a nice person, Chase. You're compassionate. Let's think about places that need people to be kind. Like customer service. Or maybe working with the elderly. You're great with Poppa. What about the manor, care and counseling? All of these would need a degree, but you could work and take a class here and there until you figure out if that's what you want to do."

In her mind's eye the look of sympathy on Kent Donavan's face when he broke the bad news flashed before her. She nearly fell out of her chair. Where the hell had that come from? As if she would ever consider suggesting a career in insurance to her son. She must be more tired that she realized. That would happen, oh . . . *never.*

Blinking, she refocused on the computer screen, but one glance at her son's face, and she knew he wasn't buying into it. Wasn't in the mood. It was probably pointless to push him.

"All right, look, spend some time thinking about it, and we can finish this up later. I doubt people are setting up appointments this week, anyway. Everyone's dealing with the tornado. Want to go say hello to Poppa before dinner?"

Chase shook his head as he closed the laptop. "Nah, I'm gonna head over to Paxton."

"Now? What about supper?"

"I'll get something there."

"But, honey, we have all this food people are bringing. I can't eat it all myself."

"I guess I could take some with me," Chase said.

Dana winced. Taking food that was intended for tornado victims to his friends somehow didn't seem right. "I don't know—"

"Better than wasting it, right?"

"Are you sure you want to drive all the way over there? That's using a lot of gas, you know. Why don't we have a quiet night here by ourselves?" Her father's warning came back to her, but he didn't understand how difficult it would be to separate Chase from his friends over there. And so far, she didn't really have a good reason to.

"Mom," Chase groaned. "I gotta get out of here for a while."

"Fine, you can make a sandwich if you want, but we can't send the food to your friends. I can always take it to the shelter. Why don't you stop and see Poppa on your way out?" She took a deep breath and plunged ahead. Might as well get it all out there. "He's worried about you."

Chase's eyes narrowed. "What's that supposed to mean?"

She studied him a moment, unsure how much to give away. "I was wondering the same thing. Want to tell me about your conversation the other day?"

"There's nothing to tell, Mom." His voice rose as his hands began flailing into the air. "He was just asking me a bunch of questions. I don't need another person asking me what I want to do with my life, okay? I don't *know*."

So he felt pressured. That wasn't good. Like a performer on a tightrope, she was going to have to find a balance – to encourage and support without nagging. She didn't want him pulling away. Dana turned toward the kitchen. "Okay, Chase. Calm down. He's trying to help. It's not so bad to have people care about you, you know."

Ten minutes later, she stood at the window and watched him drive away. She couldn't expect him to stay home, but she wished his buddies were closer, and she could interact with them the way she had when he was growing up. Not knowing them made her feel out of the loop. With a heavy sigh, she let the curtain fall into place. At least he *had* friends, she told herself. That was important.

Where would she be without her friends? Heading upstairs, she grabbed the bag of clothes from Mary. After wrestling the knot loose, Dana reached in and lifted the top few items from the stack. Her face warmed as she stared at the unfamiliar pieces – brand new clothes still sporting their tags. Sinking onto the bed, Dana fingered the soft cotton of the blue and green tie-dye T-shirt with brass embellishments. No question that Mary had good taste.

And she was generous – to a fault. Tears sprung to Dana's eyes. She knew that Mary's language of love was giving gifts. She'd been on the receiving end of a good many. Mary loved surprising people with gifts, and had the financial means to do it. But she didn't understand that sometimes her generosity felt too much like charity, and was hard to swallow. Like now.

Dana pushed off from the bed, and wandered the room. Was accepting gracefully always the right answer? She certainly didn't want to seem ungrateful. It was Mary who'd kept the kids in hats and gloves over the years. She'd have hot chocolate and sledding on snow days then send everyone home with brand new hats and gloves as though they were party favors. Oh, she employed some sneaky tactics. One year, she'd stocked up on a mountain of pool toys for the summer and invited Dana and the kids over. When it was time to go, Mary shoved kickboards and floating rings and "noodles" at them.

"Forget the pool," Mary said. "I'm drowning in pool paraphernalia. Take this stuff with you, and you can bring it back when you come here or take it with you to the city pool." As if they would be doing her a favor.

Maddie was too young to understand the word and too shy to ask. She thought Mary had said "pool parrot vanilla." Dana had tried to explain, but Maddie thought the nonsense phrase was hilarious, and couldn't get it out of her head. Eventually, she dropped the vanilla, but from then on, pool toys at Dana's house were always referred to as pool parrots. And thanks to Mary, they always had plenty of them.

Dana smiled at the memory. It had become a private joke that they didn't even bother to explain to others. With mixed emotions, she reached into the bag again, and found one of Mary's personalized notecards tucked inside. *"I couldn't resist. These will look fabulous on you. Wear them well, pal. Love ya!"*

How could she refuse?

**

The next morning, Dana threw off the blankets, determined to get an early start and run an errand before heading to the hospital.

At Sheridan's, she loaded up a small cart with snacks and goodies, then headed to the post office. She grazed a hand over the label on the package, applying a little pressure at the corners, surprised at the bittersweet emotions a simple package could evoke. This was possibly the last college care package she'd ever send to one of her kids. Maddie's final finals week. She couldn't wait to see her daughter, all grown up, walk across the stage and receive her diploma and accolades. She was so proud of her. So proud to launch a beautiful, intelligent young woman into the world.

As a mother, Dana had done her job, and done it well. Maddie was graduating with honors, and already had a job as a nutritionist lined up with the new hospital in Joplin. She'd be home for the grad party, then she'd be gone again.

Inside the post office, Dana lifted the box to the counter.

"Hello there, Dana," Milt said from behind the service area. "How are you doing? Getting things straightened out?"

"Oh, it'll take some time, Milt, but I'll get there."

The man nodded as he reached for the package. He punched some tabs on his screen then smiled at Dana. "Let me guess. Finals?"

"That's right."

"Seen a few of these in here this morning. That time of year."

Dana knew he was just making conversation, but it knocked her down a peg or two, and she laughed at herself. Okay, so she wasn't getting a mother-of-the-century award for sending her kid a care package. Still, it made her feel good to do little things like that, and she was determined that the tornado would not get in the way or cause her to forget. Maddie would be looking forward to it.

"You take care, now," Milt told Dana. "And you add me to your list if you need anything done . . . moving, packing, whatever. That's not just blowing smoke. I mean it."

"Thanks, Milt. Will do. See you later."

With a smile, and a quick wave, Dana left the post office, and tossed her purse into the car. Today, *she* was looking forward to going to work. Even bursting at the seams, it had to be less stressful than the past two days. At the hospital there was structure and order, routine steps to follow. She couldn't wait. She wanted to focus on her patients, see who'd been discharged, and how everyone was doing.

Before she could back out of the parking space, a sharp tap on the window whipped her head around. Kent Donovan motioned for her to roll the window down. Dana resisted rolling her eyes as well. She didn't have time for this.

"Hey, Dana. Glad I caught you. Do you have a minute?"

Embarrassment warmed her face, but she put on a smile and forced herself to speak to the man. "Hello, Kent. Listen, I'm sorry, but I don't have time right now. I'm on my way to work."

"John said he wasn't able to reach you yesterday."

As if he hadn't heard what she said, he rested an arm on the car door and regarded her with steady brown eyes the color of wheat after harvest.

"I do understand how hard this is, Dana. We aren't the enemy. We'll do everything we can for you. Let's get things started with your claim. There's some paperwork involved. And we need that list of the contents of your house."

She'd ignored more than one call yesterday. Couldn't they give her some time? What was the big rush, anyway? Tears threatened, but turning away, she blinked them back. Would she ever have a conversation with this guy without bawling?

Donovan's voice softened. "Is there some reason you want to wait on this?"

Dana thought about that. How silly she must look. Everyone else must be clamoring for their attention, demanding that the wheels get rolling – and fast. What *was* she waiting for? Didn't she need to get her house rebuilt?

How about just a little time to catch her breath? And process. She'd ignored calls and also put off making any. She needed to make calls to the bank and the mortgage company, to Evan and to the people on her dad's list. Her hands tightened on the steering wheel. Truth was, the whole thing was overwhelming and she didn't know where to start. *Paperwork.* Yeah, she figured there'd be mountains of that.

Kent tapped a hand on the door. "Wait here a sec."

Her gaze followed him as he did a slow jog to a black Lexus sedan a few spaces down. When he turned and headed back toward her car, a smile spread across his face. It was odd – she had the feeling that every time she met him, the past was erased, that he'd forgotten – or forgiven – any tension. Maybe it was that easy-going manner that had attracted Mary. On closer inspection, Kent Donovan reminded her of Grant Logan. Dana had never seen Mary's husband anything but calm and friendly.

Kent poked some papers at her. "I didn't get a chance to give these to you yesterday. First up, here's a check for two thousand dollars to help you get back on your feet. Use it for immediate needs like replacing clothing and everyday items, things like that."

She couldn't have been more surprised if he'd dumped a chest of gold coins in her lap. "Oh, thank you. That's . . . that's very nice."

He handed her a pen. "Just need a signature acknowledging that you received the check."

"Sure," she murmured, feeling like a shrew for not being more friendly.

"When you get a chance, read through the rest of these papers. There's a checklist of steps to take, and an outline of the things we can help you with. When you're ready, give me or John a call, okay? Numbers are on the documents."

"Good," Dana said, nodding. "That's great." She took the papers and tucked them beside the seat. Biting her lip, she looked back at Donovan. "Thanks."

"No problem. Call if you have questions, Dana. You have a good day."

Sure. "Just get me out of here," Dana whispered as Donovan retreated. She stared at the check, hardly daring to believe it was real. And she hadn't had to beg, or even ask, for it. That would be going in the bank immediately. Maybe, just maybe, the girls' trip could really happen.

Chapter Seven

Dana read the message again, and checked her watch. A management team meeting at ten. That should give her time to make her rounds. But it meant something was up. Andrew Holland, the hospital's longtime chairman, liked structure and routine, and the schedule called for a team meeting at one p.m. every Monday – not Thursday mornings. Probably just to touch base in the wake of the tornado.

At nine-forty-five she ran into Greg in the stairway. "Hey, Greg. Thanks for the notes on Mrs. Carlyle. She seems to be in good spirits today." When he wasn't in surgery, Greg meticulously followed up on patients' progress, which earned him high marks from Dana.

Greg nodded. "Yes. She's handling the new drugs much better. We ought to be able to release her in a day or two."

"Sounds good. Hey, do you know what's up with this staff meeting?"

He lifted his glasses and rubbed the bridge of his nose. "You haven't heard?"

Dana hesitated. If she read Greg's body language correctly, something was about to hit the fan. "Huh-uh. I was off yesterday."

"Berkley's given notice. Says he'll stick around six weeks to help with a search for a new administrator, but I wouldn't count on it."

"Are you serious?" Dana nearly shrieked. "I had no idea he was looking. He hasn't even been here two years." Groaning inside, she sagged against the metal railing. Another administrator already. Might as well install a revolving door in that office.

"Yeah. I talked to him. Sounds like the tornado spooked his wife and she's turned up the heat. Wants to get out of here. ASAP."

"Right." As if another tornado like that was going to blast through on a frequent basis. Dana had lived in Whitfield all her life and had never seen anything like this before. "Wait a minute, isn't she from the west coast?"

Greg thought a moment. "Sounds right, I think."

"So, get real. Has she never heard of earthquakes? She'd rather shake, rattle and roll?"

Greg simply shrugged, and Dana moved on up the stairs, blowing out her breath. "Okay, see you in a few."

Brad Berkley was notably absent from the small gathering when Dana stepped inside the conference room ten minutes later.

"Morning, Dana," Andrew said. "Nice to see you. How are things over at your place? You get it all secured?"

Dana glanced around the table. She knew her co-workers were genuinely concerned, but also figured they didn't care to hear all the depressing details. She was getting a little tired of them herself. Besides, she wasn't the only one who'd been affected. One of the part-time nurses and a custodian had lost their homes as well. In their line of work there was no room on the agenda for a pity party. She plopped into a chair. "Well, there's not much left. But we're getting it cleaned up."

Andrew jerked his head toward Amy Phillips, their HR director. "Take whatever time you need, Dana. Just work it out with Amy."

"Thanks, Andrew. I appreciate it. I'm sure I'll be taking you up on that." She hoped she wouldn't need to take a lot of time off, but she had to make calls during business hours. Her plan was to sneak away for twenty or thirty minutes each day to get through that list.

"Did you get a trailer?" Amy asked.

"No. I'm staying at a friend's place."

"Oh, good. That's better."

Andrew cleared his throat. "I know everyone's been under a lot of stress this week. You kept your cool in the chaos, and you've done an outstanding job responding to the community." His eyes moved around the table, acknowledging each person there. "The timing stinks, but we have another challenge to deal with. I guess by now you all know why we're here. Got to start a new search to replace Brad." Andrew's voice hardened as he spoke. "I'll tell you I'm getting damned tired of this. I want to find the right person this time. Someone who's going to stick around. We're going to look until we get it right."

He waved a hand toward Dana and Amy. "Once we get a good list, I want you two to put together a welcome team. We're going to wine and dine every good candidate, and show 'em what a great place Whitfield is. You know, give them some good old Midwestern hospitality."

Dana nodded her agreement and willingness to help, but didn't they always do that? She'd put together goodie bags of local products, sung the praises of the schools and safe environment, and coaxed candidates to indulge in Hannah's famous pies more times than she could count. How would this be any different than before?

"Andrew, that's fine," she said. "I'm happy to help, but there's nothing we can do to change Whitfield or make it more attractive. It's a small town. We need to focus on finding someone who can appreciate that, someone who's not looking for bright lights and big city. Brad never wanted to settle down here or raise his kids here. From the very beginning we were only a stepping stone."

What some people didn't seem to realize, was how great Whitfield was for making connections with other people. If you stuck around long enough, you could build deep, lifelong friendships. You'd have people looking out for you and your kids. At the local business establishments, you'd be a real person, not just another face in the crowd.

Andrew bounced his fist against the table. "Maybe we need someone single," he said, his eyes lighting up as though he'd thrown out the million-dollar answer. "Then they meet someone here, and – *bingo* – they settle down and get married."

Dana almost laughed. Would she be on the matchmaking committee, too? Responsible for setting the winning candidate up with dates? That was not in her job description, for sure. In more than a decade, she hadn't been successful in that department. Wouldn't that just figure, though, if she found someone else their dream partner while for herself, she could hardly find a date.

Amy's droll voice interrupted Dana's wandering thoughts.

"Andrew, have you ever heard about a little thing called discrimination?"

"I'm not saying we're going to advertise it."

"We can't even *ask* it."

"Yeah, yeah, I know that. It's just something to keep in mind."

Dana turned to Amy. "Hey, as long as we're taking orders, I'd like tall, dark, handsome, single with no ex-wife. Looking to retire in ten years with a winter home in Florida or Southern California."

Chuckles erupted around the table, and Greg sent an indulgent smile Dana's direction as he slipped his glasses on and picked up the papers in front of him. He was always the one most pressed for time. "Maybe we should read through the job requirements and see if there's anything new we want that we *can* ask for."

Dana's eyes scanned the document but she couldn't shake the weight that settled on her shoulders. Training a new person took time, and always disrupted the workflow. A new person came with new ideas and expectations. There were always changes to put in place. Always personality differences to reconcile. Change always got someone's panties in a wad. With everything on her plate, she wasn't sure she was up to the task this time around. Something about it irked her. Here the hospital had been spared the upheaval of the tornado, but they were going to twist things around, anyway.

✳✳

At noon, Dana tucked Bill Arnold's chart under her arm and adjusted the man's pillow, letting her hand rest on his arm a moment. "Bill, are you comfortable? Can I get you anything?"

He looked at his hands, twisted them across his belly, then slowly shook his head. "I'm fine."

The sad defeat on the man's face tugged at Dana's heart. Getting old was no fun. That's all there was to it. Bill was lucky that he'd pulled through another heart attack, but he was simply too feeble to go home again. At eighty-two, he was losing his home – and his independence – to old age. He'd be leaving soon, and she needed to get his discharge papers ready for the family.

Turning toward the door, Dana glanced out the window. She caught her breath as her stomach dropped. A long line of cars, starting with several black sedans and a hearse, snaked down the street below. She checked her watch. Doug Mitchell's funeral procession. According to his wife, Doug had run back out of their basement to find the family Yorkie. Both had been buried when the storm blasted in. As the church bells sounded, Dana pressed a hand to her chest and watched silently until the last of the cars turned onto the highway. They could set the broken arms and stitch up the cuts. But this town had so much more healing to do.

Dana left the hospital at the end of the day feeling like the battery of a car that had been left too long with its lights on, only a dim flicker of energy remaining. It wasn't until she saw the security checkpoint in front of her that she realized her car had steered its way home. Not that anything in her line of vision could be construed as a home. With a deep sigh, she inched forward. Might as well check the progress while she was there. Wouldn't hurt to take a few minutes to visit the lost and found, either.

When the officer motioned her through, Dana pulled up to the curb across the street from what had been her house, and slowly opened the car door, giving herself a moment to adjust to the scene. It was still such a shock, so surreal. So hard to believe her house was gone – or had ever been there. Leaning against the car, she glanced up and down the block. Where there used to be kids playing and riding bicycles, there were now work crews hollering back and forth while heavy equipment thundered and thumped between the ravaged lots. Instead of children's voices, the sound of trucks backing up to receive their next load of debris chirped around her like a late-summer swarm of cicadas.

Several neighbors had already made significant progress, their piles nearly gone. Dana stared at her property, willing an answer to materialize out of the clutter. Looking for a sign. Or inspiration. *Something*. Mentally, she wandered the rooms of her home, missing her cozy chair by the fireplace where she spent most evenings curled up with a book or her knitting.

She sucked in her breath as her hands reached for the soft crimson yarn she'd been working with, and came up empty. The cardigan sweater with the cute ruffle around the bottom had been more than halfway done. She'd hoped to have it finished by summer and then tuck it away for the holidays. A hysterical kind of giggle bubbled up. Should that go on the list? Could she even count the skeins of yarn in bags and boxes in her closet? And what was the value of a hand-knitted sweater in the eyes of an insurance company, she wondered. Simply the cost of the balls of yarn? Probably no compensation for her time or talent.

That reminded her, she'd have to check the stock of baby blankets and booties at the hospital. For the past seven or eight years no baby born at the Whitfield Community Hospital had gone home without one of Dana's blue or pink blankets hand knitted of the softest yarn she could find. Dana's mother had taught her and her sister to knit when they were young girls. Brenna hated it, but Dana had taken to it easily. She liked the clicking of the needles setting the pace for her progress. She loved the textures and colors, felt pride in creating something from a single long string of yarn. As a girl, she'd decorated her room with blue ribbons won at the county fair. Year after year, she owned the category.

Brenna had found her talents in cooking. Probably more useful, Dana mused. Maybe it was nervous energy, or her habitual need to multi-task, but Dana liked to keep her hands busy. Even if she were just watching TV or letting her thoughts wander, she could still accomplish something.

Now, as she surveyed the landscape, she wondered where all the yarn had landed. She imagined the rainbow of color swirling inside the twister, the long strands twined within the massive funnel cloud. Had it been beautiful even in its terror and destruction? Perhaps some of the strands would be picked up by birds and woven into warm, protective nests for their baby chicks. She'd have to keep an eye out. Whitfield just might have the prettiest bird nests, the most colorful fences and fields in all of the plains this year.

But there was nothing pretty about the sight in front of her. Dana pushed off from the car, then turned when someone yelled her name. From next door, her neighbor Jessica waved to her. When Dana had seen her two days ago, Jessica still seemed shell-shocked, could hardly speak. Waving back, Dana crossed the street.

"Hey, there," she said softly, wrapping the younger woman into a hug. "You doing all right?"

To Dana's surprise, when Jessica pulled back, she wore a smile.

"Better. Guess what I got in the mail today? Ronnie's sister went to one of those instant photo places and made photo books from all the pictures she's taken at the boys' birthday parties. When I opened them up, I sat down and cried. My albums are the biggest loss."

"For sure," Dana said, with a lump in her throat. "It was so nice of her to do that, and so fast. Wow." Dana had no one to do the same for her. She couldn't turn to her mom or sister to replace her photos. What was destroyed was simply . . . gone. Blinking back tears, she attempted a smile. "Where are you staying?"

"We got a trailer."

"Yeah? All moved in? Can I help you with something?" Dana asked.

Jessica shook her head. "No. They're too small to put much of anything in. Mostly a place to shower and sleep." She gave a short laugh. "Scratch that. No one's getting much sleep."

"I'm sure you're cramped, but at least it's temporary."

"Doesn't matter. We're all in one room, anyway. The boys won't sleep by themselves. All week long they've slept with Ron and me. Micah wakes up scared two or three times."

Dana squeezed Jessica's shoulder. "I'm sorry to hear that. How's his hand?" Dana counted the days in her head. "Stitches out tomorrow?"

"Yes, we'll be in at two."

"Good. Maybe when he doesn't have that big bandage as a reminder, things will settle down a bit. It might just take some time."

Jessica shaded her eyes and looked toward the missing houses. "Yeah. I think if we survive this, we can get through anything."

Dana remembered thinking the same thing in the weeks following her divorce. After the initial emotional trauma, she'd gone into survival mode. At some point, things had smoothed out. They'd found a groove, a routine. It had taken time, but somewhere along the way, surviving changed to thriving. They'd re-defined their family unit and pulled through. She'd kept her focus on her kids, and took it a day at a time.

When she compared the loss of her home to the upheaval they'd endured then and the overwhelming heartache she'd felt after the deaths of her mother and sister, the scale diminished. At this point she wondered if there was anything she *couldn't* survive. And how many times would she be put to the test?

Her mother was fond of quoting Eleanor Roosevelt from a magnet she kept on her refrigerator, "A woman is like a tea bag; you never know how strong she is until she's in hot water." Dana was strong because she had to be. When people are depending on you, there's no other choice.

Like before, she'd take it a day at a time. Prioritize. Whittle the tasks into smaller, manageable chunks. What she needed was a chart, some kind of road map to keep track of everything. It dawned on her that she didn't even have a scrap of paper with which she could begin making an outline. And no computer, of course. That old piece of junk had been begging to be put to rest for months. The tornado had put it out of its misery. She'd have to stop at the drug store and pick up a spiral or legal pad on the way to Claire's. If she worked an eight-to-five job in an office she could probably get away with borrowing a company iPad, but at the hospital, the new devices were in use around the clock. Whitfield Community Hospital was just starting to convert to electronic records and notes.

The late afternoon sun warmed Dana, and as she shed her light jacket, she decided to walk over to the storage building that Best Heating and Cooling had offered as lost-and-found headquarters a couple of blocks over. It was amazing – only a couple of blocks separated total devastation from almost untouched. "Have you recovered much from lost and found?" Dana asked Jessica.

Jessica's nose wrinkled and her ponytail swished behind her. "Not a thing."

Great. She was probably wasting her time. But if she didn't give it a shot, she'd keep wondering if she'd missed something. "Guess I'll go check it out."

"Good luck."

"Thanks. I'll talk to you later."

What struck Dana first was that only a few people milled about the shed. Took only a minute, though, to understand why. There wasn't much there. And from what she could see, the items strewn across the tables looked like something a dog had chewed up and spit out. Dana presented her ID at the counter, then browsed along the tables looking for anything familiar. Books stood on the table with their pages fanned in an attempt to dry them. They'd never lay flat again.

"Hey, Curly Q."

Dana's head jerked up to meet the eyes of Cameron Wade, a longtime classmate who could never resist the old and worn reference to her hair. Cameron was running a farming operation with his father, and making decent money, if the town chatter was true.

"Hi, Cam. How are you?"

"Not bad. Lost wheat and some fences in the storm, but got my house and family."

Dana smiled. "Yes. Thankful for that."

"I've been rounding up anything I see out in the fields and bringing it over here. Gotta tell you, though. Most of it's beat to hell."

"Yeah. Looks like." Dana wiped her hands on her pant leg. They should probably run out to the farm and do the same, though their property was on the other side of the highway and most likely had no debris.

"Sheila and I were out driving a couple of days ago and she saw one of those little flimsy strollers stuck up in a tree. People shouldn't have to see something like that, so we stopped and got it down. After that, we did a big swing around town and started hauling stuff in."

"That's really good of you."

"You lose everything?" Cameron asked, his hands on his hips as he studied her.

A lump formed in Dana's throat. "Pretty much."

"Damn. Sure sorry to hear that. Listen, you find any furniture or heavy stuff, let me know and I'll haul it out of here for you."

"Thanks. I doubt it, though." But as he turned, Dana had another thought. "Hey, Cam? I know the big things like furniture are probably easy to spot, but what about small stuff, like jewelry? Do you know if anyone's going out in the fields with metal detectors?"

Cameron rubbed his jaw, and his glance dropped to the floor. "Not sure about that, sweetheart. That would take some time. I suppose it'd be up to individual property owners to do it or to give permission to go on their land. Maybe after harvest. But who knows what kind of shape it would be in by the time the trucks and combines went through." He draped an arm over her shoulder. "This sure sucks."

"It sure does," Dana agreed. "Listen, I was wondering . . ." Her mind was already forming a plan that would commit Chase to lending a hand. Even as she spoke, she knew there was a good chance he wouldn't appreciate her efforts. Then again, maybe he'd prefer something like that to helping in the shelter. It might be easier to see the scattered trash than the displaced people. "Are you going out again to gather up things that got blown away?"

Cameron shrugged. "Not sure. But I'm keeping my eyes open."

"If you do, maybe my son Chase could go with you. He's home from school, and I'd like to get him more involved in the cleanup operation. Would you call us?"

"You bet."

Dana wrote her cell number on the back of a bank deposit slip and handed it to Cameron "Thanks. That would be great."

"No problem."

"All right, then. I guess—"

"Hey, Dana." Shifting his weight, Wade looked at the slip of paper then back at her. "Let's plan on that. I can go Saturday. What's a good time for your boy?"

That was hard to say. "Not sure. I'll check with Chase and let you know."

"Sure thing. How 'bout we try for nine or ten?"

Oh, man. Could she even get Chase out of bed before noon on a Saturday? Dana forced a smile. "Yeah. I bet that'll work." She glanced past Cameron then, and her breath caught. On a table in the next aisle over was the wooden clock that used to sit on her fireplace mantel. She'd forgotten all about it.

With a quick goodbye to Cameron, she hurried to the table. She started to reach for the clock, but her hand stilled mid-air. She swallowed hard as tears sprung to her eyes again. Not hers. Her gaze roved over the garage sale display of salvaged items, and her stomach rolled. Ravaged bits and pieces of people's lives. Suddenly, she couldn't look anymore. Turning sharply, she left, empty-handed.

After a stop at the drugstore, Dana pulled her car into Claire's driveway, and gathered up the papers from Kent Donovan. It was the last thing she wanted to do, but she'd make herself spend some time with them after supper. She had to get started on the list. The longer she waited, the more she was liable to forget.

Chapter Eight

By Friday evening, Dana wanted nothing more than a quiet night at home, and an early date with her pillow. She gave Chase a smile as he pushed back from the table and carried his plate to the kitchen sink. He was doing a pretty decent job of picking up after himself and keeping Claire's place clean. But when he walked back past her and said, "See you later," she whipped around.

"What do you mean? Where are you going?"

Chase shrugged and scooped his keys up from the coffee table. "Going out. Can't hang around here all night."

"Why not?" He hadn't been 'around here' for more than an hour or so every day as far as Dana could tell. Except to sleep. "Chase, come on. You barely told me anything about your day. I know you saw Poppa, and that's it." She'd resisted the urge to question him over dinner, hoping he'd offer some information on his own. No such luck. She hated playing twenty questions. Hated being the bad guy even more.

Chase's jaw hardened. "There's nothing to tell, Mom. If there was, I would tell you. Just quit bugging me, okay?"

Dana scooted the chair back, fighting to keep her cool. "You know, if you'd talk to me and tell me what's going on, I wouldn't have to keep asking you."

He spread his hands in front of him. "Nobody was around today. I turned in some applications."

"I think we ought to contact a head hunter."

Chase rolled his eyes, his head shaking back and forth. "God, Mom. Those are for professionals. They'd laugh me out of the office."

She let out an exasperated sigh. "Listen, I'm trying to help you."

"What do you want me to do? It's Friday night. I can't make business calls now. I can't get online. There's no internet. I mean—"

Dana held up a hand to stop him. He was right about all that. And she'd broken her resolve to let the job thing go until next week. "Fine. Where are you going?"

"Luke's."

"In Paxton?"

"Yeah."

"Why can't they ever come here? I'd like to meet them. Besides, I hate you doing all that highway driving at night." Her mother's accident had been the result of an aneurism, and had nothing to do with the traffic or road conditions, but the road from Whitfield to Paxton was a two-lane highway with a narrow bridge and railroad tracks, and there was always truck traffic. It still made Dana nervous.

"Luke's got the big screen and game system, Mom. What would we do here?"

"Claire's got a pool table downstairs, and there's a TV. Heck, you could go to Bailey's and hang out. Watch a game. You could take turns, at least."

"Maybe tomorrow."

"Or you could contact some of your high school friends. I'm sure some people are around."

"I told you, I don't know anybody here anymore."

"Have you even tried?" she asked softly.

"Nobody's home from school yet."

With that, he moved toward the door, and concern outweighed annoyance.

"Be back at midnight," Dana said. "That means no drinking, Chase. You can't be on the highway if you've had even a few beers."

"I can just spend the night there."

"No. That's not what I meant. I want you to come back, and to be sober. Period. You shouldn't be drinking, anyway. You can't afford a DUI. Also, I ran into Cameron Wade at the lost and found yesterday. He's been driving around town picking up things that have landed all over the place. You can help him tomorrow morning. He said nine or ten. What about nine-thirty? That gives you plenty of time to sleep."

Chase's grunt was muffled by the closing of the door.

Dana watched her son's car pull away from the curb as she wondered where was that adorable kid who never left the house without saying "I love you." What happened to the kid who would still allow her to grab his hand for a few moments even in high school? She missed him. With a heavy heart, Dana sagged against the wall, her face in her hands. That hadn't gone well. She didn't want to nag, but what was Plan B? She couldn't contact a head hunter for a twenty-year-old or call his former high school buddies. If she overstepped her bounds, Chase might pack up and move in with those guys in Paxton. That would be worse. Until he got some direction, she wanted him close. Maybe she could find a way to chat with some of the other moms and mention that Chase was in town. She had to try something. The real question was when would that possibly fit into her schedule?

With a heavy weariness in her bones, she slowly cleared the rest of the dishes from the table. Even pushing the start button on the dishwasher seemed to take physical effort. Then she poured a glass of wine and retrieved the notebook paper she'd bought. One room, she told herself. She had to get one done.

In red ink, Dana wrote the word 'kitchen' at the top of the page, then created columns to chart the description, age and estimated value of all the items that had been destroyed in that room. Pretty much everything, she thought grimly, doodling a star at the side of the heading. Appliances, cabinets, flooring, countertops. She visualized the room. The big things were easy, but how in the world would she list every item she'd owned?

She had to do it, though. She needed every dime she could get, and that meant listing every dish towel, plate and cup, and every box of tea, cereal and rice that had been in the cupboards. Dana's hand stilled over the paper. Is that what people really did, or would she look pathetic and ridiculous? Tears welled in her eyes, and she tossed the pen down as she drew her knees up.

Looked like she would have to call for help. *Ugh.* She considered her options, and decided Kent Donovan was the lesser of her evils. She couldn't bring herself to call John Fallon just yet. Couldn't help feeling that he was still somewhat responsible for her being in this mess.

Kent picked up his phone. As he checked the number, his pulse quickened. He'd only had that number for a few days, but he knew who it belonged to. Switching off the television that simply provided background noise while he worked, he answered the call.

"Kent Donovan."

"Kent. Hello, this is Dana Gerard. Have I caught you at a bad time?"

Her voice came soft and hesitant, and Kent figured she hadn't wanted to make the call, and probably wouldn't mind if he said yes. But he wasn't about to do that. "Not at all, Dana. How are you?"

"Fine, thanks. Working on my list." She gave a nervous laugh. "Well, starting on my list."

"Good. Glad to hear that. It's best to get started then give yourself some time to come back to it as you remember things."

"Yes. I have a couple of questions, though."

Yeah. He thought she might. She hadn't read the brochure. Not a surprise. Most people didn't. Their eyes glazed over when they hit the fine print.

Kent put away the file he'd been processing, refilled his coffee cup and leaned against the counter in the small kitchenette. "Okay, shoot."

"I'm wondering how detailed I should be. I mean, I had food in the fridge, and . . ."

As her voice trailed off, Kent broke in. "As much detail as you can provide, Dana. List everything. I know a lot of people out here keep a side of beef in the freezer. Even if the freezer isn't gone, with no electricity running, everything inside will be ruined. That's a loss."

"Uh-huh. What about hand-made items? Artist quality? I make hand-knitted sweaters. I lost several of those, plus a lot of raw yarn."

Her voice took on a defensive edge, and Kent figured those held some sentimental value as well. That just didn't figure into the equation. Knitting? Huh. That sure didn't fit his mental picture of her. Artist quality, she said. That worked. She seemed like a classy gal and might have some talent. Maybe her stuff was worth something. "Sure. List anything of value. Hard to put a price on the handmade items. Go ahead and put down what you think they'd sell for in today's market. Right now, though, it's most important that you document the losses. Give us items, quantities and age. We'll talk about value after that." He heard her heavy sigh over the line.

"This is going to take a while."

"It's not easy. We suggest you take it one room at a time." Unless she kept her yarn in the refrigerator, sounded like she was bouncing all over the place. "Tell you what we give top dollar for, though."

"What's that?" she asked, her voice guarded.

"Anything with a Jayhawk on it." There was a short pause before a soft laugh erupted.

"Is that right? Good to know."

"Saw the license plate on your car. Thought you might have more. You a University of Kansas alum?"

Surprised at the sudden turn of the conversation, Dana let a beat of silence go by before answering. "I am. So is my oldest son." Surely Donovan wasn't. What kind of degree would you need to be part of an insurance disaster team, anyway? Probably wouldn't even need a degree.

"Me, too," Kent told her, providing the answer before she asked the question.

Dana stopped pacing and propped an elbow on the fireplace mantel. She didn't want to like this guy, but he kept giving her reasons to give him the benefit of a doubt. And now she was curious. "What was your major?"

"Business."

"Ah. Is that the degree most people in insurance have?" Probably with a focus on sales, she thought.

"Little bit of everything out there. I was in the National Guard for a few years, too. Never saw any combat, but did get called out for security and natural disasters."

"Oh, I thought you might've been—" She'd wondered if he might have military background. That explained his physical condition, but she certainly didn't want to let him know that she'd noticed. She started over. "That's how you got into to this business, huh?"

"Was a good fit. I enjoy it. There's a little adrenaline rush at the beginning, you know. Then there's the satisfaction of helping people put their lives back together."

Dana stifled a chuckle. He sounded as though he'd walked straight out of a Boy Scout Handbook.

"So you from a long line of KU grads?"

She did laugh then. Not because he said anything funny, but because that question evoked so much history. Such family drama. During basketball season, anyway.

"Sort of. My mom went to KU, but my dad went to K-State."

"Ahhhh." The noise Kent made was something between a laugh and a groan. "A house divided."

Dana smiled into the phone as memories flooded in. Her mother, up and down, wanting to watch a game, but unable to sit still. Her mild-mannered mother actually yelling at the TV screen. "Only on game days," she told Kent. "And even then, my dad was a good sport. He adored my mother. He got a kick out of seeing her all pumped up. When he couldn't stand the heat or her tension, he'd go to the bar and hang out until it was over – or until he felt like it was safe to come home. My mother was such—" Dana caught herself, her face warming. *How embarrassing*. She was running at the mouth, carrying on about her family as if she and Kent were friends. Kent Donovan didn't even know her family. She squeezed her eyes shut eyes. His deep, soothing voice had lulled her into forgetting the purpose of her call. He'd answered her questions ten minutes ago.

"Dana?"

"Sorry. That was too much information."

"You lost your mother?"

Dana bit her lip, and began pacing again. Why was he prolonging the conversation? "Yes. About six years ago."

"I'm sorry to hear that."

"Thank you. Listen, I've probably kept you long enough."

"Hey, Dana?"

"Hmmm?"

"What was your major?"

Dana frowned at that. Did he really not know? She couldn't remember telling him she was a nurse, but somehow, it seemed as though he would've found that out. "Nursing. I'm head nurse at the hospital. I worked the night of the tornado and all the next day. That's why I wasn't able to save anything." She added that, lest he think she was a complete idiot. Had she been home of course she would've grabbed photo albums and jewelry.

"Got it. Wow. That would've been a crazy night. I'm sure you had your hands full. That reminds me, have you got long-term accommodations figured out?" Kent asked. "Did you sign up for a trailer or are you staying with family?"

"I'm staying at a friend's place."

"Great. You let me know if you need cash for rent or anything before we settle the claim."

"Thanks. I will." And that, Dana reminded herself, was what this phone call was all about. Donovan might not be an enemy, but he wasn't a friend, either.

Chapter Nine

Chase wadded up the note from his mom, and tossed it against the wall as he flopped onto the bed. The last thing he wanted to do was drive around town with some old dude he barely knew at nine-thirty in the morning.

He glanced around the navy blue and tan guest room. Coming back to Whitfield was a big mistake. Maybe the tornado was a sign. He'd expected to be in his room with his own stuff, where everything was familiar. Instead, here he was in a room that looked like it belonged in a hotel, with nothing but a few clothes and his computer. And his grandpa and mom riding his ass.

They were right about one thing, though. He needed a job – and fast. He needed to make some money so he could get a place of his own, or move in with the guys in Paxton. Living with his mom without a job was like walking around with a big 'loser' sign on his forehead.

His alternative was to go to school. His mom and Poppa wanted him to go to college or get into some technical program. God, he hated school, but he was running out of options. Frustrated, he laced his fingers through his hair and let his elbows fall against the pillow. What else could he do? He'd been pounding the pavement for a month and had zilch to show for it.

He punched the pillow a couple of times then turned off the light. Sleep was his best option right now.

**

Chase woke, still in his clothes, to the sound of his phone alarm. He hit the snooze button and turned over. But a few seconds later, another alarm clanged close to his ear. He bolted upright. What the–? No way. She set an alarm for him? *She set an alarm?* Shaking his head in disbelief, he smacked the clock until it finally shut up, then flopped back onto the pillow.

He thought about blowing it off, turning over and going back to sleep. It'd be easy to do. But he knew that would just get his mom all worked up. Dragging himself to a sitting position, he rubbed his eyes. Wasn't like he had anything else to do.

Thirty minutes later, chugging a glass of orange juice, he heard a car door slam. He wiped a sleeve across his mouth, and watched from the kitchen window as Cameron Wade practically jogged up the sidewalk.

The guy seemed to be in pretty decent shape for fifty-something. He had that permanently tanned look of someone who spent all his time outside. Chase blew out his breath, and headed for the door. Might as well get it over with.

"Hey, Chase," Wade said. His voice was easy, as though they were old friends. "How you doing? Hope it's not too early for you."

"Nah, it's fine," Chase said. He squared his shoulders, and followed Wade down the steps.

"Thought we'd start out by some of the fields where we've got damage," Wade told Chase as they climbed into his shiny black Ford F-150. "I know there's debris out there, just don't know if it's anything worth saving. We've been spending most of our time helping with the cleanup in town. We lost a lot of wheat, that's for sure."

Chase propped an elbow out the open window and scanned the fields as Wade drove slowly down the road. So far, all he could see was trash – bits of clothes and shingles and insulation. Funny, the insulation was all over the place. Like shrapnel, it must've exploded in the blast. Looked like they were trying to grow cotton out there instead of wheat.

"What about all the trash?" Chase asked.

Cameron shrugged. "Not worrying about that right now. Might get some volunteer crews later, but for now, we're looking for stuff that can be saved. See anything?"

"Nah." What he saw was wheat bent clear over, practically flat on the ground instead of standing up straight like it should. But a moment later, an odd shape caught his eye. "Wait, there's something. A chair maybe."

Cameron pulled the truck over to the shoulder, just shy of the ditch. "Cushion is probably ruined. Already moldy."

Chase opened the door and hopped out, then swung himself over the fence. He jogged about thirty yards into the field. Lifting the chair, he turned it over. Looked fine to him. "I think this is okay," he hollered. "It's the patio kind."

Cameron joined him and inspected the wrought iron. "Yeah, let's get that one in the truck."

"Let me run down here and see if there's anything else." They couldn't see everything from the truck. Seemed that the fields stretched on forever. Could hardly make out the rows, though. Looked as though green hay had been scattered across the land. The dirt was soft, almost mushy, under his feet. He picked up a woman's purse then saw a large square lying flat against the ground. Crouching down, he turned it over, surprised to find a landscape painting still intact. Tall yellow sunflowers diminished into smaller rows until they stopped just in front of a bright red barn. He wondered whose house it had come from. It was the kind of thing his mother would like. She'd been known to stop on the side of the road and take pictures of sunflowers.

"Hey, check this out," he called to Wade. Chase tucked the painting under his arm and started back toward the truck. He stopped when he caught up with Wade. "Look at this. The glass isn't even broken."

Wade grimaced. "The crops broke the fall." Shading his eyes, he looked out across the field. "It's a damned shame. The wheat was really going strong before this. The only income we'll see from these fields this year is what we get from the insurance."

Chase glanced around. "All of this yours?"

"Yeah. Belongs to my family. I work it with my dad and brother."

"Lot of land."

Wade sent Chase a long look, and reached for the painting. "Could've been more, you know, if your grandpa had decided to sell when he got out."

Startled, Chase stopped walking. "What do you mean?"

"Dad likes to add land whenever he can. Tried to get your grandpa to sell his after . . . well, when he quit farming."

"Oh."

Cameron hoisted the painting over his shoulder and they starting walking again.

"Your dad wants our land?" Chase couldn't help feeling defensive of Poppa. Even though he didn't know all the details, Chase knew Poppa didn't want to quit farming, but his heart was broken. Then the stroke. People shouldn't try to take advantage of other people when they weren't thinking straight. He wondered if his mom knew about it.

Wade shrugged and shot Chase a half-hearted smile. "Nothing personal, kid. He's always looking to add to the operation."

Chase jerked his head toward the south, where several shining white wind turbines spun in a slow rhythm against the blue sky. "Those new wind turbines on your land?"

"Yep. That's another way to make money in farming these days. Wind farms, they call 'em."

Rather than placing the painting in the bed of the truck, Wade tucked it behind the seats in the cab. "I'd sure hate to bust it up now after it survived the storm."

Chase nodded, and climbed back inside, his thoughts still on the land and what Wade had said. Did Poppa have a hard time making money before Grams died? His mom was always strapped for cash, but Chase couldn't remember any money trouble for his grandparents. Of course he'd only been in junior high then. Nobody would've told him anything. They still didn't. That was the curse of being the youngest. Everyone still treated him like he was a little kid.

Chase sensed Wade's eyes on him, and he flicked a glance toward the driver's seat.

"You have any interest in farming?" Wade asked.

Chase shook his head. "Nah." But as he looked at the passing fields, he thought maybe he wouldn't mind it. Wouldn't mind being outside, being his own boss. Didn't mind the heat or the cold. He'd never given farming any thought at all. Why not? Here he was in Kansas, surrounded by farmland. How come no one ever talked about farming? It'd sure be better than wearing a suit and tie and sitting in an office all day like Evan did. That sounded like pure torture.

Maybe Poppa hadn't made much money, and that's why he never tried to get Chase or Evan interested. Or maybe he didn't think they could handle it. Hell, he could learn farming just as well as anything else. His stomach fell, though. Poppa had gone to college. Had graduated with some kind of agriculture degree from Kansas State. Even farming would probably require a college degree.

The breeze from the open window blew his hair, and he remembered times on his grandpa's farm. As kids, he and Evan used to ride in the tractor with Poppa, and play in the piles of hay. He used to like the smell of fresh-cut hay. And Grams had those damned chickens. Chase looked down at his hands, as if he'd still see the peck marks and scratches from trying to get eggs out from under the stupid birds. To this day, he wasn't fond of eggs.

Wade stopped the truck and they rounded up several more items, a door, a mangled bicycle and some other junk, as far as Chase could tell. Some of it was just trash, but it was big enough that Wade wanted to get it off the wheat that already stood more than a foot tall in the good parts. For two hours, they combed the fields, gathering up assorted items from people's houses. Nothing from theirs, though. Nothing that he recognized, anyway.

Across the highway, everything looked better. It was as if the tornado had gone exactly to the edge of the road. When they stopped to pick up a hubcap, and some other trash along the fences, Chase ran a hand through the soft stalks. Over here, the wheat was tall and green and healthy. Wade and his dad must be doing something right. Neat rows stood like the dominoes he used to set up in a perfect line just to watch them topple.

"This wheat looks good," Chase said. "Too bad we couldn't have had that rain without the freakin' tornado."

Cameron shot him a smile, and slapped him on the back. "Careful, kid. You're starting to sound like a farmer."

Chase let Cameron's comment roll around in his head as they drove back toward town. Had to admit it didn't sound too bad. Trouble was, they didn't have a farm anymore. Poppa had somebody else farming his land. Chase wondered, though, would Poppa have a say in who worked there? Maybe the guy could hire him. He could spend the summer working and get a feel for it, like an internship, to see if he liked it.

An hour later, after they'd made stops at the dump and the lost and found, Wade latched the gate on the truck. "Guess that's it, kid. Jump in, and I'll drop you home."

It wasn't home, of course, but Chase didn't see a reason to point that out.

"Your mom says you're here for the summer," Wade said, as if he had to strike up a conversation.

"Yeah."

"So you working someplace in town?"

Chase blew out his breath. Always the same questions. "Don't have it figured out yet."

"Oh. Looking for a summer job?"

Chase shrugged. "Looking."

"Might be harder to find something now. What with the tornado, folks'll be stretched thin."

Thanks for the encouragement, pal, Chase mumbled silently.

"Too bad you don't like farming."

Chase swiveled, his eyes narrowing on Cameron.

Cameron tossed him a glance. "We might need a couple of guys for the summer."

103

Without warning, Chase's face warmed. What was the guy saying? Avoiding Cameron's eyes, Chase studied the hands on the steering wheel. Cameron seemed to know what he was doing, and he was easy going. Chase had heard him talking real friendly to everybody while they were unloading. People seemed to like him. Might be a decent guy to work for.

He waited until they were close, then he took a deep breath and forced himself to speak. "Hey, uh, Camer– Mr. Wade – I, um. I might be interested in a job on your place."

Wade brought the truck to a stop in front of Claire's house, and killed the engine. Chase felt his eyes on him.

"Thought you weren't interested in farming."

Chase shot him a brief glance. "Well, now I'm thinking maybe I could learn."

Wade ran a hand across his jaw as if he was thinking hard.

"You ever work your grandpa's land?"

Turning toward the window again, Chase hitched his shoulders. "A little. When I was younger." It'd been a while, but they'd had some good times. He used to look forward to weekends on the farm with Poppa.

"Looks like you've got the muscle for it. It's hard work, you know."

Chase heard the challenge, and his chin tilted upward as he met Wade's eyes. "Yeah. I know."

After a long minute, Cameron nodded, reached into his billfold, and pulled out a business card. "Tell you what, write your phone number down for me. Let me check with the boss on where we stand with our summer crew. If there's still a spot, I'll give you a call."

"Yeah?" For the first time that week, Chase felt some positive vibes. He took the card and pen Wade handed him. Not wanting to appear too eager or desperate, he gave Wade a slow smile. "That'd be great."

He hopped out of the truck with renewed energy. But as he jogged up the walkway, familiar doubt whispered in his ear. Maybe the guy was just being nice and there wouldn't be a job opening. Maybe because they lost some cows and some wheat, his dad wouldn't want to hire anyone. Like he said, people would be stretched thin because of the tornado. Slowing, Chase shoved his hands in his pockets. Better not get his hopes up.

**

Bracing for the first encounter with her son since she set him up with Cameron Wade, Dana held her breath, and practically tiptoed into the house, unsure what Chase's mood would be.

The television was on, and as she rounded the corner, she saw Chase on the couch, his laptop open in front of him. At least he wasn't asleep.

"Hey, Mom," he said as she entered the room.

The friendly pitch of his voice caught her by surprise, and she stared at him a moment before giving a too-bright, "Hi."

Smiling, she set her purse down and moved forward, resting a hand on Chase's shoulder. "How'd it go with Cameron today?"

"Good."

Dana curled into the chair kitty-corner from Chase and searched his face. He seemed in awfully good spirits. "Yeah? Did you find much?"

"Some. Not much in good shape, though. Except, get this, we found a painting of sunflowers and the glass hadn't even been broken. So weird."

"Huh. That's cool though. I hope it gets back to the owners."

"Yeah. Didn't see anything of ours, though."

"Oh, I didn't figure you'd find our things specifically. I'm glad you went, though. I'm sure Cameron appreciated the help."

"Hey, Mom. Did you know that his dad tried to buy Poppa's land after his stroke?"

Dana frowned, remembering her father's anxiety and refusal to even consider a sale. The land had been in their family for three generations. For her dad, selling was unthinkable. As far as Dana was concerned, they had the best possible solution. They still owned the land, and earned income from it, but didn't have the day-to-day

105

responsibility of a farming operation. As a teen, she couldn't wait to get off of the farm and away from that life. And she'd vowed never to be a farm wife.

"Yeah. I'm surprised he mentioned that. It was never a real possibility."

"Were there any hard feelings?"

Dana hesitated. Cam had been fine, accepting their 'no' with good nature, but his dad had pressed the issue almost to the point of creating some hostility. Surely he'd gotten past it by now. "Not that I'm aware of. Why?"

Chase shrugged. "Just wondering. Wade seems like a decent guy."

"He is. I've known him all my life. He and his fam–"

At the sound of the doorbell, Dana broke off and pushed up from the chair. "You expecting anyone?"

"Nope."

Dana looked out the side window, then yanked the door open. Mary stood on the porch with a large paper bag in hand.

"Have I got a meal for you," she said with a laugh as she stepped inside and wrapped Dana in a one-armed hug.

"You are amazing," Dana said, peeking inside the bag. "It smells delish."

"Lasagna."

Dana couldn't help grinning. Mary made the best lasagna in town. "Seriously? Get in here." Feeling as though she'd just been handed a winning lottery ticket, Dana steered Mary toward the kitchen. "Can you stay for an iced tea?"

"Best invitation I've had all day."

While Mary said hello to Chase, Dana poured two glasses of iced tea, then they dropped into chairs at the kitchen table.

Dana saw Mary glance around the room, and knew right away the direction her thoughts had turned. "It's weird to be here without Claire, isn't it?"

Mary blew out a breath and perched her chin in a hand as she rested her elbow on the table. "That it is. I sure miss that woman."

"Me, too. I bet she'll be ready for company soon."

Mary shifted as she shook her head. "Not soon enough. Sounds like she'll be at Elise's for a couple of weeks, and then on call for a while. I'd like to get up there and help her, but there's so much to do here."

"You're doing so much, Mare. What was it today?"

"Serving in the cafeteria, and making beds. I don't know when they'll be able to get everyone out of the gym. Did you hear Allen and Karen Stites are moving to Texas? Just going to pick up and leave."

Dana curled her legs under her, and let the news sink in a moment. "I didn't know that, but I'm not surprised. Not everyone will rebuild. Some people will take it as an opportunity to make a change."

"I suppose so. Anyway, how's it going with you?"

"Honestly? I feel like I've been buried under the rubble of my house."

"Oh, sweetie."

"I know everyone else feels the same way, and I just need to suck it up and keep going, but it's overwhelming. All week, I've only been over to see my dad once. Before the tornado, I was there almost every day."

Mary reached out and squeezed her hand. "I know. It's been a horrible week, and people are getting tired and cranky. Including me. I'm afraid Grant's going to start singing *The Bitch is Back* every time I walk through the door."

Dana sputtered a laugh. Not a chance. Anyone who knew them knew that Grant Logan adored his wife. But as the words to Elton John's old tune ran through her mind, she wondered if Chase might be thinking the same thing about her.

"What about some shopping tomorrow?" Mary asked, her eyes brightening as she sat straighter. "We can have a nice lunch with people waiting on us then buy you some new stuff. You in?"

Hesitating, Dana glanced toward the living room. It'd be more fun to go with Mary, for sure, but Chase needed things, too. Plus, she wouldn't mind having some one-on-one time with him.

She shook her head. "I've got to get to Paxton, but I need to take Chase with me, Mare. Besides, we'll be doing boring shopping, like looking for a new computer. And I've got to get a new camera before Maddie's graduation." Dana was committed to buying as much as she could locally, but the fact was, not everything was available in Whitfield.

As Mary's face fell, needles of guilt pricked Dana's skin. Her friend was lost without her best friend. Dana knew that Claire and Mary were closer, that they shared a special bond, and Claire's absence had left a void in Mary's life – the same way Brenna's death had left a chasm in hers. She leaned forward, "Let's plan on it soon, though. I promise I'll save the fun stuff for you."

**

On the way to Paxton the next day, Dana got her first glimpse of the tornado's wrath as it moved away from central Whitfield. The town had taken the brunt of the impact, but several farms were hit as well. The Grangers' house lay in shambles, the trees surrounding it branchless spires. Debris littered the ditches and fence lines. Flattened fields told a sad story of loss that would be felt far into the year.

"What a mess," she murmured to Chase.

"Won't be much of a harvest this year," Chase commented.

"True. And lost crops also mean lost jobs. The farmers won't need as much help."

Chase gave her a sharp look, and she could've bitten her tongue. Instead she held up her hand in surrender, and weariness crept into her words. "It was just an observation, Chase. You don't have to freak out every time I say the word *job*." She had absolutely no intention of bringing up that topic. They needed to make quick work of the shopping, and she needed his cooperation.

At the mall, Dana shared her game plan. "Okay, let's split up for clothes shopping. Give me two hours. If you're done first, go ahead and start looking at computers. See what kind of deal you can find on a PC and printer. Get a pair of shorts and some shirts. Also, you need khakis for next weekend."

While Chase wandered off toward American Eagle, Dana made a beeline for Dillard's, hoping for one-stop shopping. She'd planned to splurge on a cute dress for Maddie's graduation, but the tornado had changed everything. She needed to replace basics. With that in mind, she headed for the shoe department. When it came to shoes, basics meant at least three pairs – black pumps, walking shoes, and something casual that she could wear with shorts or jeans. But, oh, it was hard to walk past all those cute summer sandals full of bright beads and bling. Rhinestones winked at her, catching the spotlights above. She walked by without even a touch. Like she'd told Mary, she'd come back later for the fun stuff. Maybe the two of them could sneak off to Wichita for a weekend. The shopping would be even better there. Not only were there tons of other stores to choose from, there were a couple of fun antique and thrift shops where they'd found treasures before. The irony was that even though she seemed to have an endless supply of disposable income, Mary Logan could sniff out a deal like a hound on a fox hunt. With Dana's flair for repurposing, they made a dynamic duo.

When Dana passed by the men's department on her way to petites, she stopped short as an idea hit. Took only a few minutes to come up with a short-sleeved shirt in Arkansas-red for her dad to wear to Maddie's party in the park. The rest of them would get Razorback gear while they were on campus for the actual ceremony, but this would suit her dad better than a T-shirt.

Two and a half hours later, they loaded their shopping bags, along with a refurbished Dell computer and a printer, into Dana's car then headed for Outback – starving.

As soon as they'd placed their order, Dana turned to Chase. "So, what all did you get?"

Chase's mouth went dry, and he wished the waitress would hurry up with that Diet Coke. What he 'got' was a phone call from Cameron Wade. Wasn't exactly a job offer, though. More like an interview, so he didn't plan to tell his mom about it yet. But he was never good at hiding things from her, and here she was looking straight at him.

"Uh, just a couple of shirts. A pair of pants and one pair of shorts."

"Cargo shorts? Something you could wear for the party?"

"Yeah."

Drinks arrived, and Chase picked his up immediately.

"Sounds good," his mom said. "I found everything I need for now. And I got Poppa a new shirt for the party."

Chase felt his face warm at the mention of Poppa. "Cool." Dammit, he wanted to know about the farm. No, what he really wanted was to know his mother's reaction to his idea. He took a deep breath. Might as well get it over with.

"Hey, Mom, if Poppa still owns the farm land, does he have a say in running it?"

She blinked at him a minute, then shook her head. "Not really. We turned that over to Bill Jansen. His contract is renewable every few years, but the feeling is that it's a long-term commitment. I'm hoping he'll keep at it for fifteen years or so."

"Fifteen years?" Chase nearly choked. "That's a long time."

"Well, I'd like to have the continuity and steady income."

The waitress arrived with their food, and gave Chase a second to think. *Holy crap.* In fifteen years he'd be thirty-five years old. *Old.* He swallowed hard. "Does he make decent money?"

"Sure. He's a good farmer."

And they'd given him good land to work with, too. Chase remembered the big garden Poppa and Grams used to have that won ribbons at the fair. Sometimes they had so many tomatoes they gave away bags full just to get rid of them. And one year they had a pumpkin so big that Poppa had to roll it up a ramp to get it into his truck.

"Does he have anybody working for him?"

Chase could tell the second it registered with his mom what he was getting at. Her fork stopped before it made it to her mouth, and she set it down with a clump of lettuce still attached. Her eyebrows arched as she stared at him. "Chase, what are you asking?"

He shrugged. "I don't know. I think farming might be kind of cool."

Her eyes bulged then. "Farming?" she said again, like she wasn't sure she'd heard right. "You want to be a farmer?"

He might as well have said he wanted to go to the moon. Didn't have to be a rocket scientist, though, to see what she thought. His shoulders tensed. "Just thinking. Why not? What would be wrong with that? Lots of people we know are farmers. Why didn't Poppa ever try to teach me or Evan to farm the land, anyway?" He couldn't help the defensiveness that edged his voice.

His mom opened her mouth, then closed it again.

"I don't want to work in an office every day like Evan does."

She reached out and touched his arm. "That's okay. That's the sort of thing you need to know about yourself. Farming is certainly not an office job. It's long hours, sun up to sun down. I lived on that farm for a long time. Believe me, there's always something that needs to be done."

Chase slumped back in the booth. He knew it. "You don't think I can do it."

"That's not what I said. I don't know. In the first place, I'm not sure you even know enough about it to make a decision. Farming is a business, Chase. Maybe if you'd lived on a farm your whole life and were brought up learning how to do it, you could go right in as a career. But these days, you need a college degree."

"What about Poppa? Why couldn't he teach me?"

Dana winced, caught between wanting to encourage Chase, and knowing the realities of farm life. Oh, how she wished her father could still do the work and show her son the ropes. Sure, he could write a book about it. He could

111

test Chase on crop science and procedures, but there was no substitute for being in the heat or cold day in and day out working the land.

"Cameron Wade called me."

Surprised at the abrupt change in conversation, Dana frowned. "About helping him again?"

"No. About a job. About working for him this summer."

Dana's mouth dropped open. Quickly she yanked up her napkin and took a moment to dab her lips while her brain caught up. So that's what had prompted this whole conversation.

"Really? And you're thinking about it? You think you might want to try it?"

"Why not? I'd be outside a lot. He seems pretty cool."

Yeah, she could imagine a young man connecting with Cam. He *was* cool. She wished he'd contacted her first, though, given her a heads-up. "But, it'd just be temporary, right? A summer job?"

Chase leaned forward. "Same as an internship. Most of the kids at school were looking for summer internships, Mom."

He was right about that, though in her mind, Dana realized she'd been looking for something more open-ended, with long-term potential. Other kids were probably planning to go back to school in the fall, so the end date made sense for them. But this could work. If nothing else, it could aid in the process of elimination. "Did he actually offer you a job?"

Chase chewed a piece of steak, shaking his head. "Not yet. Wants me to go over and meet his dad at his place next week."

"All right. Well, that sounds fine. I think you should do that."

The ride home was silent, and Dana mulled the conversation over in her head. Could Chase learn – and enjoy – farming? It could be in his blood, she supposed. He came from a long line of farmers, after all. And they had no intention of selling their land. She wouldn't mind having one of her children close by. Hadn't crossed her mind before, but now that she thought about it, it was an interesting proposition. Of her three children, Chase had been the only one to show the slightest interest in Four-H. A memory jolted her, taking her back to when Chase was six or seven. She'd snapped a photo of him pulling a huge carrot out of the ground – the expression on his face was sheer wonder. He'd been fascinated that what they ate was buried in the dirt.

Dana stole a glance at Chase, but his eyes were closed. How she'd love to see that excitement in him again.

Chapter Ten

Dana hadn't smiled this much in weeks, but the excitement and anticipation of seeing her daughter graduate and having all of her kids in one place again kept her smile muscles engaged full-throttle. They hadn't all been together since Christmas. Six months was way too long.

She shimmied into the new jeans and clipped up her hair. Packing would have to wait. She couldn't leave town for three days without visiting her dad. Plus, she told Kent Donovan she'd try to have her kitchen list to him before she left. They could always drop that by his office on their way out of town. *If* she finished it.

After a quick scan of the reception area, Dana hurried to her father's apartment. She knocked softly on the door before entering. As soon as she stepped inside, her dad picked up the television remote and switched off the TV.

"Hi, Daddy," Dana said, moving in for a hug. She patted his shoulder then strolled to the kitchenette for a bottle of water. She grabbed two, opened one for her dad, then perched on the arm of the side chair, facing him.

"Doing all right?" she asked.

He gave her the lopsided smile. "Went out." He stopped a moment, obviously working to say something.

"You went out?"

He nodded. "Coffee. Tom."

"Tom stopped by and picked you up?"

The nod again.

"That's great, Dad. That was really nice of him. I'm glad you're keeping up with your buddies. Gosh, I haven't seen him in a long time." Oh, she owed that man a hug. Tom Simpson was a longtime friend who'd also been on the Whitfield school board for many years.

Her father began writing. *Saw the house.*

Well, shoot. Dana loved that his friends continued to think of him and visit, but couldn't help feeling that seeing the ruin of her house was unnecessary. Normal curiosity, though, she supposed.

Who's helping you?

"Lots of people. My friends, the people at the mortgage company and the insurance company, all the federal agencies. And the whole community is pitching in. Don't worry."

Where are you living?

Dana studied her dad a moment, wishing she could see inside, see which wheels were turning. "I'm at Claire's place. Remember, she moved to Wichita." Dana wondered which one of them was having the senior moment. She honestly couldn't remember whether she'd forgotten to tell him, or he'd forgotten her answer. At that thought, she reached into her bag. "I have a new crossword and a couple of magazines for you," she said. With a wink, she added, "Got a harder one this time." She hoped the puzzles would help keep him occupied and his mind sharp. Probably wouldn't hurt to do a few herself.

Her dad chuckled and lifted the crossword book for a closer look.

Dana considered telling him about Chase's proposal, but not sure she wanted to get into that conversation until he had a firm offer from Cameron. Instead, she leaned forward to tell him the more immediate news. "Hey, we're leaving for Arkansas tomorrow, for Maddie's graduation."

She waited a moment for her dad to process the information and form a response.

"What time?" he asked.

Dana smiled. For a man with nothing but time on his hands, and no responsibilities, her father still wore a watch and liked to know what was happening when.

"Planning to leave after lunch, and get there in time to take her out to dinner. There are a couple of events on Saturday, and the main ceremony is Sunday. We'll be back Sunday night."

Her dad gave his awkward nod, and began writing on the note pad. When he pushed it toward Dana, her heart twisted. *Where are we staying*, her father had written.

Tears sprung to her eyes. Oh, damn. Why hadn't she been clear and said she and Chase were leaving? Did her father really think he could maneuver a college campus? She hadn't even considered trying it. With a catch in her throat, Dana took her father's hand, trying to keep the tears at bay. She spoke softly, "Daddy, Chase and I are going. I wish we could take you, too, but we just can't. There will be bleachers and stairs, and we–"

She broke off, and had to look away. The shuttered look, the disappointment in her father's eyes, sent pain and guilt crashing over her. It was as though he'd just realized how trapped he was, how his limited mobility confined him, kept him from participating in ordinary life events.

When she looked up again, her father's blank features tore at her.

"Oh, Daddy, I'm so sorry," Dana whispered. "I wish you could go with us." She wished her mother could be there, too. And Brenna. Dana thought of all the football games and recitals and school programs her parents and sister had attended over the years. They'd been to so many events. But none of them would ever see her kids graduate from college.

"Listen, next weekend we're having a party in the park, and we'll come get you for that, okay? We want you to be there, and Maddie can't wait to see you. Evan will be home, too. We'll all be together."

Her father picked up the pen again, and Dana held her breath. But when she saw what he had written, she burst into tears. She knew what he intended to do, and it broke her heart. *Bring me my checkbook*. Shaking her head, Dana backed away. She couldn't do it. She refused to let her father be reduced to a check on special occasions. He would be part of their celebration – no matter what.

116

Dana kneeled in front of him, bringing his hand to her chest. "Absolutely not," she said, her voice quaking. "This is so hard, Dad. Please don't be hurt. You can give her a gift yourself when you see her next weekend."

**

The following day, as she packed her suitcase, excitement warred with sadness. Her conversation with her father had dulled the luster of the event. Maddie had called and wanted to invite some sorority sisters to dinner with them, so it'd be another day before they'd really be together as a family. Dana had never wanted to be one of those moms who tried to be besties with her daughter and her friends. Still, she couldn't wait to meet Maddie's friends, and to *celebrate* – to leave the grim faces and burdens of Whitfield behind for a few days.

"Get me out of here," she muttered, shoving her bag into the car. Unfortunately, she couldn't blast out of there before she stopped at Heartland's temporary office. She wanted to put that behind her, too.

"This'll just take a minute," she told Chase as she swung the car up in front of the trailer.

Unsure whether to walk right in or knock, Dana tapped softly on the door. When a voice inside yelled, "Come in," she stepped inside and found three people working, each desk piled high with files and papers. A few chairs were lined up against the side, and a coffee machine gurgled on the counter. Each person looked up as she entered, and Dana's chest gave an unexpected bounce when Kent Donovan's face broke into a wide smile.

"Hey, Dana. Come on in."

Her face flushed as she moved forward. Donovan had a way of talking that made it seem as if they were friends rather than acquaintances in a business transaction.

Standing, he moved around to the front of his desk. "What've you got for me?" He lifted a brow, and held out his hand for the papers she was clutching.

Not as much as he was probably expecting, she thought. But at least it was something. "Here's the first list," she said. She handed it over, and watched as he leafed through the pages, and nodded.

117

"Great." He motioned to the desk behind him. "I've got a few others, as you can see, but I'll get started on this as soon as I can."

"Sure. I'll be out of town for a few days for my daughter's graduation, so it'll be a while before I get the next one done."

"No problem."

She turned, and he followed her to the door.

"Hey, Dana. Just curious – how many rooms were in your house?"

She started to bristle at the thought of being pressured to move faster, but then she looked back and saw the teasing smile. "Lots," she said, with a toss of her hair.

Kent gave a short laugh, and squeezed her shoulder. "Have a safe trip."

Dana walked back to her car, still feeling the weight of Kent's hand on her shoulder. She couldn't help thinking about it, but was unsure *what* to think about it. Probably nothing. In his line of work, it was likely habit to touch people – part of the consoling persona.

Finally on their way, Dana adjusted her seat belt, and pulled onto the highway. Chase immediately placed headphones over his ears and slumped against the car door. That meant three and a half hours alone with her thoughts, and that just didn't sound like a lot of fun. These days, her thoughts brought her down and stressed her out. She didn't want to go there.

She considered nudging Chase to tell him he'd have to take a shift. But he'd been withdrawn and incommunicado all week – not quite sullen, but distant. No more mention of farming or Poppa's land. Afraid to open a can of worms, she turned on the CD player, and cranked up her own tunes.

**

Evan was waiting for them when they arrived at the hotel. Dana's heart caught in her throat and she threw her arms around her son, almost jumping up and down. She cupped his face in her hands and, on tiptoes, planted a kiss on his cheek. And she didn't care if she made a scene, or he was embarrassed.

He grinned at her. "Hey, Mom."

"Hey, yourself, buddy. Oh, my gosh, look at you." Dana couldn't be any more proud of him. He stood tall and confident in a dress shirt and khaki slacks, a grown man. She stepped back to include Chase. The two shook hands, and Evan gave Chase a light punch on the arm.

"Dude, you're lookin' good," Chase said.

Evan shrugged. "Part of the job requirements."

Dana sucked in her breath, and silently hoped that Evan wouldn't inadvertently send Chase into a foul mood at the mention of his job. She watched the two of them for a moment, so different, yet alike in some ways. There was definitely a family resemblance. They had the same clear blue eyes, but Evan's sparkled with confidence, while Chase's held a look of uncertainty. Evan's stance was tall and self-assured, but Chase still maintained that adolescent tendency to look as though he were trying to shrink into his clothes to avoid being noticed.

"Let me check in. Evan, would you text Maddie and let her know we're here? Ask her if they've picked a restaurant."

A few minutes later, they hauled suitcases into their rooms. She'd booked one room for the boys to share, and one for her. Her room also had double beds, though – just in case Maddie wanted to spend the night. Dana didn't want to infringe on Maddie's last few nights with her friends, but she wouldn't mind a sleepover with her daughter, either. She placed her suitcase on the small stand against the wall, leaving the other bed clear and unwrinkled.

The girls had chosen a Mexican restaurant on the outskirts of town. When Dana and the boys arrived, it was like stepping into a Mexican fiesta – the quick music and bright costumes of the wait staff created a party atmosphere, and Dana was immediately swept into a festive mood. She laughed when a waiter walked by her, gave a well-timed "olé" and kissed her hand. Still grinning,

119

Dana spotted Maddie and her friends already seated at a table for six.

With a squeal she couldn't contain, Dana stretched out her arms and rushed toward Maddie. When Maddie pushed back her chair and stood, Dana wrapped her in a tight hug. "Hi, sweetie. Oh, it's so good to see you!" Still holding onto Maddie's arm, Dana pulled back and greeted the other girls, Heather, one of Maddie's roommates, and Tiffany, another sorority sister. Dana had met Heather before, and recognized them both from photos. Bright, confident girls, just like her daughter. She gave Maddie another quick squeeze. "You look gorgeous," she whispered.

The three girls sat on one side of the table, and Dana took the middle seat opposite, with her sons on either side. As soon as they were situated and the hostess left, Maddie made the other introductions. She pointed to Chase. "This is my little brother, Chase; my mom, of course; and my big brother, Evan." She smiled at her friends, and unmistakable pride lifted her voice. "Evan is a financial analyst with a bank in Tulsa."

Dana set small boxes tied with red ribbons in front of each of the girls. "I found these truffles that have amazing frosting designs in Arkansas colors."

Maddie lifted hers, and peeked inside. "Cool. Thanks, Mom."

The other girls thanked her, too, but Dana noticed their eyes were drawn to Evan. She had the feeling Evan had been a topic of conversation long before tonight.

When the waiter stopped for their drink orders, Dana debated between a glass of wine or a margarita. But when the girls went first, and they each ordered a margarita, Dana caught herself. She suspected Evan would order a beer, and that would leave Chase the only one without an "adult" beverage. Hoping the caffeine wouldn't keep her from sleeping later, she ordered an iced tea, and was glad she had when Evan requested a Dos Equis. A few minutes later, she lifted her glass toward the center of the table. "Congratulations to our grads."

"Thanks, Mom," Maddie said. "So glad finals are over."

In agreement, a chorus of groans went up from the others. "So done with school," Heather added.

"Where is everybody headed?" Dana asked.

Heather spoke up first. "I'm starting a job at McEwen & Associates. It's an engineering firm in Oklahoma City."

"More school for me," Tiffany said with a rueful smile. "But I'm really excited. Law school at Georgetown."

As soon as she said it, Dana remembered Maddie telling her about Tiffany's acceptance to several top law schools. "Oh, that's right. What an achievement. You girls are amazing."

Dana couldn't help feel proud that her daughter's circle of friends were high-achieving young women bound to make their mark on the world. She pushed a basket of chips over to make room for their dinner, and the waitress set a heaping plate of enchiladas in front of her. Then Dana turned to Maddie. "Has the hospital given you a firm start date, honey?"

"They're flexible, but I said around the first. I can get into my apartment any time after Wednesday. Wasn't sure how much needs to be done at home, though. I mean, what about the house, Mom? What about all the tornado damage? Isn't there–"

Holding up a hand to stop her, Dana shook her head. "No tornado talk tonight. Or tomorrow. There's nothing you can do, anyway."

Shortly into the dinner, Dana realized she'd made a mistake. Would've been better to let Chase and Evan sit together so they could talk. As it turned out, when the girls weren't discussing graduation and future plans, they seemed to focus on Evan, and Chase was virtually ignored. No surprise there, she supposed. Two years older, handsome as hell, and working and living on his own, her eldest clearly caught the girls' attention.

She'd have to find out later if he was dating anyone. It wasn't the kind of information he'd share without some prompting.

Leaning forward, Dana interrupted the conversation. "Okay, ladies. What's the plan for tomorrow? We don't want to miss anything."

"Come to the House for brunch at nine," Maddie said. "The honors ceremony starts at eleven. Then the diploma ceremony starts at two."

"Will you meet us there, or should we pick you up?"

"I'll meet you there. It'll be easier."

"Okay, but we'll pick you up for dinner for sure. What about seven?"

Maddie's eyes went round, then flickered nervously toward Heather. "Um, change of plans. We were thinking about having some people over to our apartment tomorrow night. We could order pizzas or make subs or something. That might be easier than trying to go out with all the crowds."

Dana swallowed her disappointment as she saw the chance of any time alone with her daughter slip away like the fine sands in an hourglass. But this was Maddie's weekend, and her choice. "Sure. Whatever you want to do is fine. Does the apartment complex have a bigger space you could use? Like a clubhouse?"

"Oh, God, no. These places are so cheap. It's okay, though, we can squeeze into the kitchen and living room."

More than a few guests, and it would be a crowd, Dana thought. She'd been inside that apartment. Well, the important thing was that Maddie was having fun, she reminded herself again. That would be enough.

At nine-thirty, Dana looped arms with Maddie as they ambled toward the door. "Hey," she whispered. "You want to take the girls home then spend the night with us at the hotel? There's an extra bed in my room."

Without even a pause, Maddie shook her head. "I don't think so, Mom. We're going to a couple of parties. There are so many people to see before everyone leaves."

"All right, then. See you tomorrow. Be careful." She kissed Maddie's cheek, then, like so many years ago when she'd watched her little girl run into the school building to be with her friends, Dana watched the young women get into Maddie's car and drive off.

She turned when Chase touched her arm.

"You got keys?"

"Keys?" Dana echoed.

Evan jangled the handle on the car door. "Car's locked."

Dana started. "Oh, right. Sorry." She pushed the button on her key fob and climbed inside.

At the hotel, Dana said goodnight to her sons and bolted the door behind her. Alone in her room, her disappointment came back full force, and this time, she couldn't shake the chill in her body as a sense of loneliness stole over her. More than anything, she was confused. She and Maddie had always been close. What the hell had happened? Tonight, Maddie seemed downright disinterested. With a heavy sigh, Dana tossed her purse onto one bed then flopped down on the other one. Her daughter was probably just caught up in the excitement of graduation. Couldn't blame her for that. Next weekend would be better. They'd all be home. Sort of.

When a tear rolled down her cheek, Dana swiped it away, and chalked it up to the emotion of the occasion. She knew the symptoms, though. Truth was, she had a serious case of empty-nest syndrome. Yes, Chase had boomeranged, but that was temporary. Her daughter was leaving "home" for good.

**

The crisp, clear morning, as well as the energy at Maddie's sorority house, helped revive Dana's spirits. Couldn't ask for a more perfect day for a graduation, she thought, as she sipped her coffee and chatted with other parents.

They made their way through campus on foot and filed into the auditorium of a gleaming glass and stone science building. Once they were seated, Dana opened the program and found Maddie's name – along with the two symbols that indicated the honors she'd received. Those honors along with her grades and outgoing personality had helped her land a great entry-level job. Who knew where else they would take her?

As the candidates processed toward their reserved seats at the front, Dana grabbed Evan's arm. "There she is! Do you see her? Not quite half-way. She's—"

Evan grinned and leaned over. "Easy, Mom. I see her."

Of course Maddie and her long blond curls were easy to pick out in a crowd. Dana listened to the speeches and clapped politely as other graduates walked across the stage to accept their diplomas, then she tucked the program under her thigh and readied the new Canon. She wasn't missing this shot.

Maddie looked up, a grin lighting her face as she walked across the stage. With a matching grin, Dana snapped the photo, but knew the image was seared on her brain for good.

**

The following week flashed past like a bolt of lightning. Dana spent one more day picking through rubble at the house, but decided to wait on putting the sign up indicating they were ready for the bulldozers until the kids could take one last look if they wanted to. On Thursday, she turned her attention back to Maddie's graduation, and preparations for the party.

Maddie arrived Friday afternoon. "Hey, I'm already set up in the guest room upstairs, so why don't you take Claire's room," Dana told her. "It'll be easier. Let's get your stuff inside, then, before we do anything else, I want you to run over and see Poppa. He was so sad to miss your graduation." Dana would have liked to go, too, but there were too many details to tend to. Besides, her dad would probably love the undivided attention and time with his only granddaughter.

Two hours later, Maddie returned, almost at the same time Evan arrived. "Hey, you're just in time for a job," Dana told him after a quick hug.

"Oh, I was thinking a nap sounded good," Evan told her.

The teasing in his voice told Dana he knew better. "Uh-huh," she said, thrusting a twelve-pack of Diet Coke at him. "Let's get this pop into the coolers. We can ice it down in the morning."

He flicked open a can. "Sure."

When Chase walked in, they were down on their hands and knees among coolers, bags and boxes of supplies.

"What are you guys doing?" Chase asked.

"Loading up for the party," Dana said.

"Looks like there was another tornado."

Dana laughed. "Yeah, and we're right in the middle of it." She handed some utensils to Maddie. "Stick these in the bag behind you just in case Rebecca's dad forgets his. He offered to be grill master."

Maddie took hold of them, and glanced up at Chase. "Chase, you're coming, aren't you?" She twirled a spatula. "Hey, you could flip burgers for us. You know, get some experience for your career at McDonalds. Or did you decide on Arby's?"

Dana gasped, but held her tongue as Chase stretched his arms behind his head and answered without missing a beat.

"Thought I might go all out and try for Subway."

From outward appearances, Chase held his own and didn't seem hurt by the teasing. But Dana couldn't help wondering. Was he playing along to save face? She recognized the teasing, of course. Maddie and Chase had sparred with each other since the day Chase could form words. Dana had grown used to it – and weary from it – but had forgotten how harsh they could be.

"Maddie," she warned. Apparently Chase hadn't mentioned farming to his siblings. Maybe he'd dropped the idea. He hadn't mentioned it to her again, either.

"You know," Maddie continued, "this is going to be really embarrassing for a nutritionist to have a brother in the fat– I mean fast food industry."

He sent her a cool glance. "I promise I won't tell anyone we're related, Sis. They'd never believe it, anyway. Not with that throne attached to your ass."

Evan laughed then, and Dana shook her head. "Okay, you guys, that's enough. Let's try to act our age." She'd thought they'd moved past this petty bickering and sniping. She turned toward Evan. Would he take sides? She hadn't noticed any problems between them last weekend. Surely the two older weren't going to gang up on the youngest. That, she would not tolerate. Uncertainty kept her silent for now, though. Maybe a little ribbing would be good for Chase. If he settled for something below his level in a family full of college grads and professionals, there was bound to be some backlash. Here was a taste of real life.

But there was something in Maddie's tone that bothered Dana, and after dinner, she pulled her daughter aside. "Maddie, what's gotten into you? Why would you talk to Chase like that?"

Maddie's eyes went wide. "Like what?"

"You know what. You're being mean, and I want to know why."

"Mom, come on already. It was a joke."

"It wasn't very funny."

Maddie grinned. "It was, but you're just so uptight."

"I'm sorry. Expecting my kids to be civil to each other makes me uptight? I don't get that."

"Mom, seriously, if he's going to drop out of junior college, he's gonna have to be able to take a joke. How does it help to baby him? He gets everything he wants, but doesn't work for anything. Should we just let him to be a slacker?"

The words stung Dana like a slap in the face. It took a long moment to come to her wits. She held up a hand. "Okay, I'm going to forget you said that, 'cause there's no way I can get my head around it. When have you ever gone without a single thing you wanted, missy?"

Prom dresses, care packages, study abroad and more played across Dana's mind. If anyone did without in their family, it was *her*. Certainly not her children. And damned-sure not her daughter. Dana had busted her ass day after day to give her kids the same things all the other kids had, even though they had a lousy, absent dad.

Dana reached out and touched her daughter's soft waves. "You know, Maddie, I've been so proud of you.

For weeks, I've been excited to tell people about your graduation and your job." Dana's voice dropped, tinged with sadness. "I have to say, I'm disappointed. I'd hoped that you and Evan would talk to Chase, encourage him. Help him get back on solid ground and find a passion and a direction for his life. Last weekend you ignored him, and I let it go because of graduation. But so far this weekend, you've done nothing but criticize and make fun of him. You talk about helping people with eating disorders and all kinds of issues. Well, how 'bout helping out your own brother?"

She turned on her heel and walked away from her daughter.

In the next twenty-four hours, Dana had little time to dwell on the scene with Maddie. She was able to put it aside and enjoy the graduation festivities – so many friends stopped with gifts and good wishes. The party, it seemed, provided the town with much-needed relief from tornado cleanup. Dana was happy to help on that score.

As she watched her daughter interact with guests, the familiar pride slipped back into place. Here was the daughter she recognized. With grace and smiles, Maddie interacted with their guests, making a point to stop and speak to long-time acquaintances and family friends. When Charlie Fast wandered through the crowd, Maddie took the time to listen to him – probably listening to a story she'd heard many times before. And, bless her, she was attentive to Poppa. Dana smiled as Maddie tossed an arm around Poppa and sat on his lap, her legs dangling over the side of his wheelchair.

"That's adorable," Dana called, dashing for her camera. "Stay just like that, and let me get this." They matched perfectly – the shirt Dana had bought for her dad was a spot-on Arkansas red. It was so good to see him enjoying himself and feeling like part of the family. It would be the start of a new photo album – new memories to treasure. She'd just snapped that one when Mary nudged her.

"Hey, your turn. Get in there, Mom. I want a shot of you all."

Dana handed her the camera. "Thanks, Mare. Would you take one with mine, too?"

"You keep posing, and I'll keep shooting," Mary said.

Dana laughed, knowing the kids would humor her only so long. She certainly didn't want to start any more bickering. A few more shots, and she took the camera back, then began picking up stray plates and abandoned pop cans.

Two hours later, after the fanfare, and all the guests had gone, Dana's thoughts drifted back to her children. Perhaps Maddie had had some anxiety about moving off on her own, away from family and friends, and subconsciously envied Chase being able to return home. That might account for her earlier behavior.

Dana understood that a fundamental change had taken place. There'd been a shift in the tectonic plates of her life, and she had the feeling things would never be quite the same. Her children were grown. They had their own lives, opinions and world views. They'd been exposed to new experiences, people and ideas, and had been changed as a result. And Dana's role had changed. She would never be as central in their lives as she had been.

On one hand she was thrilled because it meant she'd done her job. At the same time, she knew it meant redefining herself – the motherhood bar on the graph of her life was shrinking and would be much smaller in the future. Tossing the last bag of trash into the bin out by the shelter, she stopped cold as a thought slammed into her. She'd always thought that her measure of success would be getting all three kids graduated from college. That had been the benchmark she'd been aiming toward.

Dana's steps were slow as she wrestled with that idea. It might not happen. Of course it wasn't the degree itself that was important. That was an achievement, but it was meant to lead to the next steps – a successful career and a happy, fulfilling life. The ultimate goal was the happy life. Oh, how she wanted that for each of her kids. How could she help Chase get to that place from a different route? She hadn't expected a detour.

128

Chapter Eleven

At seven-thirty Monday morning Dana bumped into Chase – awake and fully clothed. Startled, she let out a yelp, and clung to her mug with both hands to keep the coffee from sloshing out. "What are you doing?" she asked.

He leaned against the banister and gave her a cool look.

"Going to work."

Dana let those words sink in a moment. "Work?" she echoed. "As in a job?"

"Yeah."

She loosened her grip on the cup to put one hand on her hip. "Where, and why didn't you tell anyone?"

Chase crossed his arms, and she could see his shoulders tense. "Didn't want to take any attention away from the princess."

Dana rolled her eyes as she reached for Chase's arm, and steered him down the stairs and toward the kitchen. "Tell me."

"I'm starting to work for Cameron Wade today."

Dana's breath caught on a little laugh. "Are you really? That's awesome, sweetie." She studied his face a moment. "Are you excited about it?"

"I don't know, but I want to give it a shot. At least I'll be outside, and working for local people, not making money for some mega-company."

That was true. Whether it led to any kind of career path or not, it was forward progress. Making something happen. She had to give him credit for that.

"Well, I'm glad it worked out." She slid an arm around his waist. "What time will you be home?"

"Not sure. Maybe around six."

"Okay. Have a good day." She stood on her toes and planted a kiss on his cheek. "I've got to get ready. Congratulations. I'm proud of you." Dana freshened her coffee and scooted up the stairs, doing a happy dance inside. *Thank God.* She gave herself a figurative pat on the back as she fluffed up her hair. These kids didn't think they needed her anymore. But, hey, her set-up with Cameron had turned out to be providential. Maybe she wasn't so obsolete after all.

∗∗

Dana bounced inside Hannah's cafe. It'd been a while since she'd had a fun lunch out, and she'd earned this one. To make up for being gone for all of the graduation festivities and moving Maddie into a new apartment, Dana had put in six straight days at the hospital. Now, she was ready to plant her face into a thick slice of Hannah's famous pie. The only problem was deciding which kind. She glanced at the glass case and salivated while she waited for the hostess to seat her. Chocolate cream topped with Snicker's chunks and a drizzle of caramel didn't look half bad. Definitely a candidate.

"This way," the hostess said.

"I'm expecting Mary to join me," Dana told her, picking up the menu. She'd barely opened it when Mary stepped inside. With a quick wave, Dana flagged her down.

"Hi there," Mary said, moving in for a hug. "How are you? You look great."

"Thanks. I think I've finally caught up on a little sleep."

"Good. Nobody needs those kind of bags."

"Seriously."

"Something sure smells good in here."

"I know. It always does. I'm thinking salad and pie."

"Mmm, hmm."

They placed their orders, and Mary leaned in as if she were about to spill a secret. "Speaking of bags . . . guess what?"

Dana arched her brows. No need to guess. Mary was obviously about to pop.

"You're going to need some luggage. Talked to Claire last night. She still wants to get some kind of girls' trip together."

Dana took a gulp of water as her hands turned clammy, and she wondered just how high Claire was shooting and whether her bank account could handle it. She met Mary's eyes. "Cool. Count me in."

Mary blinked, her eyes wide. "Really?" She put a hand to her chest, and laughed. "Oh, my gosh, I thought I was going to have to twist your arm. I swear, Claire and I were ready to tie you up and toss you in the trunk of a car."

Dana grinned. "Depends on what you have in mind. It's not the best timing, of course, but I've been saving for it, and I need to get out of here."

"We're thinking about a shopping trip since you both need new stuff. And keeping it simple, maybe driving to Dallas or Chicago. We can shop 'til we drop, go to the museums, botanical gardens, whatever. What do you think?"

"It sounds awesome. I don't care about the shopping, though. I just want to get away. When—"

She broke off when the waitress returned with their salads. Then her face went hot as she stifled a gasp. Her eyes snapped to the waitress' face, but the young woman didn't make eye contact. When Dana looked for a nametag, the girl's arm blocked it.

"Can I get you anything else?" the girl asked.

Dana glanced at Mary and gave a slight shake of her head.

As soon as the waitress left, Mary frowned. "What's the matter?"

Dana sucked in her breath, unsure how to handle this. "Our waitress is wearing my mother's ring."

131

"What?" Mary gasped, her head whipping around. "Are you sure?"

"Positive." The large rectangular aquamarine with fine silver filigree setting and border were unusual and distinctive. No doubt about it.

She rested her hands in her lap, fighting back tears. "I had a feeling something like this would happen. Think how much jewelry, how many coins, keepsakes, and watches were blown away in the tornado. They had to land somewhere. Anybody could pick them up. And I have no proof. Even if I had a picture of Mom wearing it, all the albums were destroyed."

"Well, that's just not right. Everyone knows about the tornado. And she knows that ring doesn't belong to her. Anything found should be turned in. Period."

Dana picked up her fork and pushed some avocado around on her plate. "It's too much to ask. I really hoped people would be honest. But when you find something pretty and valuable like that it's too tempting to hang onto it. Plus, think about it, would you turn something valuable in to just anybody without knowing it would get to the rightful owner?"

"Maybe not, but she could leave a name and contact number with lost and found. Listen, we can very quietly tell her that it's yours."

"No, Mary. Please, don't make a scene."

Mary drummed her fingers on the table before speaking again. "Dana. It belongs to you. You can't just let her have it."

"I need to think how to handle it, Mare."

They ate in silence for a few minutes, but Dana had lost her appetite. Could hardly chew as she fought to keep the tears away. Disappointment settled in her stomach. So much for chocolate Snicker's pie.

When the girl stopped back by with the iced tea pitcher, Dana was able to see Caroline's nametag. What was the right thing to do? Should she pull her aside and ask about it? Speak to Ada, the owner? The ring sparkled in the light. She certainly wasn't trying to hide it.

As Caroline moved on, Dana waved a hand at Mary. "I'll deal with it later. Let's talk about the trip. We need to figure out some dates so I can let them know at work. I already said I'd be taking off at least a week. I should probably be here for the Fourth, though. The hospital is always busy then."

Always busy because people didn't take the dangers of fireworks seriously. Every year they treated burns and sometimes worse. It was one of the worst days of the year – and saddest – because the injuries often involved children. She dreaded it, but she had to be there.

"Right. Okay, what about the week after that?"

"That should work. Who else is going?"

Mary shook her head. "Not sure yet. I know Jane is interested, and possibly Susie and Lisa. We'll have to figure out if we want to take two cars. Otherwise, maybe just the four of us. Do you have a preference?"

"Well, Claire opened it up to everyone at book club last year. Seems like it'd be rude to restrict it now."

"True. The more, the merrier, I guess. By the way, have you heard about the street dance?"

"No. Who's doing that?"

Mary rolled her eyes. "Have you been hiding under a rock or what?"

"I wish," Dana told her. The notion of hiding under a rock for a while didn't sound half bad.

Mary grinned. "Well, you'll want to come out for this. Angels and Demons band is giving a free concert for Whitfield. Can you believe it? Next weekend."

"Oh, nice." Dana was aware enough to know that the band had Kansas roots and had recently hit the big time with a rock/country crossover. "That's a great idea." Whitfield usually had a street dance in the fall in conjunction with the county fair, but she loved the idea of having one now.

"Claire might come down," Mary added.

"Are you serious? Oh, now you're talking. That would be so much fun. I hope she can."

Caroline stopped at the table to retrieve their plates. "Pie, ladies?"

"Of course," Mary said, coolly. "What's the special today, Caroline?"

"Dutch apple."

"Hmmm. I think I'll have peach. Is Ada in today?"

Dana groaned inside. Was Mary planning something, or just toying with the girl?

"No. She'll be in later."

Good, Dana thought, but she had qualms about speaking to Ada. She didn't want to get Caroline in trouble. It wasn't as though the girl had *stolen* the ring.

Mary nudged her. "Pie."

"I guess if you're having some, I'll have a slice of chocolate Snicker's," Dana said.

When the slabs of pie arrived at the table, she wasn't sorry. It wouldn't replace her mother's ring, but it looked like heaven. She couldn't help the tears that sprang to her eyes.

"This is going to be great for Hannah's business," Mary said. There was humor in her voice, but sympathy on her face. "Everyone will think that pie is so delicious it's moved you to tears. Kind of like that scene in *When Harry Met Sally.*"

Dana laughed, and lifted her fork. "Could be worthy of an orgasm, even."

"Everything good, ladies?" Caroline asked a moment later. She met Dana's eyes, and Dana saw an honest friendliness there.

Dana put down her fork and cleared her throat. "Caroline," she said softly. "Could I ask you a question?"

The girl nodded. "Sure."

Dana touched the ring. "This ring you're wearing, it's so similar to one I lost in the tornado, and I—"

Caroline's eyes went round, and she put a hand to her chest. "Oh, my gosh! Really? Is it yours? I've been hoping the owner would come in and see it. It's so beautiful, it makes me sad to think of someone losing it." She pulled the ring from her finger, and handed it to Dana. "I polished it."

Tears streamed down Dana's face, even as she was laughing. She pushed back the chair and wrapped her arms around Caroline, making a scene for sure. "Thank you so much, Caroline. This belonged to my mother, and losing it was really hard to accept."

She gave the girl another quick squeeze. "You have made my day." Dana picked up her purse. "I want to give you a reward for returning it."

The girl shook her head vigorously. "Oh, no, ma'am. I wanted to return it. I'm so glad you said something."

"Thank you," Dana whispered again. With a catch in her throat, she sat back down, and slid the ring onto her finger, watching its facets shimmer in the light. Her mother had worn the ring only on special occasions, and Dana had tucked it away for safekeeping. Clearly not the best policy. She held up her hand for Mary to see. "I think I'll start wearing it."

"Absolutely. Pie and jewelry," Mary said, lifting her fork. "What more do you need?"

Swiping at her cheeks, Dana laughed. "A tissue."

**

The unfamiliar weight of the ring kept Dana conscious of it, and as she drove, she wondered if they'd spent enough time at the house. Had they given up too easily? It was messy, dirty work. And especially difficult to keep emotions at bay. But, obviously, things were being found. She'd been ready to call Kent and give the go-ahead on the bulldozers. Once she did that, it was all over. Damn, she should've thought to ask Caroline where she'd found the ring. Maybe the others ended up close by. She'd have to call or circle back around.

She wasn't dressed for it, but she turned toward her house, anyway. Getting out of the car, she glanced up at the mid-day sunshine. If the sun hit something just right, it could make all the difference. She stepped cautiously around a mound of debris, and stopped short as Kent Donovan turned toward her. What was he doing there?

"Hey, Dana," Kent said, backing out of the kitchen area. "How are you?"

"Good, thanks. Just thought I'd take another look around, see if I can find anything else. It's so hard to give the final go-ahead on the teardown."

Kent propped a clipboard on his hip and glanced at the wreckage. "Yeah, why don't we hold off on that for a few days. I'd like to spend a little more time in here."

"Oh, all right. I thought—" Dana's face flamed as the significance of Kent's words sunk in. She could see her itemized kitchen list on his clipboard. He was double-checking her. Oh, my God, what was he doing? Measuring drawers to see if the number of utensils she'd listed could really have fit inside? Counting the fragments of dishes to calculate whether they could add up to a full set of china?

Her chest heaved, and she pushed sunglasses to the top of her head, biting her tongue to keep from lashing out. "I thought you had all the documentation you needed," she said. "Wasn't that the point of all the photos?" She wondered if he had a legal right to be on her property. Could the insurance reps all just come and go as they pleased?

"Sure, but I can get better information if I see it for myself. The photos don't always tell the whole story. And you left a few blanks on—"

"Everything on that list is one hundred percent accurate," Dana cried, her emotions getting the best of her. "I'm sorry that I don't have a receipt down to the last penny for every item that was in my house." To her mortification, her voice shook as she spoke, but she couldn't stop the outburst. The ball was out of the cannon. "What do you want? Carbon dating on every item so you can tell exactly how old it is? Are you taking fiber samples from the wood and carpeting?"

She crossed her arms and glared at him.

Kent felt her eyes pelting him with daggers. Taken aback, he processed the unexpected tirade. Shaking his head, he raked a hand through his hair. "Dana, whoa.

Hang on a minute. You think I'm over here with your list . . ." he tapped the papers on the clipboard. "You think I'm here to double-check you? To verify what's on this list and make sure you aren't trying to cheat Heartland out of any money? Is that what you're saying?"

In spite of the defiance on her face, Kent could see those amazing crystal-blue eyes tearing up.

"Well, aren't you?"

Kent closed his eyes for a moment, his whole body sagging. Did she really think that? He thought they'd gotten past the mistrust, but she stood there with that same glacial attitude she'd had the first time they'd met. He could practically feel the frost in the air. With a sigh that came from deep within, he faced her. "No, Dana. I'm not."

He swung the clipboard around for her to see it. "You left out some of the details, so I thought I'd come over and see if I could fill in the blanks. If you don't know what kind of tile you had, then I have to go with a common commercial grade. At twenty years old, that's not going to be worth much. But if you had a high-grade Travertine tile that's twenty years old, it still had some life left in it, and that gets you a higher value."

Her pursed lips told him she wasn't convinced.

"Makes sense, right? Same with the kitchen cabinets. You said wood, but there's a big difference between painted lumber and solid maple." His eyes locked onto hers. "Here's the deal. I'm trying to help you get what you're entitled to. That's my job."

She took a step back. "Your job? Are you kidding me? I may not know how all of this works, but don't treat me like I'm an idiot. You work for Heartland Insurance, not me."

Boy, this was one wall that wasn't crumbling, Kent thought. He gestured behind him. "Look, the kitchen is where a lot of your value comes from. Outside of the roof and heating and cooling, it's got your big-ticket items. You want to get all the dollars you can out of there. But it's your call. You ready to bring in the 'dozers?"

Kent stood still then, watching her. The ball was in her court. He could see the anger change to uncertainty as she looked from him to the remains of the house. It was a tiny crack in the surface, but he'd take it. "Dana," he said quietly. "We have one more week before the cost of removal goes up. Why don't you give me a few more days? Can you get me a couple more rooms by then?"

She looked at the ground before meeting his eyes again. "I don't know."

He held the paper out, and pointed to her answers. "Look here. Can you see where I added maple? That's an automatic enhancement." Exasperated, Kent blew out a breath. "I don't know what else to do to gain your trust, Dana."

Maybe it had something to do with being a single woman that she was afraid of being taken advantage of. If she'd been burned before, he supposed it'd make sense that she was afraid to let her guard down. But *son of a bitch*, he needed to make some kind of progress. It wasn't his nature to duck and run, but this ice queen was wearing him thin. "Maybe it'd be best if I turn your file over to another agent. Would you be more comfortable with a woman?"

"Your way or the highway, huh?" She gave him a grim smile, then shook her head. "No. You're not dumping me off with someone else now. Let's just get it done."

He stepped in front of her, forcing her to make eye contact. "Dana, I'm asking you to try to trust me. At least a little. I'm going to squeeze every dime I can out of here for you."

Something about that statement almost made Dana laugh, and she acknowledged that if he weren't with the insurance company she could see him being a frugal sort. The Boy Scout in him was probably conscientious. But the question remained, where did his loyalty lie – with the victim or the company?

He interrupted her thoughts. "Was there a specific reason you stopped by today? Were you looking for me?"

138

Dana surveyed the rubble again, and her hopes plummeted. She held out her hand with the ring. "No. Someone found my mother's ring, and I got it back today. So I guess I thought there was still a chance I could find something, but . . . I don't know."

Kent looked at the ring. "That's great. I'm glad you recovered it. Matches your eyes," he added softly.

Her gaze snapped to his. Yes, it did, but she hadn't expected him to notice. She wiped the palm across her jeans in a moment of awkward silence.

Clearing his throat, Kent glanced at his watch. "I've got some time. Come on. Let's have a look."

On the downside of her emotional roller coaster, she wasn't sure she had the energy for it anymore. Still, a fresh set of eyes might have a better chance of spotting something. She let him steer her toward the remnants of her home. Earlier, she'd been focused on recovering items inside, but as she picked her way through, she glanced toward the backyard. Her entire lot was a debris field. Maybe there were treasures buried out there.

"Let's spend some time in the backyard," she said.

"Lead the way," Kent murmured.

Dana could feel Kent's eyes on her, so she avoided them, and instead began moving pieces of wood and metal – taking from one pile, and adding to another. At least he had the good sense to shut up and not try to placate or comfort her. They worked silently, and Dana took satisfaction in heaving trash across the yard. She flung a couple of shingles into the air, and watched them ricochet off the other pile.

"This would be a great outlet for someone with an anger management issue," she muttered.

"It's okay to be angry, Dana."

She hadn't been talking to him. Had almost forgotten he was there. But when he spoke, her head snapped around, and she gave a harsh laugh. "Me, angry? Why in the world would I be angry?" She shot the next shingle across Frisbee style. "See? Look. This is fun."

Looking past him, her eyes were drawn to something metal, coppery. The lamp from her bedroom. She'd love to keep that. With a quick spurt of adrenaline, Dana pushed a splintered two-by-four out of the way, and bent down to retrieve the lamp. She yanked it up, and stared. Then let it slip from her grasp. The shade was gone. No surprise there, but the top half of the stand was bent at a ninety-degree angle then twisted, the electrical component dangling limply at the top.

Sagging, she picked it up again and hurled it across the yard. Kent took a step back, and said nothing. Good to know he wasn't stupid.

A few minutes later, Dana conceded defeat. Again. She stood up and ran her arm across her face, pushing back her hair. "I'm done," she announced. "We're wasting time." She took a deep shuttered breath. "I'm not coming back. Do whatever you want, then have it cleared."

He followed her for a moment, then put a hand out to stop her. "I won't come back if you'd rather I didn't."

She simply didn't have the energy to fight about it. Or care, for that matter. "It's up to you," she told him. "Look, I'm sorry I lost it earlier. I'm—"

Kent cut her off. "You don't have to apologize, Dana. I understand. It's personal, and it hurts."

Kindness laced his words. And, yes, probably understanding. He'd seen this before. People always said they didn't want sympathy, but at the moment, she didn't mind. "You're right about that," she said, her voice low. "Still, I apologize for taking it out on you. I just—" She pressed her lips together, fighting tears once again. "I'll get the other lists to you. But don't wait on me, and don't miss the deadline. Bring in the bulldozers."

Leaving Kent Donovan standing almost where she'd found him, Dana carefully stepped around the clutter. And didn't look back.

Chapter Twelve

Dana pushed the papers aside when Chase walked in. Three bathrooms, four bedrooms, a dining room, living room, garage . . . and her head was spinning.

"Good timing," she told him as he strolled into the kitchen. "I need a break."

"Yeah? From what?"

She pressed her fingers to her temples. "Lists. Possessions. Insurance. Thinking."

He went straight to the fridge and pulled out a Diet Coke. "Yeah. That doesn't sound like fun."

"No. Did you think of anything else from your room? I need to get these over to Heartland soon. Tomorrow, if possible. I'm sick of dealing with them."

Chase shrugged. "My guitar was the main thing."

"Yep. Got it. Pull up a chair, baby. Tell me about your day." She could already tell he'd been spending time outside. His face was tanned, and he looked healthier. "Are you enjoying it?"

"Mostly following Cameron or his brother around so far. Worked on fixing fences today."

"Oh. I bet there's a lot of that needing done. Are they tilling up the damaged fields?"

"Not yet. But they will. And then I'll be working the rigs. Wade wants me to get a feel for the different equipment."

"Good. That's great." She suppressed a grin, not wanting to embarrass him by gushing. But she felt like slapping his hand with a high five, or dancing around the kitchen. He was like a different kid. Relaxed. Even, she realized with a jolt, speaking in complete sentences that she could understand instead of mumbling. She made a mental note to find a way to thank Cameron for giving Chase the opportunity.

"Smells good," Chase said, glancing around. "What's for supper?"

Dana pushed back her chair. "I've got some chicken and potatoes in the oven. Why don't you get cleaned up while I throw together a salad? And Chase? Don't forget, Claire will be here tomorrow. Make sure things are clean up there, and why don't you plan to get supper on your own tomorrow night, okay?"

Once Chase was out of sight, Dana let her head fall into her hands as relief surged through her. If she could get Chase moving in a positive direction, and make some progress on the mess at the house, maybe life wouldn't seem so out of control, and she could feel normal again.

**

The following day, Dana put in a half-shift at the hospital, focusing on administrative duties and schedules. Brad's imminent departure meant that she would temporarily assume additional assignments, including some of the community outreach programming. In conjunction with the clinic, the hospital always held summer first aid and babysitting classes as well as a blood drive.

Greg had been right about Brad's time commitment – or lack of. As far as Dana could tell Brad had mentally checked out of Whitfield and had turned his attention to "new opportunities."

Dana saved the master schedule to her desktop, then stopped to brief Valerie.

"I've got to get going," she said. "But I'll be around, so call if you need anything."

Valerie propelled Dana toward the stairs. "Would you go already? Everything is under control. In fact, Hillary and I just did rounds, and it seems like everyone is out for a little siesta."

"All right. I'll see you later."

"Hey, forget about this place for a while, and have fun with your friend."

"Thanks, Val." That was exactly what she intended to do.

Claire was due in around three o'clock and Dana wanted to be at the house when she arrived, figuring company would be better for her than coming back to an empty house with time on her hands.

But there was still that one errand.

She pulled her car up to the trailer and grabbed the envelope that held the itemized lists of the entire contents of her house – as best she could remember – down to every book, movie, Christmas ornament and hair clip. Dana noted a few other cars. Maybe Kent wouldn't have time to talk. Better yet, maybe he'd be out in the field. Their paths hadn't crossed since Dana's emotional meltdown at the house. Wouldn't surprise her if the man was avoiding her at this point.

She slowly opened the door, and stepped inside. All three desks were occupied, and Lilian and Roger Newman sat in front of Kent's. Every head turned when she entered.

"Hey, Dana," Kent said, with an easy smile. "I can be with you in a little while. You're welcome to have a seat and something to drink."

Dana shook her head, and held up the envelope. "No, thanks. I just want to drop this off."

His eyes slid to the woman at the next desk, and Jennifer held out her hand as she stood up. "I can take that for you."

Dana handed her the lists, but still moved toward Kent's desk where Lilian had risen from her chair. Dana clasped her hand. "How are you guys?" she asked. One block behind Dana, and two doors down, their home was in the same condition as hers. Flattened.

Lilian sniffled. "We're moving to Oakmont until we can get the house put back together. We're staying with Roger's sister." Oakmont was a smaller town only about twenty minutes from Whitfield. Close enough to monitor progress on their home.

"We'll see how long we can stand it, anyway," Roger added with a wry smile.

Dana laughed. "I understand. Good luck with that."

"Thanks, sweetie," Lilian said. "Hey. How's your dad doing?"

Oh, nice. A handshake with a dash of guilt. Dana glanced at her watch, and didn't see how she could squeeze in a visit with her dad today. Not with Claire due to arrive any minute. "He's well, thanks." She was going on faith, but knew that if he wasn't, she'd get a call. "You all take care. We want you back here as soon as possible."

With a self-conscious glance at Kent, Dana turned and hurried to the door.

Fifteen minutes later, Dana heard the garage door go up. She barely let Claire get inside the house before folding her into a tight hug. "Oh, Claire."

They held on, clinging to one another for a good long time, crying, hugging and rocking – holding each other up. Dana would swear the shoulder blades beneath her fingers were sharper than normal. The events of the past several weeks had obviously taken a toll on her friend.

When she stepped back, Dana searched Claire's face, but didn't let go of her. Her face was a little pink, and her eyes looked tired, but she was put together, and her gorgeous brushed-chrome hair was styled – sleekly framing her face. So Claire. "God, it's good to see you. I have missed you so much," Dana said. "How are you holding up?"

"It's been a hell of a month, that's all I can say."

"Longer than that for you," Dana said quietly, squeezing Claire's arms. "You doing okay?"

She watched Claire's eyes roam the room, and wondered if she'd be haunted by memories. Hopefully nothing would trigger a setback. If that happened, Dana knew there would be fewer and fewer visits.

"I'm better."

Dana tugged her farther inside. "Hey, it's your house. Come on in. What do you want to drink? I have Diet Coke, iced tea, and some lime Perrier. And fresh limes, already sliced." She'd polished off the open bottle of wine last night, and had taken out the recycling so there were no signs of alcohol.

"Sounds perfect. I'll have an iced tea with a slice of lime."

Dana headed for the refrigerator and let Claire take a minute to get her bearings.

"Wow. Susie really transformed the place, didn't she?"

"If you mean took all of your style and personality out of it, then yes. I hardly recognized it when I first came in."

"It looks good, though. I guess people want to envision their own things and decorating. Doesn't matter. Honestly, I don't think of it as home anymore." She brushed a hand across the back of a chair, shaking her head. "Isn't that crazy? Spent thirty-some years here, and in less than one, it seems unfamiliar."

Dana handed Claire a glass. "Come on. Let's sit. I want to hear everything about Elise and your new condo."

Claire smiled then. "You girls have to come up soon. I wish you could see it before we take our trip, so you'd know what the spaces look like. I'm going to need your opinions."

Dana laughed. "Not to worry, my friend. We'll still have plenty of those. Take some pictures and bring them along."

"That's a good idea. Wow." With a shake of her head, Claire blew out a heavy sigh. "Can't believe we're both starting over."

"No kidding. This whole thing seems like a bad dream. A freaking nightmare, in fact."

"I'm sure. What a mess. It's really gone? Everything?"

Dana leaned forward, nodding slowly. "Gone."

Claire grabbed her hand. "I'm so sorry, Dana. I still can't get my head around it."

"Wait 'til you see it with your own eyes. It's unbelievable."

"Mary mentioned shopping on our trip, but there's no way you'll be ready to buy new things, is there?"

Dana took a long drink of her iced tea, working to keep her eyes from tearing up, which they seemed to do at an embarrassing rate these days. She knew she didn't have to pretend with Claire. *Couldn't* pretend with Claire. She knew her history, and her situation.

"No. I'm afraid that's going to be a while. And I won't be able to buy everything new."

"That's okay. You don't have to replace everything at once. Take it a little at a time so it's not so overwhelming. When the timing is right, it could be fun. You're so creative, you won't need to spend as much as the rest of us do."

Dana figured they'd spend most of the trip shopping for Claire, and she was okay with that. She nodded. "Speaking of fun, hope you weren't planning to catch up on any sleep tonight. Mary's coming at seven. I've got all kinds of food and junk. I'm taking off my watch, and turning off my computer, and we're staying up as long as we can keep our eyes open."

"I'm in," Claire told her. "But remember, we'll have another late night tomorrow. Not sure I can handle two nights in a row. The batteries take a little longer to recharge these days."

At one time, Claire had been the queen of hospitality. She'd given amazing parties, had played hostess for hours, wearing heels, looking poised and gracious – and all the while making it seem effortless. Dana hoped to see that Claire this weekend. "If memory serves, you'll do just fine," Dana told her, grinning.

**

The clock said three-ten as Dana flipped off the bedside lamp. Way past her bedtime, but catching up on each other's lives made the night fly by. Being together, no fluff, no sugar-coating, was better than drugs. She was still smiling as her thoughts faded and her eyes closed.

146

A bird chirping outside the window brought her awake again, and she listened for a moment, enjoying the leisurely no-alarm wake-up. Yawning, she glanced at the clock. Even though she'd had only a few hours of sleep, she felt refreshed. And the mouth-watering aroma of something cinnamon wafting from downstairs beckoned to her. Claire must be waving her magic wand in the kitchen. Ah, it was so good to be with her friends, and to have the entire day ahead of them. It'd be a weekend to remember, for sure.

As they headed to the street party Saturday evening, Dana's thoughts went back to earlier days when they were giddy teenagers heading for the homecoming dance. They were older, for sure, but didn't look half-bad, she thought as she watched Claire mingling with a group of friends.

A couple of local bands were kicking things off, with the Angels and Demons scheduled at dusk. Already, music and laughter filled the air. In line at the keg waiting for a beer-filled plastic cup, Dana started when a heavy arm settled around her shoulders.

"Hey, there, darlin'. How are you?"

The smell of beer curled around them as she glanced up and got a full view of her former high school classmate Will Avery's outlandish grin. Dana figured this cowboy-wanna-be had been in the keg line a few times already. No surprise there. Resisting the urge to duck under his arm, she took a small step to the right. Will was a fun guy, but had a tendency to drink too much, talk too loudly, and let his hands wander a little too far.

"Doing okay. How 'bout you?"

"I'm good." He raised his cup. "Planning to buy a lot of beer tonight so's I can help out with the fundraising, you know?" One of the distributors had pledged to make a donation to the town based on a percentage of sales for the night.

"Right. Kind of you to sacrifice like that on account of others, Will." Dana was pretty sure the gut hanging over Will's jeans and belt buckle had nothing to do with philanthropy, and everything to do with weekends at the bar.

With a chuckle, he leaned in closer. "Do I detect a trace of sarcasm in your voice, Little Miss Dana? I'm deeply offended that you doubt my generous nature."

Dana laughed and moved forward in line, shooing Will away.

He didn't budge.

"Get your beer, doll, then I'll take you for a spin on the dance floor. Whaddya say?"

Dana glanced behind him at the 'dance floor,' the black top of Main Street, which had been shut down and roped off for the evening's festivities. Already a good crowd moved to the beat of a Shania Twain song. Those not in the center were on the sidelines laughing and tapping their toes, and swaying along with the tune. It was a night to forget the troubles caused by a tornado and remember friends and community.

Two years ahead of her in high school, Will had always been on the wrong side of raunchy for her, and not in her circle of friends. Still, he was a known entity, and it was just dancing. She knew he'd been working his ass off helping with cleanup, and deserved a night to let loose. And she was there to have fun, after all. She might end up wearing her beer, or Will's, but what the hell? It was time to kick up her heels and live it up a little. She smiled and held up a finger. "Give me just a minute, cowboy, then I say let's show 'em how it's done."

Dana took a couple of sips of beer as Will put a hand on her back and steered her toward the dancing crowd. Then he grabbed her free hand and gave a tug. With a quick yelp, Dana lurched forward then back, teetering a moment before gaining her balance and moving along with him. Even though she tried to hold the beer away from her, it sloshed onto her fingers and dripped on her exposed toes. No doubt, she'd smell like a brewery before the night was over. She decided she didn't care.

Laughing, she twirled around. "Now, don't try anything fancy, big guy," she hollered at Will. "I'd like to drink some of this." Please don't let him step on my feet, she pleaded silently. The strappy heels that Val had loaned her were no match for his heavy cowboy boots.

The next time he spun her around, she nearly stumbled, but it wasn't on account of their shoes. From the corner of her eye, she saw an unexpected familiar face. What in the world was he doing there? Hanging out in Whitfield on weekends, too? She looked again to see who he was with. Had he brought a date?

Kent Donovan smiled and nodded as their eyes met. She was sure that smile held amusement. Great. He already thought she was a ditzy blonde who didn't take care of her affairs. Dancing with Will Avery and swinging around a cup of beer certainly wouldn't improve her image.

When they whirled back near Claire, Dana widened her eyes, appealing to Claire to rescue her. Instead, Claire raised her cup of lime-infused seltzer, and laughed.

Finally, the music paused, and Dana caught her breath. "I need a break, Will."

"Yes, ma'am." He deposited her at Claire's side.

"You look good out there for an old man," Claire shouted at Will.

With a wicked grin, Will pulled Claire into his arms and whisked her away, her long red blouse blurring against the flashing lights.

Served her right. Chuckling, Dana stepped onto the sidewalk, and took the opportunity to wipe her beer-soaked hand on her pant leg. When she looked up again, she found her view obstructed by Kent Donovan. Even standing on the curb, she barely met the man's chin. She pulled herself up, glad she'd taken a chance on the three-inch heels. If he thought for one minute he could spoil the night with his insurance and depreciation blabber, well, he could think again. And move along.

A lazy smile spread across his face. "Hey, Dana. Nice to see you out having a good time. You look amazing."

It wasn't the opening she expected. "I, uh . . . thank you," she managed to stammer, then blurted out, "What are you doing here?" As soon as she said it, her face flamed hot. That didn't come out right. "I mean, did you come especially for the dance?"

He shrugged a shoulder and took a sip of his drink, regarding her. "Sure. Something to do. He gestured toward the dancers. "Seems like this is just what the town needed."

Dana nodded. "Yes. It's good to hear people laughing." She'd seen more tears and heard more sobs over the past four weeks than she cared to count. Her gaze landed on the charcoal gray shirt he wore tucked into a nice pair of blue jeans. Losing the khaki slacks and blue sport coat was a definite improvement. He looked . . . normal. Actually, he looked good. The shirt matched the flecks of gray at his temples, and– Sucking in her breath, she broke that train of thought and glanced past Kent. "Who are you here with?"

"Guys from the team. Wanted to come out and support the community. We've enjoyed getting to know people here," Kent added. "Under difficult circumstances folks have been friendly."

Her eyes snapped to his, and she wondered if that was a veiled dig at her. She hadn't been friendly. Kent had, but Dana still couldn't quite trust that he wasn't simply putting on a good act. As she looked at him, though, she saw no accusation in his eyes, nothing to indicate he was miffed or put out. In fact, his stance was relaxed. Here he stood talking to her as if they were friends. She took a step back and sipped her beer. Where was everyone, anyway?

The crashing of cymbals and sudden swell of drums spared Dana a response, and they both turned their attention to the band. When applause broke out a few moments later, Kent leaned toward her. "Have fun tonight."

"Thanks," Dana said. "You, too." She watched Kent walk back to his buddies, and as the band started up again, realized Kent Donovan could've asked her to dance. And didn't. She took a gulp of beer, chalking up the vague feeling of disappointment to any woman's natural pride. Maybe he didn't dance. She spotted Mary talking to Jane under The Coffee House awning, and headed their direction.

"Hey, you," Mary said, pulling her up on the sidewalk.

Dana glanced around the group. "Where's Claire?"

"Can't keep her off the dance floor," Mary said.

"Good," Dana said. "She needs some fun. Any sign of Stan?" They'd all crossed their fingers, hoping that Claire's ex-husband and his new wife would be absent from the festivities.

Mary scowled. "I'm sure he'll make an appearance. One we'll ignore. Why aren't you out there dancing?"

"Waiting for a proper invitation," Dana told her dryly.

"Oh, the hell with that. Come on. We don't need an invitation." Mary grabbed Dana's arm, and tossed a nod toward Jane. "Let's get this party started."

Lisa joined in, too, and other dancers moved back as the four of them began a line dance. Took only a minute for a few others to join in, and soon the entire crowd began clapping.

Out of breath three songs later, Dana turned to see Claire heading their direction with Kent Donovan dangling on her arm. Claire smiled, and motioned to Dana. What the heck? Puzzled, Dana walked toward them.

"Dana! Hey, I want you to meet someone. This is Kent Donovan, and he's in town with a disaster relief team. Knows all about getting government grants and helping people rebuild their houses."

Dana looked from one to the other, noting the excitement in Claire's eyes and the glint of amusement in Kent's. Playing along, she slid her hand into Kent's outstretched hand. His thumb brushed over the top of hers, sending an unexpected tingle up her arm.

"Hey, Dana," Kent said warmly.

Dana couldn't help smiling. The setting was so different tonight that it almost seemed as though she really were meeting him for the first time. Anyway, she could 'fess up to Claire later – and get the scoop on how she came into confidences with Kent.

"While you two get acquainted, I'm going to refresh my drink," Claire said, leaving them together.

"Your friend is right," Kent said, leveling Dana with a pointed look. "I know all about getting through the system. I'd love to help you."

"I accept," Dana said. "But not tonight. I refuse to talk insurance and tornadoes tonight."

"Deal." Kent shifted, and when she looked back at him, she realized he was holding out his hand.

"Care to dance?"

His smile crinkled the lines around his eyes, and she caught her breath. Did she? She had no good reason not to. If someone had asked her beforehand to name her dance partners for the evening, she couldn't possibly have been more off target.

Dana put her hand in his again, and followed him to the dance area, more self-conscious than she'd been with Will. More aware of Kent's solid build. No beer belly to work around there. For a man his age to look that good, Dana figured he must spend a fair amount of time at the gym.

As she moved in front of him, Kent grazed his fingers over the bright blue cami and lace top on her shoulders.

"This is nice. Looks like you did some shopping."

That she had. She'd put that check in the bank the day he handed it to her. "Had to have something to wear tonight." Had he ever seen her in anything other than those ugly work orthopedics? No wonder he was treating her more like a friend than a client tonight. She cringed to think how she'd looked on first impression.

"So why didn't you tell Claire we'd met and you're already working on my case?"

Kent shrugged. "Didn't know she was talking about you when she said a friend of hers could use some help."

"But when she introduced us?" Dana persisted.

He twirled her around then, and when she came back toward him, he leaned in close, "Honestly? I thought a do-over was a good idea." With that, he spun her again.

152

Laughing, Dana bent her knee, brought her heel up in the air, and tossed her head back. For a few minutes they stopped talking and just enjoyed the music. The breeze blew back her hair, and Dana found herself having fun.

When the music softened, Kent tightened his grip on her hand and pulled her closer so that she tucked neatly between his arm and chest. As her heart rate accelerated, Dana stepped back and gave a shaky laugh. "Oh, no, I really—"

He bent close to her face and said something, but she couldn't make it out. "I can't hear you," she told him. She shook her head, gulping in air. "What are you trying to do . . . whisper sweet insurance nothings in my ear? Something about claims? Secret deductions?" Maybe his unexpected nearness flustered her or the couple of beers had already taken hold. Whatever it was, thoughts escaped her mouth as they hit her brain.

Giggling, she looked up in time to see Kent's jaw twitch. Clearly he wasn't amused. Heat rushed through her as a pang of disappointment lodged in her chest. They'd been having a good time, and she'd squelched it as fast as throwing water on a match.

Kent stopped dancing. "I believe that was a rule violation," he said. "Not talking insurance tonight, remember?"

Standing still on a crowded dance floor was an occupational hazard. A wide shoulder bumped into Dana, knocking her sideways. Gasping, she stumbled, twisting her ankle. Arms flailing, she clutched at Kent, trying to avoid an embarrassing sprawl onto the asphalt. He caught her, but as he moved back, his shoe connected with her exposed toes.

Dana swallowed a scream as a sharp pain shot up her leg.

"Oh, Dana. You all right?" He swore under his breath. "I'm so sorry. Can you walk?"

"Ow, ow, ow," she chanted, hobbling toward the sidewalk, Kent half carrying her.

He eased her onto a bench along the walkway, and knelt in front of her. "Here. Let's take a look."

A warm hand supported her heel, and she wiggled the ankle gingerly. Nothing seemed broken. Probably just bruised.

"Dana?" Mary crouched beside Kent. "Are you okay, hon? What happened?"

"I twisted my ankle."

"Oh, but you're moving it around. That's a good sign. Can't be too serious then."

Dana shot her a look. "Thank you, Nurse Mary."

"You're welcome." Mary raised her eyebrows at Dana and then glanced at Kent. Leaning in, she lowered her voice, "For a minute I thought you might have had a little swoon."

"Excuse me? A swoon? Really?"

"Well . . ." Mary drawled, "it looked like it was getting kind of warm out there."

As her face flushed, Dana held up a hand. "Please stop now."

"What's going on?" Claire pushed through the people standing around. "Good lord, Dana, you've already got this man on his knees?"

Mary let out a whoop, and the two of them fell into a fit of laughter. Dana rolled her eyes, and swatted at Claire, avoiding Kent's eyes. Weren't her friends just a riot? "When you two are done being ridiculous, how 'bout you find me some ice? I'm in pain here."

Grinning, Mary patted her shoulder. "I'm on it, Nurse Ratched."

A few minutes later, the bands began to switch out equipment. Good timing. The rest of the evening would be more listening than dancing, anyway.

"Here you go," Mary whispered, thrusting a wet towel filled with ice at Dana.

She pressed the towel to her ankle as Pamela Shore, mayor of Whitfield, took the stage, flanked by cheerleaders from the high school. After thanking the crowd, the bands, and a way-too-long list of others, Pamela led a spirited rendition of the school fight song, "We are Whitfield." Of course the Whitfield locals knew every word by heart.

At the final verse, they all joined in the clapping, then Kent touched Dana's arm. "Dana, if you're okay, I'm going to find my group."

"Oh, sure. That's fine," she told him.

"Listen, I'm really sorry—"

Dana shook her head. "I'm fine, Kent. No need to apologize. It wasn't your fault." He graciously refrained from pointing out that it was she who'd spoiled the dancing, which had caused the unfortunate chain of events.

"I'll be in touch."

As soon as he left, Claire moved in. "Scootch over," she said, shimmying onto the bench. And then she pounced. "So, I guess you and the disaster relief guy hit it off, huh? He's going to help you? He seems like a really nice guy."

Dana's head fell forward, and she rubbed her temples. "Claire, don't get too excited. He's with my insurance company. He's part of their crisis management team."

"Hmmm. Looked to me like he was trying to manage a claim out on the dance floor."

"Oh, please. Enough. We are talking about an insurance man. Someone who takes money from people and proceeds to rip them off. Not interested, thank you very much." She took a long swallow from the bottle of water Mary had brought. "He's part of a special team — the team that comes in to share the bad news with a great smile. Tries to make you believe everything's going to be okay." Her lips trembled. Damn it, tonight they were supposed to put all that aside and have fun. Celebrate what they had, not worry about what they'd lost. She swiped at a tear that escaped despite her efforts to blink them back.

Claire's arm slid around Dana's shoulder. "Hey, everything *is* going to be okay. Forget about the insurance guy. Forget about everything. We're going to sit here with the breeze on our faces and enjoy the music."

Dana nodded, but her eyes pulled in the direction Kent had gone.

**

Kent stopped for a fresh beer, and chugged half of it before joining the rest of the group. He listened to the band, but couldn't get into it. Couldn't shake the feeling that he'd done something wrong.

Was he setting himself up for a conflict of interest where Dana Gerard was concerned? Well, conflict anyway. Interest? Was he interested in the woman? Her junior-high level taunting irritated him, but why did he let it get to him? If he had any sense, he'd turn around and run. At least turn her account over to Jennifer or some other agent.

Something about her got to him. And tonight, well, who could blame him. For a little while, she'd been like a different woman – more fire than ice. Fun, sexy, and . . . yeah, interesting. He glanced across the street for another glimpse. Not that he needed another physical sighting to conjure up the image. The little blue number she was wearing had offered a tantalizing view he wouldn't soon forget.

Looked as though she'd settled into the place where he'd left her, and was flanked by friends. Had to smile at that. He had a feeling those women could be a handful – and maybe a lot of fun. It was good to know she had friends who had her back.

Damn, it seemed like they'd taken a huge step forward, maybe found some common ground. Now she'd be reminded of the pain he'd caused every time she took a step. He nearly choked on his Bud Light as a familiar ache tightened his chest. What would Meredith think of his *interest* in Dana Gerard? People were always telling him that Meredith would want him to be happy, to move on, find someone else. Maybe he hadn't found happy, but he'd finally found equilibrium, and that had been hard enough.

At any rate, here was a woman who could use his help. Meredith would expect him to do his best. And he intended to – if Dana would let him.

156

Chapter Thirteen

The scent of freshly brewed coffee met Dana in the hallway Monday morning. She thought she must be dreaming, until she saw Claire at the kitchen table, cup in hand.

"Hey, there. Good morning," Claire said, getting up from the table.

"Morning. Why are you up so early? Did you have trouble sleeping?"

Claire poured a cup of coffee and handed it to Dana. "Not really. Just wanted to see you before you left for work. Now listen, I'm having lunch with Mary, but I'm not in a big rush this morning, so tell me what I can do to help you out."

"You just did it," Dana said, sipping the rich brew.

"No. I mean it. I can cook, do laundry, shop for your dad, whatever you need. What does Chase like to eat?"

Dana's throat constricted. She was so used to doing it all herself. An extra set of hands and a little more time would sure be nice, but she couldn't take more from Claire. She was already helping so much. And so far refused to even discuss the issue of rent. "Claire, I really don't—"

"Dana. You're stressed. Let me help you out. It's what friends do."

"Jeez, is it that obvious?"

Claire toyed with her napkin as if having to choose her words carefully before she met Dana's eyes. "I thought you looked tired that first night, but you know what really did it? You let things get to you Saturday night – the insurance guy, the teasing. Normally, the Dana I know would've dished it right back. You would've laughed it off, flirted even, had fun with it. Tells me you're worn out. All your fun has fizzled, and we've got to fix that."

Dana swirled her mug.

"Unless I'm reading this wrong," Claire added softly. "You have a thing for this Kent guy?"

At that, Dana's head snapped up. Good thing she hadn't been taking a bite of the apricot croissant Claire placed in front of her. She'd need the Heimlich. "You're kidding, right? Me and an insurance guy? Like that could ever work."

Claire raised her brows, the smile on her facing taunting. "I've seen more unlikely couples. He's nice-looking. And was rather gallant attending to your ankle. You like that schmaltzy stuff."

"Schmaltzy? I like gentlemen. What's wrong with that?"

"I'm not saying there's anything wrong, I'm just noting that you tend to go for the knight-in-shining-armor type. The emergency-team-to-the-rescue guy might have some potential in that department."

Shaking her head, Dana gave a low chuckle and pushed back her chair. "So, you made my morning by having coffee ready, then you go and ruin it by bringing him into it."

"See what I mean?" Claire sipped her coffee and regarded Dana with a smirk.

"Oh, whatever," Dana said, with a roll of her eyes as she headed for the stairs. "I need to get ready. I'll be down in a few minutes."

"I'm not going anywhere."

Dana normally did some of her best thinking in the shower, but now she was running late, and had no time to think. Might be a blessing, she decided. Her brain could use a break, especially from dwelling on Claire's topic of conversation.

Twenty minutes later, she was back in the kitchen wishing she didn't have to tell her friend goodbye.

Claire held out a pink envelope. "Hey, I almost forgot, this was in my mail, but it's for you."

"Someone is sending me mail at your house? I got a P.O. box."

Claire shrugged. "No big deal. Lots of people know you're here."

Dana looked at the return address, and smiled. It was from the Needle Nook, a local craft shop where she bought yarn and sometimes attended, or taught, classes. A place that could make her happy just by running her hand across the shelves filled with soft, colorful balls of yarn. It'd been too long. Maybe she could run by there after work. After Claire left.

A sense of melancholy stole over Dana. She wanted to turn back the clock to a time when their lives weren't so fragmented, a time before death and divorce and loss. With a catch in her throat, she reached out to Claire. They hadn't had nearly enough time.

"You'll be gone by the time I get off work, won't you?" Dana asked.

Claire nodded. "Yeah. I have to get back."

"Miss you," Dana whispered, her throat clogged.

"Me, too. I'll call you."

At the same time, they moved in for a hug. "Take care of yourself," Dana told Claire. "I'm coming up for a visit just as soon as I can get away."

Claire squeezed harder. "There's always a room waiting for you."

**

Monday morning hung in the air like a thick fog as Dana entered the hospital and made her way to the nurses' station. Everyone she passed nodded politely, but there was little conversation. Caffeine had not yet pumped its way through the veins of the hospital and its staff. It'd be an hour or so before the humans replaced the zombies. A good time to get reacquainted with her office.

Dana spotted the large file on the desk beside her computer as soon as she walked in. Several file folders, in fact, held together with a giant rubber band. *And so it begins*, she thought, sinking into her chair. She set her travel mug on the desk, and lifted the heavy stack of files, knowing exactly what they were without even a glance – her extra workload.

She glanced at her watch. With any luck, Amy would have some information for her at the one o'clock team meeting. They needed to get the new part-time nurse on board soon. HR was checking references on the three candidates Dana wanted to interview to help fill the gap while she took over some of Brad's duties for the summer. Since they wouldn't be paying Brad's salary while they searched for a new administrator, the hospital could afford some part-time help.

The community classes always started the second week of June to give the teachers a week off. That meant the summer schedule started next week – and Brad's last day was Friday.

Like a ghost she'd conjured out of thin air, the man's reflection appeared on Dana's darkened computer screen.

"Dana, great. I see you're already diving in."

She swiveled, but remained seated. "Hey, Brad."

He rubbed his hands together, nodding toward the folders in Dana's lap. "So, we're all set?"

Dana blinked. "Oh, you mean on the classes?"

"Yeah. You have everything you need?"

She stood then, puzzled by his question. Did it mean the folders were all she got? No overview, no update, no additional information? "Well, yes, I suppose so, as long as everything in here is current. I've just started looking. Are all the classes fill–?"

"Yep. It's all in there. Just holler if you need anything else. But holler quick." The wide grin on his face reminded her of the Cheshire cat – as though he were getting away with something. Really, if he disliked Whitfield so much, why had he taken the position in the first place? Andrew

160

was right. They needed to find someone who would connect with the community and embrace it.

Dana pasted on a smile. "I hear you're looking at Portland."

"Right. We're heading to Kansas City first. That'll be home base while I interview. Don't expect to be there long, but it'll give the kids a chance to visit my folks."

"Yes, that'll be nice," Dana said, suppressing the urge to shoo him out the door.

"Well, guess I'll see you later."

"Sounds good."

Dana was surprised to find Brad seated at the conference table for the management meeting. Probably had nothing else to do since he'd already dispersed his responsibilities.

Andrew began the meeting by going over routine business items and the budget. "Almost half-way through the year, and our numbers look good," he said. "Especially considering the increase in people receiving service on account of the tornado. Brad and I have been working on filing for some federal grant money to help offset those costs.

Dana processed that information. She hadn't heard anything about it. "When's the deadline?" she asked. She could've sworn Andrew shot Brad a stern look before replying.

"Should have it all wrapped up before Brad leaves on Friday."

"I'll have the documents ready for you to sign by end-of-day tomorrow," Brad said smoothly.

"Good deal," Andrew said. "And this is a good a time to thank Brad for his service to Whitfield Community. We appreciate your work on the hospital's behalf and wish you the best in your new place."

Polite applause broke out around the table.

"Thank you," Brad said. "I've enjoyed working with you all."

"And that takes us to the next step," Andrew said, his eyes on Amy. "Fill us in, Amy."

"First, we've got the ad for the administrator's position out all over the country – medical journals, health care associations, hospitals. All the usual places. As we discussed, the deadline is July fifteenth. That gives us time to review the apps and interview by the end of summer. With any luck, we can have someone around Labor Day." She glanced up at Andrew. "I've already had several calls. I expect résumés will start coming in this week."

Amy slid a folder across the table to Dana. "Just sent you an email. I've done the background checks on these applicants, so you can start interviewing."

Exactly what she'd hoped to hear. "That's great, Amy. Thanks. Shouldn't take too long."

As the meeting broke up, Amy lingered. "So how are you doing, Dana?"

She shot her a wry smile. "I'm upright, fully clothed and made it to work, so I guess I'm doing all right."

Amy laughed. "Yes, I'd say that qualifies. Your house?"

"Gone with the wind. Bulldozers finish it off tomorrow."

"Oh, wow. You going to watch?"

Dana shook her head. Did not sound like a fun thing to do at all. "No, ma'am. I'm working tomorrow."

Amy removed her glasses, and Dana felt like some kind of lab specimen under her probing eyes. "Dana, you sure? It's okay if you want to take some time and be there."

She drew a shaky breath. "I don't." Maybe it was cowardly. Maybe it would provide closure, and someday she'd regret not being there, but right now it seemed like putting herself through unnecessary pain.

"All right, then. What about your son? Did our interviewing tips land him a job?"

Dana smiled. "Honestly, I don't think so. But he did get a job."

"Yeah? Where at?"

"Working on the Wade farm. I don't think the interview process was anything like what we expected."

"Oh. That's not really the direction you . . ." her voice trailed off.

"Not what I had in mind," Dana confirmed. "But so far he seems to be enjoying it. And you just never know where something might lead."

"True," Amy agreed. "Well, good to hear he's set for the summer. One thing you can check off the list, right?"

"Exactly." She waved the folder Amy had given her. "Now, I guess I'd better get on to the next. I'm scheduling these right away."

"Sounds good. Keep me posted."

By mid-afternoon Dana had set up appointments with all three candidates. Just to be on the safe side, she also confirmed that the space at the community center was reserved and ready for classes next week.

"I'm glad you're handling this, Dana," Elaine Ashfield, director of the community center, told her when she called. "I spoke with Mr. Berkley several weeks ago, and he told me to do exactly what we'd done last year. So I went ahead and ordered the same first aid booklet. I hope that's all right."

Dana wanted to hug the woman. "Absolutely, Elaine. Thanks so much for handling that. Have they arrived?"

"Oh, yes. They're here, so we're all set on our end. Now, last year you all handed out bandages and magnets with emergency numbers on them. Will we have those again?"

Dana groaned inside, wishing she'd anticipated the details when she first learned of Brad's resignation. Looked as though a trip through the supply closets was in order. "I'll check the status of those," Dana said, not wanting to admit she had no idea. "I'm sure we'll have something." Of course they'd need freebies. If necessary, she could call in a favor from some of the vendors for free bandages or wet-wipes and anything else she could get her hands on.

"And do you know which nurse we'll have?" Elaine asked.

"Yes. Her name is Hillary Jenkins." That had been Dana's decision, and she knew for a fact that Hillary was trained and ready to go.

"Perfect. Just let me know if you think of anything else."

Dana said goodbye to Elaine and immediately headed downstairs to rummage through the supply closets. With any luck, they'd have magnets and pencils left over from last year. She was pretty sure the cost of emergency printing was not in her budget.

The office materials closets offered nothing, but finally, the shelves of a miscellaneous store room revealed not only magnets but box after box of what Dana considered freebies – bulk quantities of key chains, pens, pads of paper, purse-sized hand sanitizer, Neosporin, bandages, and . . . what in the world? Dana frowned as she studied the contents of one of the boxes. Hundreds of individual packets of condoms stared back at her.

She checked the delivery details on the box, then the others. All were delivered to Brad Berkley. Good grief. He must have asked every vendor they had for free stuff as a routine request. But condoms? Who were those for? They certainly wouldn't be handing them out to students of the first aid or babysitting classes. Why hadn't he sent them over to the clinic where they might actually be of some use? Shaking her head, Dana pushed the box behind the others. Looked as though Brad had a thing for getting free merchandise. Or . . . she surveyed the number of boxes in the room. Perhaps it was a power thing. Did he require vendors to suck up by offering freebies? Did he make decisions based on who gave the most? And, Dana couldn't help wondering, was the giving always for the benefit of the hospital?

Friday, she thought, couldn't come fast enough. With each day that passed she was more ready to usher the man out the door. Switching off the lights, she blew out her breath. At least they had plenty of items for the classes. She'd have a couple of the girls start bagging those up. It'd be a good task for the night crew.

**

Energized by the accomplishments of the day, Dana decided she'd stop by her dad's place after work and visit with him before dinner. Or maybe have dinner with him if she didn't hear from Chase. She hadn't done that in a while. The food at the manor was usually quite good, but the setting could be depressing. So many of the residents were older than her father, in much worse condition, and couldn't offer much conversation. The Needle Nook could wait another day.

She slid into her flip-flops, wincing just a little as she flexed her foot. The toes were still tender. She considered taking a couple of aspirin, but indulging in a glass of wine with her dad sounded like a better option. Sometimes, they'd sit in the courtyard before dinner, and while she sipped the wine, her dad would enjoy a scotch and water. They hadn't done that in a while, either. It was about time.

Inside the manor, Dana made her way to her father's wing, then stopped short at the sound of yelling down the corridor. "No! You don't get it. That's not what I'm doing."

What in the world? Heart pounding, Dana broke into a sprint. She recognized those voices.

Dana flung open the door to her father's apartment, and nearly barreled into a red-faced Chase. She put a hand up to stop him. "What is going on in here?"

Hanging on to Chase's arm, Dana stepped around him to see her dad scowling from his chair. "Daddy? What's the matter?"

Her father flailed his arm, pointing toward Chase. "He– Him–" In his agitated state, he could hardly get a word out. Dana let Chase shrug out of her grasp as she moved toward her dad, making soothing sounds. "Shhh. Come on, now. Everybody just calm down." She patted his back, glancing back and forth from one to the other. "What is this all about?"

"He thinks Wade hired me to try and get his land." With his hands on his head as though he wanted to rip his hair out, Chase's voice rose again. "He thinks I'm so stupid that I would fall for some kind of trick and find a way to turn it over to Cameron and his dad."

Dana frowned. This made no sense at all. Chase had nothing to do with the land. Only her name and her dad's were on the deeds now. The Wades would know better.

Chase kicked the door. "*God.* Why does everybody think I'm stupid? He doesn't even know what the hell he's talking about."

With that parting shot, Chase yanked open the door and stormed out. Still stunned, it took Dana a moment to decide who needed her most. But her protective instincts won out, and she ran after her son. Heading for the entrance, she made a quick stop at the front desk and requested a nurse to her father's apartment. "I'd like to check his blood pressure," she told Shannon.

"Chase," Dana yelled when she got to the parking lot.

He stopped, but didn't turn around. Panting, she caught up with him and grabbed his arm. "No way. Don't you dare get in that car and drive away mad." Her voice shook with fear. She knew that could be almost as bad as getting behind the wheel drunk. "Come back and take a minute to settle down."

He flung her hand away and sagged against his car. "I'm not going back in there."

"All right, fine. Let's sit here on one of the benches and talk." Chase's eyes held unshed tears, and Dana knew they'd taken a step backward, that his new-found confidence had taken a beat-down. The frustration of that was almost enough to send her into a fit of screaming as well.

She scanned the grounds for a bench in the shade, and took hold of Chase's arm. "Come on. I want to hear this." Thankfully, he walked with her, and flopped onto the bench.

"Tell me what happened."

"He just went ballistic, Mom. I was telling him about working with Cameron and old man Wade, and he freaked out. He kept saying 'you can't do it, you can't do it.' At first I thought he meant I couldn't farm. Then he started writing that the farm was his and that I need to stay out of his business, and that I didn't know what I was doing."

"Oh, honey." Dana slipped an arm around Chase's shoulder and leaned into him.

"He's not gonna help me learn the business. He thinks I can't do it. Everybody thinks I'm too stupid to do anything."

"Now, stop. That doesn't even make sense. Think about it. If we thought you were stupid, why would we assume you could handle going to college, hmm?" She patted his knee with one hand while the other circled his back. "Chase, like I've said a million times, you have so much potential. You can do whatever you want. You need to believe in yourself."

"Yeah? What good does that do if no one else will?"

"Chase." She waited until his eyes met hers. "*I* believe in you."

He ran a sleeve across his face. "I'm tired of this shit, Mom."

"Hey, let's cut Poppa some slack, okay? He just got scared and confused. He knows you don't have the ability to sell the farm. I'll talk to him, but I don't want this to cause permanent damage between you two. Let's help him understand, because when he's thinking straight, he can teach you so much."

She squeezed Chase's hand. "He wants to see you happy and successful. You know he's been worried about you. That's because he *loves* you."

When he didn't respond, Dana stood. "I'd better get back in there and check on him. Why don't you head over to Bailey's in about an hour, and I'll meet you there, okay? I don't feel like cooking tonight." She'd have to put dinner with her dad on hold.

Satisfied that Chase had calmed down enough to drive, Dana hurried back inside the manor. Oh, boy, she was definitely going to need that drink. Maybe the aspirin, too.

Her father still sat rigid in his chair, as if on high-alert, a scowl she rarely saw settled on his face. She took his hand in both of hers, and sat down so she could be eye-level. "Wow, Daddy. That was kind of crazy. You all right?" When he didn't answer, she let go of his hand, and tore off the older pages of the legal pad. Flipping to a new page, she pushed it toward him. "Tell me what's wrong." While he wrote, Dana folded the old pages and shoved them into her pocket to read later – maybe.

His eyes still hard, her father pushed the pad her direction. *What's he doing on the farm? He has no business there.*

The door opened, and the nurse came in with a monitor. "Here we go," she said.

Dana waited while Linda took her father's blood pressure, her eyes moving from her dad's face to the numbers on the machine.

"Looks like 152 over 117," Linda announced. "That's a little high, Mr. Hatfield. Do you want to lie down and rest?" She turned and spoke to Dana. "Would you like me to help get him into bed?"

"I don't think that's necessary, but please have someone check on him a couple of times this evening. He just got upset over a misunderstanding, that's all."

"Will do. Don't you worry. Is that all for now?"

"Yes, thanks, Linda."

Dana blew out her breath and rearranged the pillow behind her father. The last thing she expected was that she'd have to be a mediator between her dad and son. She'd been hoping the two might form a bond over farming. She picked up her dad's hand again. "Hey, I'm sorry Chase upset you, Dad, but I sure wish you wouldn't have talked to him like that. You really hurt his feelings. I want you to sit still and listen for a minute so I can tell you what he's doing, all right? Everything is okay at the farm. This is good news, Dad. Chase has a summer job working for the Wades."

She backed toward the kitchen as she spoke. Reaching into a cupboard, she pulled down a glass tumbler and her dad's Johnnie Walker. "I'm going to fix you a drink. That sound good?" Not expecting an answer, she added a couple of ice cubes then headed back toward him.

168

"Here you go. Enjoy." Facing him, she smiled, and rubbed his arm. "You know what, Daddy? Chase might turn out to be a farmer, like you, one of these days. If we give him a chance."

Within in a few minutes, Dana could see her father start to relax. When he finally leaned back in his chair it seemed to release his tension. She kept talking, filling him in on all the kids, but especially Chase. Damn it, someone in this family besides her was going to give this kid some encouragement.

"I could use some help here, Dad. I'd like for you to work with him. Give him a sense of what it's like to run a farm. Help him understand the big picture while he gets a taste for the day-to-day work from Cameron. He needs our support."

While she spoke, an idea formed in her head. Maybe a drive out to the farm would spark some memories or conversations. And maybe it would put his mind at ease to see everything intact. It'd be impossible to push a wheelchair into the fields, but they could drive in far enough that he could see how the wheat was doing. Maybe they could even go out on one of the tractors once Chase had some experience with them. Getting her father out of the manor more often would probably help keep him grounded in reality. With the exception of Maddie's graduation party, and the visit from Tom, he'd been stuck there for days on end.

"Hey, Dad, why don't we plan to run over to the farm this weekend. Harvest will be starting soon. Would you like to see that?"

Finally, her father's lips lifted in a lopsided smile, and he began writing.

Yes, he wrote. *Let's watch the harvest.*

It could be kind of fun, she told herself. As soon as the thought hit her brain, Claire's words came back to her. *Your fun has fizzled*, she'd said. That was probably true. She could do better.

Her father shook the pad, and she glanced at it again. *Tell Chase I'm sorry.* Nodding, Dana patted her father's shoulder then carefully tore the paper from the pad. "I will."

Maybe the three of them could go to the farm together before she left on the girls' trip. They could have a picnic, take a bottle of wine and go in the evening. In full force, harvest lasted until dusk. When the setting orange sun hit the gold wheat it could be just as beautiful as an ocean sunset. With a catch in her throat, Dana made a mental promise to make it happen.

Chapter Fourteen

Seated across from Chase, Dana picked up her glass of sauvignon blanc and stretched her legs out under the booth. It was oh-so-tempting to lean back and close her eyes, but nodding off was a definite possibility. Forcing her eyes open, she gave her son a weak smile.

"So, other than the freak-out with Poppa, how was your day?"

Chase looked away, his jaw set.

Apparently the mad wasn't going away easily. Dana leaned forward with a heavy sigh. "Chase? Listen, sweetheart, you've got to let it go. Poppa obviously still remembers that the Wades were interested in our land, and he jumped to some crazy conclusions. Cam's dad is a decent guy, but he saw an opportunity, and he was a little too intense."

She dug the folded paper out of her pocket and pushed it across to Chase.

He looked at it, then at her. "What's that?"

"A start."

He thrummed his fingers on the table a moment before picking up the paper and slowly unfolding it. His eyes scanned what Poppa had written, but he remained silent.

The waitress interrupted, setting burgers and fries in front of them. "Let me know if you need anything else."

Chase reached for his burger, and Dana let him take a few bites before sharing her idea of visiting the farm, figuring he'd be in a better mood with food in his stomach.

"Did he say he wanted me to go, too?" Chase asked.

"Well, not specifically, but that's kind of the point. To get Dad over there and out of the manor, sure, but I want him to feel as though he's helping you, Chase. Even if you decide farming isn't the kind of life you want, Poppa has so many stories he can share. That in itself will be good for him, and probably relieve some of his anxiety." She paused for a bite of her own burger, then added softly, "We're all in this together, you know? We're a family."

"Did you tell him that?"

"Chase, for heaven's sake. Those exact words? No. But I did tell him that he hurt your feelings and it was wrong to talk to you like that. And he's apolo—"

Her phone rattled against the table to tell her she had a new text message. She picked it up, and debated whether to read the message or not. From Kent. Curiosity won out, but she wasn't prepared for the emotion his words sparked.

Dana, your property is slated for eight in the morning. Call if you want to talk or have questions.

She stared at the words, and struggled a moment to catch her breath.

"Mom? What's the matter?"

Pressing her lips together, she shook her head. "They— they're clearing the debris tomorrow morning."

"That's good, right?" Chase asked. "I mean, then we can get the house rebuilt. Did you hire a contractor?"

Dana nearly choked on her water. In an attempt to assure Chase she had things under control, she'd told him she had a list of names of builders in the area. Sure, she had their names and phone numbers and brochures and recommendations all tucked inside a lovely Vera Bradley file folder that Claire had given her. Hire one of them? She hadn't even spoken to one of them.

"Not yet," she told him. "I'm still working on some grant and loan applications with the insurance company. It's going to take some time." Glancing at Chase, she saw the unspoken concern in his eyes. "Don't worry sweetie, I'm sure Claire isn't going to kick us out any time soon. You focus on your job, and I'll deal with the house." She tried not to let Chase's anxiety fuel her own. In the past, when she'd been young and optimistic, she'd dreamed of someday building her own house. But in the years since then, she'd heard so many horror stories of delays, added costs, and unreliable crews that it sounded more like nightmare than dream-come-true. Not to mention the thousands of decisions to be made. With a complete do-over, the possibilities were endless.

Dana's mind wandered to the colorful displays of paint chips at the hardware store. The possibilities *were* endless . . .

**

At seven forty-five the next morning, Dana pulled into the hospital parking lot after successfully resisting the invisible current that seemed to be tugging her toward her house.

Inside, she kept herself busy, reviewing all the patient charts and doctor's notes from the previous night.

"Hey, Jeanie, I see Dr. Talisman increased the dosage for Mrs. Phillips last night. How'd she do?"

"Much better. I think the poor woman finally got a decent night's sleep. We checked on her several times, but she slept right through."

"Good news."

"Yeah, I may have to ask Greg for some of that. I swear, with all the bulldozers and hammering and pounding going on out there, I'm not sure when I'll ever get any good sleep."

Dana hadn't thought of that. Of course for people close to the devastation, sleeping during the day would be almost impossible. And here she was dragging her feet, dragging out the process. "Oh, Jeanie, I'm sorry. Do you want me to adjust the schedule so that you aren't working as many nights? I could see if Val or Sarah would take a few more."

"More what?" Val asked coming into the nurses' station. "I think maybe I've had all I can take." The

173

comment was tinged with humor in her voice, and Dana laughed.

"With all the tornado clean up and reconstruction, Jeanie can't get a decent day's sleep. I'm looking for an alternative to drugs."

Val shook her head. "Boy, no one's escaping the tornado completely, are they? Listen, since it's summer, I could probably do another night shift. Sam would have a conniption if I took any more, though." She turned to Jeanie with a wink. "But hey, I know where you can get some good drugs if you decide to go that route."

Smiling, Jeanie grabbed her purse and hitched it over her shoulder. "Thanks. I'll keep that in mind. Giving earplugs a shot today. See you girls later."

As Jeanie headed for the stairs, Dana couldn't help glancing at the wall clock. Eight forty-five. She sucked in a deep breath. How long would it take to brush away the remnants of someone's home, anyway?

Val touched her arm. "Hey, you okay?"

"Sure. I–" Butterflies fluttered in her chest.

"Spit it out."

"Sarah's here, isn't she?"

Val's face went blank, and she glanced around. "Yeah. She's getting lunch requests ready."

That wouldn't take long. They had plenty of staff on hand.

"Dana, what's the matter?"

"I need to leave for a few minutes. I just want to check something at my house."

"Your house?" Val echoed.

Dana was already hurrying to her office to grab her purse. "I won't be long, and can be back in less than five minutes if you need me."

She parked a few houses down the street, and got out of her car. Shading her eyes, she looked at the activity. Sure enough, a huge dump truck sat in her driveway. And the mountains of rubble had been reduced to small hills. Several men stood in the yard. As she moved closer, she could hear one of them shouting directions to the man in the front-end loader.

174

Dana hung back, unsure of her welcome, and not wanting to be in the way. Arms crossed, she watched the proceedings, surprised to find it more interesting than personal. It just looked like boards and trash, so she had a hard time believing it was actually her house.

A few minutes later she couldn't believe her eyes when Kent Donovan came walking up the street – bearing two tall cups from The Coffee House. When he reached her, he smiled and offered her one of the cups. "Caramel latte. The least I could do."

Dana's mouth dropped open, though she reached for the cup. "How did you–"

"Saw your car as I drove past. Was hoping you'd still be here." He lifted his cup. "I prefer mine black."

Dana gave a little laugh. "Thank you. That was very thoughtful." She took a sip of the coffee, impressed that he'd remembered what she'd ordered that day they met at The Coffee House. She couldn't help but wonder if he was this attentive to all his clients. Or – her chest tightened – was it just her? It took some imagination, but she had to admit she wouldn't mind feeling a little bit special. Wouldn't mind that warm smile in his eyes being specifically for her. Her gaze lingered on his profile for a moment. But when he turned, she quickly looked away, her face flushing.

"How's it going?" he asked. "You been here since eight?"

"No. I've only been here ten or fifteen minutes. Looks like they'll be done soon. And I should get back to work. Do I need to do anything – sign off or inspect it?"

"Nope. You're welcome to walk around once it's cleared, of course. They'll put up the temporary fencing when they're done."

She nodded, and they stood silently as the loader deposited a scoop of debris from the last pile into the waiting truck. There was such a feel of unreality in the scene. With the house and rubble gone, she'd expected the lot to look larger. Instead, it looked small and empty. Hard to believe a four-bedroom house had stood there.

175

"Think you'll make any changes to the plan?" Kent asked.

Her head snapped around. "What plan?"

He cocked his head toward her property. "Your house. The floor plan. You thinking about making some changes? This would be the time to do it."

Dana stared at him while that notion sunk in. The bedrooms were so small. She could enlarge one and add a bathroom. She could put two twin beds in one for times when the boys were both home. And, oh, man – the washer and dryer were moving upstairs for sure. No more lugging baskets full of laundry down a flight of stairs to the basement.

She nearly laughed as the ideas raced through her head. "You know," she told Kent with a smile. "I just might."

He grinned. "Good. You should."

"I'd better get back. Looks like they're about to wrap up, anyway."

When Dana turned toward her car, Kent followed suit, walking alongside her, and when the sharp beep indicated it was unlocked, he opened the driver's door. Her mind still imagining improvements to her house, she gave him a distracted, "Thanks."

"Hey, Dana."

"Mm-hm?"

"I've got some of those applications ready for you to sign. I could bring them with me to dinner."

She stopped cold, her mouth hanging open in the breeze. Did he really just say that? "You– you want to come to dinner?"

Kent let out a sharp laugh, and threw his head back. "No. That's not what I meant. That came out all wrong. I'm suggesting I swing by with my forms, pick you up and take you to dinner."

Heat rose in her cheeks, and Dana gave a flustered laugh.

Bending his knees, Kent met her eyes. "I'd like to make this a little easier for you. Nothing wrong with not cooking after putting in a day at work, is there?"

He had her there. "No. Not cooking sounds wonderful."

His smile widened. "How does six-thirty on Wednesday sound?"

"Perfect."

"All right. See you then."

Dana slipped into the car. She didn't know whether it was his motivation or not, but Kent Donovan had just ensured she wouldn't spend the rest of the day thinking about her house.

**

The following afternoon, Dana glanced at the seat beside her and the stack of files she was dragging home, and decided she couldn't face them. Not yet. Time for a quick detour – or maybe not so quick. The card from the Needle Nook had generously included a gift certificate, and her fingers itched to spend it – and to start a project. Even something as simple as a baby blanket that she could create by memory would help her relax and free her mind to wander, which, in turn, would help her think. She needed to do something normal, to reclaim the pieces of her life that were outside of work and responsibility.

She pulled into the parking lot that joined up with a small freestanding blond-brick building. Profuse flowers cascading from beer-barrel pots stood on either side of the door, and a hand-painted sign above it welcomed customers. Dana stepped inside, and at the tinkle of the bell attached to the door, a few heads swiveled around.

Patricia Lyons, the store's proprietor, jumped from her seat, arms outstretched. "Dana Gerard! Get yourself in here." The arms wrapped around Dana, rocking her. "Oh, honey, it's so good to see you. How are you?"

"Hey, Trisha, I'm fine. Thank you so much for the gift card and your sweet note, and for those amazing meatballs you left for us."

Trisha waved a hand. "Oh, it's nothing."

"And nothing is exactly what I've got," Dana told her with a laugh. "I really need a project. Something easy and mindless."

"I hear you. Come on in and let's get you set up."

The laughter coming from the back gave Dana pause. She probably knew some of the people there, and should go say hello, but she wasn't in the mood to talk about her house, and she figured that would be the first question out of anyone's mouth. These days the tornado eclipsed everything else. People had stopped asking about her kids or her work. Of course, she could never divulge information about a patient, but she could talk about the classes now under way and the search for a new administrator. Normal things that were a big part of her life. Then again, sometimes people asked about Claire. And sometimes that bordered on gossip, so Dana wasn't inclined to discuss that topic, either.

"I've got one of my crochet groups in this evening," Trisha said. "Go on back, if you want."

Dana put a hand on Trisha's arm, and spoke in a low voice. "If you can get me some basic needles, maybe sevens and tens, that would be great. I need a minute just to look."

"Will do. You take your time."

The rainbow of color created by the cubbies of yarn that stretched nearly floor-to-ceiling on three sides of the room was delicious eye candy for Dana. She wanted some of everything. With a deep breath, she reached out and ran her fingers along the rows.

A few minutes later, Trisha was at Dana's side again. "Hey, I know you must be crazy busy with everything that's happened, but some of us are making blankets to donate to tornado victims." She nodded toward the back room. "Stacey St. Johns is here. She lost her house, too. The knitting helps her take her mind off of it for a little while."

Dana smiled. "That's a great idea. I'd love to help."

"People won't need many blankets now, but by the time we get them all done, they will," Trisha said. "It's one thing they won't have to buy, you know?"

"Absolutely. I'm in."

"Knit or crochet, whichever you prefer. Steve and I are donating yarn. I'll bag some up for you."

178

Dana told Trisha goodbye and left the store with two large sacks of supplies, and a warm, satisfied feeling. She tossed the yarn in the back seat and glanced out across the highway. On this side of town, she wasn't far from the farm. Chase wouldn't be home for another hour, so Dana stopped at the convenience store at the corner for a large iced tea, then swung onto the blacktop. She drove the two miles of highway, and turned onto the county road that ran the length of the farm. Just off of the highway, she pulled to the side of the road and parked. No need to alert anyone to her presence. She just wanted to look at the fields – and have a few minutes alone.

Tucking her purse under the seat, she grabbed the drink, then crossed the road and ducked between the bars of the metal gate. Easier than unwinding the chain that held the gate to the thick fencepost. Walking along the rows of wheat, she let her thoughts drift. She'd never loved living on the farm, but the light breeze and quiet solitude of the open land had a way of helping her regroup. Dana had no shortage of time alone with her thoughts, but alone with nothing but the wind and open fields was different.

You could always count on the breeze, she thought, tugging the clip from her hair. It wasn't always soft and cool, though. Sometimes it was hot and dry like a furnace blast. She shook her head and let the wind blow across her face. And sometimes, it took on a murderous fury that could lift houses and rip them apart.

Perching on an old stump at the edge of the crop line, she gazed out at the wind turbines in the distance, the steady movement of the giant white blades almost hypnotizing. She had a new appreciation for them – for the way they harnessed the power of the wind and used it for good. Some people hated the look of them, and there had been resistance and town hall meetings and neighbors at war with each other. But to Dana, they were graceful, like synchronized swimmers, and created a dramatic kaleidoscope against the bold blue evening sky.

And they showed progress. That's what she liked best. The newfangled windmills were proof that people in

179

small towns on the plains of Kansas could be progressive and forward thinking.

Progress. Dana blew out her breath. Boy, the twist of those clouds had certainly blown her backward. But it was simply a twist of fate. Though it was a setback for her and so many others, there was nothing she could do about it. That was life. She had to deal with it and move on. Dana looked westward to where the house she'd lived in as a girl used to sit. She couldn't remember an emotional attachment to it, but for some reason, she'd been attached to the house that she'd raised her own children in.

Would it feel the same when it was new? It would be so different. But she couldn't stay in the past. She had to let go, to plan a new place. It wouldn't be grand, but it'd be enough. Chase could do some of the work. They could paint. It might be fun to work together on a project. They'd cut expenses where they could. Maybe she'd skip the fireplace.

**

Kent pulled onto the highway, heading back to town after his second house call of the day. Two of his rural clients had lost rentals in town, and it was more convenient for them if he did the driving. He didn't mind. The drive time was down time. A few miles from Whitfield, he glanced at the fields to his right, then hit his brakes hard, and pulled the Lexus onto the shoulder. At sixty miles an hour it was hard to say for sure, but that looked like Dana Gerard's car. And that probably meant car trouble. Watching the rearview mirror, he saw no cars coming behind him, so he slowly backed up, careful to stay on the shoulder and out of the ditch. Aware that it was a dangerous maneuver, he swiveled around, checking for traffic in all directions.

He turned onto the smaller road and pulled behind the white Highlander, recognizing not only the license plate, but the tiny indentation in the left side of the fender. Certain now that it belonged to Dana, he climbed out and jogged forward. The driver's door was locked, but there was no sign of the driver. Kent walked around the car, checking all the doors and tires. Locked with no sign of breakdown. No flat tires. No flashers blinking. The hood was closed. Huh. He shielded his eyes with the side of his hand and scanned the fields surrounding him. Had she walked down the road looking for help? Had someone picked her up?

At that thought, a sense of uneasiness set in. Where the hell was she? "Dana?" he called into the expanse of open air. Cupping his hands, he put his face to the tinted window and peered inside again. No purse.

Hands on his hips, he looked around again, thinking through the possible scenarios. It'd be dusk soon – and dark soon after that. Thoughts running wild now, he broke into a sprint, alternately searching the ditches and fields. When it suddenly dawned on him to use his cell phone, he let out a nervous laugh, berating himself for jumping to conclusions.

Digging his phone out of his pocket, he made the call, and waited. After four rings, her voice message came on the line. He shoved the phone back in his pocket, and ran a hand through his hair, unable to keep his heart rate from accelerating. Now what? He considered driving on up the road and see if there was a farmhouse nearby. Hell, she'd probably happened along someone she knew and was inside having a drink or something while he was standing around like an idiot. He looked up half-expecting to find a hidden camera laughing at him.

Turning back toward the cars, he still couldn't shake the feeling that he ought to do something. On impulse, he cupped his hands to his mouth, and shouted again, fear creeping into his voice. "Dana? Dana!" Twice he stopped and shouted again, as he made his way to the cars. Then from the other side of the road, he saw a woman heading his direction, silhouetted against the low sun.

He waited a moment, watching her approach. Sure enough, Dana, with her hair loose around her face walked toward him. He jogged across, and grabbed hold of the metal gate, relief washing over him. "Dana!"

The surprise on her face changed to confusion, and her brow wrinkled. "Kent? I thought I heard someone call—"

"Yeah, that was me."

"What are you doing?"

"Was on my way back to town from the Norton's place. Saw your car, and thought you had a breakdown or something. I mean I thought your car might have broken down and you needed help."

She laughed then, but her words were dry. "No, I think *I'd* be more likely to break down than my car."

Kent let out a breath he hadn't even realized he'd been holding. "So, everything's all right?"

"Um, sure. Thanks."

In an awkward silence they faced each other. "This is—"

"What are you do—" They spoke at the same time.

Dana hitched a thumb behind her. "This is my family's farm."

She looked at him as though that explained everything. But Kent's brain put up a road block. That might explain what she was doing on the other side of the fence, but it sure as hell didn't explain anything else. Her family had a farm? Why was she so worried about money then? Why was she living at a friend's place? He shook his head. "I don't understand."

To his surprise, she nudged him over, and slipped between the bars of the gate. That she had the agility and size to do that was both impressive and intriguing.

"I just like to come over sometimes. It's kind of relaxing."

"No. I mean, you have a farm? How come—"

She put up a hand to cut him off. "Long story."

Kent rocked back on his heels. He wouldn't pressure her, but wanted more than that. He'd been worried about her. And now he was confused. "I'd like to hear it."

Crystal blue eyes met his as she tucked a strand of hair behind her ear. "Are we still on for dinner tomorrow?"

"I hope so."

"Can it wait until then?"

The fact that she hadn't told him it was none of his business or accused him of stalking her by showing up there, and actually remembered the dinner date nearly left Kent speechless. Resisting the urge to subdue the wayward blond curls again, Kent shoved off from the gate and took her arm. "Absolutely."

Chapter Fifteen

Dana hadn't mentioned the meeting-dinner-whatever-it-was to anyone but Chase. In typical twenty-year-old fashion, he'd grunted and read nothing into the plan as far as she could tell. She counted it a small blessing.

For her own sake, she settled on the term business date. He had, after all, said he'd like to take her to dinner. Didn't sound like going dutch. Nor did it sound like a simple client meeting.

At six-twenty, she was ready to go, and already casting frequent glances out the front window. Chewing her lip, she pondered the business date, wondering if Kent could possibly be any help with contractors. Maybe he'd worked with some before, or at least had heard of them. Since they were discussing her house, anyway, surely he wouldn't mind looking at her list . . . unless he considered it an actual date. She pulled the folder and list of contractors out of her computer bag. It wasn't.

When the doorbell rang, Dana met him at the door, ready to go. Inviting him in would just be awkward. She still wasn't sure what to think of his behavior yesterday. He hadn't explained why he'd been out by the farm in the first place. She nearly laughed out loud every time she thought of him wandering the road yelling for her. At the same time, though, it was kind of endearing. He *had* sounded concerned, after all. That run-to-the-rescue trait must run awfully deep.

He greeted her with his usual friendly grin. "Hey."

"Hi."

"All set?" he asked.

"Sure." She stepped onto the porch and pulled the door closed.

"You're a brave woman."

Dana paused a moment, confused by his opening line. "What do you mean?"

"Wearing sandals. Around me."

"Ah." She chuckled, glancing down at her freshly painted nails that she'd rather not conceal. "I forgot about that. Well, for tonight, I'll live dangerously."

"Note to self," Kent said. "Do not kick Dana's toes." He opened the door for Dana, then slipped in beside her. "How are they by the way? Your toes?"

"Much better, thank you." She may have forgotten about the toes, but now that he brought up their ill-fated dancing, what she remembered most was how he'd tucked her between his arm and chin when the dancing slowed. Dana turned to the window, afraid her warm cheeks might give her thoughts away.

"How would you feel about the Country Chef for dinner?" he asked.

It was the nicest restaurant in Whitfield. Good food and service without the pretentious fluff that a restaurant in a big city would have. "Sounds great."

Ten minutes later, they settled into a quiet booth. As soon as they'd ordered drinks, Kent motioned to the folder she'd tucked under her purse.

"What've you got there?"

Troubled eyes met his. "These are builders who've been suggested to me. I wondered if you might know any of them, or know their reputations."

Their waitress set drinks on the table. "Do you folks need a few more minutes?"

Dana spoke up when Kent glanced at her for confirmation. "Oops, sorry," she told the waitress. "Haven't even looked at the menu."

"No problem. I'll be back in a minute."

When Dana reached for the menu, Kent reached for the folder. "Let me take a look at those."

She pushed it toward him, then turned back to the menu.

Kent leafed through the bits of paper and brochures, recognizing most of the contractors listed, and very glad she'd sought his advice.

The waitress returned, and after Dana ordered a side salad and chicken-mozzarella flatbread, Kent requested a KC strip and loaded baked potato.

"Have you interviewed all of these people?" Kent asked as soon as the waitress left.

"No. I've only contacted a couple of them. Seems like they're pretty busy already."

"Yeah. Everyone who regularly works in this area will be for a while. But don't worry, they'll hire extra crews, and others will come in for the opportunity."

"Is there anyone you'd recommend?"

"Not this one." Kent swung the paper around so that she could see. "This guy is mostly retired. His sons have taken over, and they're known to cut corners."

"Really? Oh, my gosh. That's too bad. My dad knows him. That's where I got the name."

"Yeah. It's a shame. From what I understand, he used to do excellent work. The boys are riding on his reputation for now, but that won't last much longer."

"Hmm. Good to know."

"Let me email you a couple of other suggestions." He'd put in a couple of calls himself, if necessary. That was one project he didn't want going south.

His offer was rewarded with a bright smile that sent a warm thrumming through his veins.

"That would be great. Thanks."

Kent had hoped she'd open up and fill him in on the family farm, but she seemed to have forgotten about it. He hadn't. Of course he wouldn't – not while that picture of her walking toward him, her hair blowing softly around her face, remained front and center in his brain.

"So, you can't stay at the farm until your house is rebuilt?" That seemed like a decent segue to him.

186

She shook her head. "Oh, no. There's no house anymore. That was torn down years ago. It was old and rundown, and instead of putting money into it, my parents moved into town when I was fifteen. There are a couple of barns and sheds, but no place to live."

"Ah. Too bad."

She gave a lopsided smile. "Honestly, at this point, it would just be one more thing to take care of."

"At this point?" Her entire body seemed to lift as she drew in a deep breath.

"Yeah, my dad can't farm it anymore. He's in assisted living due to a stroke."

"Ah, I'm sorry to hear that. And you'd lost your mom . . ."

"Yes. My mother and sister died a couple of years before the stroke. It really wiped Daddy out."

She paused, and Kent could see the pain flash across her face. Holy Christ, this woman could use a break.

"The thing is, he let the farm go until it slid into bad shape. I had no idea how bad until it was too late. I hadn't taken over his finances. I talked to him every day, and checked in on him, but I was still working and raising kids. I thought the responsibilities of running the farm would be good for him, help keep him busy."

"Sure," Kent said.

"But he started doing crazy things. He bought an expensive tractor and let it just sit out in the fields. He bought space at the grain elevator, but never delivered the crops. And he wasn't paying bills. Thank God some were on auto payment." Frosty eyes met his. "His insurance was cancelled. We had to get an attorney involved to reinstate his health and homeowner insurance, then we had to agree to much higher deductibles."

Kent groaned inside. Another strike against him. He was about to apologize for the entire industry when she continued.

"One night I took dinner over, and Dad didn't come to the door. All the lights were off. I went in, and found him sitting in the dark in the living room crying. He hadn't done anything all day." She paused for a sip of her drink.

187

"That's when I started looking for a housekeeper for him. But a week later, a friend went over, and found him in the tractor bent over. Thought he had a heart attack, but he was just out of it. Stroke. By then, the damage was done."

"No other siblings? No one else to help out?"

Slowly she shook her head. "Just me and my kids," she said, her voice barely above a whisper.

"What happened to your mom and sister?" The words slipped out before he could stop them. What the hell was wrong with him probing like this? Clearly it was emotional for her. He didn't want to come off as an insensitive clod. "Look, I'm sorry. It's none—"

"No. It's all right. It's what started the whole thing. My mother had an aneurism and crossed the center line on the two-lane between here and Paxton. A truck hit them head-on."

Kent sucked in his breath, and stared at her. That hit too close to home. Another truck . . . "Oh, Dana. I'm so sorry." He rubbed a hand across the back of his neck, squeezing his eyes shut. God, those memories. When he looked up again, he saw the confusion in her face. "I know exactly what you went through," he said, his voice tight.

Her eyes widened. "What do you mean?"

"I lost my wife and son in a wreck, too."

"A wife and son?" she echoed. "Oh, Kent . . . I had no idea."

He saw her eyes shoot to his left hand, which was missing the gold wedding band that used to reside there.

"It's been a long time," he told her, wishing he'd kept his mouth shut. She'd opened up about her family and the farm, how could he not do the same? "They were heading home from a soccer tournament in Topeka. It was dark, about ten o'clock. Where it happened, there wasn't much space between her lanes and the opposite traffic – just a narrow grassy median, and no guardrails. The trailer went off the road, and smashed right into Meredith's van. The only mercy was that they were both killed instantly."

A hand flew to Dana's mouth, and horror filled her eyes. "Oh, my God, Kent," she said, the pitch of her voice mirroring her expression. "I'm so sorry."

Kent swallowed hard as his throat constricted, but forced himself to finish the story. "Andy was nine at the time. It's been seventeen years." He looked past her as the years rolled through his head. "Hard to believe."

A soft touch on his arm brought him back to the present. His eyes met Dana's and he saw the tears welling in hers. This was when most people started fidgeting, uncomfortable and unsure what to say, ready to bolt at the earliest opportunity. So far, Dana wasn't exhibiting any of those reactions. But the touch must have been automatic, and when she realized her hand was still on his arm, she snatched it back. He hadn't minded it being there in the least.

"Did– did they figure out what happened?" Dana asked quietly.

Kent took a long gulp of his beer then swiped a hand across his mouth before answering. Here's where the story could still make him so angry. "Yeah. Driver fell asleep. Logged too many hours."

"Oh, no," Dana breathed. They fell silent for a moment, then her brow wrinkled. "Wasn't there a settlement? Did they prove the guy shouldn't have been driving?"

"Oh, yeah. The shipping company knew it. And they tried to cover it up. Everything came out eventually."

Dana stared at him, confusion on her face. "So then why are you–"

"Why am I not out playing golf? Living a life of leisure? Seeing the world?"

Dana gave a tiny shrug. "Well, *something* else."

He couldn't help the hardness that crept into his voice. "I've seen a lot of the world. And don't particularly like much of what I've seen." He shook his head. "No. This is better. This keeps me going. I'm not selling insurance, Dana. I don't have any sales quotas. I'm not trying to save the company from paying out. I'm here to help people."

She held his gaze for a long moment, then said softly, "Help other people put *their* lives back together."

Kent blew out his breath. "I can't fix everything. People die in natural disasters all the time. But I do what I can." He declined to mention that in every disaster he worked he picked out a project, made some kind of community donation from his own accounts. This time around he was struggling. What he'd really like to do is help Dana Gerard, put some money in a trust or an escrow account for her. In his head, he'd played around with some ideas, how to make it anonymous and untraceable. No matter how hard he tried, though, Kent couldn't come up with a way that wouldn't look like a conflict of interest that could potentially put Heartland in a bad situation. The goal, after all, was to help, not cause more trouble.

It's all he'd done with the money in the fifteen years he'd had it. The only thing he could justify. Couldn't shake the feeling that it was dirty. Money's what caused the nightmare in the first place. Greed. People pushing for more and more. One more mile, one more load, one more buck. That's really what killed his wife, his son and the truck driver.

"So you just travel around from disaster to disaster?"

"Yeah. I finally sold our house seven years ago. At first I couldn't part with it. So many memories. For a while it was surreal, still felt like they were going to walk through the door. But then it started to feel cold and empty, and that's when I knew it was time. Funny things, houses."

Turning away from the bright tears shimmering in Dana's eyes, he pulled a file folder from the seat beside him and opened it flat on the table. It was good to see a softer side of her, to make her understand she didn't need to fear him, but he didn't tell his story for sympathy. It was time to change the subject. "How 'bout we build you a new one?"

With a choked laugh, Dana swiped at her eyes, and nodded. She dug a pen out of her purse and attempted to look at the first document Kent shoved toward her. But she couldn't stop the tears from spilling over. Putting the pen down, she reached for the small package of tissues in her purse. Dana dabbed at her eyes, then took a sip of iced tea, trying to get herself under control. Her thoughts and feelings were bouncing all over the place. So similar to her own loss. Such life-altering tragedies they shared.

She looked across the table and met a wan smile from Kent. "You all right?"

"Kent, we don't have to do this right now if you'd rather not."

At that, he leaned across the table and picked up the pen, shaking it at her. "Dana, if you don't sign these right now, I'm going to start forging your signature."

He'd obviously told as much as he could for one night and needed to move on. To keep from drowning in his own grief and sorrow, he turned his attention to others. She held up her hands in surrender. "Okay, okay. I can't be responsible for your fall into illegal activities." She took the pen.

"You'll also need to add some personal info. . . . debt, income and your social. I've marked each place you need to sign."

Of course he had. The man was obviously meticulous. A moment later, she looked up in surprise as the waitress stopped by, and Kent ordered her a glass of chardonnay. But she didn't object.

"Seems like it's time to ditch the caffeine," he told her.

"Yeah, I think you're right. Thank you."

"Let me know if you have any questions."

Dana gave a little snort. "You know I'm not reading all this, right?"

He shot her a pointed look. "Does that mean you're trusting me?"

The pen stopped mid-air. Something tightened in Dana's chest, and she took a deep, shaky breath. "I suppose I am," she managed. Where was that glass of wine, anyway?

With exaggeration, he pumped a fist at his side. "Maybe I should get that in writing, too."

She flashed him a playful grimace. "Maybe you shouldn't push your luck."

"Not pushing, not pushing." He ran a thumb along the side of the papers, fanning them a little. "You can't just sign that last page. Has to be filed online. I've got all the links and passwords ready. All you have to do is go in, fill out your part, and hit submit. Do it soon. It's a grant application, and you don't want to be last in line."

The glass of wine arrived, and she sat back a moment, her eyes meeting Kent's. "It feels like a waste of time, Kent. I mean, really, what are the chances I could land any kind of grant?"

He gave her a lopsided grin. "I don't suppose you have any blood relatives who are minorities. Native American ancestry?"

Dana lifted a chunk of blond hair. "What do you think?"

"Well, it's too bad your daughter just graduated. A kid in college would help, but with your son under twenty-one and living at home, that still puts you in the single mom category. You've got a shot."

She had a hard time believing it, but Kent's smile held such confidence, Dana caught his optimism. She lifted her wine glass toward him. "Can't hurt to try."

"Would you like another?" Kent asked when Dana set her empty glass back on the table several minutes later.

"Oh, no thank you." She glanced at her watch, surprised to see they'd been there more than two hours. "I should be heading home." Another glass of wine would make her foggy, and her brain was already feeling scrambled from trying to fill out the forms and process everything Kent had told her at the same time.

"I'll get those other names to you ASAP," Kent said, sliding out of the booth.

"No rush. The Fourth is coming up, and I'll be gone for several days after that."

"Oh, yeah?"

"Yes, some friends and I have been talking about a girls' trip forever, and we're finally doing it."

"When will you be back?" he asked as they walked to his car.

"We'll be gone four or five days."

192

"Maybe we'll hear something on these applications by the time you get back."

He walked her up to Claire's porch, and Dana hesitated. Inviting him in was more appealing than it had been at the start of the evening. She couldn't tell from his body language whether he was expecting an invitation or not. It'd been an emotional couple of hours.

"Thanks for joining me for dinner," Kent said. "I'm glad we got all of that done."

"Yeah, me too."

"My pleasure."

"Kent?" Dana hesitated a moment, not sure what to say, but feeling that she needed to offer him something more.

"Hmm?"

"You're good at what you do. Thank you."

The warm kiss he brushed against her cheek sent tingles down her spine, and Dana found herself disappointed that he drew back so quickly. Before she could figure that out, he took her hand. "Friends?" he asked.

Dana laughed, though her throat had tightened. "There you go, pushing again."

"This time, I am."

"Yes," she said, her voice soft. "I suppose a friend in the insurance business could be a handy thing to have around."

"You have no idea." Grinning, he squeezed her hand again, then turned and started down the steps. "I'll be in touch," he called over his shoulder.

Dana waved and stepped inside, mulling over her last words. Once the disaster relief was officially done, Kent Donovan wouldn't be "around."

Chapter Sixteen

With the phone cradled between her ear and shoulder, Dana flung the suitcase borrowed from Mary onto her bed. "I'm packing now," she told Maddie. "This should take all of five minutes." What she had to pack wouldn't fill even half of the case, but hopefully, it'd be filled with bargains for the trip back home. Images of the Macy's summer clearance racks danced in her head.

"What time are you leaving?"

"Trying for nine o'clock, but that's pretty optimistic with this group."

"All four in one car? That'll be cozy."

"No, we decided to split up. Gotta have room for shopping bags on the way back. Claire is looking for things for her new place, and you know how Mary loves to shop. I think she'll start buying Christmas presents." Dana needed a few things, but mostly she planned to have fun helping her friends spend their money. "We drew straws. Mary came over with these caramel chocolate ice cream pops after dinner, and when we were done, she gathered up all the sticks, and wrote our names on them. Kind of silly, but it worked. Jane and I are riding down together, I'm rooming with Claire, then Mary and I will be together for the ride home."

"Sounds fun."

"I can't wait. I want to come see you, too, sweetie. And I will as soon as things settle down a bit at the hospital. You can always come to Whitfield, you know."

"I know, but the weekends are pretty busy here. I'm working with some Girl Scout troops to get their health and foods badges. It's a lot of fun."

"What about Allison? Do you spend any time with her?" Maddie's new roommate had a boyfriend, and Dana had wondered whether she'd be part of Maddie's social circle.

"Oh, yeah. Us, a few people from the apartment, and a couple of girls from work kind of hang out together."

"That's great. So what's on the agenda for this weekend?" Dana absently tossed a pair of shoes into the suitcase, then grabbed her jeans. But she didn't miss the slight hesitation before Maddie spoke again.

"I have a date tonight."

Dana let go of the jeans, and sat down on the bed. "Yeah? With whom?"

"An intern. His name is Zach."

"Uh-huh. Tell me more." Dana's thoughts immediately went to the only "date" she'd had in recent memory. She'd known the time would come when she and her kids would potentially be dating at the same time, but it felt weird. Not that she was dating Kent Donovan. But she had to admit her respect for Kent had gone up about a thousand percent since their dinner out, and she'd enjoyed his company. Knowing more about him had made such a difference. Anyway, she wasn't mentioning Kent to Maddie. She would not be trading date stories with her daughter. Didn't keep her from wanting to know about Maddie's, though.

"Well . . . he's totally cool. Cute, smart, funny."

"Funny, huh?"

"Oh, he's hilarious. Very quick-thinking."

Dana smiled at the excitement in Maddie's voice. Oh, to be twenty-two. Dana hadn't had many men in her life. She'd put dating on hold years ago. She'd heard too many horror stories of stepfathers abusing their stepchildren, and refused to ever expose her children to any possibility of that. Her kids had always come first. "I'm glad you're meeting people," she told her daughter. "Can't wait to hear all about it."

"Hey, Mom, I'm looking at my calendar. What about after you get back? I could come down that next weekend. Would that work?"

"Of course. That's great. I'll make sure I'm not scheduled to work. Okay, sweetie, I'll touch base with you once we get to Dallas. Night."

Next, she dashed off a quick email reminding Evan that she'd be out of town. Probably wasn't necessary, but she'd want to know if any of them were away from home for several days. She'd already said goodbye to her dad and Chase.

Chase had left for work earlier, and he planned to spend a couple of nights in Paxton while she was gone. The rule was he couldn't have friends at Claire's house when Dana wasn't there. Seemed as though they weren't too interested in venturing to Whitfield, anyway. It annoyed her a little that Chase was always the one driving, but he'd been working so much lately, and staying in town, that she couldn't complain. The kid deserved to have some kind of social life.

**

Laughing and squealing like preteen girls at a One Direction concert, Dana and her friends shoved suitcases into cars at nine a.m. sharp. "Get me out of here," Dana said, meaning it.

"Amen," Mary seconded. "Here, I divided snacks into two bags." She handed one to Dana, who shook her head. Trust Mary to provide for everyone.

"Thanks, Mom," Dana said, taking a peek inside the loaded goodie bag.

"Hey," Mary said. "If you can't bring enough for the whole class, then don't bring any at all, right?"

"Just bring it and let's go already," Claire called, motioning Mary to the car.

Mary twirled around with a flourish. "My chariot awaits, ladies. See you in the rearview mirror."

Seven-and-a-half hours later, they pulled into the SpringHill Suites that would serve as home base for the next four nights. True to their word, Mary and Claire had scaled the trip to something between bargain basement and first-class. With a grin she couldn't contain, Dana climbed out of the car ready to stretch her legs, then stretch out on a poolside lounge chair with an ice-cold beverage. Never mind that she didn't own a swimsuit yet. A cami and shorts would be just fine. Slinging her bag over her shoulder, she nearly charged the sliding glass doors. *Let the fun begin.*

**

On the first morning of vacation, Dana tried to sleep in. For a while she listened to Claire's soft breathing from the other bed, hoping it would lull her back to sleep, but it was no use. Their internal clocks operated on different frequencies. Dressing quickly, and as quietly as possible, Dana tiptoed out the door and down the long corridor to the elevator. In the lobby, she ordered coffee and made her way back to the pool, settling in to enjoy the slow pace before the day's revelry began. Today, shopping. Tomorrow, perhaps the botanical gardens or a museum. And then, probably more shopping.

She heard her companions before she saw them, heard the laughter and easy banter. Not even nine o'clock, and the fun had begun. As her friends made their grand entrance into the restaurant, Dana watched the heads turn.

"Oh, my," Mary exclaimed. "Would you look at this spread?" She spoke to one of the young women wiping down the counter. "Honey, this is spectacular. It all looks wonderful." Dana had to smile. Though Mary looked as if she could be some kind of celebrity, decked out in high style, she always made a point to be kind to workers and service staff. It was an extension of her generosity, and one of the traits Dana admired. She rose, ready to stake her claim as one of those women meeting the day head-on with exuberance and cheerfulness.

**

By dinner, some of that exuberance had waned. They collapsed into a padded booth ready for sustenance and rest. Dana closed her eyes, and let her head fall back for a moment. "I need caffeine," she said.

"Coming right up," Claire said. She ordered pitchers of iced tea and Diet Coke. When they arrived, she nudged Dana. "You gonna sit up and drink this, or were you wanting an intravenous drip?"

"Hmmm. A drip would be nice," Dana said. But she lifted the glass and enjoyed a long drink of the ice-cold liquid. "Ah. That's better."

As soon as they ordered dinner, the conversation turned from the day's events to children. It always happened. Any time she got together with friends to get a break from home and kids they ended up talking about . . . kids.

"I think this one might be the one," Mary said. "Wouldn't surprise me if Annie shows up with a rock on her finger any day now."

"Oh, fun," Jane said. "A wedding."

"About time," Mary added. "It's not fair. Claire's got two grandkids, and I have none."

Claire nudged her. "It's not a competition."

"Like hell," Mary said, her voice tinged with humor.

"Oooo." Claire grinned. "Guess that means I win."

Dana laughed. "You two fight like sisters."

"She started it," Claire said.

After they'd settled back down, Mary waved a hand toward Dana. "Dana, what about Chase? He getting along all right with the Wades?"

Dana's mommy pride bubbled to the surface. "You know, I think he's having a good summer after all. I'm really proud of him. He's working hard. Some mornings, he's actually left the house before me."

"That in itself is a major accomplishment," Claire said. "Think it could turn into more than a summer gig?"

"Oh, for a crystal ball," Dana groaned.

"Yeah, get in line, sweetheart. We could all use one of those," Claire said.

198

"Well, I really don't care if it extends past summer. What I hope most of all is that it gives the kid some direction. I hope something will grab him and he can pursue a degree or a career, whether it's agriculture, food processing, crop science, chemical stuff, I don't care. I just want him to have a goal. I think that would make college easier for him."

"No doubt," Jane said. "It's hard to figure out the path when you don't know where you want to go."

"Exactly," Dana said. "If nothing else, this experience should help rule out farming if it's not his thing."

"Narrowing the field would be good," Claire added, scraping her plate as she scooped up the final bite of flourless chocolate torte and raspberry sauce. "Speaking of . . . what are we doing tomorrow, ladies? We've got lots of options."

Dishes were cleared away, and the conversation turned to their own agenda.

"Something Dana can wear that little yellow number to," Mary said.

Dana had scored a darling yellow sundress deep-discounted on the sale rack at Macy's. At that moment, it was the trendiest item of clothing she possessed. Yes, she wanted to wear it. "I can wear that anyplace," Dana told her. "Since it's about all I own, you'll be sick of seeing it because I'll wear it all the time."

"How 'bout the arboretum?" Jane suggested. "Perfect place for a cute little dress. If we go in the morning, we can be done before it really heats up."

"Sounds like a plan," Claire said. "Listen, let's get out of here. I'm about ready to turn in. I've officially shopped until I'm on the verge of dropping."

At the hotel, they scattered, ready to slip into comfy pajamas and relax. "Hey, why don't you go first," Dana told Claire, motioning toward their room.

A few minutes later, Dana heard Claire rustling in the bathroom, so she quietly entered the bedroom to change clothes. She didn't mean to eavesdrop, but Claire's words, and the anxiety in her voice, carried.

"It's so unnatural," Claire said. "We're sitting around laughing and talking, eating chocolate, and this is when a glass of wine makes sense."

There was a pause before Claire continued. "No. I wasn't craving it. It's just that it seems so fake. Normal people would have a glass of wine."

Frowning, Dana listened harder.

"I don't know whether the girls missed it or not," Claire said. "They wouldn't say anything, of course. They've all been great about it."

Dana's head dropped to her chest. So that was it. Claire had to be speaking with her AA sponsor. How often, Dana wondered, did her friend have to be talked off the ledge, convinced she didn't want a drink? How long before not drinking would be the norm? Would it ever? Recovery could be a rough road. Dana had seen drug and alcohol patients in the hospital, but usually only during an episode, when they hurt themselves or needed their stomach pumped. For follow up they went to other doctors or treatment centers.

She moved away from the door and pretended to be busy collecting her purse, checking her phone for messages to give Claire some privacy. But when the door opened and Claire entered the room, Dana crossed over and took her arm. "You doing all right?"

Claire sank onto one of the beds and yanked up a pillow. "Not fooling anyone, huh?"

Dana sat beside her. "No, that's not it. I'm sorry. I overheard some of your call. How often do you talk to her?"

Claire's head fell onto Dana's shoulder. "Every damned day. Sometimes more than once."

Dana slid her arm around Claire. "That's good, though. I'm so glad you have someone to talk to. I'm sure it's different than talking to me or Mary, but you know you can talk to me about this any time, right?"

Claire sat up straighter, and shot her a rueful smile. "I know, but I don't want our conversations to be about that.

I don't want it to get in the way of other things. And some days I'm just so tired of talking about it."

Dana choked out a laugh. "I know what you mean. I feel the same way about this tornado. It's as if the tornado now defines me. I have no other life. Oh, wait, that might actually be true."

Claire swatted at her. "It is *not* true. But to veer off topic just a little, have you seen Mr. Rescue recently?"

No need to ask whom she meant, but Dana wasn't sure she wanted to go there. Claire's eyes widened, as she obviously read something into Dana's silence. For some reason, she'd told Claire that Kent had helped her with loan applications and researching contractors, but she'd purposely withheld the fact that they'd had dinner. And she'd kept his concern for her the day he thought her car broke down at the farm a secret that she visited alone, sometimes just before she fell asleep. Some nights, her thoughts bounced around like the little silver ball in a pinball machine, and she convinced herself that Kent might actually feel something for her. Then she'd remember the quick – but very warm – brotherly peck he'd landed on her cheek. The one that had her wondering what would have happened if she'd turned her head or leaned into him a tiny bit.

"Didn't I say he might grow on you?" Claire demanded.

Dana held up her hands. "Okay, okay. I admit, I like him better than I did at first. He's been very helpful." That was as far as she was willing to go on record.

"Good. Has he asked you out?"

Well damn.

"Claire, I think it's about time for bed. You can have man dramas in your dreams."

Claire shot up, hands on her hips. "Why, Dana Gerard, I do believe you've been holding out on us. How could you go out with a man and the entire town not know about it before you even got home?" She put a hand to her chest. "Oh, *my*. Something actually got past Mary Logan. Quick! Check the news stations."

Dana had wondered the same thing at the time. She'd practically tiptoed around the hospital over the following days wondering who would mention it first. The fact that no one did proved that she was now a statistic. "Like I told you, in the eyes of the rest of the world, I'm a tornado victim. Nothing more."

"Well, the rest of the world doesn't have a clue," Claire said, heading toward the door. "Hey, slip into your jammies, then come on out. We're not done yet."

As Dana pulled the nightshirt over her head, she heard Claire razzing Mary with glee in her voice. Those two could never resist one-upping each other, and she was sure to be the subject of their banter – she and Kent Donovan. Since Claire was heading back to Wichita, there wasn't too much to worry about, but if Mary linked their names together in conversation around Whitfield . . .

She shook her head and braced for the onslaught. But when she opened the door, she was greeted by three wide grins. "What's going on? You all look like the Three Stooges or something."

Her friends stepped back to reveal a stack of packages on the coffee table in the sitting area. Stumped, Dana stared at the girls. It wasn't her birthday. Wait. Was it? In her current state of mind, she could certainly be guilty of forgetting her own birthday. But she hadn't.

"Have a seat," Claire said, flopping back onto the small sofa. Jane pulled Dana forward.

"Just a little something from the three of us. You know how we like presents," Mary said.

"And shopping," Claire added.

"And you," Jane said.

"Aw. All this is for me?"

"And for your new house." Mary said, handing Dana a package wrapped in bright pink and orange polka-dot paper and tied with an iridescent pink bow.

"Oh, my gosh, Mary. This is beautiful." She carefully untied the bow and slit the tape at the back. Opening the lid of the sturdy box, Dana peeked under the tissue paper.

Stacked inside were three identical white wooden frames with brushed silver embellishments at the corners.

"One for each kid," Claire said.

Dana smiled. "I kind of figured." If only she'd backed up all the photos she had of her kids and kept those someplace safe. That's what she should have had in her safe deposit box. She swallowed hard. "Thanks, guys. These are gorgeous. Maybe at Christmas I can get a solo shot of each of them."

"Yeah, and maybe you can get them matching sweaters, too," Claire said. "They'd love that."

Mary laughed. "Hey, don't make fun. I still get mine matching pajamas."

Claire rolled her eyes. "You would."

Jane reached over and scooted the large flat box toward Dana. "This one next. Careful. It's heavy."

Again, Dana turned the package over and unfastened the tape.

"Rip it, girl," Mary said. "I'll turn into a pumpkin soon."

"Okay, okay," Dana said, tearing the paper down the center. "Oh, my gosh," Dana breathed. She ran a hand over the glass in front of the watercolor painting of giant sunflowers, then stared at Mary. "How did you get this?"

"I'm on the Arts Council, remember? Tracked the guy down from the entry forms for the fair last year. Fortunately, we don't throw anything away around there."

The painting, or one similar to it, had caught Dana's eye at the county fair, and she'd fallen in love with it. But purchasing original artwork was definitely not in her budget. "Oh, Mary. This is too much. You guys—"

Mary held up a hand. "Gift. It's a gift. A simple thank-you will do."

"I wasn't sure I'd bother to replace the fireplace in my house, but now I have to," Dana said, her voice almost a whisper. "This is so going front and center." Standing, she braced the picture against the wall, and admired it. "I absolutely love it."

Grinning, she looked at each of her friends, "thank you, thank you, and thank you."

"You're welcome."

"Last one," Claire said. She deposited the box into Dana's lap as she sat back down.

"Another one?" Dana screeched. It was too much, but she had to admit, it sure was fun. This time, she tossed the bow in the air, and with a flourish, ripped the paper from the box.

"Now you're getting the hang of it," Mary said. "Nicely done."

Nestled in heavy cream tissue paper was a beautiful leather photo album. "Oooooo. This is exactly what I need," Dana said. "I haven't got around to making prints from Maddie's graduation, but they are going in here, for sure. Thank you."

"Aren't you going to open it?" Mary demanded.

Dana glanced around, lifting the giftwrap she'd strewn on the floor. Had she missed something?

"The album," Claire said.

Dana held it up. "I opened it. It's beautiful. I can't wait to start—"

Claire nudged her. "Turn the page."

And then it dawned on Dana, as she looked at the expectant expressions on her friends' faces. They had done something amazing. Holding her breath, she opened the album. The proud smiles of her parents on either side of Evan in his high school cap and gown greeted her. The image quickly blurred, and tears streamed down Dana's face. "Oh, my God."

She flipped through the pages, hardly able to see, but pretty sure there were photographs of swim parties and school events, photos of her and her kids. The tears came harder, and she closed the album to keep it from getting drenched, hugging it to her.

"We copied everything we could find," Mary told her. "By the time I was done, *my* house looked like a tornado had ripped through it."

Dana shook her head. "You have no— no idea." She tried to speak between sobs, but couldn't complete a sentence.

Claire's warm arms wrapped around her. "Dana. Hey, come on. It's okay."

She couldn't stop crying.

"Jeez, we thought you would like it," Mary said, her words tinged with humor.

Dana sputtered something between a choke and a laugh, and Jane handed her a tissue. "Thank you so much." She dabbed at her eyes, and they filled again. "This is incredible." She ran her hand over the smooth caramel leather, then opened the album again. "I can't believe you found so many," she whispered. "My kids, my folks . . ."

"And us," Claire said, tapping a photo page. "Check out those pool babes."

"And the bikinis," Mary added. "Woo-woo!"

Dana grinned. She, Claire and Mary were stretched out on lounge chairs around Mary's pool. Shades on. Drinks in hand. Oh, they'd had some good times. "We look so young. I can't even remember looking like that."

"We've been doing this friend thing a long time," Claire said.

Dana caught Claire's hand, but once again her throat clogged, and she could only nod.

Mary shot out of her chair. "Group hug." She moved in close and turned her head, but not before Dana saw the sparkle of bright tears in her eyes as well.

Feelings so hard to put into words bounced in the vibration of all four of them patting each other's backs – like Morse code tapping out a message of friendship.

**

On their last night, they opted to stay in and watch chick flicks, starting with *Working Girl*.

"This is going waaaay back," Dana said.

"A classic," Mary said. "There's no harm in looking at Harrison Ford in his younger days for a couple of hours." She picked up the remote and handed it to Jane. "Here.

You're the techie in the group. See if you can figure out how to make this thing go."

With an indulgent smile, Jane swiveled toward the television, her ponytail swishing behind her. "Jane, with your hair up like that you look about as old as those kids at the high school," Dana said. Jane worked part time in the high school office and with her computer background had made herself a reputation for figuring out cords, connections and other computer wizardry that challenged the rest of the staff.

"No kidding," Claire agreed, opening two bags of chocolates and spreading them across the table in the center of the small sitting area. "That should get us started," she said, flopping back onto the sofa and kicking up her feet.

Dana chose a dark chocolate toffee. "You always get the best stuff, Claire."

"That's my mission."

"Mission accomplished," Mary said, examining the contents of the table. "Speaking of, what's everyone doing when we get back? Dana, you ready to start construction?"

Dana licked the Dove chocolate from her finger before answering. "Not quite. Not sure when that's gonna happen. I haven't got the timing figured out."

"When do you leave for New Zealand?" Claire asked Mary.

"Next week," Mary said. "I feel bad leaving with the whole town still such a mess, but Grant really wants to get away. And we've planned this for so long. The words peaceful and romantic came out of the man's mouth. I kid you not. We're going!"

"Of course you have to go," Dana said. "You've done so much for everyone, Mary."

Mary reached out and touched Dana's arm. "Hey, my place is yours while we're gone. I mean it. Go over and use that pool. Relax a little."

"Thanks, Mare. I might. Oh, that reminds me, Claire, do you mind if I host a dinner or two at your place? We'll be interviewing candidates for the hospital administrator's position soon, and I'm on the hospitality committee."

Mary's head jerked up. "Why the hell are you on hospitality? You should be front-runner for the job."

"No duh," Claire added.

Dana's hand stopped before it reached her mouth. "Are you kidding? They wouldn't hire me. I'm a nurse, not an administrator."

"I thought you were both."

Dana shifted, surprised by the force behind Mary's words. "Well, that's true. I handle the nursing admin." Actually, that took more of her time than nursing these days.

"You could probably do that job in your sleep, but would you want it?" Jane asked. She settled back into her chair, the movie on hold.

Three sets of eyes stared at Dana.

Flustered and unused to being the center of attention, Dana reached for more chocolate. At this rate, she'd outgrow all the clothes she'd just bought by the time they hit the Whitfield city limits. New clothes, new house . . . did she want a new job, too?

"I don't know," she hedged. "I've never given it much thought."

"Why not? Seems like you've gone as far as you can in nursing. Might be the next logical step," Claire said.

"And a promotion, right?" Mary added.

"Well, true. It'd be more money." That gave her pause. She could sure use the money. She didn't know the exact salary, but the range was certainly a couple of levels above hers.

"But would you want it?" Jane asked again. "Or would you rather be nursing? Seeing patients?"

Dana shrugged and curled her feet under her. "I don't know. But it doesn't matter. I don't have the management degree."

"No, you've just got the management *experience*. How many hospital administrators have you trained, anyway?" Mary asked, her eyebrows arching.

For a moment, Dana felt as though she were being scolded or cross-examined. "A fair few," she admitted. In her head she did a quick count. Easily five or six. They stopped through, got their two-to-three years of experience and then moved on to more prestigious hospitals in bigger cities. No one wanted to stick around permanently. Same with the doctors. Doctors, and their wives, wanted more bang for their med-school buck. They wanted private schools and fancy country clubs and upscale shopping. Things Whitfield didn't offer.

"Exactly," Mary said. She snapped her fingers. "You give them the experience to go on and get even better jobs. You make them look good, and it's about time you got the credit you deserve. Show 'em who really runs things around there, babe. I mean it. Talk to the board and toss your name into that hat. Hospitality, my ass." She nearly choked on the last words, laughter bubbling up as soon as she said them. It was a full five minutes before Claire and Mary could stop laughing.

Finally, Jane tapped the remote against the coffee table. "Okay, guys. This is queued up. You ready?"

To Dana's relief, Jane pushed play without waiting for an answer, and they turned their attention to the television.

While the familiar story played out on the screen, Dana's thoughts remained on the drama unfolding in her own life. Should she apply for the administrator's position? The deadline was only days away. Could she even put together a résumé by then? She hadn't written one in years, and would have to start from scratch. All of her experience and references would come from Whitfield Community.

Those details aside, would she want the job? Was she crazy to even consider it with everything else she had going on? Or was it crazy to miss this potential opportunity? Andrew was looking for someone to stick around longer this time. The position might not come open again for several years.

A shriek from Mary brought Dana's attention back to the movie. "What's the matter?"

Mary flailed her arms. "Oh, that woman! So nasty."

Dana glanced at the television where Sigourney Weaver's character was systematically taking credit for another woman's hard work.

Work again. Sitting up, Dana ran a hand through her tangled hair. Was she due for a promotion? For years, Dana's policy had been to keep her nose to the grindstone, do whatever was asked of her even if it meant extra hours or responsibilities without additional compensation. The goal, of course, had been to keep the job, secure her place there, and make sure she could provide for her kids. She'd accepted small raises in accordance with annual performance reviews, but had never considered asking for more.

Had she been a pushover all these years? Good ol' Dana, *making everyone else look good*, Mary had said. Was it time she got recognition for it?

She glanced at the TV screen again. The girl, Tess, didn't have the background for the job she was doing, but she had the skills and the smarts – and the ambition. She just needed someone to take her seriously.

If Dana applied for the admin position, would the Whitfield board take her seriously? Dana imagined turning in her résumé to Andrew or Amy, the shocked looks on their faces – or sitting in front of board members for an interview. They might offer her an interview out of polite duty, she supposed. But whisper behind her back? She drew her knees up, dismissing that idea. No, she was liked and respected at the hospital. Even if they declined to consider her a serious candidate for the admin position, surely they wouldn't laugh.

When it came to her administrative duties, she was strictly internal, dealing with scheduling and procedure compliance. Part of the supporting cast behind the scenes, not front and center. Yet, here she was doing community outreach, taking over Brad's duties – doing his job. Considering her seniority, she probably knew more than anyone about how that place operated.

"Take that, lady," Mary yelled at the television.

Dana smiled. This one had a great ending. She hummed along as the music started behind Tess in her unexpected new office with huge windows and amazing view.

Dana thought of her closet-sized office behind the nurses' station. No windows. No desk. Just a couple of cabinets and a work surface for her computer. The admin's office certainly wasn't extravagant, but it did have a nice view of the manor's courtyard next door.

Jane picked up the remote. "Does everyone want a break before we start the next one?"

"What's next?" Mary asked, her words distorted around a lion-sized yawn.

"You've Got Mail," Claire reminded her.

"No, what I've got is a strong desire to drift off to la-la land." She swung her feet to the floor. "You girls watch if you want. I'm pooped."

There was a chorus of agreement, and when Jane switched off the set, they all trudged to their beds with little conversation.

As soon as Claire said goodnight and switched off the small lamp between the beds, Dana snuggled into the cool sheets prepared to drift into instant sleep. Unfortunately, Mary's words came back once again to haunt Dana in the quiet darkness.

After an hour of rolling back and forth, Dana considered getting up and going down to the lobby. Her incessant tossing and turning might be keeping Claire awake. She couldn't stop thinking about Mary's challenge. And Jane's question.

Mentally, Dana ticked off reasons for giving it a shot. She was already doing part of the job. She'd been in her present position for almost ten years, and a change might be good. It could give Val or someone else a chance for promotion. The extra money would be nice. Would she miss seeing patients? Maybe, but there was no reason she couldn't look in on patients, especially when she knew them or their families. That was her edge. She already knew these people, already had ties to the community.

Dana had lived there all her life. She loved Whitfield. Why bring in someone else and try to forge a new relationship where one already existed?

A little surge of excitement ran through her. Just maybe, right there in front of their noses, *she* was the answer to their problem. Dana closed her eyes, only to have an image of the large box of condoms from the hospital storage room flash in her brain. That did it. There wasn't a doubt in her mind that she could do the job – and do it better than Brad Berkley.

Chapter Seventeen

Chase grinned as he pulled the Mazda up to the Wades' barn. Almost looked as though Sandy, one of the retrievers, was waiting for him. He jiggled the key, and when the car gave a final hiccough, climbed out.

Sandy's tail thumped the ground, and Chase held out a hand. "Hey, girl." As he scratched the dog's head, it occurred to him – she *was* waiting for him. Chase chuckled as the dog followed at his heels. Better than a secretary with a cup of coffee, he thought, or a stack of messages.

Cameron looked up from a pad of paper when Chase walked in. "Morning, Chase."

"Morning." A few of the other men standing around sipping coffee or whatever they'd brought in their Thermos jugs nodded his direction.

Cameron addressed Chase again. "Got you on the baling crew today. Time to get this straw collected and stored. You'll go out with Willie."

"Sure," Chase said. Maybe he'd get to run some of the equipment, or at least drive the tractor. He was ready for something new. Willie Young was the oldest guy on the crew. About a hundred pounds overweight, he reminded Chase of Santa Claus, minus the white hair and beard. Wasn't the most agile, but he knew his stuff, and Chase figured that's why Cameron paired them up. He tucked his water bottle under his arm, and listened while Cameron gave instructions.

"Want to get as much done as possible today, but don't rush. You push that baler too fast, and it's gonna choke. I don't want to spend half the day fighting with equipment. If we get far enough, we'll start stacking it in the north barn."

Chase smiled to himself, remembering Poppa's words. When he looked up, Cameron's eyes were on him.

"Want to share?"

Chase's face warmed. "Just thinking of something my grandpa said the other night."

"Yeah?"

Chase shifted, and gave a shrug. "Said sometimes it feels like a farmer is really a mechanic in overalls."

Poppa used to own a lot of equipment, and he'd given Chase a report on just about every piece along with a story about every breakdown they'd had when he and his mom were at the farm over the weekend. He'd practically filled up one of those yellow legal pads. By the time they'd got him back to the manor, Chase's head hurt from all the terms, but he had a new appreciation for Poppa's work. The old man knew his stuff.

Chuckles broke out among the group, and Cameron grinned. "Your grandpa's a smart man. And he's right. Nothing shuts an operation down faster than broken equipment. You've got to know the condition and capabilities of every piece. The baler happens to be in the senior citizen category. Go too fast, and it'll jam, or the twine'll get tangled up. We want tight, uniform bales, so let's take it nice and easy."

Did Willie not hear the same speech, Chase wondered an hour later when the older man shifted and practically gunned the engine for the second time. Yeah, it was hard to be gentle in the heavy work boots, but surely the guy could get somewhere between all the way or nothing at all. He gave a shrill whistle, and signaled Willie to stop.

Over his shoulder, Chase saw Cameron come around the barn. Damn. Must've heard the whistle. What they didn't need was an audience – especially with the boss.

"Willie, just a minute," Chase yelled. "The twine's coming out again." As soon as the parts stopped moving,

213

Chase re-attached the spool then tossed the loose straw back out of the bin. At the rate they were going, the bales would look like something out of a Dr. Seuss book.

Cameron motioned to Willie then jerked his head toward the tractor. "Why don't you two trade places for a while? Chase, you want to take a ride in the cab?"

"Sure," he said, even though he was thinking *hell yes*. He shot a glance at his partner, hoping the older man wouldn't be put out.

"Fine by me," Willie said, taking a swig from his water jug. "Damned if that cab didn't shrink over the winter, Cam. Can't you boys afford the wide model?"

"Flat broke, big fella. You're just gonna have to suck it in."

"I see what you're trying to do here," Willie said, wagging a finger toward Chase. "You're trying to increase my productivity by setting me up with this kid. You learn that in some corporate bullshit class?"

The two were jawing at each other, but Chase knew it was friendly fire. At least he thought so. He watched Cameron's face.

"Nah, this is straight from my HR consulting firm," Wade countered, confirming Chase's suspicion. Cameron knew about business, but there was no way he'd ever hired a consulting firm. These guys made fun of Corporate America every chance they got.

"It's a ten-step program," Wade added. "'Course for an old dog like you, we might have to make it fifteen steps."

Willie looked at Chase. "You hear how he's talking to me? Think I could sue for harassment?"

"Age discrimination," Chase said, with a quick grin at Cam.

"Damn right."

"Go ahead and check your employee handbook on that," Wade told him.

"My wha–?" Willie threw back his head and laughed. "Employee handbook. Right. You mean the one that says 'get back to work before I fire your ass'?"

Wade chuckled. "That's the one."

"All right, Chase. You heard the man. Let's get a move-on."

Chase climbed into the cab, and at Willie's signal moved forward – nice and easy. A couple of times Willie slowed him down, but by noon, their truck was full and ready to go to the barn.

While Chase and Willie unhitched the baler, Chase caught Cameron inspecting the bales. "How do they look?" he hollered. If something was wrong, he wanted to know before they did any more. Cameron gave him a thumbs-up, and headed their direction.

"After lunch, Patrick and John will ride over and give you a hand unloading, then you can start on the other field."

Chase looked at his watch. They'd lost track of time. Patrick and John had already eaten, so Chase wolfed down his turkey sandwich and chugged a Gatorade.

"You boys head on over, and I'll meet you in a few," Willie told them.

As they shuffled out of the barn, Chase couldn't help wonder if Willie was staying behind on purpose – that purpose being to give Wade a report on Chase's performance. He thought he'd done a decent job.

The second field was different, though. Tougher. The baler kept jamming up.

"Well, bite my ass," Willie huffed, climbing out of the cab and inspecting the machine for the second time. "Something's just not right."

Chase crouched down running his hands across the chain. It looked solid. But there were about a million moving parts that all had to work together. If the timing was off, the whole thing broke down. "Hey, Willie, why don't you get inside and go as slow as you can. I want to see if I can tell where it's getting hung up."

Maybe he could at least isolate which area was causing the problem. He'd tinkered with cars enough to know a little something about mechanics. In high school, he spent a fair amount of time at a friend's dad's shop just to keep his own car running. Couldn't afford to have someone else do it. Besides, he kind of liked figuring it out

– the way he had the night he met Luke and Kyle for the first time, both of them standing in the parking lot of a pizza joint looking under the hood of Luke's car without a clue what they were doing. While they stood around with their hands in their pockets, Chase had knocked corrosion off the battery and adjusted some belts enough to get the car running again.

Muttering under his breath, Willie tromped back to the cab. Chase swiped his hand across the beads of sweat that threatened to trickle into his eyes, and watched closely as Willie inched the baler forward. There. "Hang on, Willie."

Willie hauled himself out again. "Find something?"

"I need some tools."

"Inside." Willie returned with a small tool kit and held it out to Chase. "You sure you know what you're doing?"

Chase grinned up at him. "No, but I think I see where the problem is."

"Good enough for me."

Chase removed a couple of cover plates, then turned the crank inside. Or attempted to. "It's caught." He crawled under the machine. "Aw, man. There's a piece of twine wrapped around it. No wonder it's not going anywhere. Can you hand me those needle nose?"

Ten minutes later, Chase held up a strand of orange twine that had choked the small wheel. "Got it."

Willie slapped him on the back. "Atta boy. Let's get the show back on the road."

It was nearly six o'clock when they made the last pass and loaded the last bale into the truck.

"Bring it in," Cameron hollered at them. "We'll stack it on Monday."

Sweaty and dusty, they made their way to the horse stable. "Cold brew and checks in the office," Cameron said.

The "office" was a small room at the front of the stable, across from the tack room. As far as Chase could tell, the Wades kept the farm operation separate from the three houses on the property. Wade's parents still lived in the big house with a pool in back. Two other houses sat on opposite ends of the county road, one belonged to Cameron's family, and his brother lived in the other one. Even though they lived separately, it was kind of cool how they were all right there. The farm was their whole life. Chase wondered how things would have been if Poppa and Grams had stayed on the farm. It wasn't quite as big as the Wade spread, but there was plenty of room for a house – or two.

When Willie picked up a Bud Light and held it out to Chase, Cameron gave a slight shake of his head and sent an apologetic glance to Chase. "Sorry." He handed him an envelope. "Have some fun this weekend. You worked hard out there today. Nice job."

Embarrassment sent a warm flush up his neck. For a while he'd been one of them, not just a kid. He'd been part of the team, and accomplished something. Sure, it was hot, dusty work, but he– A funny feeling hit him in the chest. He could honestly say he'd had fun out there.

Willie threw an arm around Chase's shoulders. "Damn, boy. How old are you?"

"Twenty."

"When's your birthday?"

"November."

"November!" Willie yelped. He clapped Chase on the back. "That's a shame. Well, there it is. We owe you one, kid."

Chase grinned. "Thanks, Willie." It was good to know that the men wouldn't mind him being there. Maybe even expected him to still be around in another three months. Avoiding Cameron's eyes, he stuffed the check in his pocket.

By the time Chase got back to Claire's and got cleaned up, it was seven o'clock. And he was starving. The forty-five minutes over to Paxton sounded like forever. He opened the refrigerator door already knowing it would disappoint. His mom would've stocked it, but he said he'd go to Paxton. Letting the door slam shut, he turned and grabbed his keys. Guess that's what he was going to have to do.

217

His phone buzzed with a text for about the tenth time. This time the message from Luke surprised him. *Coming to get you. Five minutes.*

Cool. Maybe he wouldn't have to wait an hour for food after all. He could get a burger and fries at any of the bars they went to. He could get a beer, too, with his fake ID. Wouldn't be the same, though – not like being with the crew and celebrating the end of the work week. That would've meant something. Anybody could sit in a bar and have a beer. Didn't make 'em part of anything.

**

When Chase opened the front door, Luke and Kyle were both on the porch, and beer breath hit him in the face as soon as Kyle opened his mouth. *Great.* Chase jingled his car keys.

"I'll drive," he said.

"Good," Luke said.

Yeah, Chase figured he wouldn't get any argument even though he almost always helped pay for gas. By midnight he wasn't sorry he had his own car but he was sorry he also had Kyle and Luke so he couldn't just split. They'd ended up in Oakmont, closer than Paxton, but still twenty minutes from Whitfield. The greasy burger settled heavy in his stomach, and his eyes burned. Spending ten hours in the heat tossing straw around was probably the cause of that. But he was tired, too. And bored. Tired of drinking in the bar. Seemed like that was all Kyle ever wanted to do.

Chase nudged him. "Let's go do something."

Kyle put the beer to his lips and gave Chase a hard glare. "Like what?" he sneered around the bottle.

"I don't know. Something besides drink."

"What's the matter? Can't handle booze?"

That was the other thing – when Kyle got drunk he got mean and difficult to deal with. Luke drank, too, but it just made him stupid. God, he needed to make some new friends. But where? He hadn't kept in touch with anyone from the college. Hadn't really clicked with anyone. Most of the people were from Paxton or farther west.

Maybe he could hook up with some of the guys from high school. Might not be so bad now that he had a job and was doing something. It'd be weird at first, but he and Spencer had been pretty tight for a few years. Still, the ones home from college would be leaving again soon. The ones who hadn't gone to college were drifters or already married.

Luke leaned in, interrupting Chase's thoughts. "Anything happening in Whitfield tonight? There's nobody hot here, and the band sucks."

"Whitfield?" Kyle laughed. "No way. Town's a joke."

Chase's jaw clenched, but kept his mouth shut. He didn't need to get into it with Kyle.

"Well, we gotta go back there anyway to get my car."

Kyle swiped his mouth and set the bottle hard onto the bar. "Fine. Let's go."

When they hit the Whitfield city limits, Luke turned toward Chase. "What about your place? We can get online."

Chase squirmed. Not happening. To Luke, getting online meant watching porn or dumb videos on YouTube. "Nah, man. I told you, we can't go there. It's not our house."

He knew his mom wanted the guys to hang out there more, but not when she wasn't around. And for sure not when they'd been drinking. He saw Luke glance behind at Kyle with a smirk on his face. Luke was keyed up good. He was usually all right, but tonight he'd been a jerk, too. Maybe they should just call it a night.

"Hey, thought you needed to get gas," Kyle said from the back seat as they approached the Quick Stop convenience store.

Chase glanced at the fuel gauge. He hadn't planned on driving tonight, and had forgotten about the gas. "Yeah, I do." He made a sharp left, then swung into the station, sending his bladder into a tailspin.

He opened the door and reached for his wallet.

"What the hell is that?" Kyle asked, giving a loud whoop.

Chase bent down and looked into the back seat. "What?"

Kyle pointed across the street, and when Chase straightened, he saw Charlie Fast dancing around at the park.

"Just an old guy." He swiped his credit card, then turned back to the guys. "Hey, I'm going inside for a sec." Claire's house was only a few minutes away, but he had to go, *now*. "You coming?" he asked Luke, who'd climbed out of the car.

"Nah. We'll stay here."

Waiting in line behind a fat dude, Chase hoped the guy wouldn't do more than take a piss. Relieved several minutes later, Chase left the men's room and scanned the glass cases of the convenience store for a Gatorade. The couple of beers he'd had in Oakmont had left him thirsty. He waited again to pay, then headed back out to the car. He did a double-take. Where the hell did they go?

Then he heard Kyle laughing from the park across the street. What was– *Oh, no!* Kyle was dancing around holding Charlie Fast's goofy gold cap in his hands like a tambourine. "Leave him alone," Chase yelled. Quickly, he tossed the Gatorade in the car, then grabbed the gas nozzle. Well, shit. It didn't fill. He pulled out his credit card, and swiped it again, squinting to read the message on the tiny digital screen. *See cashier.*

Groaning, he looked back at the park. What was their problem? "Hey!" he shouted at Kyle and Luke. "Stop it. Come on."

"Tweet, tweet," Kyle hollered at Charlie, taunting him. "Are you a birdie, old man? Sing like a crazy bird for us again."

Shoving the handle back into place, Chase rounded the car and started for the park. "Would you guys knock it off?" He flicked a glance at Charlie. From the distance, he looked kind of dazed. Probably scared the pee out of him.

Luke walked toward Chase, and Kyle gave one last gesture toward Charlie. Almost looked like he'd given him a little punch.

"What the hell?" Chase said, stopping in the street.

"Oh, back off, Gerard. Just having a little fun. Crazy old fart was over there dancing and singing Zip-a-Dee-Doo-Dah at the moon." Luke and Kyle cracked up like it was the funniest thing they'd ever heard.

"So what? Just leave him alone."

"Uh-oh, look out," Luke told Kyle. "Farmer Boy's got a corncob up his ass."

"You guys are such assholes sometimes," Chase muttered as they walked toward his car. "The pump's not working. I gotta go inside."

"What's the matter? Your money no good here, Gerard?" Luke asked, leaning against the back fender. "We gonna have to push this piece of crap or what?"

"Guess you could walk," Chase told him.

He jogged back to the shop, and when he returned, both Luke and Kyle were on the other side of the car, laughing and stumbling around. Chase glanced across the street where Charlie was retreating farther into the park. Good. He should stay out of the way, especially on Friday and Saturday nights.

With the tank finally full, Chase twisted the gas cap back on, and climbed into the car, ready to send the guys on their way. He shook his head as he started the engine. What a waste of a night. He should've stayed at Wade's place. If he'd hung around longer maybe the guys would've invited him to play poker or something. At least they did stuff. Some of them liked to go fishing, he'd heard them talking about it over lunch before. Even though it was awkward to hang around without having a beer, next weekend he'd give it a try.

He pulled up to the curb, and locked the car as soon as Luke and Kyle dragged themselves out. He didn't stick around to offer an invitation. "See you later."

Chase jumped the step up to the front porch, and opened the door, but he didn't go inside. He felt bad about Charlie. He might be a crazy old fart, but he didn't bother anybody. No reason to mess with him like that. Hesitating, Chase wondered if he should run back by the park and make sure the guy was all right. Make sure he got home.

When Luke's tail lights disappeared around the corner, Chase locked up the house again, and climbed back inside his car. Slowly, he circled the park, looking for Charlie. When he couldn't see him from the car, Chase parked across from the Quick Stop and wandered into the park, past the light where they'd seen Charlie earlier. He spent several minutes looking around, but there was no sign of Charlie.

He blew out his breath. Looked like he'd already left. Chase was ready to go home, too, and forget this night had even happened. Tomorrow night he'd be busy. If Luke or Kyle even called.

Chapter Eighteen

Sleeping in sounded good, and that was Chase's plan for Saturday morning. What was the point of getting out of bed if he had nothing to do? But at eight o'clock he gave up. Dragging himself to a sitting position, he yanked on a T-shirt from the end of the bed and slipped it over his head. He mulled the possible activities for the day – and came up with a pretty short list.

He told his mom he'd visit Poppa. That wouldn't take long. He'd been fine since the weekend they'd gone out to the farm, but still it wasn't like they had a lot to talk about or could do anything. It occurred to him once again that if they still ran the farm there'd be tons of things to do. Downstairs, Chase poured a tall glass of orange juice. He'd actually rather be working than just hanging around. Maybe he'd wash and wax his car. Hadn't done that in a while.

Glass in hand, Chase opened the back door, and stepped onto the patio, staring westward. Maybe he could still do something at the farm. He wouldn't have to be paid. His family still owned it, so he had a right to be there, didn't he? He could check fences or clean equipment. Heck, why would Jansen say no to free labor? That was something he could talk to Poppa about.

Chase chugged the rest of his OJ and rinsed the leftover pulp down the sink then headed upstairs to get dressed. He pulled on a faded Kansas City Chiefs T-shirt and jeans then laced up his work boots. Might as well have them on in case he ended up in the fields. He'd made up his mind. Even if Poppa didn't want him working at the farm right now, he was going over to introduce himself to Bill Jansen. First, though, he'd make the stop at the manor.

Chase was about to knock on Poppa's door when he thought he heard voices inside. He put an ear to the door. Sure enough, another man's voice carried to the hallway. Could be a friend or an aid. He debated whether to interrupt, knowing that sometimes an interruption was actually welcome if someone had just stopped by but was having trouble getting away. He could always duck his head in and say hello then come back later.

He knocked softly on the door.

"Come in," Poppa's raspy voice called.

Chase opened the door a crack to find Poppa in his recliner and another man sitting on the sofa with his arms dangling over his knees. A guy he'd never seen before with a weathered face and deep lines around his eyes. Younger than Poppa, but completely bald. Chase looked from one to the other. "Hey, Pops. Sorry to butt in. I can come back later. You need anything?"

The other man stood and took a couple of steps toward Chase, his arm extended.

"Howdy. You must be Chase," the man said, in a deep gravelly smoker's voice.

"Uh, yes, sir."

"Good to meet you, finally. I'm Bill Jansen. Your grandpa's been telling me all about you. Says you might be heir to the Gerard lands one of these days."

Chase gaped at the man before he came-to and shook his hand. Did Poppa really say that? "Nice meeting you, too," Chase said, his glance switching back to Poppa. What was he supposed to say? "I, um. Well. We'll see," Chase stammered.

"I understand you're working for the Wades."

"Right."

"That's a good outfit. As good a place as any to learn the ropes. You doing any studying?"

"Studying?" Chase echoed.

"You know, learning about seeds and soil types, irrigation."

The breath whooshed out of Chase's lungs, and he shoved his hands into his pockets. Was this guy testing him? Trying to make him look bad in front of Poppa? He didn't seem angry or unfriendly. But the question caught Chase off-guard. It was a good one, he supposed. Maybe that's what he should be doing with his weekends.

"Not really. Not for the summer."

"Well, listen, if you're interested, I got all kinds of textbooks and manuals at the house if you want to come on by and pick up a few."

"Yeah?" He looked at Poppa for his reaction, and almost laughed. Poppa had leaned forward and seemed to be staring at Chase waiting for *his* reaction. "Sure. I could do that."

"You know where we are?"

"No, sir."

But once Jansen described his redbrick house with gray clapboard and black shutters only a couple of miles from their farm, Chase knew exactly where he meant. He'd driven by it a hundred times.

"Why don't I let you and your granddad visit a spell. I gotta get on to my chores, anyhow. I'll be back at the house in a couple of hours if you want to come out."

"Yeah. I'll do that," Chase told him. No sense washing his car if he was going out to the farm. This was a better option, anyway.

Jansen held his hand out and shook Poppa's. "Sure good to see you, Arlen. Let's hope we get another batch like this one next year. You take care now."

As soon as Jansen closed the door Chase turned to Poppa. "You all right with this? Me getting some books, maybe helping out around the farm?"

Poppa gave that half-sided smile and started writing on the tablet in front of him.

Chase read the note, and nodded. *Bring the books. We'll do some lessons.* His throat tightened when he read the next line. *I'll teach you.*

Chapter Nineteen

On Sunday morning, Chase stretched out on the sofa and hauled a thick book about irrigation systems onto his chest, figuring he could get up to speed on the mechanical stuff pretty easily. By the time he headed over to Poppa's later in the afternoon, he should be able to talk about it, anyway. He smiled to himself. He was about to impress the old man.

About half-way through chapter one, the doorbell rang. Barefoot, he padded to the front door. A police cruiser sat at the curb, and two officers greeted him on the porch. What the–? Oh, no. Chase's stomach churned. His mom was due back this evening. Did she have an accident on the road?

"Uh, hey," he stammered, his heart pounding.

"Chase Gerard?" one of the officers asked.

Barely breathing, Chase nodded.

"We'd like to talk to you a minute."

"Okay."

"Mind if we come in?"

Chase backed up. "Sure. What – uh, what's this about?"

"Chase, I'm Officer Riley. This is Officer Hamilton. We'd like to know if you had any interaction with Charlie Fast in the park on Friday night."

"What?" It took Chase a minute to switch gears.

"Surveillance cameras show you were at the gas station across from the park that night."

"Yeah. I was getting some gas."

"Uh-huh. Anyone with you?"

Chase's chest began to pound. What was going on? Should he name Luke and Kyle? Warning bells clanged in his head. He was being questioned by police. Should he call an attorney? What the hell did they want?

"I was with a couple of guys," he hedged.

Riley opened a notepad, and raised his brows at Chase. "Their names are?"

Oh, holy crap. Chase shifted, and shoved his hands in his pockets. "What do you want their names for?"

"We're interviewing anyone who might have been in the area that night."

"Why?"

Riley's hard eyes bore into him, and Chase's throat went dry.

"We're investigating the death of Charlie Fast."

**

Chase sat rigid in the chair in the living room, holding his leg to keep it from bouncing up and down. Charlie Fast was dead? He *died* Friday night? Chase tried to listen to the policemen, but the words were foggy. They kept asking the same things over and over. He just wanted them to leave so he could think.

"Now let's see," Riley said, drawing out his words real slow. "One of your friends drives a blue Nissan, is that right?"

"Yeah."

"Is that Luke? Luke Abrams of Paxton? Is that correct?"

Finally Chase couldn't stand it anymore. "If you already know, why are you asking me? I don't get what any of this has to do with me."

Riley held up a hand. "Calm down. We just want to make sure we've got it all straight."

"All *what* straight?" Chase said, more agitated by the second.

"Who's the other friend?"

Chase clenched his fists, unsure what to say.

227

"Son, make it easy on yourself. You might as well cooperate. We're going to find out anyway."

He swallowed hard, staring at his feet. He was not a snitch. No way could he name Kyle. He'd never live that down.

"They both from Paxton?"

"Look, I got nothing to hide. We were just getting gas."

"You boys been drinking that night?"

The breath whooshed out of Chase's lungs. Had they already traced them to Oakmont? Have them on camera there, too? If he said no, they'd catch him in a lie, but if he said yes, they'd know he'd been drinking under age. *Shit.* He wished he hadn't ignored the texts on his phone earlier.

So what if they tracked down Luke and Kyle, too? What could they say, anyway? Charlie had been perfectly fine when they saw him in the park. Hell, he probably had a heart attack. They didn't have anything to worry about. They hadn't done anything. But he couldn't help remembering that last jab Kyle had taken at Charlie.

Straightening again, Chase answered the question with a shrug. "A little. But when we saw Charlie we were sober. I remember he was fine, dancing and singing. You know, just having fun."

"Did you speak to him?"

"Not really."

Riley's eyebrows arched.

"Did anyone approach him?" Hamilton spoke up.

"Uh. I was in the store, but the other guys went over to the park. Just for a minute."

"Why?"

He shrugged. "They were hanging out waiting on me."

"But then you went over, too?"

Jesus Christ. What did they have on surveillance? Could they see the park? He hoped so. Then they could see that Charlie was fine when they left. Chase's stomach rolled. Could they see that Kyle had been messing with Charlie? "Yeah, to get the guys."

"Uh-huh. What time was that, Chase?"

228

Chase rubbed a hand across his face, thinking. "I guess it was around twelve-thirty. Something like that."

"What'd you do after you left the station?"

"Came home. Here."

"Your friends, too?"

"Nah. They left."

"In the blue Nissan?"

Chase wanted to scream. What was this guy's problem? It felt like he was talking to Dumb and Dumber. "Right."

"Did you hear from them after that? Get a text or anything when they made it home?"

"Nope."

"Have you talked to them since then?"

"No."

"Why'd you go back to the park?"

Chase's heart pounded. Oh, fuck. Did they think he went back and hurt Charlie?

"We know you went back, Chase. Why?"

Chase thought he might be sick. He couldn't tell them he wanted to make sure Charlie was okay or they'd know something was wrong. But if he lied . . .

Licking his lips, Chase hitched a shoulder. "Thought I'd lost my wallet."

"Uh-huh," Riley said.

Chase heard the suspicion in his voice. God damn it. He'd just lied to a cop.

"Did you find it?" Riley asked.

"Yeah. It was in the street here when I got back. Guess it fell out of my pocket when I got out of the car."

"I see." Riley closed his notepad, and stood. "Well, that's all for now. May want to talk to you again."

Chase heaved a deep breath. "Sure. But for the record, when we saw Charlie in the park, he was fine. Singing and dancing."

"Yeah. Singing and dancing."

"Right. And that's all I know about Charlie Fast Friday night. What makes you think anything happened anyway? He was old. Maybe he just died."

Riley nodded. "Maybe."

Chase forced himself to step onto the porch, and stay there until the cops had turned the corner and were out of sight, hoping to give the impression to anyone watching that nothing was wrong. He ought to drive over to Paxton right now and beat the living crap out of Kyle Norton.

It was a lucky break his mom hadn't been home, but Chase couldn't help wonder how many versions of the scene she'd hear in the next twenty-four hours. That's all he needed.

He called Luke first, exploding as soon as Luke picked up. "I just had a freaking visit from the cops, Luke. They were questioning me about that old guy in the park Friday night. He's dead! He died Friday night. What the hell?"

"Hold your shit, Gerard. They came to my place, too. It don't mean anything. They're snooping around, that's all. No big deal."

"No big deal? Are you crazy?" Chase shouted. "He's dead. Did you guys do something?"

"What are you talking about? You were there. What'd you tell the cops?"

"That we stopped to get gas. But a surveillance camera shows us going to the park." Chase flopped into a chair, his head in his hand. Luke's words turned his stomach. Chase hadn't been there the whole time.

"What happened while I was in the gas station, Luke?"

Chase waited for an answer. And didn't get one.

"Oh, Jesus Christ," Chase screamed. "What did you do?"

"Nothing," Luke said.

But Chase heard the fear in his voice.

Chapter Twenty

Dana spotted the two police cars as soon as she pulled into the hospital entrance Monday morning. Oh, shoot. Looked like there'd been some trouble last night. Back at Claire's and in a room of her own, Dana had slept more soundly than she had for a week, and hadn't heard any sirens. Hopefully it was nothing drastic. They sure didn't need another tragedy. She pulled around to the employee spaces, and hurried inside.

After dumping her purse into her desk drawer, she headed to the nurses' station while she adjusted the clip in her hair. She'd practically blown in on the stiff wind out there today.

"Hey, what's up?" she asked Rachel, who was standing at one of the computers. "Saw some cop cars outside."

Rachel shook her head, sadness flickering in her eyes. "Charlie Fast died over the weekend."

Dana's stomach dropped. "Oh, no. What happened?"

"Not sure exactly. At first they thought it was a heart attack, but they might do an autopsy to be certain."

"Why cops?"

Rachel shrugged. "They're talking to the doctors, trying to figure out what happened. And I think they're trying to track down his kid."

Jeanie swung around from her computer. "Hey, speaking of cops. Did something happen with Chase while you were gone? Vivien Rogers told me she saw police at your place yesterday."

Dana blinked, as a chill swept through her. "Cops at my place?"

"At Claire's."

"Huh. I don't know. I got in late last night, and only saw Chase for a few minutes. Then I rushed out this morning to get here early. Must not have been a big deal or I'm sure he would've mentioned it." She spoke the words with confidence, but inside, questions pummeled her. What was going on? Dana considered texting him, but he should be at work by now, and she hated to interrupt him. Surely if it was something big, he would've told her. She just hoped there was no drinking involved.

Sagging against the counter, she blew out her breath. What a crazy morning already. "Guess I'll find out soon enough. It's too bad about Charlie. He was an odd duck, but he was part of Whitfield. I always liked him."

Rachel nodded. "Me, too. I hope the kid has some money and can at least give him a decent burial."

Dana wasn't optimistic. No one had seen Charlie's son, Everett, around town in years. It was common knowledge that they'd had a falling out when he was young, and he'd split. Surely the town would give him a funeral. She couldn't imagine half the town not showing up. After all, like the spire on the Methodist church, he was a Whitfield fixture. Who knew, Charlie might have money of his own tucked inside a mattress or cookie jar. Wouldn't surprise her a bit.

Rachel handed her an iPad. "Here are the notes from overnight. Charlie was already gone when they brought him in Saturday, so we don't have a report. I think you'd have to get the coroner's report for the details."

"Sure," Dana murmured. "Thanks, Rachel. See you tomorrow."

Dana sank into a chair, but didn't open the notes, taking a minute to recover from the unexpected news – and wondering what had happened that would put cops on her doorstep.

"Hey, lady. Welcome back!"

Val slid a hand across Dana's shoulder, and Dana attempted a smile but knew it was half-hearted.

"Uh-oh. What's up?" Val leaned close, her eyes questioning.

"I just heard about Charlie Fast."

"Oh, yeah. Such a shame. But you've got to know the guy didn't take care of himself. I bet he had all kinds of health issues."

"I'm sure that's true," Dana said, picking up the iPad as she stood. "How are you? Since I didn't get any phone calls, I assume you managed to keep the place running."

"Like the well-oiled machine it is," Val told her, grinning. "Not so much as a hiccup, I'm telling you."

"Glad to hear it," Dana said.

"So the trip was good?"

Dana hesitated a moment. It was tempting to see what Val's reaction would be if she told her about applying for the administrator's job, but figured it probably wasn't appropriate. And if she didn't get it, the fewer people who knew she'd applied, the better. Digging up her file of past performance reviews was on her list of things to do today. So was getting a few minutes on Andrew's calendar, though just thinking of it made her stomach flutter. Claire would most likely be her lone confidante in this one.

"It was great," Dana said. "We had a lot of fun."

"And how was the shopping? Find any good bargains?"

That she had, including a classy black-and-white patterned jacket that she planned to wear with her basic black skirt in the event of an interview opportunity. They'd stumbled across a well-stocked second-hand shop only a few blocks from the hotel, and not one of them had left empty-handed.

"Let's say my suitcase felt like I'd added a couple of rocks on the way back. And I didn't bust the bank."

"Atta, girl."

Dana couldn't help grinning. "All right, we'd better start morning rounds."

Dana stopped outside room three and picked up the chart. Who was Dylan Jones? Oh, a young boy . . . only nine years old. Admitted yesterday with a concussion and a couple of cracked ribs after falling from a second-story deck. Looked as though the poor kid was lucky to be alive. Thoughts of Kent's son slammed into her brain. Nine years old. Such an active age, when they were still carefree and full of energy. The age of farts and stupid jokes, the age when a simple soccer goal or baseball hit could bring sheer joy – children for only a few more short years. Questions drifted through her head. What had Kent's boy been like? Was he a good soccer player or just one of the herd as happy picking dandelions in the grass as kicking the ball? Had his team won that final match before his death? It didn't matter, but she wished she'd asked more about him. At least to see a picture. She imagined Kent's son with big brown eyes and a happy smile. And then imagined the anguish of losing a child at such a young age. It had to be almost unbearable.

Sidetracked for the second time that morning, Dana shook her head. "Focus," she whispered to herself. With a deep breath, she stepped inside the room, and greeted her patient with a smile. "Hi there, Dylan. I'm Nurse Dana. How are you feeling this morning?" She adjusted the settings on the bed, then turned to the couple hovering at the side, and extended her hand.

After talking with Dylan and his parents, Dana recorded vitals for two other patients, then made for her office. Today she needed to spend some time there. Not only did she need to look at the online application, she absolutely had to connect with some contractors. Since it was her first day back from vacation maybe no one would raise an eyebrow if her almost-always-open door were closed.

With a fresh cup of coffee in hand, Dana settled into her office chair and loosened her shoes. All the walking she'd done in Dallas had renewed an occasional twinge in her left toes. She made quick work of perusing and answering her hospital-related emails, then opened up her personal account to retrieve Kent's list of builders. Before she got to that one, though, another email from Kent

234

caught her attention. Her throat constricted as she read the topic line. "Heartland closing temporary office."

She flopped against the back of her chair. *Rats.* That meant Kent would be leaving, too. Claire was right. He'd grown on her. She'd come to find his easy smile reassuring, the caramel brown eyes soothing. For a moment, Dana wondered if he'd had any say in the decision or if it'd come down from corporate. The timing was unfortunate. He'd just opened up to her about his wife and son – they'd discovered a common bond.

On one hand she was sorry to see him go. He was without question the most interesting man she'd met in years. She'd never expected to find *that* under these circumstances. Funny, it was like looking for a missing item around the house – it suddenly appeared when you stopped looking. Dana brushed her fingers across her keyboard, thinking. On the other hand, it must mean they were close to wrapping things up, and she'd probably have a settlement soon.

She wondered if he was expecting a call from her. This would certainly be a good excuse. Maybe this evening. Right now she needed to focus on the tasks in front of her. Closing that email, she forced herself to change directions and start on the contractors. Reaching for the phone, she opened a new Word document for making notes.

**

Kent stared hard at the computer screen, fighting the urge to put a fist into it. The numbers were worse than he expected. If he approved the amount, Dana could have a check in a few days. Trouble was, approving it happened after sharing the number with Dana. He was no coward, but throwing himself in front of an angry bull sounded like a better option at the moment.

They could appeal it, though in his experience that rarely yielded big bucks, so not worth the extra time and aggravation. He didn't know how much Dana owed on her mortgage, but he knew she'd need nearly twice what Heartland was offering her to build a new house. Numbers filled his brain as he considered ways to make this work. Once again he pondered ways of offering an anonymous grant. The company wouldn't like it – if they ever got wind of it. Even though he was a contract employee, he'd been their representative for this event. And any question of favoritism or impropriety would bring unwanted questions and possibly bad press. What about a zero-interest loan? Could he find a way to set it up so that she made payments to a third party to make it look legitimate?

He switched over to the FEMA website. What about those loans? Why hadn't anything come through yet? He knew they were busy, but come on. People's lives were on hold. At least Dana had gone on the trip with her friends before this news came in. The numbers may have kept her home, and he was glad that hadn't happened. A silver lining in there somewhere, he supposed, albeit a slim one. She was probably swamped with catch-up work today. How many emails did the head nurse at a small hospital get, he wondered. The closing notice had gone out, but had she seen it yet? It was possible she still didn't know.

Kent opened Dana's file. Had they missed something? Had *he* missed something? Damn. After all that talk about how he was going to help her. What had he come up with? Not much. He remembered telling her friend – bragging, really – how he could work the system. As that thought punched him in the gut, he considered something else. Could he somehow work through her friend? She'd contacted him about the library, and they'd talked a couple of times. Maybe Claire could say she was doing a renovation on her kitchen to help it sell and somehow offer appliances to Dana. He raked a hand through his hair. Ridiculous. She'd never buy it, and her friend would never lie to her. At least from what he could tell, they wouldn't keep secrets like that from each other.

But he had to do something. In the words of Mission Control, *failure was not an option.* Kent grabbed his sunglasses and keys, then headed for the door. Looked like it was time to make friends with some folks at National Bank & Trust of Whitfield. Maybe he could make her believe that the loans were deposited directly into an escrow account. Dana would never need to see an actual check or loan document.

236

At least he could investigate the possibilities.

**

She'd been on his mind so much that day, Kent at first thought he'd imagined Dana's number popping up on his cell phone. When the third ring confirmed her call, he shut down iTunes and picked up.

"Hey, Dana."

"Kent, hi. How are you?"

"Doing all right. How was the trip?" He held his breath as though waiting for a verdict, figuring her answer would reflect her mood.

"Really nice, thanks."

He heard the soft smile in her words, and let out a sigh of relief. She deserved that. "Glad to hear it."

"Yeah. Hey, I hear you're closing the office."

Kent ran a hand across the back of his neck. Right. Not a social call. "Yep. Moving the trailer out end-of-day Friday."

"So . . . what does that mean for me? For anyone not settled up yet?"

"No worries. We'll continue to work those claims out of the Wichita office. Except for me."

"Not you?"

"I'm sticking around for a couple of weeks at least. Tying up loose ends. I'll be working from my motel room."

"Oh, I see. I guess I'm one of those loose ends, huh?"

"You are. Did you have any luck with those contractors?"

"Actually yes. I have some appointments set up this week."

"Ah, that's great. Once you get someone lined up, things will really start moving."

"Yes. Speaking of moving, any word on when we'll finalize the money side of all this?"

Gulp. Kent didn't want to break the news to her over the phone. He thought fast. "Was just about to get to that. Any chance you'd want to meet me over at The Coffee House?" Or not. At seven-thirty, it was still ninety-two degrees out. Not to mention their last meeting at The Coffee House had been a disaster. What was he thinking? "On second thought, what about the Tasty Cream place in that little strip center on the north side? How does something cold sound?"

He tried to analyze the silence that greeted his suggestion. Was she pondering the menu options or reading something into his invitation?

"You want to go for ice cream?"

Her voice lifted, and Kent would swear she was amused. Or at least interested in the prospect. "Sure. You like ice cream, don't you?"

She laughed then, in a soft voice that sounded relaxed. "Of course I like ice cream. Who doesn't?"

"Well, I hear it's the place, so let's give it a try."

"Oh, believe me, I've been there. It's a good thing it's not downtown. I'd weigh another hundred pounds."

Kent doubted she could even claim one hundred, but knew it was best to steer clear of discussing weight with a woman. "Sounds like an endorsement to me. Want to meet me there?" he asked. "Or I can swing by and pick you up."

"I'll meet you. Give me ten minutes."

With mixed feelings, Kent lingered on the sidewalk, waiting while Dana pulled her car into the only open parking spot in front of Tasty Cream. When she spotted him, and smiled, something twisted inside. How many minutes before that smile turned to tears? "Hi, there," he said when she joined him. "Nice timing. Pretty busy around here."

"It always is," she told him, her glance shooting toward the small glass-front building painted with smiley-face ice cream critters. "But it turns over quickly, so we should be able to get a table inside."

"Perfect. Speaking of busy, I'm guessing you had a crazy day." He opened the door and they stepped into a line about six deep.

"Oh, yes," Dana said. "I'll be paying for that vacation all week long."

"But worth it?" he asked.

238

Her smile widened. "Every minute. We had so much fun."

"Glad to hear it." In that moment, he changed his mind. They were just two people out for ice cream on a warm summer night. No way was he going to spoil her mood.

They inched forward and Kent turned his attention to the cases in front of him. As they moved up, he had to stop himself from putting a hand on Dana's back. Why did it seem so natural to slide a hand across her shoulders when doing so would probably earn him an elbow to the chest?

He'd met dozens of single women in the years since Meredith's death, but nothing sparked. Something about Dana Gerard sent a little hum through his system. Probably not the least of which were her incredible sky blue eyes. Especially when they twinkled the way they did now as she gleefully surveyed the tubs of ice cream in the case in front of her.

"Cherry nut, please," Dana told the girl at the counter. "A single on a cone."

"Just a single?" Kent asked.

She shot him a look. "One is plenty. Oh, and an iced tea, please."

"Better make it a big scoop," he told their waitress. "And I'll have one of those Oreo shakes."

He'd only been teasing, but the woman took him seriously, and handed Dana an iced tea and a heaping cone with ice cream billowing over the sides.

When she turned, Kent winced.

"What?"

"It's very, um . . ."

"Pink," Dana finished. The coloring had clearly been artificially enhanced.

"Yeah. Let's go with that."

"And try to forget that I'm probably ingesting an unhealthy dose of red dye number whatever."

"Makes the sugar seem like health food then, right?"

Her lips curved into a wry smile. "Good thinking."

They jostled through the crowd to a tiny high-top table. Dana nodded to acquaintances, but didn't stop to talk. If she didn't start on this ice cream soon, it'd be dripping down her arm.

For several minutes, they kept the conversation light, focusing on the people-watching opportunities.

"Can't believe it took me more than two months to discover this place," Kent said.

"Me either. It's famous around these parts, pardner," she said in her best Western twang.

Kent laughed. "So I see."

When Dana finished her ice cream cone, she took a long drink of her iced tea and looked across the table at Kent, curious that he hadn't brought up the topic she thought they were there to discuss. Not that she minded forgetting about the money part of the ordeal for a while. But it was hanging out there like laundry in the breeze, waiting to be dealt with.

"Well how was it?" Kent asked when he met her eyes.

She nodded. "Very tasty, thanks. And your shake?"

"Excellent. I have a feeling I'll be back."

"You should since you only have a couple of weeks left."

Her words hung in the silence between them.

Kent leaned forward. "I've been talking to your friend Claire."

Dana blinked. What was that supposed to mean? "Claire?" she echoed.

"Heartland's commercial division has the policy for some of the county properties, including the Whitfield Library."

"Oh. Yes, Claire is the library's biggest champion. She was going to chair a major renovation a couple of years ago, but then–" Dana broke off, her face warming. That was not her story to tell.

"I know," Kent said quietly. "She told me about her son."

"She did?"

"Yeah."

That was probably good, Dana thought. For so long Claire couldn't even speak about Ben. It struck her then that Claire and Kent also had a common bond. They'd both lost sons.

"I'm thinking about helping to get the library rebuilt."

Dana frowned. "Heartland is, you mean?"

He shook his head. "No, not officially. The additions Claire has in mind are based on the previous plan that never got implemented. So, of course, the improvements won't be covered by the insurance."

"So what does that mean? A capital campaign, bond issue? It's bad timing. People will be stretched thin already. And–" She caught herself again. "I'm sorry. I don't mean to be negative. I'd love to see the library rebuilt."

"Remember that settlement I told you about?"

Slowly, she nodded. "Yours?"

"Yep. I'm thinking of making a contribution. Andy loved books. Before he died, he'd started reading a bunch of non-fiction on weather and things like fires and volcanoes." Kent looked past her a moment, a sad smile on his face, obviously remembering his son. When he looked at Dana again, he clapped his hands together. "Might be a good way to spend some of that money."

"It's a great idea. But are you sure you want to do that in Whitfield rather than Wichita?"

"Absolutely. This is where the need is. And I like Whitfield." His eyes wandered the shop. "It's a great town. Friendly people. Thinking about sticking around a while."

Dana sucked in her breath. "Really?"

Steady eyes met hers, and her chest fluttered. Quickly, she looked away, not wanting to read anything into his words.

"I think I'd like to see that rebuilt. It's important for the community. And for me, it's the payoff, you know? I like to be in on the fun stuff."

Dana sniffled, and gave a shaky smile. "Sure." She smoothed her napkin against the table, trying to keep from thinking about her own rebuilding. Would she get to the fun part? Or did the fun come only if you had money to play with? She couldn't begrudge Kent one second of fun, though. Not when she knew the source of his money, the pain and heartache he'd endured. No amount of money was worth that.

He cocked his head, his eyebrows raised. "What are you thinking?"

She took a deep breath. "I'm wondering why you haven't mentioned my rebuilding project."

Kent toyed with the straw in his shake while she waited for an answer. When his eyes met hers again, he sat back. "It can wait."

Dana thought her eyes would pop out of her head as she gaped at him. "Wait? I thought I was slowing the process down." Surely the settlement wasn't just a ploy to get her out for ice cream. Was it? Confused, she shook her head. "Kent. If you have some information for me, spit it out, okay?"

"Truth?"

"Yeah. Please."

"I hate being the one to give you bad news. Didn't want to spoil your mood."

She gave a little smile and leaned toward him. "Did you think ice cream with a cherry on top would soften the blow?"

To her surprise, he reached out and squeezed her hand. "Maybe."

She grinned then. "Am I so scary? Come on, spill."

He drew some papers from his back pocket. "I'm sorry. The preliminary offer is lower than I expected."

"Well, believe me, I have low expectations."

Kent coughed out a laugh. "Thanks for the vote of confidence."

"Nothing personal." As soon as the words escaped, she regretted them. Somehow, chatting over ice cream with Kent Donovan seemed rather personal, especially when he scooted his chair closer to hers to share the documents. Holding her breath, she kept her eyes fixed firmly on the papers in front of her.

He tapped his pen at a number in bold about two-thirds of the way down the paper. She stared a moment. It was lower than she was hoping for, too. Those numbers didn't add up to a house.

Suddenly, Kent scooped the papers up and they disappeared behind his back. "I'm not satisfied with this," he told her. "With your permission, I'm going back to corporate. Since you haven't started building, we have some time. We can appeal."

She stared at him, unsure whether she wanted to drag it out any longer. "Kent, do you really think it will do any good? Maybe we should just be done."

His jaw twitched. "It's your call."

Dana thought a moment, then released a heavy sigh. "I have appointments set up with three contractors this week. Why don't we wait and see what they have to say. I don't have to have the best of everything. I just need a simple place to live. Besides, if I get the admin promo–"

She broke off, groaning inside. Where the hell had that come from? Here she was worried Mary would let the word out, and instead she slipped up herself.

Kent didn't miss her goof. "You're up for a promotion?"

For another thirty minutes, they talked, and Dana told him about developments at the hospital.

"I know you're not asking for my advice," Kent said after she fell silent for a moment. "But it might be a good time to do something for yourself. And it would give you something to focus on besides your house."

"Sure. There are pros and cons to the–" She broke off as Cameron Wade came through the door. When she caught his eye, Dana waved, and motioned him back. Funny that she'd see Cam before she saw Chase. They'd missed each other all day, and she'd had three calls about the visit from the police yesterday. There was a question that needed answering.

"Cam, hi. How are you?"

"Hey, Dana, doing great. You?"

"Good, thanks." Dana made introductions then turned to Cameron. This wasn't the ideal setting, but she'd been waiting for a chance to speak to him about Chase.

"How are things going at the farm? Chase seems to be enjoying it."

Cam grinned. "The guys and I enjoy having him around."

"Oh, I'm glad to hear that. Thank you so much for giving him the opportu–"

He held up a hand. "No worries, Dana. He's a hard worker, and a good kid."

Pride swelled inside Dana, and she nodded.

He hitched a thumb toward the line. "I better get in this line, before it gets any longer. Got a whole houseful of folks waiting for ice cream. Could get ugly, you know?"

Dana laughed. "Yes. You better scoot, then."

"Good to meet you, Kent," Cameron said, then moved away from the table.

"My son is working for him this summer," Dana explained to Kent. She glanced outside, where the sun was slipping away, the sky turning a deep blue. "Speaking of work . . ."

"The work day comes early, I know," Kent said, sliding off of the barstool. When he held out his hand, Dana took it, and hopped down, grateful for his assistance. High-top tables and chairs could be difficult for short people to maneuver gracefully.

Outside, Kent braced an arm against her car. "Can I ask you a question?"

Dana hitched her purse over her shoulder, and smiled. "Of course."

"If we didn't have this insurance business and I asked you out for ice cream, or dinner, would you come?"

Dana hadn't dated for so long, she hardly knew how to act. But she knew one thing for sure – she had no interest in playing games. She found him attractive, and found his moral character refreshing. Meeting his eyes, she nodded. "I would." It was hard to read his face in the dim light, but the quick grin he flashed was unmistakable.

"Good to know. I'm not sure how the week's gonna shake out with closing down the office, but keep your phone handy, would you?"

244

Dana reached for her car door with one hand and held up her phone with the other. "Will do."

**

Dana hurried inside, anxious to finally talk to Chase.

"Hey, sweetie," she said when Chase strolled in from the patio. "Sorry I didn't get to see you this morning. Did you get dinner?"

"Yeah, I had some pizza."

Dana ran a hand across his back. "Hey, did something happen while I was gone? I heard the police were here yesterday."

"Yeah, I figured you'd hear about it."

"What happened?"

"Nothing. The police came to ask me some questions."

"Questions about what?"

"Did you hear that Charlie Fast died?"

Confused by the change of topic, Dana nodded. "Yeah."

"Well, I was getting gas at the Quick Stop across from the park Friday night, so they wanted to know if I saw anything. That's all."

"Did you?" Her hand flew to her chest. Oh, she hoped not.

"Saw Charlie for a minute. He was fine then."

"Huh. I wonder what's going on. There were police at the hospital today, too. I suppose any time there's a death, they have to look into the circumstances."

"Yeah, I guess. It was kind of weird, though, to have them come here."

Dana breathed a sigh of relief. How ridiculous that it'd prompted so much concern, and had nothing to do with Chase at all. "I'm sure it was, but don't worry about it. They're just doing their job."

"Yeah."

As he turned, Dana noticed he had something tucked under his other arm. She did a double-take. "What's that?"

He looked back at her. "What?"

She pointed. "That."

Chase raised the object in his hands. "A book."

245

"Oh, okay." Puzzled, she watched him head to the stairs. That looked like a big book – and that was not Chase's usual evening activity. No arguments from her about that, though. "Hey," she called as Chase started upstairs. "I saw Cam tonight at Tasty Cream. He says you're doing a great job."

"Cool."

"I'm proud of you," she hollered. Hands on her hips, she watched until he disappeared from sight. She'd love to know what he was reading, but he hadn't seemed inclined to share. A funny feeling settled over her. What was that all about?

Chapter Twenty-One

Getting time on Andrew's calendar had been easier than Dana expected. She wished she had nicer shoes and clothes to change into, but all she had was a black cardigan sweater that she often pulled on when the air conditioning got a little too chilly. She might not look like management material in the plain scrubs, but at least they proved she knew about life on the floor.

Vickie, the hospital's executive secretary, greeted Dana when she approached Andrew's office. "Go on in," she said. "He's expecting you."

She peeked around the door and caught Andrew's attention before entering the room. "Hey, Dana, how are you?" He beckoned her toward the chairs in front of his desk.

"Fine, thanks, Andrew. How about yourself?"

"No complaints. What can I do for you?"

Dana put a smile on her face and met Andrew's eyes. "I want to bounce an idea off of you."

"Fire away," Andrew told her, his peppered gray brows lifting a bit.

Deep breath. "How would you feel about me applying for the administrator's position?" She watched as mild interest turned to surprise, and then something like confusion.

"Brad's job?"

"Yes." Like a fissure in a frozen pond, she felt a tiny crack in the confidence she'd forced herself to present. It wasn't as though a light had gone on in Andrew's head. He didn't slap his forehead and say, "Why didn't I think of that?"

Instead, Andrew began twirling a pen from his desk. "You're not happy in your current position?"

"Oh, Andrew, of course I am. It's just that I've done it for ten years, and I thought . . . well, I thought this might be a good change. As you know, I'm–" She licked her lips. This was tricky. She didn't want to sound whiny. "I'm doing some of Brad's job now. And since you mentioned wanting someone who would connect with Whitfield," she let out a nervous laugh, "I'm pretty well-connected."

Andrew sat back in his executive office chair, nodding his head as he studied her. "That you are. I suppose I have no objection if you want to apply."

Dana's heart sank. Not exactly a vote of confidence. No offer of a glowing recommendation. She swallowed hard. "All right. Well, if it's okay with you, I'd like to use your name as a reference."

He gave her a polite smile. "No problem, Dana. That's fine."

She pulled her résumé out of her daytimer. "Would you like a copy of my résumé?"

He waved her off. "Give that to Amy. And be sure to submit the online application. We're starting to interview."

"Before the deadline?"

"We've already identified a few obvious candidates, so there's no reason to wait," Andrew explained.

"I see." Dana stood, pretty sure that was the end of the conversation. She knew she'd caught him off guard, but still, couldn't he at least feign interest if not enthusiasm? Good thing he wasn't trying to bluff a poker hand. Hoping her disappointment wasn't as obvious, she smiled and tucked the paper back inside the planner. "Sounds good. Thanks, Andrew."

Concentrating on the doorknob across the room, she turned and managed to walk to the door, though her legs were like mush.

In the corridor, doubt enveloped her. Now what? Should she even bother taking the résumé to Amy? She supposed she had to now. Andrew would be expecting to see her name on the candidate list. She groaned inside, wondering if she'd just opened Pandora's box.

Dana slipped inside the ladies room to regroup before heading back downstairs. When she lifted her hands to readjust her hair clip, her mother's ring twinkled in the overhead lights. She'd forgotten to take it off before coming to work. Slumping against the counter, she fingered the fine silver filigree. "What should I do, Mom?" she whispered. Was it a time to politely bow out or to throw caution to the wind and charge ahead? Her mother would most certainly encourage Dana to stand up for herself, but she'd also tell her to think quietly and decide what *felt* right. Do the right thing.

In her heart, Dana felt sure that having someone who knew and loved the people of Whitfield at the hospital's helm was right. And win or lose, it seemed like it was time to imagine herself in a new light. Being stuck in a rut wasn't good for her or the hospital.

Determined to finish what she'd begun, Dana retreated to her office and began transferring the information from her résumé into the online form HR was using for the job opening. Answering the short open-ended questions was harder – she didn't lack confidence in her abilities, but tooting her own horn didn't come easily. By the time she finished, her fingers ached from being frozen over the keyboard while she agonized over every word, and her brain hurt from the sheer mental energy of making sure every sentence was well-crafted, and sounded positive and upbeat.

As a reward, she reached into her purse for one of Claire's toffee chocolates that she'd stashed away. Then, for the second time that morning, she headed to the administrative offices. She walked past Vickie and gave a quiet knock on Amy's open door.

"Oh, hey, Dana. Come on in," Amy called. "How are things?"

"Great."

"Erika doing all right?"

Dana nodded. The new hire had hit the ground running, quickly relieving the workload of the other nurses. "She's terrific."

"Excellent. So what brings you in here? If you're looking for a lunch date, I'm open."

Dana smiled. "I wish, but I can't get away today. I'm sneaking out a little early to meet a contractor at my place this afternoon."

"Oh, okay." It was a statement, but the tone of her voice carried a question.

Taking a deep breath, Dana held her résumé out to Amy.

"I want to give you this and let you know I'm applying for the administrator's position. I've already talked to Andrew and just submitted the online application."

Amy's mouth opened. Then closed again.

"Dana. Wow. That's great." She reached for the paper. "I'll take that. Thanks."

Dana hesitated. "Are you getting many applications?"

"Quite a few, actually." Amy pressed her lips together. "Just out of curiosity, why'd you wait so long?" She held up a hand. "I'm sorry. I know you haven't had a lot of time, dealing with your house and all."

Still, she heaved a sigh as though something else was on her mind.

Dana shifted. "You're right. I had too many other things going on, and it finally hit me that this could be an opportunity."

Amy nodded, her eyes troubled.

"Is there a problem?"

"Oh, not at all. I'm glad you decided to apply. It's just that—"

She licked her lips again, and Dana's patience wore thin. Apparently no one was supportive of the idea. Fine. Couldn't they put on a professional façade? Maybe a smile, for heaven's sake? "Amy, just tell me. What's up?"

"Listen, Dana, I probably shouldn't say anything, but here's the deal. Andrew has gotten pretty involved this time around. I mean, he's been making calls, encouraging people to apply. I'm sure he hasn't made any promises. He knows better than that. Still, I can't be certain he hasn't set up some kind of expectation. You know what I mean?"

So that was it. That totally explained Andrew's lackluster response. Damn.

"Yes. I get it."

"He's pretty annoyed that we're hiring again, and that Brad left without much notice. Anyway, I know he's talked to a lot of people about the job."

Dana thrummed her fingers on the desk. "Well, I've submitted the application, so I guess I'm officially applying. Thanks for letting me know. At least I won't get my hopes up."

Amy stood. "Oh, Dana. I'm so sorry. I wish we'd known sooner. Heck, I wish I'd thought to ask you about it." She held up her hands. "It makes so much sense."

"Thanks, Amy. It's not a problem, really." She attempted a smile. "Maybe after I get my place rebuilt I can take a couple of management classes and be ready for next time, you know?"

"Sure. That's a good idea."

"I'd better get back on the floor."

"All right. We'll keep you posted. I'm sure you'll get an interview. We've been sorting applications as they come in and have already narrowed it down."

That took Dana by surprise. "Really? What about hospitality?"

Amy's face pinched with a guilty wince. "With your vacation and the situation with your house, plus doing some of Brad's work, Andrew decided you had enough going on. We had the gals at Sheridan Drug put together a couple of gift bags." She gave a little laugh. "So you're off the hook."

"Oh. Okay." No complaints there.

Dana tried to put the job quandary out of her mind for the rest of the day, lingering with patients as much as she could. But as she walked slowly up and down the hallway with Mrs. Garrison on her arm, she realized the seed had taken hold. Though she enjoyed her patients, a younger nurse with fewer credentials should be doing this. With her other hand, Dana pushed the hair back from Mrs. Garrison's face. "Your color's better today," she said. "Dr. Talisman says you'll be going home as soon as you get your strength back, Julia. Are you ready?"

"Oh, yes," the woman said.

Dana watched the floor, careful not to trudge on Julia's slipper-footed toes, and reminded herself that she absolutely could not start feeling dissatisfied with her job. As a supervisor, she knew that a nurse who didn't want to be there didn't give the best care, didn't connect with patients, and was easy to spot. She refused to be that nurse. Swinging around, she grasped both of Julia's hands. Walking backwards, she faced her patient and gave her a wide grin. "Let's get our groove on, Julia," she sang out. "You're doing great."

At four-thirty, Dana left the hospital. She was ready to go home and put the day behind her, but she couldn't do it quite yet. Not until she met with Gary from Ace Builders. His truck was already in her driveway, and two men were standing out front.

Dana climbed out of the car. "Hello," she called.

One of the men strode toward her, arm outstretched. "Hello, Ma'am. I'm Gary Matthews. You must be Mrs. Gerard."

"Yes. Dana, please. Thanks so much for coming today."

"We took the liberty of looking around. This is John, by the way. We've got our measurements. Now, we've got a few questions."

As did she.

"Are you wanting to use the same foundation and floor plan?"

"Is that cheaper?" She could see her vision of a new laundry room growing dim already.

"Yes, ma'am, generally. That's not to say things can't be moved around within the space, though."

She listened while Gary went over various options and the company's timeline. "We could probably get you started in October. 'Course then we start getting into bad weather. I'm guessing we could finish up next May. That's a guestimate."

"Of course. As I mentioned on the phone, I'm on a tight budget," Dana reminded him. "I need good, solid construction without a lot of bells and whistles."

"Yes, ma'am. We understand. That we can do."

Thirty minutes later, he shoved a folder at her. "Here's where we start. You look through here and see if anything catches your eye. Everything can be changed, but it gives us something to work with. There's a chart that outlines materials and the square footage of your home in a good, better, best scenario."

"That's perfect. Thanks so much."

"We'll follow up with you next week. In the meantime, don't hesitate to call if you have any questions."

Dana waved as the men climbed into their truck. Okay, one down, two to go. That wasn't so bad. Progress, anyway. She looked down at the thick folder in her hands. Definitely an after-dinner-with-a-glass-of-wine project.

**

Dana looked up from the documents she'd spread on the kitchen table, trying to visualize the dimensions listed in the documents. Then she remembered there was someone she'd intended to speak to tonight.

With the day crammed full, she'd pushed last night's enlightening conversation with Kent to the back burner, but now it came forward full force. Claire Stapleton was up to something with Kent. That was one thing. And then that other. Dana sucked in her breath. She wanted to tell Claire about her application – needed someone she could trust to help her analyze the situation. There was no way she could go through the entire process and not have someone to hash through it with her. Or vent to. Wasn't that what friends were for?

Dana pulled her cell phone out of her purse. Two rings later, Claire's voice came on the line.

"Hey, there," Claire said.

"Hi. How's it going?"

"Not too bad. What's up with you?"

"I did it."

"Uh-huh," Claire drawled. "Pretend you're talking to a slow, clueless friend. Define *it*."

"I applied for the admin job."

Claire's tone quickly changed. "Oh, that's great, Dana. Good for you. I'm glad you put yourself out there. Do you know anything about the timeframe or the competition?"

"I know they want to move fast, and I found out Andrew has made a few calls trying to round up candidates. So I'm sure there'll be competition."

"Oh, too bad. Well, not to worry. At least this gets you off of hospitality, right?"

Dana heard the humor in Claire's voice, and knew her friend was trying to help her stay positive. "That's one way to look at it," Dana told her. "The bad thing is now I don't get to meet the candidates. This could come back to bite me, you know?"

"But now you'll be the one to be wined and dined. That could be fun."

Dana hadn't thought about that. Would she? Or would they only wine and dine the people they brought in from out of town? She knew from past experience that the wining and dining was offered only to the top candidates. *Ugh*. One more thing to add to her radar. "Hmm. Not sure. I guess if I don't get that, I'll know I'm not at the top, huh?"

"Not necessarily. They don't need to spend as much time getting to know you. The good thing is you've already got a job you love, so it's no sweat if it's not your time. Like you said before, you've got a lot on your plate."

"Yes, and speaking of, that brings me to another reason for calling."

"You need a reason to call?" Claire asked, feigning hurt feelings.

"Most of the time, no, but it just happens that today I do have another reason. His name is Kent Donovan."

There was a moment of silence before Claire responded. "What about him?"

"I hear you may be working together."

"Now don't get testy," Claire said. "He thinks he might be able to get some funding above the insurance payoff to help rebuild the library. I swear I did not ask him. He volunteered that Heartland always contributes to some public property in a big disaster like this. And since the library was just about the only public property destroyed . . ." Her voiced trailed off. "You're not mad, are you?"

Dana sputtered out a laugh. "Of course not. What is there to be mad about?" She responded to Claire, but her thoughts went back to her conversation with Kent. The story didn't quite match. Kent alluded to spending his own money on the project, not Heartland's. Huh. Maybe he didn't want Claire to know about his money. Dana couldn't help feeling a little spark of pleasure that Kent had apparently shared his personal history with her only.

"Nothing," Claire said. "In fact, I may be doing you a favor."

"How's that?"

"By keeping him in town a little longer."

As her face warmed, Dana was glad Claire couldn't see it.

"How do you know about it, anyway?" Claire demanded. "You must've been talking to him."

"Yes, I talk to him regularly, you know."

"I could see him sticking around Whitfield," Claire said. "I think he likes it." She sniffed into the phone. "Just saying."

But for how long, Dana wondered. Until the next natural disaster? Would the adrenaline rush he got from working an event lure him away, or was he really ready to sign on for a permanent address again? Maybe she'd get some insight tomorrow night. She'd agreed to a mid-week dinner date since she wasn't available this weekend. It'd be their first time to get together on a strictly social basis. Her eyes tracked back to the brochure. That is, if she could keep from asking his opinion on her contractor options. As she thought about it, though, she wouldn't mind getting his read on their offers. In fact, she realized with a thud to her chest, she wanted the man's opinion.

Chapter Twenty-Two

The next morning, Dana lingered on Claire's porch a moment, her mind still on her house and the upcoming date with Kent. Already she could hear the sounds of rebuilding in the distance – trucks and hammering. They were starting early, she supposed, to beat some of the heat. She glanced up at the high clouds that still held a pinkish tint. They'd be gone in a hurry, as would any hint of cool air. With temperatures soaring into the high nineties, they were starting to get heat-related issues at the hospital.

As she drove to work, she made a mental note to touch base with the fire department about making rounds with cold water and checking on known shut-ins.

She'd barely stepped inside her office when her phone rang.

"Dana Gerard."

"Dana, it's Amy. I need to set up an interview with you."

Dana knew they wanted to move fast, but she was surprised to get Amy's call so soon. "Wow, you guys aren't messing around," she said, with a little laugh.

"No reason to," Amy said. "Will tomorrow work for you?"

As if she'd say no, Dana thought, a tremor of excitement shooting through her. "Of course. What time?"

"Why don't you come up to the conference room at eight forty-five?"

"Perfect. Amy, thank you so much. I'm thrilled to have the interview."

"No problem. You're a strong candidate, Dana."

Her heart bounced. Was she? "I don't suppose you can tell me how many other strong candidates there are?"

"That, I cannot. But I can tell you I think we'll have a decision next week."

"Seriously?"

"We'll make an offer. Of course it could still take several weeks to start someone if they have to give notice in their present job."

"Right." Fine by her. The sooner, the better. It'd be a relief to have it decided one way or the other. "Sounds good. Thanks, Amy."

Dana inhaled a deep breath. Either way, it meant big changes were right around the corner.

**

By the time Dana slipped back into her car that afternoon, she felt as though she'd worked an entire week, and was already looking forward to another weekend off, due to Maddie's visit. Normally, Dana would've scheduled herself to work both Saturday and Sunday to make up for her vacation.

It wasn't lost on her as she headed home that the hospital administrator would work neither. It would be so strange to work a straight eight-to-five shift Monday through Friday – no more weekend shifts, except when they held special events like a health fair. Of course, it meant she'd have to let go and trust her staff even more than she did now.

No different than the night shift, she told herself. She didn't have to worry about that. In fact, tonight she was determined not to – it was almost time for her date with Kent.

Inside the house, she dropped her purse on the kitchen table. The one good thing about her limited wardrobe was that it made choosing what to wear easy – the new yellow dress was the obvious answer.

First, a quick shower, then– Dana stopped short, and tiptoed to the couch where Chase was sprawled. She

258

peeked over and saw that he was sound asleep. Resisting, the urge to run a hand across his cheek, she glanced at the coffee table. That it was littered with a Dr. Pepper can and an open bag of pretzels was no surprise, but the spiral notebook and several books were curious. Stepping cautiously around the couch, she took a closer look. In addition to a current edition of The Farmer's Almanac were a textbook on farm management and a handbook on soil conservation. She shot a swift glance at Chase.

Dana took a step back and dropped into a stuffed armchair. Chase was clearly studying. Where'd he get this stuff? Had he enrolled in an online class?

He must have sensed her staring at him because he shifted and opened his eyes. He looked at her a moment before he came fully awake and sat up. "Hey."

"Hi, sweetie." She motioned to the table. "Looks like you've been busy."

Chase looked at the table then back at her with a sheepish smile. "Oh. Yeah." He began stacking the books.

"So what's going on? Are you taking a class?"

"Nah. Just doing some stuff with Poppa."

Dana's chest fluttered. "Really? Where'd the books come from?"

"Jansen. He let me borrow them."

Dana shook her head, trying to understand. "You and Jansen and Poppa have some kind of study thing going on?"

"Yeah."

Both puzzled and pleased, she let out a laugh, "Well, that's great. Why didn't you tell me?"

He shrugged. "No big deal."

A giddy kind of relief swept through Dana. He did this on his own. He'd found something he was interested in. She licked her lips. "Is it– How's it going?"

"Good."

"Oh, honey, I'm so glad. Wow. Looks like cool stuff."

"Most of it."

She smiled. "Are you going out tonight?"

He picked up the can and took a drink before answering. "Nah. I don't think so."

"Really? Just hanging out here? What are the other guys up to?"

Another shrug. "Not sure."

He could've knocked her over with a feather. As far as she could tell he hadn't been out since Friday night. Dana watched him for a moment, searching for any clues in his body language, wondering if something was up. "Tired?"

"I guess."

"All right, well, this is kind of funny – I actually am going out tonight," she told him, pushing herself up from the chair. She ran a hand through his hair. "You need anything before I leave?"

"Nah, I'm fine." He stood, and picked up his keys. "Think I'm gonna go get a pizza or something."

"Okay, I better get ready." And obviously, she needed to find time to check in with her dad. Maybe she could get a few more details out of him. From the looks of things, true to his word, he'd taken Chase under his wing. "Thank you, Daddy," she whispered.

**

Back downstairs, it occurred to Dana that Chase had spared her an awkward introduction. As far as he knew, she was simply going out with friends. She remembered Kent standing on the porch once before and she'd declared that they were friends. So, technically, that was true.

She smiled inside, looking forward to the evening. And when Kent pulled his car up to the curb, she stepped outside with a smile for him as well.

"Hello," she called.

He met her at the porch. "Wow. You look stunning," he told her.

"Thank you," she said. She'd parted her hair to one side and left it loose, and added some night-on-the-town make-up that accentuated her eyes.

"Hey, I made reservations at the Country Chef. Hope that's okay. I know we've been there before, but–"

"It's perfect," Dana said.

"We could go to Paxton if you'd rather."

Dana shook her head. "Not at all. No reason to drive all the way to Paxton. Besides, I like keeping the business in town."

The miniature lights twinkled at the restaurant entrance and inside the bar, though it wasn't dark enough to get the full effect. Dana glanced around the dining room. Each table was set with a white tablecloth and dotted with fresh flowers. She made a mental note to tell owners Stella and Jim Englewood how nice the place looked.

"Right this way," the hostess said.

Kent's warm hand rested lightly on Dana's back as he followed her. A glance to the left stopped her though, and her head whipped around as she looked again. She sucked in her breath. Seated at a table near the window were Andrew and his wife, a couple of hospital board members and a woman Dana didn't recognize. She recognized the scenario, though. The wining and dining of candidates had commenced. Right here. Right under her nose.

"Is this a habit," Kent whispered under his breath, "or are you testing my reflexes? Or do you want a matching pair of beat-up toes?" He took her arm and walked beside her when she her legs began to move again.

Dana shook her head. "Oh, Kent, I'm so sorry. I didn't mean to—" She grinned up at him. "No, I don't need a matching pair, so thank you for that quick evasive maneuver. Very impressive."

"You're welcome."

When the hostess stopped at a small booth and placed menus on the table, Dana debated whether it would be better to watch the proceedings or ignore them. In the end, she couldn't help herself. She took the seat with a view of the group. This way, she could look at Kent, and easily let her gaze slide behind him now and then.

But she struggled to keep her eyes on the menu. Her head kept bobbing up, her gaze veering that direction. The woman looked about Dana's age, wore a beige suit with dark grey blouse and a single strand of pearls. Very traditional. Her short brown hair appeared to be teased in front, coming to a point just at her earrings.

Kent swiveled, then looked back at Dana. "I have a feeling I've lost you. What's going on back there?"

Dana winced. It wasn't her intent to offend her dinner date. "Kent, I'm sorry." She leaned toward him with a slight nod of her head. "Don't turn around. I'm sizing up the competition."

His eyebrows hitched up. "Oh, yeah? You sure?"

"Oh, yeah."

"Well, maybe I should come sit by you so we can compare notes."

Dana grinned, grateful for his good humor. "Actually, I like having you there to block their view of me."

"Glad to be of service. It's a wonder you don't have whiplash from when you first saw them."

Laughing, Dana rubbed her neck. "You know, I think I might."

Kent ordered a bottle of wine, and they fell into easy conversation.

When the waiter returned and filled two glasses, Kent lifted his toward Dana. "To business that becomes pleasure."

She swirled her wine and met his eyes. "Bet you never thought that was going to happen."

His eyes crinkled as his smile widened. "Some challenges are worth a little extra effort."

"Well, thank you for making the effort. You've been so patient and helpful. I don't know what I would've done if you'd given up on me."

Kent shook his head. "You'd have been fine. Sometimes you have to go through all the steps – the anger and frustration and sadness – before you can catch your second wind and get going again."

She took a deep breath. "Not sure I'm there yet, but working on it."

"You'll get there. A day at a time."

In the pause, Dana glanced behind him. The candidate was speaking, gesturing with her hands. Probably explaining an idea, promoting herself. Or was she charming them? Regaling them with a humorous anecdote, perhaps?

Kent jerked his head toward the table. "That could be part of it, you know. Change can be energizing. So can rebuilding. You get out of your comfort zone and see new possibilities."

Dana smiled at his optimism, figuring that forcing himself to stay positive had been the way he'd survived his own dark days. "True." She turned her attention back to him. "Tell me about your ideas for rebuilding the library."

Something flickered across his face, maybe melancholy. "It's about the kids. I want it to be a fun place with computers and big screens where kids can play with words, use their imaginations, find adventure. Claire's talking about a storytelling stage and reading nooks. It won't appeal to every kid, but it's just as important as providing good schools and parks and fields for physical activity."

"You must have been such a great dad," Dana said softly.

"Wasn't until Andy was in the third grade, not long before he died, that I realized how short a time there is to really work with a kid, to encourage their curiosity and get them on track to love learning."

"Did you coach or run Boy Scouts, anything like that?"

Kent heaved a visible sigh, as his shoulders lifted. "That last year I'd committed to helping out one of the other dads with the Boy Scout Troop. After Andy died, I tried to keep it up. I wanted to keep a connection alive, but it didn't work."

Troubled eyes met hers. "It was too hard. Not just on me, but on the kids and the other parents. I made everyone uncomfortable. Nobody knew what to do or say, you know?"

Dana nodded. "I totally understand wanting to keep a connection, though."

"I had to pull back. For a while, I tried to stay in touch with other families, but it was hard. When his class of kids graduated from high school I felt like I should be there. My sister warned me against going, but I went anyway."

He set his glass on the table and stared into it a moment before his gaze came back to her. "Dumb. Didn't make it half-way through the ceremony. I didn't belong there. I think that's when I finally realized I had to let go."

"Oh, Kent. I can't even imagine how hard that must have been."

"So now I do things from a distance. Works a lot better. It's a kind of therapy, I suppose. I can help other kids without having that personal attachment."

"I think the library project sounds wonderful. And if you decide you want to work more closely with kids, there's always a need for helpers in Four-H. Whitfield has a pretty active organization."

He sent her a long, thoughtful look. "Good to know. Might have to check it out one of these days."

When movement from the table near the window caught her eye, Dana glanced at her watch – and realized she'd paid no attention to those proceedings for the last hour. She'd been completely engrossed in her conversation with Kent.

Their waitress refilled drinks and set a dessert menu on the table.

Kent raised his brows. "Care for dessert? Or we could run over to Tasty Cream." He rested muscular arms on the table, a smile in his eyes. "Or . . . dessert here, and ice cream tomorrow night?"

Dana smiled while she shook her head. "I appreciate the offer, but I have to tell you, I can't go out with you if all we ever do is eat." As soon as the words left her lips, she regretted them, realizing that left to interpretation – and imagination – other things they could do. A hot flush spread over her face, and the gleam in Kent's eyes told her his thoughts had taken the same route.

His voice dropped to a warm drawl. "I'm open to other ideas."

She choked out a laugh, and reached for her glass of ice water, trying to come up with something clever to

264

suggest, but failing. "Well, hmm, let's see," she stammered. "There's a movie theater."

Kent cracked a smile. "Uh-huh. We could go to a movie."

Dana gulped more water, and let the awkward moment pass, but knowing she'd revisit it on her own later.

They declined dessert, and after Kent took care of the check, they moved to the door. And an idea popped into Dana's head. She made sure not to stop walking while she talked, however.

"Have you been out to Crawford Lake?"

"No, but I've heard of it."

"It's a pretty place to walk and watch the sunset. Only about thirty minutes from town."

He opened the door, and they stepped outside where the sun was already well into its descent. "A little too late for tonight, but there's always next weekend. You said no food, but can I bring a bottle of wine?

Dana caught her breath as the scene played in her head. That he had suggested it was testimony to the fact that he was like no other man she'd ever dated. She'd taken her kids there for afternoon picnics, and she knew they'd been out there for fishing with buddies. There were generally a few couples holding hands walking the trails, but she'd never been one of them.

"That sounds lovely. I'll come up with some glasses we can take." If she couldn't find anything left in Claire's cupboards, she'd run by the five-and-dime and pick up some plastic tumblers.

Back at Claire's house, Kent parked at the curb and walked Dana up to the porch. "How about Friday night?"

"Sure. That'd be– Oh, rats. That won't work. Remember, my daughter's coming to visit." Conflicting emotions surprised Dana. She was looking forward to seeing Maddie, but an evening at the lake with Kent sounded . . . well, romantic. She shot him a glance. Could she have both?

"I'm not positive she'll be in Friday night. She could decide to drive in Saturday morning. I'll check and let you know if Friday's open."

"Sounds good." His voice dropped, and Dana knew even before he leaned in that she was about to be kissed. And not on the cheek this time.

Her eyes closed, and Kent's warm lips met hers.

"I had a nice time tonight," he whispered before pulling back.

Dana smiled. "Me too. Thank you."

"I'll see you later."

Dana couldn't quite bring herself to hope that Maddie wouldn't come until Saturday, but it would be all right if she didn't. Then again, there was no reason she and Kent couldn't go to the lake on Sunday, or next weekend. That lake wasn't going anywhere. And, she thought rather happily, neither was Kent Donovan.

Chapter Twenty-Three

On Thursday morning, Dana slipped into the new jacket, humming the tune from the *Working Girl* soundtrack while she mentally reviewed her bullet points of accomplishments as head nurse and goals for the hospital. The feather in her cap, of course, was that she'd played a key role in successfully handling the biggest disaster in the history of Whitfield – and it was still a hot topic of conversation. Whenever possible, she'd also add evidence of her long-time ties to the community. Maybe a little name-dropping here and there, too, she mused.

She glanced at her watch. In anticipation of her interview, she'd gotten up early. Too early. Going to the hospital and hanging around all dressed up would be ridiculous. Instead, she headed back to the kitchen, refilled her coffee and picked up the newspaper. She flipped it open, and a second later gasped in disbelief at the headline.

"Oh, no. Oh, God, who would do such a thing?"

"What? What happened, Mom?" Chase's wide eyes stared at her from across the kitchen table.

She couldn't help it. Dana sank into a chair, her eyes tearing up. After all these years, what would compel someone to hurt a harmless old man? Of course no place was insulated, but in Whitfield? What was *wrong* with people?

"What's the matter, Mom?"

She pushed the newspaper toward Chase. "Charlie didn't have a heart attack. It was subdural hematoma . . . internal bleeding and swelling inside his brain. They think someone hurt him, and that's what triggered it."

"How would they know that?"

"Autopsy, and other injuries. I guess someone called the police and said they'd seen something going on over at the park that night. That's why they've been investigating. That's why they were talking to everyone who was at the park or gas station that night." She stared at Chase. "You didn't see anything?"

"Saw Charlie, but he was fine then."

Chase looked from his mother's face to the newspaper, hardly daring to skim the article. Who saw? And what did they see? Could they identify anyone? Was it Kyle and Luke? He hadn't heard from either one of them since then, and the police hadn't been back. He'd just started to breathe a little easier. In his mind, he'd figured they'd decided it was an accident, and that's why they hadn't pursued it. Hell, the guy was old and crazy. Besides, it was dark. What could anybody see?

Another thought had his heart pounding. If it *was* Luke and Kyle, would they implicate him? What if they got caught and thought he ratted on them? They'd been in scrapes before. He knew they were in trouble a few years ago over some kind of Halloween prank, but nothing really serious. He wished he knew whether the video showed the park, or just the gas station and the street. Still, he reminded himself, Charlie had been fine when they left. He probably fell down on his way home.

Chase stood up and grabbed his cereal bowl. "Wow. That's weird," he said.

He thought for a minute, hoping the running water would drown out the sound of the spoon in his shaking hand clanking against the bowl. Play it cool. There's no evidence. Don't freak. Buying some time, he put the bowl in the dishwasher, but suddenly his insides churned. He had to get out of there. With his stomach in knots, Chase stopped beside his mother. "Mom, you gonna be all right? I, uh, I gotta get going."

His mother nodded, and reached for his hand. She smiled up at him, but still had tears in her eyes. "Sure, sweetie. I've got to go, too. I have my interview this morning." She swiped a hand under her eye. "Guess I'd better fix my make-up."

"Okay. Good luck."

"Thanks. I'll see you later."

**

Cameron was still giving instructions, going over the plan for the week, when Chase saw the black police car pull into the drive. His blood turned to ice as he watched the car, as if in slow motion, snaking along toward the barn, dust billowing around it.

Pete nodded his head. "Looks like trouble caught up with you, Cam."

Cameron turned, then shook his head. "Hang on a sec. Let me see what this is all about." He moved toward the driveway, waiting for the tricked-out Ford Explorer to come to a complete stop.

Chase waited, too, his throat as dry as the fog of dust that still hung in the air. He held his breath as Sheriff Howard Tandy climbed out of the car. Officer Riley stepped out from the other side.

"Morning, Howard," Cameron said. "What brings you out this way?"

Chase could see Tandy's eyes shift to the rest of the group. To him, he'd swear. The blood pounded in his ears, about to explode.

"Need to speak to one of your employees," Howard said.

"That right?" Surprise lifted Cam's voice. He motioned behind him. "Well, your timing's good. Everybody's right here."

"I need Chase Gerard."

Chase's face burned hot as all eyes turned to him.

Cam took a couple of steps back. "Chase, come on over here. How 'bout everyone else go ahead and get started?"

The crew shifted and shuffled, but as far as Chase could tell, nobody left. On legs that were stiff as rusted-out tractor gears, Chase moved forward. When he reached Cameron, his boss put a hand on his shoulder and walked with him the few remaining steps to Tandy.

"Chase Gerard?" the man asked. As if that hadn't already been established.

"Yes, sir." Chase glanced at Cameron who hadn't budged. He wished he'd leave. The fact that the sheriff had shown up in front of everyone was humiliating enough already. He figured this wasn't going anywhere good.

Meeting Tandy's eyes, Chase forced his shoulders down. Be cool. You did nothing wrong, he chanted inside.

Tandy squared himself in front of Chase, then unfolded a piece of paper.

The words "warrant" blared at him from the top of the page. Chase's mouth dropped open as his eyes met Tandy's. "A warrant? For what?" Chase stood, clenching his fists.

"It's a search warrant, son. We'd like to take a look inside your car."

"For what?"

Tandy ignored the question. "We need you to unlock your car."

"Fine," Chase mumbled. What the hell? What did his car have to do with anything? He yanked his keys out of his pocket and stormed to his car, ready to get this over with.

"The trunk, too, please," Riley said. He shot Chase a cool look. "We talked to your buddies."

Chase's hands tightened around his keys. What was that supposed to mean? He was pissed because he'd had to do his job, because Chase didn't rat on people? Well, too bad. Ignoring Riley, Chase opened the trunk, and Tandy began opening the other car doors, starting with the back seat.

"This your cap, son?" Tandy asked, straightening.

Frowning, Chase moved forward. What cap? His stomach twisted when he saw the checkered cap that Charlie Fast wore every single day. And every person in

Whitfield would recognize. Shock rooted Chase to the ground. What the hell was it doing in his car and how did it get there? Groaning inside, he put the pieces together. That stupid Kyle. He'd taken Charlie's hat. *Shit.* How did Chase not think to make sure he gave it back? He'd been in such a hurry to get them out of the park, he'd forgotten about the hat.

Chase swallowed hard before meeting Tandy's eyes. "No, it's not. I don't know how that got in there."

"Know who it belongs to?" Tandy held up the cap, and when he turned it over, Chase sucked in his breath. A dark red splotch stained the back of Charlie's cap. Blood. Oh, holy shit. That had to be blood.

"Hey, Riley?" Tandy hollered at his partner, but his eyes never left Chase.

"Yeah?"

"I'm going to need a plastic bag."

"Sure thing."

Riley jogged to the SUV and returned with a plastic bag. He held it open, and Tandy dropped the hat inside. He held Chase's eyes. "So maybe now you'll want to tell us about those friends, huh?"

Leaning against Chase's car, Tandy faced Chase. "You're saying you don't know whose hat it is or how it got in your car?"

Chase clenched his jaw. Maybe he ought to tell Riley to go ask Kyle about it. He could give the cops the idiot's address and cell number. A sinking feeling hit Chase like a punch in the gut. Did Kyle take the hat and hurt Charlie? Could it have happened that fast? But he'd seen Charlie walk away. Charlie was fine.

"Yeah, that's right," he finally told Tandy. "I don't know."

With a shake of his head, Tandy pushed off from the car. "Chase Gerard, you're under arrest. You have the right to remain silent . . ."

He heard the infamous words, but his brain refused to accept them. This could not be happening. Oh, God. While the sheriff said his spiel, Chase heard Cameron mutter "shit" under his breath.

Chase flinched when Riley came around and stood beside Tandy – holding a pair of handcuffs. No way.

"Whoa, hold on," Cameron interrupted. "Wait a sec, Howard. Cam turned to Chase. "Do you know what this is about?"

Chase kicked at the ground. "Yeah, but they're wrong."

"You don't have to answer any questions."

Chase met his eyes. "It's about Charlie Fast, and I've got nothing to hide."

"I'm sure you don't," Cam said, his voice calm and reassuring. "Just the same, I want this done right."

"In that case, we better get on down to the station," Tandy said.

Riley started forward with the cuffs, and Cam stepped in. "Howard, come on. Surely that's not necessary."

The sheriff waved Riley off, then motioned toward the SUV.

Chase licked his lips, trying to think of an alternative. "What about my car?"

"You can deal with that later," Tandy said.

"Are you charging him with a crime, Howard?" Cam spoke up again.

"Not yet," Tandy said, his voice clipped.

"Then he can take his own car, right? Why can't he follow you to the station?"

"Sorry, Cameron. Can't do that."

Riley opened the back car door.

Cam nodded at Chase. "You go on. I'll call your mom. I'm sure this can all be resolved, but it's best to follow the rules, so just sit tight until you have that attorney, all right?"

"No," Chase croaked. "Don't call my mom." God, no.

"Do you know which attorney to call?" Cam asked.

Chase's mind went blank. Who the hell was their attorney? He knew his mom had a divorce attorney. They'd talked to attorneys when his grandmother and aunt died, but he couldn't come up with a single name.

Cam rested a hand on Chase's shoulder again. "Chase. I'll call her. Don't worry. It'll be fine."

Head down, Chase willed himself not to cry as his face burned. He couldn't look at the rest of the guys.

**

"You look so sharp," Val whispered, poking her head into Dana's office at eight-thirty.

Dana had finally broken down and spilled the secret to Val. It was just too hard not to, especially showing up in obvious interview attire. "Thanks."

"Oh, boy, I hope they—"

Dana held up a hand to interrupt her. "Just a sec. That's the third time my phone has rung in less than five minutes." She pulled it out of her pocket and frowned. The same number three times. But she didn't recognize it. "Let me find out who this is." She pushed send to redial the last caller. It picked up immediately.

"Dana?"

"Yes. Who's this?"

"It's Cam Wade."

Sudden alarm bells blasted in Dana's head, and her heart hammered. Oh, God, had there been an accident at the farm?

"Cam, what's up? Is something wrong?"

"I'm not sure, but—"

She heard the heavy sigh before the pause, and her fear escalated. "But what?" she cried.

"Listen, try to stay calm. The sheriff was here a few minutes ago. He, uh, he took Chase. They're on their way to the station."

What? Dana frowned into the phone, her mind trying to switch gears. "Cam, what are you talking about?"

"Don't worry, I told him not to answer any questions without an attorney."

"An attorney?" Dana echoed. This made no sense. "An attorney for what?"

"Something about Charlie Fast."

"Charlie Fast? Why would—" Oh, God. No. The blood drained from her face, and she let out a strangled

273

cry. Val reached for her, but Dana stepped back, fear nearly doubling her over.

"Dana, what is it?"

"Dana?" came the distant voice from the phone.

"Yes," she whispered. "I'm here."

"You might want to get over there and see what's going on. I'm sorry, angel. He's under arrest. They read him his rights."

"What?" She screeched then clamped a hand over her mouth. They read him his rights? *Chase?* Her little boy? Oh, no, no, no. That wasn't right.

"Can you go?"

"I– of course. Oh, God, Cam. I'm going now." Her numb fingers fumbled with the lock on her desk drawer. When it finally released, she yanked up her purse and headed for the door.

She waved a hand toward Val. "I've got to leave."

"Now?" Val grabbed her arm. "But– Dana, wait. What about your interview?"

Dana stopped cold. "My inter– I don't know. But I can't. I've got to go. Now." She turned with Val on her heels.

"What should I tell them?"

"I don't care!" Dana shouted. "Tell them I had to leave." At the top of the stairs, Dana turned back. "Tell them I had a family emergency."

She didn't make it to her car before her phone pealed again. With shaking hands, she took the call. "Chase?"

"Hey, mom," came the familiar voice.

Tears choked her. "Oh, Chase. What's going on? Are you all right?"

"I'm fine. Have you talked to Cameron?"

Dana slipped into the car and jabbed her key at the ignition. It took several tries before the key hit its mark. "Yes. I'm on my way."

"Okay, but don't freak out. They just want to ask me some questions."

"Why?" Dana cried. "You said they already asked you questions. I don't understand."

"I don't know what they're thinking, Mom. But–"

274

Dana heard the hesitation. "But, what, Chase? Do you know something about this?"

"Here's the deal. Luke and Kyle might know something."

Dana's heart pounded. "Oh, no."

"I don't know for sure, Mom. Luke said they didn't do anything, and I wasn't with them. I need an attorney, though."

"That's exactly right. Don't do anything until I get there."

Dana found their family attorney's number in her directory and punched it in. While she frantically told Mitchell Dodd the little she knew, Dana drove to the police station, Cam's word playing over and over in her head – an unwelcome voice that had burst in and shattered her day.

Rushing through the door of the police station, she looked around, searching for her son, but was met by a brick wall and a large window, its tall panes presumably made of bullet-proof glass. Imposing and unfriendly steel doors set back on one side of the window.

"Ma'am?" An officer pushed off from the counter and stepped in front of her. "Can I help you?"

Her blood pressure skyrocketing off the charts, Dana figured she looked like a crazy woman. She took a deep breath and tried to speak calmly. "I'm Dana Gerard. I need to see my son. He– He came in with Howard." The man's eyes looked her up and down, then glanced behind the glass panel. "Marcia, tell Sheriff Tandy Mrs. Gerard is here."

While Marcia picked up the receiver, the officer motioned Dana to a small sitting area in the lobby. "Why don't you have a seat? Can I get you something to drink?"

Something to drink? She wanted to scream. Was he kidding? They were holding her son, and he was offering politely ridiculous gestures? "No, thank you," Dana ground out. "I want to see my son." Crossing her arms, she remained standing.

A moment later, Marcia signaled to them. "Howard says come on back."

275

On quaking legs, Dana followed Officer Collins through the heavy steel door. Inside, she saw Howard speaking to another officer. When his eyes landed on her, he shifted, and the look of regret on his face turned Dana's blood to ice, a fear like she'd never known before rocked her. Her steps faltered, but Howard loped toward her. "Tell me what's going on, Howard," she said, her voice hardly more than a whisper.

"Listen, Dana, we need to talk to Chase. He's not a minor. I can't talk to you."

"About what?" She didn't care about legalities. She cared about her son, and she wasn't budging.

Pursing his lips, Howard turned away for a moment. "We're looking into the death of Charlie Fast, and we have reason to believe Chase might have . . ."

His voice trailed off, and Dana could tell he was choosing his words carefully. Every nerve in her body screamed against the picture she was drawing from Howard.

". . . some information," Howard finished. "And that's all I can tell you."

Dana fought down panic. "I want to see him."

"You contacted an attorney?"

"Yes. Mitchell Dodd will be here soon."

"All right." He jerked his head. "This way."

Dana followed Howard down the hallway, and in a moment, an officer arrived with Chase. "Oh, sweetie."

"It's okay, Mom," Chase said, meeting her eyes. "I had nothing to do with it."

Choking on a sob, she threw her arms around his neck, clutching him to her. "Oh, God, baby. Oh, God." She took a tiny step back, and rested her hands on his cheeks. "Okay. Don't worry. We're going to get it all sorted out." Dana shot Howard a scowl as fear turned to outrage, and she didn't take her hand off Chase's arm. How dare he act as though Chase was some kind of criminal?

With renewed vigor, she drew herself up and faced Howard. "What's the charge against him, Howard?"

He shook his head. "There's no formal charge yet. Let's wait for Mitch, and he'll answer all your questions."

Yeah, she had about a million of those. Number one being why the hell did they think Chase knew anything? Being at the gas station across from the park that night was not enough of a reason to arrest him. And why did she have to wait for Mitch for answers? Another officer opened the door, and motioned to Howard. She couldn't make out their words, though.

Pasting on a smile, she turned to Chase, ignoring the officer who was standing guard over him. "It's all going to be fine. Mr. Dodd will explain everything to us, and he'll be in the room with you. He's a good guy." As she spoke, she remembered the last time she'd talked to the man – when they'd settled all the legalities of her father's financial affairs. He carried himself with a strong and professional demeanor, but he was also kind and understanding.

A moment later, the door opened again, and Mitch stepped inside. She met him in a few quick strides.

He rested a hand on her shoulder. "Hey, Dana. You doing all right?"

"Fine. Thanks for coming. They aren't telling me anything, and I want to know what's going on."

"I'll take care of it."

"Tell me how this works. Can I be there for the questioning?"

Mitch shook his head. "I doubt it, but let me get up to speed. I'll talk to Chase and Howard."

The sheriff stepped forward, and the two men shook hands. "Good to see you, Mitchell." He handed Mitchell a file, and gestured toward a small office. "You can use this room."

Looking at Chase, Mitch tipped his head toward the room.

Hugging herself around the middle, Dana hung back when he mouthed to her, "don't worry," then disappeared into the room with her son.

The minutes ticked by like hours, and Dana waited, every muscle in her body tense as a stretched spring. When the door opened again, another man joined them, and to

Dana's dismay, the three of them disappeared into an office. Alone.

Another agonizing thirty minutes passed before Mitchell appeared in the doorway. Dana shot up from her chair. She reached out for Chase, but spoke to Mitchell. "Can we go now?"

He grimaced toward Howard, then herded Dana a few steps away. "Not quite. Listen, Dana. Legally, they can hold Chase up to forty-eight hours without charging him with anything."

"But why would they?"

"Lots of reasons."

Dana stepped back, the fury rocketing through her causing her voice to rise. "Are you telling me they want to keep my son in jail for forty-eight hours without a specific reason?" Hands on her hips, she glared at her attorney. "Am I hearing this right?"

"Mom," Chase raked a hand through his hair and looked at the floor before meeting her eyes. "I need to tell you something."

Fear shot like a dagger through her heart. "What?" she whispered.

"They found Charlie's hat in my car." He held up his hands. "Let me explain. I think Kyle ran over there and took it while I was in the Quick Stop, and he left it in my car when I dropped them off."

"Oh, Chase." Dana gulped, trying to take in the implications of that.

"I didn't know anything about it. I swear."

"I believe you, honey." Tears welled in her eyes, and Mitch took her arm.

"Let's go outside and talk."

"Oh, no." She shook her head until the clip holding her hair sprung loose. "No way. I'm not going anywhere." She snatched the clip out, and shoved it into her pocket, then turned when Mitch look past her.

Howard jerked his head. "The room's all yours." The third man slipped behind Howard and headed toward the outside door.

"Who is that?" Dana asked.

"Prosecutor," Mitch said, his voice clipped.

That one word sent shivers up Dana's spine. "What?"

Mitch ushered Dana into the room and closed the door.

For the next hour, Dana listened to Chase's recount of Friday night, then received a lesson in law and police procedures.

"So what does all of this mean specifically for Chase?"

"Right now they're holding their cards very close, and they don't have to show them for forty-eight hours. That's it. They're on a fishing expedition right now. Trying to see what they can hook and reel in. They have the surveillance video from the gas station that puts Chase and his friends at the park where Charlie was last seen. It was Friday night, and there were a lot of cars coming and going. At this point, they're trying to track down anyone who might have seen something. And they're making sure everyone's story matches up. But they aren't going to tell us who knows what. Not yet."

"And the hat?"

Mitch blew out his breath. "I have to tell you, that doesn't look good. There's blood on the hat."

Dana squeezed her eyes shut, her head reeling. "But that's Chase's word against Kyle's. How can anything be proven?"

"That's what the DA's office will decide. Frankly, I'm not seeing anything that would prove beyond a reasonable doubt that Charlie's death wasn't an accident."

"Is there anything we can do?" Dana wanted action, something positive to do.

"Let's see how the next twenty-four hours play out." He stood then, and Dana slowly rose.

Her voice shook. Her whole body shook. "You mean just wait?"

"Exactly. Either Chase will be released, or I'll get a call from the prosecutor's office."

"You'll get a call?"

"That's right. They'll communicate through me now."

Dana held her stomach, surprised it hadn't released its contents by now.

Outside the room, Chase sat on a bench, flanked by two police officers. When she approached, one of them moved aside. Standing, Chase took her hand. "Mom. You should go home. Go back to Claire's. This is all gonna be over soon. They've got nothing. They can't. There's nothing to get."

"Can I bring him some things?" Dana asked Mitch.

They both looked at her.

"Like what?" Mitch asked.

"Books? Snacks?"

Mitch glanced at the officers, and shrugged. "I don't see why not."

"Do you want me to?" she asked Chase. "It might make the time pass faster."

"Sure, Mom, but you don't have to. Wait. Don't you need to get back to work? What about your interview?"

Dana shook her head, ignoring the pang of regret to her chest. She refused to think about that right now. "I'm not– that doesn't matter."

"What? Sure it does." Chase kicked at the floor, then met her eyes. "You missed it, didn't you?"

"Chase, it's not a big deal. I can do it next week."

"Are you sure?"

"Of course. All we need to worry about is getting you out of here. Now, I'll run home and get some things for us to do this afternoon." She glanced at her watch. "I'll get some lunch, too. Anyway, we might be out of here by five o'clock. We all know there's no reason–"

Shaking his head, Mitch stopped her. "Dana, look, they're not going to let you hang around here all day. Chase is right. You should go home or back to work. Try to stay busy and let this play out."

He nudged her toward the door as he spoke. "Listen, there's the prosecutor over in Paxton to consider, too. This might not all get done today. My hunch is they're trying to pressure these guys a little. Looks like they may be the last people to see Charlie alive, and they did have some interaction with him. Right now, what happened, if anything, is unclear. The prosecutor will study all the evidence and determine whether there's enough to press charges."

"Why can they not accept that it was an accident? Why do they need to blame someone?" Dana nearly shouted. "It's very likely that Charlie fell. Nothing deliberate at all."

Mitch held up a hand at her tirade. "I know. And that's why I'm telling you to be patient. I'll be in touch as soon as I hear something."

Warring emotions sent adrenalin surging through Dana as she drove the short blocks to Claire's house. Inside, she quickly gathered up the two textbooks from Chase's bedside table and some granola bars. Her knitting bag caught her eye as she blasted through the living room, and fresh tears burned. Why couldn't she stay there? Were they going to spend the rest of the day badgering him? That thought sent blood pounding to her head.

She tossed everything in the back seat, then took out her cell phone, steeling herself for a conversation with Cameron. In her first lucky break of the day, the call went straight to Cam's voicemail. She left a brief message, and glancing down for a second, realized she had missed several calls. Dana slipped the phone into her purse. She couldn't deal with those right now, and she couldn't go back to the hospital. She'd do nothing but worry, and would be a distraction for everyone else.

✶✶

By five p.m., the slow burn that had simmered inside her all afternoon rolled to a full-scale boil. Dana hadn't heard from Mitchell. Her knitting needles clinked furiously as she fumed inside. How long was she supposed to sit here with no updates? She glanced at the clock again. Maybe she should make a surprise visit.

This time, the officer led her downstairs and to a dim, narrow hallway. At the end of the corridor were two jail cells. When Dana saw Chase sitting on a padded bench, her knees nearly buckled. She rested her forehead against the cold metal bars, as a long string of expletives exploded inside her.

"Oh, Chase, what are they doing?" she wailed. "Has Tandy been in this afternoon?"

Chase approached the bars. "No, but the prosecutor has. Same questions over and over."

"This makes me furious." Dana ground out the words. Then she turned back to the officer who was still lurking behind her. "Could you please see if Sheriff Tandy is available?"

He ran his fingers across the thick mustache at his upper lip. "Ma'am, I believe the sheriff has gone home for the day."

"Home?" she cried. "Without telling us? What are we supposed to do now?"

The man towered over her, feet spread, hands on his hips. "My information is that your son will be spending the night here and Sheriff Tandy will be in tomorrow morning."

Dana gasped. The words stung as though she'd been slapped. How dare he leave without giving them any more information? The coward. She whirled around to Chase.

"Oh, honey. Damn them. I'm so sorry." Tears flooded her eyes. "They have no right to do this to you. Let me try Mitchell again."

Chase gripped the bars in front of her. "Mom," he said in a weary voice. "Let's just do what they say and get it over with. I'll read for a while, and go to sleep early if I can. In the morning, they'll get it all sorted out. Can you call Cam for me?" Chase looked at the floor. "Just tell him I need to take a couple of days without pay. I'll work the weekend to make up for it."

Dana clutched her son's arms, her heart breaking. Those were the words of a decent, hard-working, *law-abiding* young man, not some derelict who beat up defenseless old men. She didn't want to let go. But what choice did she have? "I don't want to leave you here," she whispered. "I can't."

"I'll be fine. I promise." He squeezed the hand that still rested on his arm. "I'll see you in the morning."

Dana felt the presence of the man behind her and reluctantly turned. Still in her heels from this morning, her steps echoed down the hallway. She turned back once, but could no longer see her son. On quaking legs, she climbed the stairs. When they reached the top, the officer closed the door behind her, pulling it into place with a sharp, final snap.

Chapter Twenty-Four

Dana ended the call with Mitchell, and climbed into her car, slamming the door behind her. Patient. Right. If he said that to her one more time, she was going to lose it. Easy for him to say – *his* kid wasn't sitting in jail. Patience meant time. And time meant money.

Money. It was always money. Back at Claire's, Dana bolted into the house. Even if they didn't charge Chase with anything, the prosecutor only worked through an attorney. That would cost money. If Howard called Chase as a witness later, he'd need an attorney. Mitch would expect to be paid for today. It took no time at all for legal bills to soar into the thousands. She didn't need to do the freaking math – that was a simple fact. She sank into a chair at the kitchen table, head in her hands. Oh, God, if they did charge him, the bills would be astronomical. And bail. She'd have to post bail. Her fists clenched. Her son would not spend a minute more in jail than he absolutely had to. He could probably qualify for a public defender, but Dana cringed at that thought. No way would she put her son's future in the hands of some stranger who might resent the free work and not give it his best effort.

It was bullshit. Dana knew the only reason for keeping Chase, for holding any of them, was to keep them from talking to each other. He wasn't a flight risk. He had no prior record. It was a bullshit maneuver to try and play them against each other.

Like a wildfire, fury erupted inside her. Why was this happening? It was so wrong. Her stomach knotted. She'd been wrong. She hadn't taken her dad's warning back in May seriously. She hadn't insisted that Chase bring the guys around more so that she could interact with them and observe them. Truth was, she didn't even know those guys. She had no idea what they were capable of. But she believed in her son, and knew without a doubt that he was telling the truth. He'd done nothing to hurt Charlie Fast.

Tears that had threatened many times over the past several hours could not be held back any longer. Sobs racked her body. Chase had been doing so well, had been excited about working at the Wade's farm. He'd actually been studying voluntarily, and– She pushed the chair back and paced the floor. Cam was probably expecting a call. He deserved an update, but, oh, she didn't want to tell him that Chase wouldn't be at work tomorrow morning. Would Cameron believe Chase? Cam had only known him a couple of months. Could he fire him for being arrested?

Just like that it came back to legalities. Attorneys – and attorney fees. Every little question, every phone call was billable time. Those bills would come to her, and she'd have to find a way to pay. She could ask Mary. Mary would give her the money no questions asked. Although her husband might want to know why thousands of dollars were missing from their accounts. And how could she ever pay it back? Anyway, Mary was on a plane to New Zealand. She and Grant had driven to Kansas City last night so that they could make a seven a.m. flight.

Poppa had the money. Dana had power of attorney, and her name was on all the accounts. Of course it would take a few days to cash out some investments. Could she get away with using her dad's money without telling him? Dana slammed a fist into her palm. She could not tell him about this. Just thinking about it rolled her stomach.

But it reminded her that she'd had very little to eat all day. Dana stared into the refrigerator wondering if there was anything she could eat without either choking or throwing up. The idea of eating practically gagged her, but she had to keep herself together through the ordeal, stay hydrated at the very least.

The nurse inside her took over. For a queasy tummy, it was the BRAT diet – bananas, rice, apples, and toast. Maybe she could handle some applesauce and crackers. With unsteady hands, she carried the plate of bland food to the table, then took a glass from the cupboard, debating between tea and water. She could probably do without the caffeine.

At the sink, she swiped a hand across her wet cheeks, and filled a glass with water. But as another thought struck her, the glass slipped from her hand and crashed into the sink. She had money. Not in her bank account, but coming. Shaking, she turned off the water, and sagged against the counter. Kent said she could have the money any day now. Right now. Thoughts warred inside her brain. Could she do it? Could she use the money from the house for Chase? Of course she could – it was her money. Hell, she could sell the lot and rent an apartment if that's what it took. Relief flowed through her. That's exactly what she'd do. She didn't care about the house. The only thing that mattered was getting Chase out of this.

Dana picked up her phone, and remembered the calls she'd ignored earlier. She flopped into a chair and forced herself to thumb through them. She recognized two from Andrew, one from Claire, and there was one from Mad– Oh, no. *Maddie*. Dana sagged against the table. Wow. Anytime she thought something couldn't get worse, she was quickly proven wrong.

Damn, damn, damn. She should've told Maddie not to come until Saturday. By then it could all be over. But tomorrow night . . . Fresh tears erupted. If they kept him the full forty-eight, he'd still be there tomorrow night. She jumped up again, pacing the room. She'd just have to tell Maddie that Chase was spending the night with a friend. She'd have to lie. It went against the grain, though. She'd always tried to be honest with her kids, and expected the same from them.

Gathering her nerves, she listened to the message. Maddie planned to be there between seven and seven-thirty, in time for dinner. Any other time, Dana would love to have the girl time with her daughter. But this– She clenched her fists, remembering Maddie's teasing of Chase. If she dared to say anything negative about her brother, how in the world would Dana keep from lashing out? Worse and . . . worse.

She winced at the next call on the list. Andrew. He'd want to know what had happened, and of course, she'd have to let them know she wouldn't be at work tomorrow. She'd be worthless, probably dangerous. Her hand slid across her forehead. The timing was a disaster. All of the board members had probably already assembled by the time they learned she wasn't showing up for her interview. Not the best impression. But they'd have to understand that she had no choice. A family emergency. She'd better come up with a story for that. Another lie? If her chances of getting the job were slim before, they'd be zero if she told them her son was in jail. Oh, God. She imagined the headlines – "Hospital Administrator's Son Jailed in Connection with Suspicious Death."

It wouldn't matter that it was all false. It'd be bad publicity, bad for the hospital's image. Gritting her teeth, Dana pressed the key to retrieve the message.

Dana, please give me a call at your earliest convenience, the latest message said. In a rather curt voice, Dana thought. Though understanding, Andrew was probably annoyed, planning to have the interviews wrapped up by the end of the week. The first message sounded much more concerned. *Ugh.* She didn't want to call him. She glanced at her watch. What she needed to do was call Kent and get the wheels in motion to get her money. Not that she *wanted* to make that call, either.

She decided to try her powers of persuasion on Maddie first. She could fish around and see if there was something going on in Joplin tomorrow night that she might not want to miss. It would be a godsend to have this behind them before Maddie arrived.

Maddie picked up on the third ring.

"Hey, Mom. Did you get my message?"

Just act normal, Dana reminded herself. "I did. So in time for dinner, then? Did you have something in mind?"

"No. We could grab a burger or something easy if you want."

"Okay. So, you're sure there's nothing going on there to stick around for?"

"What do you mean?"

"Nothing. I just wondered about, well, are you still going out with Zach?"

"He's going home this weekend, too."

Rats. "Ah. All right."

"What's the matter Mom? You sound funny."

"Funny? What does that mean?" Damn. Acting was never one of her talents. She'd better get this done before she gave herself away.

"I don't know. Do you have a cold?"

"I'm fine. Maybe a little tired. But I'll be good as new tomorrow, and I have the whole weekend off."

"Awesome. I'll see you around seven-thirty."

"Great! Bye, sweetie. Drive carefully."

She ended the call, and sank into a chair. She'd have to do better than that if she ended up having to fake her way through dinner tomorrow night. With a heavy sigh, Dana considered her next call. Maybe she'd do better with something not so personal.

The professional thing to do was to call Andrew immediately, and she refused to look anything other than professional. Drawing herself up, she retrieved his number, and hit call.

"Dana?" Andrew's voice came on the line.

"Yes. Hello, Andrew. I'm so sorry I wasn't able to make the interview today. Something's come up with one of my son's, and I–"

"Yes, Val told us. Is everything all right now?"

Dana licked her lips. How to answer that. "Not really. But, listen, I might be able to get to the hospital for an hour or so tomorrow. Would that work?"

"Barry Gilmore had to get back to Tulsa this afternoon. The rest of us were planning to meet tomorrow

288

and make some decisions. Only a few of the board members live near Whitfield, you know."

Of course she knew that. They were from other hospitals and health-related fields, people experienced in hospital and business management. "Yes, I know, and I'm very sorry to throw a wrench in the plan. Could I possibly run in before your meeting?"

"That might work," Andrew agreed. There was a pause before he spoke again. "Dana, I'm wondering if the timing is right on this thing."

Her heart hammered. He knew something. She could hear it in his voice. "What do you mean?"

"Well . . . I mean your house, and now this thing with your boy. Maybe now isn't the best time for you."

Dana's blood ran cold. "What do you mean, this thing with my boy, Andrew?"

She could hear the heavy sigh. "I heard something about it today. Don't worry, I haven't mentioned it to the rest of the board. I– I've sung your praises pretty good, Dana, but I don't know about this. How can I recommend you to lead this hospital with this hanging over you? I thought you might want to withdraw your application."

Dana was speechless. But only until her indignation caught up with her brain. "Andrew, I don't know what you've heard, or how, but I can assure you, it's all a huge mistake, and my son is not implicated in any wrongdoing."

"Dana," Andrew said softly. "If that's the case, why were you gone all day? Why did you miss an important interview? Now I understand nothing's been made public, and I don't want to upset you. If you still want to come in tomorrow, I'll see if I can make that happen, but I can't guarantee anything."

Disappointment lodged in Dana's throat. He'd sung her praises. She'd actually had a shot at the job. But he wasn't willing to stand behind what he knew – that she and her entire family were upstanding members of the community.

"I understand," she told him, her voice quiet, but firm.

"I'll be in touch."

"Thank you."

Dana hung up, and before she could unleash her thoughts about the call, she sent a text message to Valerie to let her know that she wouldn't be at work tomorrow. At least she could count on Val to cover for her.

And then Dana collapsed onto a chair, her mind replaying the conversation with Andrew. How had he found out? Her face burned. If he'd heard something, how long before the whole town knew?

It wasn't right that this should smear Chase's name – or hers. Nothing was official. A fishing expedition, Mitchell had called it. Using her son for bait.

Dana shook her head, clutching the sides of the table. What was going on? It was as though her town had turned against her. Her house had been wiped away. The sheriff was treating her son like a common criminal rather than a life-long part of the community. One of their own. And now her boss couldn't give her the benefit of a doubt after twenty-some years of service? Where was the support network?

How ironic that she'd have to turn to an outsider for help. What had Kent said at dinner the other night? That Whitfield was a friendly town? She used to think so, but now . . .

Fine. She didn't need them. She'd deal with it on her own, and they'd apologize later. She'd make sure of that. Yanking up her phone again, Dana found Kent's number. Her finger hovered over the send button. She did not want to make this call. But what choice did she have? She wanted that money. If they thought for one second about holding Chase longer, she wanted the cold cash in her hands and ready. Most of what was happening was completely out of her control – but maybe she could control this one thing.

Taking a deep breath, willing herself to sound normal, she pushed the button.

"Hey, Dana," came the warm, easy-going response. As if it were just another friendly call. She swallowed hard and forced herself to continue.

"Listen, I need to talk to you."

"Sure thing. I've got some time."

"I wondered if we could meet somewhere."

"Of course. Or I could come to you.

"You could?" She licked her lips. That would be better. Out of the public eye. "Would you?" she asked.

"I can be there in ten minutes."

Dana squeezed her eyes shut, her breath coming in quick gulps. "Really?"

"I'd be happy to." She could hear the questions in his voice, but he thankfully refrained from asking them.

Dana ended the call then said a quick prayer. "Please let this work," she whispered. She put on a pot of coffee then paced the floor, making frequent glances out the front window.

When she heard knocking she couldn't be sure what was louder – her heart hammering or Kent at the door.

"Hey," he said when she opened the door and stepped back to let him in.

"Hi," she said. "Come on in. I've got coffee in the kitchen."

Kent sent her a puzzled look, but followed her into the other room. "Coffee? You know it's about ninety degrees outside."

Dana pushed her hair back. "Oh, right. Do you want something cold?"

"Nah. I'm just teasing you. Coffee's fine."

She poured two cups and set one in front of him, then sat down, an awkward silence closing around them.

Kent cleared his throat. "So, what's up? Are you having issues with the contractors?"

Slowly she shook her head. "No. I, uh–" Dana looked past him. "I have a bigger problem than rebuilding that house. I need–" She broke off. Did she have to tell him the whole story?

Kent's eyes narrowed, and he leaned in. "Dana, talk to me. You have a bigger problem than the fact that your house was blown away? Seriously?"

Tears burned, but she blinked them back. "If we settle up right now, how soon can I get a check from Heartland?"

His eyes widened as he stared at her. She held his gaze a moment, but when her lips trembled, she looked into her mug, her knuckles white around it.

"Well . . . it'd probably be a couple of days, I'd guess. We'd need to cancel the appeal, get everything in order. Are you sure you want to do that? I mean, you don't want to sell yourself short."

"I need the money now." She pushed back her chair and stood, wringing her hands. "What about a partial settlement? Could you get me a check for say fifty thousand dollars toward the full amount?"

"To use for something other than replacing your house?"

She faced him then. "What difference would it make what I used it for? It's my money, right?"

She watched him rub a hand across his jaw, obvious frustration on his face.

"Dana, why don't you have a seat and tell me what this is all about. Maybe I can help."

"No, I don't want to tell you. I just want my money." Her words were hard, but when she looked back at Kent, the concern she saw on his face broke her defenses. She flopped into a chair, put both elbows on the table and rested her head in her hands. "I need the money for my son," she whispered. "For legal fees. Possibly bail."

Kent leaned forward and ran a hand along her arm. "Wow. Okay. Let's talk about this."

Standing, he moved into the kitchen then returned with a box of tissues. He handed her one, then raked a hand through his hair. "You could go to the bank and get a quick short-term loan against the value of the property."

Her head snapped up. "Would that be faster?"

"Maybe."

"Would they need to know what it was for?"

"I wouldn't think so, not if you've got collateral." He set his coffee mug on the table then gently moved her hands away from her face, and crouched down. "Are you a hundred percent sure you'll get the money back?"

A huge sob wrenched her shoulders. "Yes," she cried. "Yes! I'll get it back. He's not going anywhere. He's innocent. It's all a mistake."

She raised her eyes to Kent's. "They haven't charged him with anything yet, but they're keeping him in j–jail tonight. If they do charge him, I've got to have the money ready to get him out of there."

Kent pulled her up from the chair, and to her complete surprise, folded her into his arms.

"Okay, just take it easy," he murmured as his hand moved across her back.

She sobbed into his shirt, soaking in the comfort he offered, at least for a little while. It felt good to be wrapped in his warmth – even if it was ninety degrees outside.

Long moments later, he pulled back and took her hand. "Tell me what happened?"

"He's been accused of hurting someone who later died."

"Son of a bitch."

"He did *not* do it. I know he didn't. Chase has always been a nice kid. So sensitive. He was always the one who'd stand up for other kids or be nice to someone who was hurt or bullied. I know my son. He would never do this."

"But the evidence points to him? How'd he get implicated?"

"Stupid friends. The guys he was with the night it happened *might* have done something."

"What'd they do?"

"Last weekend, Charlie Fast, a harmless, defenseless old man who wanders around town – or used to – died from swelling in his brain. There was a witness who said she'd seen some guys in the park earlier that night and they were fighting or something. The police think they beat Charlie up and a blow to the head prompted the swelling that killed him. The two guys were friends of Chase's. And now they're all facing possible charges."

Her voice went whisper-soft, and Kent swore under his breath.

Through thick tears, Dana continued. "Chase figures the other guys think he turned them in, and that's why they aren't telling the truth. They aren't telling the DA that he wasn't involved. They started something with Charlie while Chase was in the gas station across the street."

"How do they know all that?"

"Surveillance cameras." Her lips trembled. It was more than that for Chase. "And–"

"What?"

"The hat. The damned hat. One of the other boys left Charlie's hat in Chase's car."

"Oh, sweetheart."

Dana stood again. "It's just not right."

Kent took her hand. "Let's go."

Dana blinked. "Go where?"

"My place. To get my checkbook."

"What? No way, Kent. Forget it."

He bent his knees to face her at eye level. "I'm not letting you worry about this one more minute. We'll let the appeal keep going. You can pay me back when you get the money. Period."

Dana stood with her mouth open. Would he really do that for her? "Are you serious?"

Kent brushed a thumb across her cheek. "Absolutely. I'll do whatever I can." Without even meaning to, Kent pulled her against his chest as relief flooded through him. Relief that, finally, he could do something for this woman. Something huge. He'd never felt more heroic. He landed a quick kiss on her forehead. "Don't worry. We're going to fix this."

He gently nudged her to the sofa. "Let me get you something cold to drink, and let's figure out the next move."

When he returned to the living room with two glasses of ice water, she'd curled up on the sofa, her head resting on her arm.

"Thank you," she said, taking the glass. "I don't know what I was thinking when I put on that pot of coffee. Just something to do, I guess."

"I'm guessing you had a couple of other things on your mind." He sat down on the coffee table, facing her. "Have you talked to an attorney?"

"Oh, yes. He was there when they questioned Chase this morning."

"What did he say?"

She rubbed her hands over her face before meeting his eyes. "Told me to be patient. How can I sit here and do nothing while my son is sitting in jail?"

"Did you tell your attorney you've got bail money?"

"No. Hadn't thought of it. Get this, his idea is that if they charge Chase, we should ask for release without bail because he has no record. And that could take two to three *weeks*," she screeched. "As if I'm going to let my son sit in jail for no good reason for that long."

"You know, it might not be as much money as you think. They only require a percentage for bail. When do you expect to hear something?"

"I have no idea. He said the DA's office was holding their cards close."

Dana's head fell into her hands. Kent could feel her frustration, but he wasn't sure how to make it easier for her. No mom would let her son stay in jail without a fight. He moved to the sofa beside her. Throwing an arm around her shoulder, he pulled her against him. "What would make the time go faster? Do you want to talk? Watch a movie? Go for a drive?"

"Funny, the last thing Chase said before I left was that he'd go to sleep to make the time pass. I wonder if he can."

"It's not a bad plan."

"I'm so proud of him. Honestly, he's handling it very well. He's been calm and polite." Her eyes met Kent's. "Probably over-compensating to keep me from freaking out."

"Sounds like a great kid. Listen, you say the word, and I'll scoot out of here so you can get some sleep, too."

She looked past him toward the darkened patio, and the silence grew heavy. It took a moment for Kent to realize she was watching him in the reflection of the glass doors.

Finally, she shifted, turning toward him. "Do you have to?"

Kent stood, and lifted a throw blanket from another chair. "Have to what?" he asked, tucking the blanket around her.

"Leave."

His hands stilled, and his throat went dry.

Chapter Twenty-Five

Dana stared across the room at the image projected onto the wall. The early morning sunshine cast a silhouette of the blinds, each slat straight and uniform in neat and tidy symmetry. Nothing crooked. Nothing out of place. Just strong, solid lines. How she craved that kind of structure. What the hell had happened to her life? Everything was a mess – out of place, out of sync.

She knew without looking at the clock on the bedside table that it was time to get up, but thoughts of facing this day scared her. Had she been twelve, she would seriously consider tucking a few personal possessions and some snacks inside an old flannel shirt, and running away.

Really, what was keeping her here, anyway? Her family's reputation hung in the balance. The situation with her job could be a fiasco, and she didn't have a home to call her own. Hell, maybe she should just pick up leave. Start over somewhere new. She could work anywhere. Every city had hospitals, and assisted living centers that could care for her dad. Claire had done it – started a new life near her daughter. Dana could do the same. Take Poppa and Chase and go to Joplin or Tulsa close to Evan or Maddie. Chase needed a fresh start, for sure. Maybe that would be easier for him in a new place.

She squeezed her eyes closed. *"Oh, dear, God,"* she whispered. *"Please get us through this ordeal with Chase. Make it right."*

It was so tempting to roll over and duck back under the covers, to pretend it was a bad dream that she'd wake from soon. But she couldn't. Wouldn't. She had to be there for her son. And that meant showing up at Mitchell Dodson's law firm then making her presence known at the Whitfield sheriff's office.

Dana lurched upright at a sound from downstairs. Holding perfectly still, she listened. And then remembered – she had company downstairs. She dressed quickly in a fresh top but the same black skirt from yesterday. She had to look professional to deal with these people.

At the top of the stairs she clipped her hair back, and grinned when the scent of fresh coffee greeted her. *Nice.*

"Good morning," Dana said when she reached the entrance to the kitchen.

Kent spun around. "Morning. How you feeling?"

"I'm okay."

He handed her a mug. "Cream or sugar?"

"A little cream would be great."

Kent took the small carton from the refrigerator.

"Thank you. I do like a man who can find his way around a kitchen."

Leaning against the counter, he sent her a lazy smile. "Glad to hear it."

Dana took a sip of coffee, and licked her lips, unsure what to say. There was a man in her kitchen. A kind and generous man who'd kept her company on one of the worst nights of her life. Under other circumstances she may have invited him into her bed, but last night wasn't the right time. Last night, she'd simply needed the comfort of a friend. The fact that he'd given her exactly that made him all the more endearing this morning.

"I suppose you have a crazy busy day today," she said. It was both a statement and a question.

"I do, but not like yours. I need to check in at the office, and make sure they're ready to roll out of town this afternoon, but I'm flexible. I'll run by the bank first thing. Want to get me a deposit slip?"

"A de–" Their conversation from last night flooded back in. "Oh, Kent. We don't have to do that right this minute. Let's– let's wait and see what happens."

"Wait? For what?"

She shook her head. "I don't know. I just–"

He put down his mug and stood in front of her. "Dana, I know this isn't easy for you, but now is better than later. What if something happens at ten o'clock tonight when the banks are closed? To take a personal check, they'll want to run it through the check-verify system and make sure it clears. The money's got to be there."

Her lips trembled, and Kent pulled her close, his warm hand circling her back. "It'll be okay. Let's just take care of everything we can."

Dana nodded. "Yes. You're right." Reluctantly, she stepped out of his arms then took her purse from the counter and tore a deposit slip from her checkbook. "Be sure to give me one of yours, too," Dana said when she handed him the slip. Refusing to give in to her fears, she forced a shaky smile. "I expect to put it right back tomorrow."

"Deal," Kent said.

He sealed it with a firm kiss that left her lips buzzing.

**

Her first stop was Mitchell's law office. Never had Dana imagined such a scenario – that she would be rushing to an attorney's office about her son who'd just spent a night in jail. Her heart pounded as she mounted the steps.

The receptionist looked up from her coffee mug wide-eyed when Dana burst into the lobby. "Good morning. May I help you?" the woman inquired, setting the mug on a credenza behind her.

"I'd like to speak to Mitchell, please. Is he in?" Dana asked.

The woman glanced at her watch. "Is he expecting you?"

"Not exactly. Well, yes. He should be. He's handling a situation for me, and we need to talk."

Sheryl offered a polite smile and held up a finger. "Let me ring. May I have your name, please?"

"Dana Gerard."

"One moment, Mrs. Gerard."

When Sheryl turned back to Dana, she shook her head. "I'm sorry, Mr. Dodd isn't in yet. You're welcome to—"

At that instant, Mitchell walked through the front door. Dana wanted to cheer over the good timing. There would be no getting past her now.

"Dana. Good morning. Wasn't expecting to see you this early. I don't have anything for you yet. Let me check my messages."

He moved forward as if to walk past, but Dana didn't budge. "Nothing from the DA's office?"

Shaking his head, he inched toward the interior hallway. "I'm sure they'll be in touch soon, but I have to tell you, I'm due at the courthouse at nine." He turned to Sheryl. "Could you get our guest something to drink? Dana, give me a few minutes."

Dana crossed her arms, disappointment lodging in her chest. What a fool, running in here as if he'd be able to rush right to the DA's office. As if he'd had no clients until she called yesterday morning. She swallowed hard, and accepted the cup of coffee Sheryl offered. "Thank you."

Dana retreated to the leather chairs behind her, wishing she could call and check in with Chase, but the bastards had taken his phone.

Ten minutes later, Mitch appeared in the doorway again.

Dana shot up from her chair. "Any news?"

"Nothing. But it's still early."

She heard the slight censure in his words. Too bad. She couldn't have slept another minute if she'd tried. "So what can we do to get things moving?"

He put a hand on Dana's arm. "I know this isn't what you want to hear, but it's probably going to be lunchtime before I get any answers. I'm sorry."

Shoulders sagging, Dana moved toward the door.

"I'll be in touch," Mitch told her.

She nodded, then jumped when her phone rang inside her purse. She didn't dare ignore it. Grabbing hold of it, Dana checked the number. Oh, no. *Andrew.*

Quickly, she stepped outside. "Andrew?"

"Hello, Dana. We're ready for you. Can you come?"

"Oh." Could his timing be any worse? She could not leave Chase hanging another hour. "Do you mean for the interview?"

"Yes. We're in the conference room. Just come on up when you get here."

"Now?"

"Is that a problem?"

Conflicted, Dana hesitated. If she blew it off, she made the decision for them. Made it easy for them.

"Dana?"

"Yes. I can be there in ten minutes." They'd never know if she took five minutes to run by the police station. All she needed to do was see her son, and assure him they were making some progress. She had to.

At the station, Dana whirled out of the car and dashed inside. "Hello. I'd like to see my son, please. Chase Gerard. I just want to see him for a minute. I don't have a lot of time. Please."

"You are?"

"Dana Gerard."

"Just a moment, please."

The dispatcher backed away and picked up her phone. Dana hovered, but couldn't hear the woman's conversation. Waiting was agony.

When she turned back around, the officer pointed toward a door to the side. "Through there."

Dana sprinted to the door, which was opened by an Officer Thomas. "This way," he said.

Back down the unfriendly corridor, every step reverberated, escalating her anger once again.

Chase looked up from a book when they stopped at the tiny cell. "Hey, Mom."

Dana let out a choked cry, and pushed her hands through the bars, running them up and down Chase's arms. "Hey, sweetheart. Are you okay?"

"I'm fine."

"Were you able to get some sleep?"

He shrugged. "It was fine. So what's going on?"

Oh, how she wished she knew. "Listen, I've got to get to the hospital for my interview, so I can't stay. I just wanted to see you and let you know Mitchell's working everything out. He's talking to the District Attorney's office, okay?"

Chase hitched his shoulders, and shoved his hands in his pockets. "Do you think I'll be out today?"

"I hope so. We're doing everything we can."

His chin dropped to his chest. "I should be at work today."

"I know, but Cam will understand. Try to stay positive." She put her hand to her lips, then rested it on his cheek. "I'll be back in an hour or so."

Feeling as though she were on a treadmill, Dana rushed back out to her car.

At the hospital, she hurried up the back stairs, avoiding the nurses' station, and arrived at the conference room out of breath. Swallowing hard, she switched off her phone, then tapped on the open door.

Six sets of eyes stared at her.

"Come in, Dana," Andrew called.

Most of the attendees were seated on one side of the table. Smiling, Dana pulled out a chair on the opposite side. Then wondered if she'd be able to remember anything she'd planned to say.

"Why don't you get something to drink, and we'll get started," Andrew said, nodding toward the cart behind him.

"Oh, that's a good idea. Thanks." She opted for a bottle of cold water. As soon as she settled into the chair, Andrew began introductions.

Dana forced herself to smile at each person, and concentrate on their name and position rather than the other elements of drama going on in her life at the moment.

"Why don't we start with the résumé," Andrew said.

"First, I'd like to thank you all for giving me this opportunity," Dana spoke up. "I'm very sorry to have put a snag in your schedules." Maybe it wasn't smart to remind them that she'd stood them up, but she felt she needed to clear the air. She couldn't pretend it hadn't happened.

There were polite murmurs. "Is everything all right now?" one of the women asked.

Dana shook her head. "Not yet, but we're dealing with it. Thank you for asking."

For the next thirty minutes, Dana answered questions relating to her background and experience. And then the man at the end of the table, Phil Newman, owner of a large medical equipment company in Paxton, interrupted. "We have the basic information on paper. Why don't you sum up how your experience makes you a good candidate for hospital administrator, Ms. Gerard?"

Dana heard the challenge in Newman's voice. She had some work to do here.

"Of course. I believe my knowledge of the community along with my knowledge of the hospital, the procedures as well as the physical facility, make me a good candidate. I'm familiar with compliance issues, emergency procedures, community outreach programs, and I've worked closely with all areas of the hospital, from Procurement to Human Resources, to the cafeteria."

"What makes you a leader, Ms. Gerard?"

She'd been prepared to discuss her leadership potential, but the man's hostility caught her off guard. She had no idea whether it was personal, or he simply wasn't a fan of women in management positions.

Dana took a drink of water, and met Newman's eyes with a friendly smile. "First, I lead by example. By caring about this hospital and its patients. I lead by knowing and following rules and regulations, and by hiring the best people I can, and setting high expectations."

One of the women asked the next question. "How much hiring have you done for the hospital?"

"Almost all of the current nursing staff are my hires," Dana said. "We have an excellent—"

"Can we back up a minute?" Newman cut in. "Ms. Gerard, you said lead by example, by caring about the hospital and its patients. Now I'm having a hard time understanding that statement in terms of what took place here yesterday. You left the hospital for personal reasons. I'm told you never returned to work the rest of the day, is that correct?" Before she could answer, he spread his hands on the table. "I don't see that as an example of caring about this hospital or leadership."

"Phil," one of the women said, admonishment in her tone.

"I think it's a fair question," Phil argued. "When something personal came up, she made a choice and abandoned the hospital. Is that what we can expect in the future?"

It was hard to keep her cool when fire flared inside. This guy was going to get his answer. Gathering her courage, Dana gripped the arms of the chair, and pulled herself erect. "Thank you. I'd be happy to address that, Mr. Newman."

She glanced around the room, making eye contact with the other people, who shifted uncomfortably and looked as though they'd like to be anywhere else.

"Mr. Newman is correct that I left the hospital," Dana said, keeping her voice as calm and steady as possible. "But I didn't abandon it, and there really was no choice to be made. If anyone on my staff had received the phone call I did yesterday, I would expect them to follow my example, and do exactly the same. And," she let her gaze land on Phil Newman. "I would expect the rest of the staff to step up, fill in, and get the job done. No questions asked."

She flicked a glance at Andrew. "That's what we do here. I left the hospital and its patients in the hands of skilled, well-trained individuals who look out for one another. This is Whitfield Community Hospital. That means we're part of the Whitfield community, but it also means we're a community inside as well. We've got each other's backs. We cover for each other. That's

304

community." She paused, but only for a second. Only long enough to let her words soak in.

"Nurses who come to work worried about kids or elderly family members or some issue at home, aren't going to be their best, and that's unacceptable. I want nurses who are happy to be here, not resentful. I want my staff to come in smiling about their kids' school play, not grumbling because they missed it.

"You want to know if I care about this hospital? I've spent almost my entire career at this hospital. My children were born here. My family has been part of this town for three generations. You want to know my leadership potential? I get things done. I hire good people. I'm on a first-name basis with the mayor. I know shop and restaurant owners, bank executives, and school board members.

"And for the record, when this town was hit with the biggest disaster in its history, I was here. While my house was blown to bits, and then drenched, I was here. I didn't leave this place for two and a half days. I was busy taking care of the people in this town." She braced her hands against the table. "Here's the bottom line, ladies and gentlemen. I'm sure you can hire someone with more management skills, more degrees, more initials behind their name, but you aren't going to find someone who cares more about the people of Whitfield and this hospital."

With trembling lips, she glanced at a speechless Andrew. "I'll see you on Monday," she told him. Quickly, Dana pushed back her chair, and tossed her purse over her shoulder. "Thank you all for your time. It's been a privilege to meet with you."

**

At eleven, Kent showed up at Claire's. Dana sagged against him.

"Hey, take it easy," Kent said, drawing her into the living room. "You all right?"

"I'm going out of my mind," she told him. "Waiting and waiting. I haven't heard from anyone, and I—" She bit

305

her lip as the reality of what she'd done hit her in the chest.

"What?"

"I'm pretty sure I blew my interview."

"Now that I don't believe for a minute."

She nodded. "Believe it. I sort of went off." Dana flopped onto the couch and told him about her tirade.

"Wow."

"Yeah." When she looked up at Kent, expecting some kind of disgust, she saw a glint of humor in his eyes. She cracked a smile. "He did have it coming, though."

"Sounds like." He took her hand and pulled her up. "Let's get you some lunch. Want to go somewhere or carry out?"

"Oh, I haven't even thought of food." She had no idea if there was anything in the fridge. But she hesitated. If people were talking about her was it better to avoid them until the whole thing was over, or meet them head-on?

"Going out might make the time go faster," Kent said.

Dana let out a sigh. "True." And maybe it would feel more normal. "Yeah, let's go. Maybe if I'm not sitting here waiting for a call, it'll come."

At Hannah's, Dana smiled until her cheeks hurt. Maintaining the "normal" façade took some effort. She took a long drink of her iced tea, and tried to keep up a conversation.

The familiar tune of her phone rang at the same time a slice of fresh banana cream pie arrived. Dana shot out of her seat. "I'll be right back."

"I'll save some for you," Kent told her as she pushed back her chair.

She fumbled with the phone on her way to the door. "Mitch?"

"Hey, Dana. Wanted to let you know that the prosecutors are looking at all of the evidence this afternoon. I'm hoping we'll know something end of day."

Dana's jaw clenched. That was it? More hoping. More waiting.

"I know it's hard, but try not to worry."

Dana held her stomach, afraid to ask the next question. "It's Friday afternoon. If they decide to bring charges, would that happen today, or do you think they'd wait until tomorrow morning." God, she wanted him out of there before Maddie arrived.

"It's hard to say, Dana. I'm sorry. I just can't predict. I've seen it go both ways."

She ended the call, and walked slowly back to the table to fill Kent in. She took a mouthful of what she knew was a delicious slice of pie, but she couldn't taste it.

Chapter Twenty-Six

At seven o'clock Dana dabbed at her eyes with a fresh tissue, trying her best to keep from looking a blood-shot mess when Maddie got there. With every second that passed, Dana's hopes of getting Chase out tonight plummeted. And she still hadn't decided whether to tell Maddie, or fib and say Chase was in Paxton for the night. The problem – aside from the fact that she did not lie – was, she could get a call – and get caught in the lie – at any moment.

A few minutes before seven-thirty, she heard a car door slam. She took a deep breath, and opened the front door to greet her daughter.

"Hey, do you need some help?" Dana hollered.

"No. I've got it." Maddie hoisted a small bag onto her shoulder, and pulled a rolling one behind her.

As soon as she reached the porch, Dana pulled her into a tight hug. "Mm, mmm. So good to see you." She grabbed the rolling case. "Would you rather be in Claire's room like last time, or upstairs with me?"

"Upstairs is fine."

"Okay, we can leave this here for now." She put the suitcase near the steps. "I'll let you freshen up a minute. Want something to drink or are you ready to go eat right away?"

"Either way, Mom. Be right back."

When Maddie returned to the living room, Dana pointed to a stack of movies on the coffee table. "Hey, I thought maybe we'd stay up half the night and watch movies. I pulled out some old goodies, but we can also look at what's available to download." Maddie didn't know it, but that was code for, 'I have to stay up as long as possible, so that I'm exhausted by the time I go to bed.'

"Sure. Sounds fun. Want to go shopping tomorrow?"

"You mean with my credit card?" Dana asked wryly.

Laughing, Maddie kicked off her shoes and pulled her feet onto the couch. "I didn't say that. I'm a working girl now, remember?"

Dana gave her another quick hug. "Yes, and you look fabulous. What do you need to shop for?"

Maddie shrugged. "Maybe a couple more skirts."

"Ah, need more business attire, huh?"

At a noise from outside, Dana twisted around to look down the hallway. Sounded like a knock at the door.

"Hellooo," a deep voice called out.

What the–? She stared as Evan came through the door.

"Hey, Mom."

"Hey, yourself, buddy. What are you doing here?" In a flash, she had him in her arms. "Oh, my gosh, am I glad to see you." She closed her eyes as love poured through her. How had he known she needed him?

"Guess Maddie beat me."

"By only a few minutes." Dana pulled him into the living room, and looked from one to the other. Had they planned this? "What's up?"

Evan ran a hand across the back of his neck. "Well, Maddie said you sounded funny on the phone yesterday, and I–" A grimace crossed his handsome face. "I heard something about Chase yesterday. I didn't have plans for the weekend, so . . . here I am."

Dana sank into a chair. She had no choice now.

"Mom? You okay?"

Dana reached for his hand. "Sit down."

"Listen," her gaze switched back and forth, but straight into their eyes. "Chase is in some trouble." Her voice quivered, as she knew it would.

"What kind of trouble?" Evan asked.

"It's serious. Remember I told you Charlie Fast died?"

Two nods. Two puzzled faces.

With a deep breath Dana launched into the story. "So these friends of Chase's have implicated him. He–" Her voice broke as she choked on the words. "He was arrested yesterday morning. So he's– Oh, God. He's in jail."

"What? They think Chase had something to do with it?" Maddie shot up from the sofa. "That's ridiculous. No way. Chase would never do something like that."

With a catch in her throat, Dana lunged toward Maddie and swept her into a hug. "I know. I know." Relief poured through her. It was the validation she needed.

"So you think these guys are lying to get Chase in trouble, too?" Evan asked. "Thought they were friends."

"Yeah, some friends," Maddie said.

"We don't know for sure who's saying what. The DAs were supposed to meet to go over everything this afternoon, but nothing's happened. I'm going crazy waiting."

"How do we get him out? Have you talked to an attorney?"

Sniffling, Dana nodded, taking a moment to catch her breath. "I've talked to Mitchell Dodd. He thinks the police are waiting for one kid to rat the other out. Right now, it's Chase's word against theirs."

"Wow. This is crazy."

"That's for sure." Dana turned to Evan. "Tell me how you heard about it."

"Paul Maynard texted me. His older brother works for Wade, too. Guess he saw the arrest. I can't believe they'd go to the farm and do that in front of everyone. That's crap."

"I know, let's sue the cops for publicly humiliating him," Maddie said.

310

Dana attempted a smile. "I am so happy to have a couple of cheerleaders on our side."

"So he has to stay there tonight, too?" Evan asked.

"Unless we hear otherwise. They can only keep him until eight tomorrow morning without a charge."

"Jesus, the kid is probably scared to death. Let's go see him."

Dana glanced at Maddie.

"Heck, yes, Mom. Will they let us in?"

"I don't know, but we can try." She'd go pound on Howard Tandy's front door if she had to. She let out a little laugh, and threw her arms around them both. Her heart swelled. All these years she'd tried so hard to be there for her children. And here they were – for her. It was a moment she'd never forget. "Let's go."

They waited in the drab, unwelcoming lobby of the police station for several minutes, but finally Officer Riley, who Dana recognized, ushered them inside. "This isn't really normal," he told her.

As if she cared. Having her son in jail wasn't either. But in an effort to stay on good terms, she said, "We won't stay long."

Another officer stepped from the small basement office into the hallway when the three of them – four, including their escort – started down the corridor.

Hands on his hips, he watched them approach. "What's going on, Riley?"

"They're here to see Gerard."

"Yeah? Nobody told me it was visiting hour."

Dana bristled, ready to make good on her threat to storm Howard's house. Before she could speak, Riley held up his hand.

"It's fine."

"Okay. Inside or out?"

"Open the door."

When Chase appeared at the bars, Dana pushed past the officers.

"Mom, what's going on?"

"Hey, sweetie, look who's here."

The officer slid the door open, and they crowded around Chase.

Twenty minutes later, her phone buzzed. It was tempting to ignore it. She hated to interrupt their visit, but she couldn't take that chance. Her heart stopped when she checked the number. "I need to take this call," she said, almost breathless. She took off at a sprint to get upstairs where she'd have a stronger signal.

"Mitch?"

"Hey, Dana. Got some good news for you. I'm heading over to the police station now. They're going to release Chase."

Dana let out a sharp scream and jumped up and down. Heads swiveled her direction, and when she caught Riley's eye, she was sure he already knew. With relief, Dana sagged against the wall. "Oh, God. Oh, thank God. When can he leave?"

"In a few minutes. You can meet me there if you want."

"I'm already here."

Dana whirled to head back down the stairs, and nearly barreled into Evan and Maddie.

"The guy told us to leave," Maddie said.

A moment later, the lanky officer shoved through the door with Chase.

Officer Riley motioned to him. Dana watched as Riley opened a box, and held it out to Chase. She clutched at Evan as Chase pulled out his keys and cell phone.

"You know, Gerard, you dodged a bullet here," Riley said. "Let me tell you something for future reference – when a law enforcement officer asks you a question, give him a straight answer."

Dana sucked in her breath. Had he not?

Chase gave a slow nod, and Dana had the feeling she didn't need to press that particular issue. Perhaps Chase had learned a lesson. When he turned, the relief she felt was mirrored in his eyes.

She brushed at the tears that spilled onto her cheeks, and Evan tossed an arm around her. "Take it easy, Mom."

Mitch arrived, and they waited for the formalities to be taken care of. He pulled Dana aside. "Here's the deal. The kid named Luke came clean. The other one, Norton, apparently gave Charlie a push that knocked him down. Smacked his head on the concrete, but didn't knock him out, so they thought he was okay. That one might get some kind of assault charge, and Chase could get called as a witness later, but I'd expect a plea bargain. Turns out the hat proved Chase wasn't involved. Surveillance shows Norton carrying it back across the street before Chase got over there."

Dana listened, and nodded, but didn't take her eyes off of Riley. She figured something like that would happen. As soon as the words "You're free to go," left Riley's mouth, Dana burst forward and folded Chase into her arms. "Oh, baby. I'm so sorry you had to go through this."

"Yeah. Let's get out of here."

∗∗

Since none of them had eaten supper yet, they decided on Bailey's. It was perfect, Dana thought. It'd be loud, so they could laugh and talk, and celebrate, but more importantly, it would be busy on a Friday night – and that meant lots of people would see her and all three of her kids. No one in jail. No one in trouble. All having fun. Let *that* circulate around town.

It wasn't until after they were seated that Dana saw Kent. "Oh, my gosh!" She sprang out of the booth and met him halfway. The grin across his face told her he'd seen them come in, and figured out the rest.

"Hey," he said, sliding an arm around her shoulders. "This looks like a celebration."

Dana's head bobbed up and down. If they'd been alone, she would've thrown herself at him. But she realized none of her kids had met Kent, and only Chase even knew of him. Taking his arm, she steered him to their table. The timing was a little awkward, but she was too happy to care.

She made introductions, then motioned to the next table. "Pull up one of those chairs," Dana told him. With a bright smile, she ignored the wide eyes and questioning glances shot her direction. Oh, boy, she'd be bombarded later.

When the waitress arrived with drinks, Kent lifted his glass to the center of the table. "To moving past the rough patches," he said. Dana knew he was talking about Chase's ordeal, but couldn't help wondering if there was double meaning in his words.

It was almost midnight when Chase crossed his arms and flopped against the back of the booth. "Man, I'm beat."

Dana squeezed his shoulder. "Of course you are. I bet you could use a nice shower and a real bed."

He closed his eyes. "For sure."

"But Chase," Maddie cut in. "That was a really nice looking cot they had there at the police station."

"Yep, swanky accommodations. I bet you were jealous."

"Okay, you guys, let's go," Dana said. She wasn't about to let the conversation deteriorate at this point. They shuffled out of the booth, and when they started toward the door, Kent took Dana's elbow. "Want to stay for a few minutes? I can run you home."

Dana glanced at Maddie, who'd stopped beside her. She reached into her purse and pulled out her keys. "Hey, Mad, want to drive my car back? I'll be there in a little bit."

"Sure."

Maddie took the keys, but Dana didn't miss the raised eyebrows.

As soon as the kids left, Kent steered Dana to the bar, and helped her hop onto a barstool.

"Wow," he said.

Dana put a hand to her face, and shook her head. "Yeah. Thank God that's over."

Kent brushed back her hair. "It was great to see you so happy."

She met his eyes then and realized he'd never seen her that way. It'd been one ordeal after another since the day they'd met standing in the debris of her house. "I'm glad you were here to see it," she said softly.

314

Chapter Twenty-Seven

Dana's head began pounding as soon as she swung out of bed Monday morning. No surprise there. And she knew it had nothing to do with the celebratory glasses of wine she'd had last night. She couldn't decide if the fact that she'd received no calls or emails from Andrew or Amy was a good sign or bad. Apparently, at least for this morning, she was still employed.

While she dreaded the one o'clock staff meeting, she refused to feel bad for being gone or for her impromptu speech on Friday. Her priorities were straight. She hoped Andrew had already heard that Chase had been cleared of suspicion in Charlie's death, but then she knew rumors had a way of fizzling when the juice ran out.

She showered and dressed on autopilot. It'd be a tough day for her, but also for Chase. He'd have to face the crew at Cameron's farm for the first time since they saw him being arrested, including the one who had flapped his trap to the friend of Evan's. Hopefully Cam could help smooth things over.

The coffee pot gave its final gurgle as Chase padded barefoot into the kitchen. Dana poured a cup, and greeted him with a smile. "Morning, sweetie. How are you feeling?"

"Good, I guess."

She glanced at the clock. He seemed a little behind. "Not going early today?"

Chase shook his head. "Nah. Cameron told me to come at eight-fifteen today."

"Oh." Dana thanked Cam in her head, and made a mental note to talk to him soon. "That's nice of him. I bet he's going to get all the explanations out of the way before you get there."

"Maybe."

"It might be a little awkward, honey, but you have nothing to be ashamed of. Keep your head up and just do your work, okay?"

"That's the plan."

"All right. I'll see you tonight. Love you."

Dana planned to follow that same advice. At work for the first time since she tore out of there four days ago, she gave Greg and her supervising nurses a quick overview of what had happened, then shut herself in her office to try and regroup.

Several times she considered calling Amy, but didn't. It would be unfair to put her on the spot if she knew something. Since she hadn't been summoned to Andrew's office, maybe he was going to act as though nothing had happened, and they could move on. As far as Dana was concerned, that was a best-case scenario, though she would like an apology from him for believing the worst about her son.

Concentrating on patient files, she got up to speed on the twelve patients currently on the floor. They'd had a couple of releases, and two new babies over the weekend. Those, she wanted to see. Just before lunch, she visited the nursery to take a peek at the babies, one boy and one girl. Her chest tightened as she gazed at the tiny infants so fragile, so full of promise. She ran a finger along a soft cheek – a newborn's cheek had to be the softest thing on the planet. Babies brought such joy, but, oh, man, the many ups and downs before those adorable little faces made it to adulthood. Tears pricked her eyes. Her baby boy had become a man in the last few weeks. He'd spent most of Saturday at Cam's place, then he stayed to talk to Poppa after Maddie and Evan left yesterday. She knew that couldn't have been easy for him, especially since Poppa had been the one to warn him about his so-called friends.

Figuring she'd better get out of there before she had a meltdown, Dana headed for the cafeteria. But she still couldn't trust herself not to burst into tears at any moment, so she grabbed a turkey-and-avocado sandwich and took it back to her office.

A few minutes before one, she freshened her lipstick, and picked up her calendar. Never had she been so relieved to go to a team meeting. Let's roll, she thought. She was tired of the suspense.

Both Andrew and Amy were already seated at the conference table. Dana smiled at each of them. She stopped beside Andrew and bent down. "Could I have a minute with you after the meeting?"

He nodded. "I was planning to ask you the same thing."

"Great. Thanks." She wiped her clammy hands against her pants, then took a seat across the table, and quickly struck up a conversation with Neil Redding, who managed the pharmacy for both the hospital and clinic.

Once everyone had assembled, Andrew gave a general greeting, then each department head took turns sharing reports for their areas. Dana took the opportunity to let her eyes roam. Not one person seemed uneasy or flustered. It was as though nothing had ever happened. With relief, she realized everyone else had simply gone about their business

By her turn, she felt more relaxed, and with renewed confidence, she updated the group. "The babysitting classes were a hit again this year, with sixteen attendees, and the first aid classes wrap up next week. I hope by now you've all met our new part-time nurse, Erika. She's doing an excellent job. And we had two perfectly healthy babies born over the weekend."

With the routine reports out of the way, Amy spoke up. "And now, for the biggest news of all," she said, smiling as she looked around the table. "Andrew?"

All eyes turned to Andrew, who cleared his throat. "Yes. As you know we did an extensive search to replace Brad, and we interviewed a number of excellent candidates. And now, it's my pleasure to announce that we have a new hospital administrator."

Dana's fists clenched in her lap. Wow. That was fast. They must not have received any interesting applications in the final couple of days. She wondered if the decision had already been made even before she submitted her application. Pasting on a tight smile, she looked from Andrew to the door, expecting Vickie to usher in the winning candidate – Dana's new boss.

Instead, Andrew stood and leaned across the table, his arm outstretched. "Congratulations, Dana."

Dana's face went white-hot as a wave of something between shock and nausea engulfed her. The blood pounded in her ears. What?

When clapping erupted, she stared at Andrew. A moment later, Amy stood also and flashed a wide smile. "Dana, he means you!"

The words slowly sank in, and Dana rose on wobbly legs. Finally, she reached across and took Andrew's hand, which he squeezed in both of his. "We're all very excited about this, and looking forward to a smooth transition."

Dana's throat was so tight she could hardly choke out a word. "Oh, my gosh. I'm– I'm honored. Thank you."

She spent the next hour talking with Andrew, and then another thirty minutes with Amy.

"I'm so glad it's you." Amy told her. "You'll be great. Plus, it makes the training process a whole lot easier."

Dana grinned at her. "I honestly cannot believe it. I thought I'd totally blown it."

Amy shook her head. "I think Andrew was impressed that you showed a lot of courage and spunk even when you were under so much stress." She opened her calendar. "Let's try to get a block of time, maybe a couple of hours, every day this week to start the process. And let me know what day you can go to lunch. We have to celebrate."

"Absolutely."

318

Dana left Amy's office feeling almost numb. With shaking hands, she yanked open the first door in the hallway – a supply closet. She didn't care. She stepped inside then slid down the wall until she hit the floor, and let the tears come.

**

Dana moved through the rest of the week in a kind of fog, a mixture of relief and elation taking her to the brink of exhaustion. By Friday afternoon, she was ready to jump off the roller coaster. Visions of a quiet weekend floated through her head as she made her way to her car. With that goal in mind, she returned Kent's call as she walked.

"Hey, there. How are you?" Kent asked.

"All I can say is T.G.I.F."

He chuckled. "Been a crazy week, that's for sure."

"I'm fried."

"I know what you need," Kent told her.

His voice sounded vaguely suggestive, and Dana's heart slammed against her ribs. "Oh, really?"

"How about a quiet night out?"

"Okaaay," Dana drawled. Clearly the man had a plan. "What does that look like?"

"I've got a bottle of chardonnay chilling. What do you say we pick up some cheese and crackers and head out to the lake? We've been sidetracked for a couple of weeks."

Sidetracked was one way to put it. "That sounds like heaven," Dana told him, a fluttery feeling in her chest. "Give me a few minutes to change, then I'll get some things together."

"I've got it taken care of," Kent said. "I'll be by in a few."

Dana took a quick shower, and slipped into shorts and a cotton blouse. She tucked her cell phone into her pocket, then grabbed a light jacket for later just as Kent pulled up. Grinning, she didn't wait for him to get out of the car. He was right. She did need this. She hadn't really had a chance to unwind from the stress of the previous weekend and then the job announcement on Monday.

319

Kent leaned over, and planted a warm kiss on her lips before she managed to buckle in. "Hi."

"Hi," she murmured.

"You ready to relax a little?"

"Absolutely."

As Kent started the car, Dana pulled out cell phone. "Let me just check in with Chase real quick."

"Sure."

"Hey, sweetie," she said when Chase picked up. "You still at work?"

"Nope. I'm at the farm."

"Oh. What's going on?"

"Just looking at a couple of things Poppa asked me about."

"Okay, well, I wanted to let you know I won't be home this evening."

"That's fine."

"Do you have any plans?" she asked softly. He was without friends, of course.

"Not really. Hey, Mom, did you know we have some big sunflowers growing out here?"

"Oh yeah? Must be freelance. I sure didn't plant any."

"Huh. Kind of cool. Maybe a dozen."

"We're just leaving the house. Stick around a minute, and we'll stop by." She glanced sideways at Kent, who nodded.

"Where are you?"

"East gate."

"Do you mind a quick detour to the farm?" she asked Kent.

"Of course not."

"Just pull up where you did that day you thought I had car trouble."

They pushed the gate open, and Dana looked around for Chase.

"Over here," he called.

He waved at them from several yards down the other fence line. As they got closer, Dana could see a grove of tall sunflowers with heads about nine inches in diameter, just starting to show some color. Very similar to the ones she'd planted at the house before the storm hit.

"Oh, wow. These are going to be fabulous. I wonder if the Bakers planted a field this year." She turned to Kent. "In case you haven't realized, I love sunflowers. They're so cheery."

"I did get that," Kent said, smiling.

"You know, I thought about skipping a fireplace in the rebuild to save some money, but my friends bought me this incredible watercolor painting of sunflowers. It's so gorgeous, it deserves a fireplace. I want it to be front and center." The painting would be a constant reminder of her generous, amazing friends. She couldn't wait for Mary to return from her trip. They'd get with Claire and celebrate so much. If not for them, and Jane, she wouldn't be the new administrator of the Whitfield Community Hospital.

She hopped up on the lower rung of the wooden fence that surrounded the property to see if there were more sunflowers. Gazing across the field toward the west, there was– she caught her breath. "Oh, my gosh." Her head snapped back to the men. "We could– You know what? I have an idea."

Two puzzled faces stared at her.

"What?" Chase asked.

"This could be the place for our new house." She shaded her eyes with her hand again, talking to them and thinking ahead at the same time. "I can't believe I didn't think of it before, but it makes sense. We already have the land. I can sell the other property and use the money from that to help build a new house here."

"Mom, are you serious? You never liked living on a farm."

She let that comment hang a moment. He was right. She didn't love it. It would put her farther away from the conveniences of grocery and drug store – farther from friends, and from the hospital. There would be more dust and dirt to deal with, and snow to plow. But as she looked across the fields, the peacefulness of the setting struck her, as well as a sense of history and belonging. This place had

321

been home to her parents and grandparents. Maybe they'd come full circle. And maybe those other things didn't matter as much. She might not love living in the country, but she could adjust. She could compromise because it made sense on so many levels.

Dana blew out her breath. "I didn't. But that's because I was a teenager, and it made it harder to be with my friends, especially before I could drive. Now . . . well, now it would be different. We don't have to have chickens and livestock or a big garden. There's so much space here. We can spread out, and make it easy for Poppa to visit with ramps and handrails. Plus, I won't be on the second-shift rotation at the hospital anymore."

Every door and every room on the ground floor could be wheelchair-accessible. Of course she'd need her father's blessing on the idea. But why would he object? It could solve so many problems, and might be a good thing for the future. On a roll, her thoughts, took off – if Chase ended up running the farm, he might want to raise a family there someday. Mentally, she constructed the necessary rooms and configuration. She'd make sure the house faced south this time with plenty of big windows to let the sunshine in.

Dana swung down from the fence and took Chase's arm. "What do you say? Would you want to live here?"

A slow grin spread across her son's face. "Sure. That sounds great. It'd be kind of cool to make it a family farm again. We could fix up the barn, and maybe get some of those wind turbines going out here."

She turned to Kent. "What do you think? Would someone want to buy the other lot? Just the land and build their own house?"

"It'd definitely give you more money to build with. Sounds like a good idea to me if it works for you." He caught her hand, twining his fingers through hers, and leaned in close. "I think you just got your second wind."

Dana looked up and met warm eyes. Her heart fluttered as her thoughts returned to the new house. How she'd love to see that warmth radiating through the rooms,

322

wall to wall, enveloping her, permeating every nook and cranny.

It was a lot to ask of some two-by-fours and drywall. But after all they'd been through, it didn't seem such an unreasonable request. She smiled at Kent, and a sense of peace flowed through her. The new house might bask in the sunshine, but it would glow from the inside out with love that resided there.

THE END

Acknowledgments

Many thanks to my friends and family for their support of this book and all of my writing endeavors. I appreciate the assistance of my critique partners and beta readers, Michelle Grey, Janice Richards, Amy Miller, and Sandra Alig; and my editor, Toni Ferro.

Special thanks to Susan Alig, local assistant district attorney; R.N. Marcia Kruse; and all of the professionals who assisted with my research.

Darlene Deluca writes contemporary romance and women's fiction from her suburban home in the Midwest. You can visit her author pages at Facebook, Amazon or Goodreads, and her website at www.darlenedeluca.com.

18387381R00190

Made in the USA
San Bernardino, CA
12 January 2015